ALL THE WEYRS
OF PERN

ALL THE
WEYRS
OF PERN

ANNE McCAFFREY

BALLANTINE BOOKS • NEW YORK

THE DRAGONRIDERS OF PERN is a trademark of Anne McCaffrey. Reg. U.S. Pat. & Tm. Off.

A Del Rey® Book
Published by Ballantine Books

Copyright © 1991 by Anne McCaffrey

http://www.randomhouse.com/delrey/

Library of Congress Catalog Card Number: 97-93880

ISBN: 0-345-41935-9

Design by Ann Gold
Map by Shelly Shapiro

Manufactured in the United States of America

First Hardcover Edition: December 1991
First Mass Market Edition: December 1992
First Trade Paperback Edition: September1997

10 9 8 7 6 5 4 3 2 1

This book is most respectfully dedicated

to

DOCTORS JACK AND JUDY COHEN

who have enriched my life so much

ACKNOWLEDGMENTS

The author gives full credit to Dr. Jack Cohen once again for making fact out of her fiction and rationalizing the whimsies of her imagination.

The author would also like to thank Elizabeth Moon for her kind permission to use her poem, which is credited to Journeywoman Harper Elimona, in Chapter Fifteen.

The author and Dr. Jack Cohen are fully aware that some of the procedures and developments of new products suggested in these pages would probably take many more months, years, to produce and effect than is here suggested. However, there are certain licenses that an author, and her advisor, may take to produce a novel. Then, too, the Pernese had Aivas to help them, didn't they?

PERN

Benden Weyr
Bitra

Benden Hold

Red Butte
Keroon

Half-Circle

Nerat

SEA

ld

Cove

Monaco Bay

Landing

Jordan R.

Cardiff

Paradise R.

Black Rock R.
(Rubicon R.)

Cathay

Xanadu

Caspian Lake

Eastern Barrier Range

55

ALL THE WEYRS
OF PERN

PROLOGUE
▼▼▼▼▼▼▼▼▼

The Aivas felt its sensors responding to a renewal of power from the solar panels on the roof above it. The wind must have become strong enough to blow the clogging dust and volcanic ash away from the panels. There had been enough of these incidents over the past 2,525 years so that Aivas had been able to maintain function, even if only at a very low maintenance level.

Running through the main operating circuits, Aivas found no malfunctions. Exterior optics were still obstructed, but once again the Aivas was aware of some activity in its vicinity.

Was it possible that humans had returned to the Landing facility?

It had not as yet completed its priority assignment: to discover a means to destroy the organism that had been termed "Thread" by the captains. It had received no significant input to allow it to complete that task, but the priority had not been canceled.

Perhaps, with the return of humans, that assignment could at last be completed.

Power began to swell its resources as the panels were uncovered; the removal was not haphazard, as would be caused by wind and weather, but was consistent with a workmanlike activity. As more of the panels were cleared, solar energy recharged the long-unused power collectors. The Aivas responded by distributing the revitalizing energy through its systems, running rapid function checks through circuits long dormant.

Aivas had been efficiently designed, and as power continued to be available, it found itself in full running order by the time the exterior sensors had also been uncovered.

Humans had returned to Landing! Many of them! Once again humankind had triumphed over tremendous odds. Aivas duly noticed through its adjustable optical elements that they were still accompanied by the creatures called fire-dragons. Noise, too, was now filtering through the audio channels: human voices speaking in unusual word patterns. A lingual shift? In 2,525 years, that was entirely likely. Aivas listened and interpreted, measuring the altered vowels and slurred consonants against the speech patterns that had been programmed into it. It organized the new sounds into groups and checked them with its semantics program.

Within its vision came an immense white creature. The descendant of the bioengineer's first production? Aivas did a rapid extrapolation from the biolab's files and reached the inescapable conclusion that the so-called dragons had also matured and prospered. It searched for, but did not find, "white" in the parameters of the engineered species.

Not only had humankind survived the incursion of Thread for 2,525 years of Threadfall, but it had flourished. The species had the tenacity to survive where others succumbed.

If humans had been able to return from the Northern Continent, had they also managed to destroy the organism? That would be well done. What must Aivas then do if its priority was superseded?

Humans, with their insatiable curiosity and restlessness, would undoubtedly have new tasks which an Artificial Intelligence Voice-Address System could undertake. They were not, Aivas knew from its memory banks, a complacent species. Soon those who worked to clear the debris of centuries would uncover the entire building and reach its position. It must, of course, react as its program ordained.

The Aivas waited.

1

PRESENT (NINTH) PASS, 17TH TURN

By the time the Aivas had finished its recital of the first nine years of the colonization of Pern, the sun Rukbat had set with an unusually fine display. Not that many of the reverent listeners of the history that the Artificial Intelligence Voice-Address System narrated were aware of such externals.

During the hours that the Aivas's resonant tones had filled the chamber and penetrated to the hallway beyond, more people had crowded in to hear what it said, jostling each other to get an occasional look at the incredible moving pictures with which Aivas illustrated its narrative. Those Lord Holders and Craftmasters hastily summoned by fire-lizard messengers willingly crowded into the stuffy inner room.

Lord Jaxom of Ruatha had asked his white dragon, Ruth, to summon the Benden Weyrleaders, so they were the first to join the Masterharper Robinton and Mastersmith Fandarel. Lessa and F'lar slid onto the stools that Jaxom and Journeyman Harper Piemur vacated for them. Piemur frowned at his mate, Mastersmith Jancis, when she started to get down and gestured to Breide, standing gawking in the doorway, to bring more seating. When F'nor, the Benden Wingleader, came, he sat on the floor, where he had to crane his neck to see the screen, though he quickly became too engrossed in the history to notice any discomfort. Room was made in the small, crowded chamber for the Lord Holders, Groghe of Fort, Asgenar of Lemos, and Larad of Telgar. By then, Jaxom had been pushed back to the doorway and politely but firmly refused entry to anyone else.

Subtly the Aivas increased its volume so that the tale was audible to all those in the corridor. No one seemed to mind the stifling closeness of room and corridor, though matters improved when someone considerately passed around water and redfruit juice and, later, meatrolls. Someone also had the foresight to open as many of the windows in the building as possible, thus circulating some air down the corridor, though little enough reached the Aivas chamber.

"The final message received by this facility from Captain Keroon was to confirm that Fort Hold was operational. This message was logged in at 1700, fourth day of the tenth month, eleventh year after Landing."

When the Aivas ceased speaking, there was a profound and awed silence, finally broken by small scufflings as people shifted, almost apologetically, from long-held positions. A few polite coughs were quickly muffled.

Feeling it incumbent on him to make some response to these historic and unexpected revelations, the Masterharper cleared his throat.

"We are deeply indebted to you, Aivas, for this amazing tale." Robinton spoke with deep humility and respect. A murmur of agreement circulated room and corridor. "We have lost so much of our early history: It's been reduced to myth and legend in many cases. You have clarified much that puzzled us. But why does it end so abruptly?"

"There was no further input from the authorized operators."

"Why not?"

"No explanation was given. Failing prior instructions, this facility continued observations until the solar panels became clogged and power was reduced to the minimum needed to retain core integrity."

"Those panels are the source of your power?" Fandarel asked, his bass voice rumbling with eagerness.

"Yes."

"Those pictures? How did you do that?" Fandarel's usual reserved manner was discarded in his excitement.

"You no longer have recording devices?"

"No." Fandarel shook his head in disgust. "Among many of the other marvels you mentioned in passing. Can you teach us what we have forgotten?" His eyes glowed in anticipation.

"The memory banks contain Planetary Engineering and Colonizing data, and the multicultural and historical files considered relevant by the Colony Administrators.''

Before Fandarel could organize another question, F'lar held up one hand.

''With respect, Master Fandarel, we all have questions to ask Aivas.'' He turned around to signal Master Esselin and the ubiquitous Breide to come to the door. ''I want this corridor cleared, Master Esselin. This room is not to be entered without express permission from one of us present now. Do I make myself plain?'' He looked sternly from one to the other.

''Indeed, Weyrleader, perfectly plain,'' Breide said, his manner as obsequious as ever.

''Of course, Weyrleader, certainly, Weyrleader,'' Master Esselin said, bowing with each use of F'lar's title.

''Breide, make sure you report today's event to Lord Toric,'' F'lar added, knowing perfectly well that Breide would do just that without permission. ''Esselin, bring enough glowbaskets to light the hall and the adjacent rooms. Bring a few cots or pallets, as well, and blankets. Some food.''

''And wine. Don't forget wine, F'lar,'' Robinton called. ''Benden wine, if you please, Esselin, and make that two wineskins. This could be very thirsty work,'' he added in a conversational tone, grinning at Lessa.

''Well, you're not going to drink up two skinsful, Robinton,'' Lessa said at her sternest, ''talking yourself hoarse with Aivas. Which I can see is what you have in mind. I'd say you already had quite enough excitement for one day. It's certainly more than I can believe in one day.''

''Be assured, Madam Lessa,'' Aivas said in a placatory voice, ''that every word you have heard is factual.''

Lessa turned toward the screen that had displayed marvels to her, images of people who had turned to dust centuries before and objects totally foreign to her eyes. ''I don't doubt you, Aivas. I doubt my ability to absorb half the wonders you have described and shown us.''

''Be assured that you have achieved wonders of your own,'' Aivas replied, ''to survive the menace that nearly overwhelmed the settlers. Are those immense and magnificent creatures ranged on the slopes outside the descendants of the dragons which Madam Kitti Ping Yung created?''

"Yes, they are," Lessa replied with proprietary pride. "The golden queen is Ramoth—"

"The largest dragon on all Pern," the Masterharper said in a sly tone, his eyes twinkling.

Lessa started to glare at him but instead burst out laughing. "Well, she is."

"The bronze who is probably resting beside her is Mnementh, and I am his rider," F'lar said, grinning at his mate's discomfort.

"How do you know what is outside?" Fandarel blurted out.

"The exterior sensors of this facility are now operational."

"Exterior sensors . . ." Fandarel subsided into silent amazement.

"And the white one?" Aivas went on. "It—"

"*He,*" Jaxom said firmly but without rancor, "is Ruth, and I am his rider."

"Remarkable. The bioengineering report indicated that there were to be five variations, imitating the genetic material of the fire-dragons."

"Ruth is a sport," Jaxom replied. He had long since stopped being defensive about his dragon. Ruth had his own special abilities.

"A part of *our* history," Robinton said soothingly.

"Which," Lessa said with another stern glare at the Harper, "will wait until some of us have rested."

"My curiosity will be contained, Madam."

Lessa darted a suspicious look at the dim screen panel. "You have curiosity? And what is this 'madam'?"

"Gathering information is not restricted to humans. Madam is a title of respect."

"Lessa's respectful title is Weyrwoman, Aivas," F'lar said with another grin. "Or Ramoth's rider."

"And yours, sir?"

"Weyrleader, or Mnementh's rider. You have already met Masterharper Robinton, Harper Journeyman Piemur, Mastersmith Jancis, and Lord Jaxom of Ruatha Hold, but let me make known to you the Mastersmith Fandarel, Lord Groghe of Fort Hold, which we have always known was the first to be founded—" F'lar hid a grin at Lord Groghe's suddenly modest demeanor. "—though certainly not why. Lord of Telgar, Larad, and Lord of Lemos, Asgenar."

"Lemos? Indeed." But before the listeners could react to the mild surprise in Aivas's tone, it continued. "It is good to know that the name Telgar survived."

"We have lost the knowledge of the naming," Larad murmured.

"And are prouder to know that the sacrifices of Sallah and Tarvi are remembered so lastingly."

"Aivas," F'lar said, standing squarely in front of the screen, "you said that you were attempting to discover where Thread came from and how to exterminate it. Did you come to any conclusion?"

"Several. The organism known as Thread is somehow attracted to the eccentric planet which, at aphelion, pierces the Oort Cloud; as it approaches perihelion, it drags matter with it into this sector of space. This trailing cloud disgorged a little of its burden into the skies of this planet. Calculations at the time indicated that this would continue for approximately fifty years, at which time the material in Pern's orbit would be exhausted. Calculations also indicated that there would be recurrences of the phenomenon at intervals of two hundred fifty years, give or take a decade either way."

F'lar glanced about to see if anyone had understood what the Aivas was saying.

"With due respect, Aivas, we do not understand your explanation," the Harper said wryly. "A great deal of time has passed since Admiral Benden and Governor Boll led the settlers north. We are currently in the seventeenth Turn—what you call a year, I think—of the Ninth Pass of the Red Star."

"Noted."

"It has always been *assumed*," F'lar said, "that Thread came from the Red Star."

"It is not a star: the most reasonable explanation is that it is a stray planet, probably drawn out of its native system by some odd event, traveling through space until it was attracted by Rukbat's gravitational pull and became trapped in this system. The matter you call Thread does not come from its surface. It originates in the Oort Cloud of this system."

"And just what is an Oort Cloud?" Master Fandarel asked ingenuously.

"According to the Dutch astronomer Jan Oort, the eponymous cloud is composed of material orbiting a sun far beyond the orbit of its outermost planet. Cometary material leaks from the cloud into the inner part of the system. In the particular case of Rukbat, some of the material is hard-shelled ovoids that change in a peculiar manner, losing their outer layers and attenuating on contact with the upper atmosphere, falling to the surface as what has been termed 'Thread'; this resembles a voracious organism that devours carbon-based organic material."

Fandarel blinked in his attempt to digest the information.

"Well, you did ask, Master Fandarel," Piemur remarked with a mischievous expression.

"Your explanations only confuse us, Aivas, for none of us have the learning to understand them," F'lar said, lifting a hand to indicate that he was not to be interrupted. "But if you knew, and presumably our ancestors knew, what Thread was and where it came from, why didn't they destroy its source?"

"By the time this facility reached those conclusions, Weyrleader, your ancestors had removed to the Northern Continent and did not return to receive the report."

A depressed and defeated silence prevailed over the room.

"But we are here now," Robinton said, straightening up on his stool. "And we can receive your report."

"If we can understand it," F'lar added drolly.

"This facility has educational programs that can supply remedial teaching in all branches of science. The prime directive given this unit by captains Keroon and Tillek, as well as Admiral Benden and Governor Boll, was to gather information and formulate a course of action that would end the threat posed by these incursions."

"Then it is possible to remove the threat of Thread?" F'lar asked, carefully schooling his expression to reveal none of the hope that he was feeling.

"The possibility exists, Weyrleader."

"*What?*" was the incredulous response of everyone in the room.

"The possibility exists, Weyrleader, but will require tremendous effort from you and quite likely the majority of your population. First, you must be able to understand scientific language and learn to work with advanced technology. In addition, access to the main banks of the *Yokohama* must be obtained to add to relevant data on asteroid positions. Then a course of action can be initiated that could probably result in the cessation of these incursions."

"Possibility? Probably result? But the possibility exists?" F'lar strode to the screen and put a hand on each side of its subtly glowing blankness. "I would do anything—*anything*—to rid Pern of Thread."

"If you are prepared to relearn lost skills and perfect them, the possibility does exist."

"And you *would* help us?"

"The end of these incursions remains the first priority of this facility."

"Not half as much as it is of ours!" F'lar replied. F'nor fervently seconded him.

The Lord Holders exchanged quick glances, hope warring with surprise. The destruction of all Thread was what F'lar had promised them nineteen Turns before when he had become leader of Pern's then single Weyr. Benden's wings of brave dragons and riders had been all that stood between the certain reduction of humankind on Pern to hunters and gatherers by the totally unexpected resumption of Threadfall after a lapse of four hundred Turns. In their extremity, the Lord Holders had promised support of all his emergency measures. Struggling with the exigencies of the Pass, they had quite forgotten his vow. But all three were quick to perceive the advantages to *them*—if they could also see the disadvantages to the Dragonriders—to be quit of their ancient responsibilities. Jaxom, as both rider and Holder, regarded F'lar with consternation. Yet there was no doubt the Benden Weyrleader meant exactly what he said—that he would do all he could to rid Pern of Thread forever.

"Then there is much to be done," Aivas said in a brisk tone. Almost, Master Robinton thought, as if the thing was relieved to have employment after so long a recess. "Your Records, Masters Robinton and Fandarel, would be of immense value in assessing your history and potential, and what knowledge of science you currently possess. Certainly a synopsis of your own history would assist an evaluation of the educational programs required to achieve your goal."

"The Harper Hall has assiduously kept accounts," the Harper said eagerly, "though the oldest of them have become illegible over the hundreds of Turns which have passed. I think the more recent Records of the twenty Turns of this current Pass would inform you adequately. Jaxom, could you and Ruth possibly go to the Harper Hall and collect them?"

The young Lord Holder immediately rose.

"If you wouldn't mind, bring Sebell and Menolly," Robinton added, glancing at F'lar, who nodded emphatically, "back with you?"

"The Records of my crafthall," Fandarel began, inching forward on his stool, wringing his huge hands together in an uncharacteristic gesture of tension, "are missing so many words and explanations— perhaps even one about this Oort Cloud. Generally what's missing is just where we cannot possibly figure out from the context what was meant. If you were able to tell us what words were missing or corrupted, you would be granting the most invaluable assistance to our efforts at self-improvement."

He was about to continue when Robinton's hand on his shoulder stopped him. They all heard Master Esselin come bustling down the corridor, directing those who carried food, cups, and wineskins to hand them over to Jancis and Piemur. He peremptorily gestured those carrying pallets and blankets into the smaller adjacent rooms. At a nod from F'lar, he hurried back down the corridor, out of earshot.

"A moment, dear friend," Robinton said when Fandarel was about to continue his request for help. "Aivas, you may have all the information the colonists considered relevant, but I don't really think we should dispense it without due consideration."

"Exactly what I was about to say," F'lar added.

"Discretion is a built-in feature of this Aivas model, Masterharper, Weyrleader. You should discuss among you who is to have access to this facility and in exactly what ways it may be of use to you."

The Masterharper groaned, holding his head in both hands, and was immediately surrounded by Lessa, Piemur, and Jaxom.

"I'm all right, I'm all right," he said testily, waving them off. "Have you all realized just what this source of knowledge can mean to us?" His voice was rough with emotion. "I've only now begun to absorb how profoundly this discovery could change our lives."

"I've been struggling to absorb that myself," F'lar said with a grim smile. "If this Aivas knows something about Thread and the Red Star that would help us . . ." F'lar halted, his hope too precious to express aloud. Then he smiled wryly and held up his hand. "First, I believe it is extremely important to decide the question of who should be permitted into this room. As you pointed out, Robinton, Aivas cannot be accessible to everyone."

"Definitely," Master Robinton said. He took a long swig of the wine he had poured for himself. "Definitely. Considering that crowd in the hall, there's no way we can censor the discovery of Aivas nor," he added, holding up his hand at the protests, "do I think we should. However . . ." He grinned. "We can't just have anyone who wants to popping up here and monopolizing—this—"

"Facility," Piemur put in, his expression genuinely thoughtful. "When word of Aivas gets about, there'll be any number of people who'll want to talk to Aivas just to say that they had, because they don't grasp its significance."

"For once I agree with you, Piemur," Lessa said. She looked around her. "I think there's enough in this room right now with a real need to talk to Aivas and the common sense and courtesy to know when to stop." She paused to cast a stern eye on Master Robinton, who grinned back amiably. "Certainly we are representative of the planet—Weyrleaders, Masters, and Lord Holders—so no one can say Aivas is being monopolized by one group. Or is that too many, Aivas?"

"No." For some reason this easy acceptance made the Masterharper grin. Aivas went on. "The authority may be expanded or contracted as may be deemed necessary. To recapitulate, it is permitted for you . . ." And all those in the room were named in pleasant baritone tones.

"And Jaxom," Piemur added quickly, since Jaxom had gone on Robinton's errand and someone needed to speak up for the third party to the original discovery of Aivas.

"And Lord Jaxom of Ruatha Hold," Aivas amended, "to command my services. Is that correct? Very good. The necessary voiceprints have been registered, including Lord Jaxom's, whose voice I registered earlier, and this facility will respond to no others, or in the presence of others, until further notice."

"As an added precaution," Master Robinton said, "to change that roster, there must be one of the Weyrleaders, one Master, and one Lord Holder present in this room." He glanced about to see if that precaution was acceptable.

Just then, Esselin bustled down the corridor to ask if there were any further orders for the night.

"Yes, Esselin, assign the most responsible and least curious of your men to guard the building's entrance. Only Lord Jaxom and those who accompany him are to be permitted to enter the building tonight."

By the time Esselin had assured F'lar of his total cooperation, a rather tense discussion had started between Fandarel and Larad as to which crafthalls should have precedence in learning from Aivas.

"If I may interject a suggestion," Aivas said loudly, startling them all, "it is a relatively simple matter to expand this facility to accommodate many requirements." When the silence lengthened, Aivas added in a milder, almost apologetic tone, "That is, if the contents of the Catherine Caves are still intact and undamaged?"

"Do you mean the caves at the southern side of the grid?" Piemur asked.

"Those would be the ones." To the bewilderment of the watchers, images of a variety of items appeared on the screen. "And these are the objects required to supply additional stations."

"Your beaded panels, Piemur," Jancis said, clutching at his sleeve with one hand and pointing excitedly with the other.

"You're right," Piemur said. "What are they, Aivas? We seem to have boxes and boxes of them, all different sorts."

"Those are computer cards." To the listeners, it sounded as if Aivas's measured tone betrayed a discreet excitement. "Were there also any of these objects?" And boxes were displayed with screens that were smaller replicas of the screen facing them, along with rectangles resembling what Aivas had identified as a touch panel.

"Yes," Master Robinton said with surprise. "I couldn't think what they might be when I saw them, swathed in that thick film."

"If there are sufficient parts in good working order, then there need be no contention for access to this facility. These were the remainder of the ordinary processors. All other voice-activated units were packaged for shipment to the north and, it seems, lost, but these elementary models will admirably suit the current need. With sufficient power, up to twelve stations can be accommodated without affecting response time."

Once again the audience lapsed into numb silence.

"Do I understand you correctly?" Fandarel began, after clearing his throat. "You can *divide* yourself into twelve segments?"

"That is correct."

"How can you do that?" Fandarel demanded, spreading his arms wide in disbelief.

"Surely, Mastersmith, you do not limit yourself to one hearth, or anvil or forge, one hammer, one fire?"

"Of course not, but I have many men . . ."

"This facility is not a single hearth or fire or hammer, but many, and each can work as diligently as the others."

"This I find very hard to understand," Fandarel admitted, scratching his balding pate and shaking his head.

"Before you is a machine, Mastersmith, which can be segmented, and each discrete part can function as a separate tool."

"I don't begin to understand how you can do that, Aivas, but if you can, it would certainly solve the problems of priorities," Master Robinton said, grinning from ear to ear. Oh, the questions of past paradoxes that could now be answered by this marvelous creature! He took a large pull of his wine.

"To create these separate tools," Aivas went on, "will, in itself, provide the first of many lessons that must be understood before you will be ready to attack your primary objective, the annihilation of Thread."

"By all means, let us begin then," F'lar said, rubbing his hands together, infused with the first stirrings of real hope he had felt during the last few grueling Turns of the current Pass.

"There isn't enough space in here for a dozen of us all talking with a dozen of you, Aivas," Lord Larad of Telgar said reasonably.

"There are other rooms in this building that can be utilized. Indeed, it would be wise to have separate offices, and perhaps one larger room where many could observe and learn. It is best to begin at the beginning," Aivas said, and suddenly sheets began to roll out of a slot to one side of the main screen. "These are the items that will be needed in the morning, the tools that will be required to construct the additional stations, and a diagram of how to redesign this building to accommodate them."

Being nearest, Piemur caught the sheets as they were spewed out. Jancis came to his aid.

"More material will soon be needed for the printer," Aivas went on. "Rolls should be stored in the Catherine Caves with the other supplies. Paper would be an acceptable substitute."

"Paper?" Larad exclaimed. "Wood-pulp paper?"

"If nothing else is available, that will do."

"It would seem, Asgenar," F'lar said with a chuckle, "that the skills of Master Bendarek were not developed a Turn too soon."

"You have lost the skill of extruding plastic from silicates?" Aivas asked. Master Robinton thought he heard a note of surprise in its voice.

"Silicates?" Master Fandarel asked.

"But one of the many skills we have lost," Robinton said ruefully. "We will make diligent pupils."

The flow of sheets stopped, and as Piemur and Jancis sorted them, they realized that there were six copies of each page. When they had assembled the sheets, they looked around expectantly at those in the room.

"Not tonight," Lessa said firmly. "You'd break your necks stumbling about those caves in the dark. We've waited this long, we can wait until morning. And I think that we all should"—she swung around to pinion the Masterharper with a stern eye—"either seek a bed for the night or go back where we belong."

"My dear Weyrwoman," Robinton began, pulling himself erect.

"Nothing, absolutely nothing, including your direst threat would compel me—" And suddenly he seemed to wilt and fold in on himself. Piemur caught the cup before it fell from the Harper's hand. As he supported his Master's limp body, he had a smug smile on his face.

"Except of course the fellis juice I put in his last cup of wine," he said by way of explanation. "So let's get him to bed."

F'lar and Larad immediately started forward, but Fandarel held up one huge hand. Picking up the long Harper in his arms, he nodded to Jancis to show him where to put the sleeping Robinton to bed.

"Piemur, you haven't changed, have you?" Lessa accused with a mock scowl that turned into a grin. Then, because she wondered at what the machine would think of what it had seen, she added, "Aivas, Masterharper Robinton often lets his enthusiasm get the better of his well-being."

"This facility is able to monitor for physical stress," Aivas said. "The Masterharper emanated considerable excitement but nothing harmful."

"You are a healer, as well?" F'lar exclaimed.

"No, Weyrleader, but this facility is equipped to monitor the vital signs of those in this room. However, the medical information stored in files was updated to state-of-the-art at the time the expedition departed for this system. Your medics may wish to avail themselves of this information."

F'lar's groan was audible. "Master Oldive must come here as soon as possible."

"Half the planet must come as soon as possible," Lessa said tartly. She gave a gusty sigh. "I doubt twelve of Aivas will be half enough."

"Then let us organize ourselves," Fandarel said, returning from his errand. "We must contain our excitement and direct our energies in the most efficient way . . ." There were chuckles at the Mastersmith's use of his favorite word. "You may laugh, but you know it is only sensible and time-saving to work efficiently, and we are each going in several directions at once tonight. We cannot but be stimulated by this sudden gift from our ancestors, but we should do nothing hasty. I will go back to Telgar crafthold now, if F'nor and Canth will be so kind. I shall make suitable arrangements and draft the services of those who can help us delve into the caves to find the required materials, and to find people to understand the diagrams Aivas has given us. But tomorrow is soon enough. F'nor?" And, raising his hairy eyebrows at the brown rider, Fandarel nodded to one and all, bowed courteously to the screen, and took his leave.

"A moment, F'nor," Larad said, "for I should return to Telgar. Asgenar, do you join us?"

Asgenar looked about him and smiled ruefully. "I think I'd better leave now. My mind is seething with questions to put to Aivas, yet I don't think I could actually come out with a sensible query. I'll bring Bendarek with me in the morning."

Lord Groghe, who had said very little but looked exceedingly thoughtful, asked N'ton to return him to Fort Hold.

"Jancis and I will stay here in case Master Robinton wakes," Piemur told Lessa and F'lar. Then his mischievous grin surfaced. "And I won't ask my eight thousand five hundred and thirty-two burning questions all in one breath, either."

"Then I think we all bid you good night now, Aivas," F'lar said, turning toward the dark screen.

"Good night." The lights of the room dimmed to a faint glow. One pulsing green light remained at the bottom left-hand corner of the screen.

T wo hours later Jaxom and Ruth arrived with both Harper Masters, Sebell and Menolly. The white dragon was festooned with sacks. By considerably reducing the level of klah in the beakers Esselin had provided, Piemur had managed to stay awake while Jancis got a nap.

"One of us has to be alert tomorrow to organize people," she had told the young journeyman harper. "I'm better at that than you are, love." She had given him a kiss to sweeten the comment.

Piemur had no quarrel with that; with a mock-paternal kiss he settled her on a pallet in the room beyond Master Robinton's.

Despite his joke about not asking questions, when Piemur returned to the Aivas room he found that he couldn't immediately formulate a single intelligent query. Instead, with a cup in hand and the beaker beside him, Piemur sat, bereft of words, in the semigloom of the chamber.

"Aivas?" he began tentatively.

"Yes, Journeyman Piemur?" The room brightened enough for Piemur to see clearly.

"How do you do that?" Piemur asked, startled.

"The panels that you and Journeywoman Jancis exposed yesterday are capable of drawing energy from the sun: it is called solar power. When all the panels are exposed, an hour's bright illumination will power this unit for twelve hours."

"You're not going to have ordinary usage from now on," Piemur said with a snort.

"A query: You apparently utilize the luminescent organism in handlights, but do you not have some sort of power generation, perhaps hydroelectric power?"

"Hydroelectric?" Piemur's quick ear allowed him to repeat the unfamiliar words accurately.

"The production of electric current by the energy of moving water."

"Master Fandarel uses water wheels in Telgar Smithcrafthold to drive the big hammers and the forge bellows, but 'electric' is an unfamiliar word. Unless that's what Fandarel does with those acid tanks of his."

"Acid tanks? Batteries?"

Piemur shrugged. "I don't know what he calls them. I'm a harper. Whatever 'electric' is, so long as it is efficient, Master Fandarel will love it."

"Would Master Fandarel's equipment resemble this structure?" The screen suddenly lit up with a diagram of a water wheel.

"That's it. How did you know?"

"This is the most frequent primitive application. Have you explored the Landing site, Journeyman Piemur?"

"I don't need my title all the time, Aivas. Piemur is enough."

"No disrespect would be construed?"

"Not from me, Aivas. Some of the Lord Holders get a bit touchy, but Jaxom doesn't, nor Larad and Asgenar. Lessa can be sticky, but not F'lar, or F'nor, or N'ton. And yes, I've explored the Landing site. What should I be looking for?"

The screen displayed a complex mechanism, set at the base of the river hill.

"Nothing like that there now," Piemur said, shaking his head.

"As Mastersmith Fandarel already uses water wheels, a new installation can be erected so that this facility is not dependent on the solar panels, which will be inadequate for the projected demands just discussed."

"They didn't store away any of your panels in the caves?"

"No."

"How can you be sure?" Piemur found such didacticism irritating. It would be totally unfair if this—this intelligence was always right.

"The list of items in the Catherine Caves is available data and does not include spare panels."

"It must be nice to know everything," he said.

"Accuracy is required of an Aivas system—and a very large data base, what you would call 'knowledge.' You must not believe that the data base *can* contain 'everything.' But sufficient to realize the priorities of the programming."

"A harper has to be accurate, too," Piemur said sourly. Master Fandarel's search for efficiency had always had, for Piemur, its humorous side. He wasn't sure if he could be as tolerant of Aivas's rectitude.

"A harper—one who plays a harp, an instrument?" Aivas asked.

"I do that, too," Piemur replied, his capricious humor revived as he realized that Aivas did not know very much at all about present-day Pern. "The primary function of the Harper Hall is, however, to teach, to communicate, and at need, to arbitrate."

"Not to entertain?"

"We do that, too—it's a good way to teach, as well—and there are many who only do that, but the more skilled of us have multiple duties. It would be presumptuous of me to usurp Master Robinton's right to enlighten you on that account. Although, in actual fact, he is no longer *the* Masterharper of Pern. Sebell is, because Master Robinton had a nearly fatal heart attack and was made to retire from active service to the Harper Hall. Not that he *has* retired, despite being in Cove Hold now, because of all that has happened since Jaxom discovered Landing and the Ship Meadow, and then the caves." Piemur halted, realizing that he was rattling on. It was just like him to want to impress Aivas with his knowledge; more than that, Piemur was experiencing an intense need to anchor his personal values in the presence of this superior intelligence.

"Sebell, who is now Masterharper of all Pern, is on his way with the Records," he went on. "And Menolly. They may look young to you, but they are the most important people in the Harper Hall." Then he added deferentially, "But you should know that Master Robinton is the most honored and respected man on Pern. The dragons kept him from dying. That's how important he is."

"The dragons then have been a successful experiment?" Aivas asked.

"Experiment?" Piemur was indignant and then subsided with a

rueful chuckle. "I wouldn't let the Weyrleaders hear you calling their dragons 'experiments.' "

"The advice is appreciated."

Piemur eyed the screen for a moment. "You mean that, don't you?"

"Yes. The culture and societies of your present-day Pern have evolved and altered considerably from the early days of the colony. It is incumbent on this facility to learn the new protocol and thus avoid giving unnecessary offense. The dragons have, therefore, become important above and beyond their initial role in the aerial defense of the planet?"

"They are the most important creatures on the planet. We couldn't survive without them." Piemur's voice rang with pride and gratitude.

"Without intending any offense, is it currently acceptable to maintain the sports of the breed?"

Piemur snorted. "You mean Ruth? He and Jaxom are exceptions—to a lot of rules. He's a Lord Holder and shouldn't ever have Impressed a dragon. But he did, and because they thought Ruth wouldn't survive long, he was allowed to be raised."

"That is contradictory."

"I know, but Ruth's special. He always knows *when* he is in time."

The resultant pause did much to assuage Piemur's feelings of inferiority. He had stumped the Aivas.

"Your remark is unclear."

"You did know that dragons can move instantaneously *between* one place and another?"

"That was a basic ability of the fire-dragon from whose genetic material the dragons were originally bioengineered. It was similar to the teleportation ability demonstrated by some species on several other planets."

"Well, dragons can also move *between* one time and another. Lessa did, and Jaxom." Piemur grinned, being one of the few people to know exactly when and why Jaxom had moved *between* one time and another. "But it's an exceedingly dangerous ability and severely discouraged. Very few dragons have Ruth's sense of time and space. So, if a dragonrider times it without his Weyrleader's express permission, he gets royally reamed—if he hasn't come to grief messing around with timing, that is."

"Would you be good enough to explain in what circumstances timing is permissible?"

Piemur had already berated himself for mentioning Jaxom's little excursion. He should have kept it to Lessa's adventure, which was already part of the fabric of recent history. So he switched to a less sensitive subject and told Aivas in detail the tale of Lessa's heroic ride on Ramoth: how she had brought the five lost Weyrs of Pern forward in time to save those in the Present Pass from annihilation. Even if he said so himself, Piemur thought he recited it with considerable flair. Though Aivas made no comment throughout, Piemur sensed that his unusual audience heard—and remembered—every word.

"A spectacularly brave and daring exploit, clearly of epic proportions despite the considerable risk she ran in losing both herself and the queen Ramoth. The results clearly justified the journey," Aivas stated. It was more praise than Piemur had expected. He grinned with satisfaction that he had managed to impress the thing.

"You mentioned that the Long Interval caused the decline of the Weyrs' authority and its prominence in your society," Aivas said. "Do you know how many times the cycle has been similarly altered?"

"The cycle?"

"Yes. How many times has the orbit of what you call the Red Star failed to bring Thread to Pern?"

"Oh, you mean how many Long Intervals? There have been two recorded in our history. We were told that long intervals would occur, but I don't know who knew that. That's why so many people were so certain, right up till the time we had our first Fall of this Pass, that Thread had actually disappeared forever."

From her favorite spot, wrapped loosely about Piemur's neck, his golden fire-lizard roused and gave a warning cheep.

"Sensors register that the lump on your shoulder is actually a creature clinging to you."

"Oh, that's only Farli, my queen fire-lizard."

"The creatures have remained in contact with you?"

"Yes and no." Piemur did not think there would be time to give Aivas the recent history of the fire-lizard. "She just told me that Ruth and Jaxom have returned with the records and Sebell and Menolly." Piemur stood up, draining the last of the klah from his cup. "Then you'll know all that's happened this Pass. Which hasn't been dull at all, but you—you sort of cap it."

Piemur could hear the exchange of low-voiced conversation down the hallway, and he started to the entrance in case Esselin's guards were being officious. He had taken no more than a few steps when Jaxom, Sebell, and Menolly, bowed under the weight of the sacks they were carrying, came striding down the hall. Menolly, her dark hair still tangled from her flying cap, reached Piemur first.

"Where's Master Robinton?" Menolly asked, looking about, her narrow, elegant features reflecting her perpetual anxiety for her mentor.

"In there, Menolly," Piemur said, pointing. "As if we'd risk him."

She thrust her heavy sack at him and ducked into the room to reassure herself, while Piemur smiled tolerantly.

"And they left you to mind Aivas all on your own?" Jaxom asked in a whisper. "Learned all the secrets of the universe yet?"

Piemur gave a snort. "As it turned out, I answered his—its—questions. But it was interesting all the same," Piemur said. "And I gave him—it—a few tips to the wise." He laid his finger along his nose, grinning. "Which is a harper function."

Sebell, looking browner than ever in the dimly lit corridor, gave Piemur the slow smile that added considerable charm to the handsome, intelligent face of the tall Masterharper.

"According to Jaxom, this Aivas of yours is a tale spinner to shame the best of us, with knowledge of all that we were, and what we can be."

"Well, I suspect Aivas might well create more problems than he solves," Piemur said, "but I guarantee you it'll be exciting." He helped Jaxom remove the Records, carefully, from the sacks. "Aivas is right interested in you and Ruth, too."

"What have you been telling him?" Jaxom asked in what Piemur privately called his Lord Holder attitude.

"Me? Nothing you'd object to, friend," Piemur hastily reassured him. Jaxom could still be touchy about other people discussing Ruth. "I spent more time reciting Lessa's ride, which he said was of epic proportions." He grinned broadly.

As Piemur talked, Sebell had been taking in the details of the room, studying the strange wall furnishings. Sebell rarely rushed in the way Piemur did.

"And this Aivas has preserved itself from our first days on Pern?" Sebell let out a long, soft whistle. He tapped one of the clear panels and looked around the room. "Where does it store its records? Jaxom said it displayed amazing pictures of our past, as well."

"Aivas, speak for yourself," Piemur suggested cockily, wanting to see how Sebell—or Menolly, who entered just then—handled the entity. "Aivas?" he prompted. "This is Sebell, Masterharper of Pern, Master Robinton's successor, and Master Menolly, Pern's ablest composer." When there was still no response from Aivas, Piemur felt his irritation rising. "They've brought the Records for you to read."

Aivas remained silent.

"Maybe it's used up the power stored in the sun panels," he said, forcing himself to keep his tone light as he wondered how the Aivas could be forced into answering. He scowled at the unresponsive screen and the green pulse winking in the corner. The feckless thing was awake, so it had to be listening. "I don't understand," he said to the others, disgusted by the inactivity. "He was talking up a storm to me just before you came—oh, shards!" He slapped his forehead dramatically with one palm. "Neither you nor Menolly are on his list yet."

"His list?" Jaxom asked, frowning in irritation.

"Yes, his list," Piemur said. He sighed wearily and sagged onto the nearest stool. "The people he is authorized to speak to. Master Robinton and the others decided to limit those who have access to Aivas."

"But *I* was here," Jaxom exclaimed.

"Oh, he'll probably talk to you once Sebell and Menolly leave. It got set up so that it takes a Weyrleader, a Lord, and a Masterharper for Aivas to add someone to the privileged list."

"Well, I'm Lord Holder of Ruatha," Jaxom began.

"Piemur's not a Master yet, and there are no Weyrleaders present," Menolly said with a little laugh. "Aivas is doing as he was told, which is more than you always do, Piemur." She grinned at him.

"Yes, but now would be the best time for Aivas to catch up on our history while there's peace and quiet. And before Fandarel returns to monopolize him," Piemur said, scrubbing at his face. The effects of a very exciting day were catching up with him.

"I'm on the list though, am I not?" Jaxom asked, a touch of asperity in his voice.

"Yes—you, me, Jancis, Master Robinton, all of us who were in the room when Aivas woke up."

"And he talked to you when you were alone," Jaxom said. "Maybe, if Sebell and Menolly leave—sorry about that—he'll talk to me, and I can feed the Records to him."

"Our feelings won't be hurt," Menolly said, glancing up at Sebell to see him nod in agreement. Sebell's good sense and equable nature were two of the many reasons she loved and respected him. "There're other empty pallets, Piemur; you look to be out on your feet. You and Sebell go sleep in with Master Robinson, and I'll join Jancis. If this Aivas has waited—how many Turns did you say, Jaxom? Twenty-five hundred—" She gave a little shudder for such a long span. "—we can wait until tomorrow."

"I shouldn't leave it all to Jaxom . . ." Piemur said, definitely tempted by the thought of lying horizontal for a while. That last cup of klah had made no dent in his fatigue.

Menolly took him by the hand. "I'll even tuck you in, the way I would Robse." She grinned at his disgusted snort. "You're no better than Master Robinson in taking care of yourself. Come, get some sleep, now. You, too, Sebell. Tomorrow—no, it's already today here, isn't it—well, I suspect everyone is going to rush about like headless wherries. So it'll behoove us to stay cool and calm."

When the doors had closed quietly behind them, Jaxom turned to Aivas.

"There's just me here now, Aivas."

"That is obvious."

"You were obeying your orders, then, weren't you?"

"That is my function."

"All right, then it is my function to show you the Records of our history, as Master Robinson wanted."

"Please place the Record facedown on the lighted plate."

Carefully, with full regard that Master Arnor, the head archivist at Harper Hall, would have his guts for garters if he damaged a single one of the precious pages, Jaxom opened the first Record, Present Pass One, and laid it on the green glowing panel.

"Next!"

"What? I barely had time to place it," Jaxom exclaimed.

"Scanning is instantaneous, Lord Jaxom."

"This is going to be a long night," Jaxom remarked, and obediently opened the Record to a new page.

"Journeyman Piemur said your white dragon is an exceptional beast," Aivas said, "with many unusual qualities."

"Compensation for him being small, white, and uninterested in mating." Jaxom wondered what Piemur had said about Ruth, even though he knew the journeyman was devoted to both him and the white dragon.

"Was the journeyman correct in saying that Ruth always knows *when* he is, and that he has traveled in time?"

"All the dragons can travel in time, at least backward," Jaxom said a trifle absently, his attention focused on turning the pages carefully, as well as quickly.

"Timing is also prohibited?"

"Timing is dangerous."

"Why?"

Jaxom shrugged as he changed pages. "A dragon has to know exactly the time *when* he is going to, or he can come out of *between* at the same spot he's inhabiting at that earlier time. Too close, and it is thought that both dragon and rider will die. Equally, it's unwise to go any place you haven't already been, so you shouldn't go forward, because you wouldn't know if you were there or not." Jaxom paused to smooth some pages flat where the binding was particularly tight. "Lessa made a particularly spectacular flight."

"So Journeyman Piemur told me. A brave feat, but apparently not without debilitating consequences. The method of teleporting was never fully explained, but judging by the journeyman's account, an abnormally long period spent in such travel causes sensory deprivations. You and your white dragon have also timed it?"

"That is the term," Jaxom said in a flat tone that he hoped would discourage further questions. But Aivas was not human, he realized, and might not perceive his reluctance from tone or words. "The episode is not common knowledge."

"Understood," Aivas replied, to Jaxom's surprise. "Would you object, Lord Jaxom, to a discussion of the duties of the various social groups that have been mentioned in the Records so far? For instance, what are the responsibilities and privileges of a Lord Holder? Or a Weyrleader? A Craftmaster? Some terms are so well understood by the scribes that they are not defined. It is necessary to have a firm grasp of such terms to understand the current political and social structures."

Jaxom gave a little chuckle. "You'd do better to ask one of the more experienced Lord Holders: Groghe, for instance, or even Larad or Asgenar."

"You are here, Lord Jaxom."

"Yes, am I not!" The quickness of the Aivas amused Jaxom. So, as talking would certainly relieve the tedium of turning pages, Jaxom complied—and found it very easy indeed to talk to Aivas through the long night. Only later would he realize how skillfully he had been queried. He could not even guess how valuable his explanations would prove to be.

Jaxom had worked his way through five Turns of the Present Pass when the muscles in his shoulders began to tense. He needed a break. So when he heard someone stirring, he called out softly.

"Who's up?"

"Jancis. You came back—oh!" She grinned as she entered the chamber. "Shall I take over? You look exhausted. Why didn't Sebell or Menolly do this?"

"Because Aivas will have nothing to do with them until they've been formally introduced to him. By a Lord Holder, a Masterharper, and a Weyrleader."

Jancis's expression was rueful. "Sometimes we outsmart ourselves. Here, I'll take over, Jaxom. Get yourself some klah. It should still be good and hot." And taking the Record from his hands, she spread the pages on the panel. "Master Robinton, and the others here then, quite rightly decided it was wiser to limit who could talk to Aivas."

"Hmm, yes, there's no telling what people will ask Aivas," Jaxom said, thinking of the way he had rattled on and on, although Aivas had done all the asking.

By the time he had finished the klah, which was not as hot as he liked but did stimulate him, Jancis had finished that volume. She started on another.

How soon, Jaxom wondered, could he get his lady, Sharra, admitted to the roster? She had been so excited when he had told her about the medical knowledge Aivas claimed to possess. She had two cotholders, suffering intense pains that she was unable to alleviate with fellis. They were slowly wasting away. Master Oldive, whose advice had been sought, was also baffled by their declines. Then Jaxom reminded himself that Oldive, being Masterhealer, would have precedence with Aivas. Jaxom was careful about using his privileges as Lord Holder, and yet, in a case of life or death, could he not make an exception?

"That will be all for now, Journeywoman Jancis," Aivas said in a muted voice. "The energy supplies are nearly exhausted. An hour of good sunlight will be needed to restore power. If the remaining panels could be cleared, there would be more power available in the future."

"Did I do something wrong?" Jancis asked Jaxom in confusion.

"No," Jaxom said, chuckling. "It gets its power from those panels you and Piemur uncovered on the roof. Sun power. Sun's been down for hours now." He yawned hugely. "It's late. We should both get some sleep."

Jancis considered the idea, then reached for the nearly empty klah beaker. "No, I'm awake now. I'll brew more klah. We'll need plenty of that when people start arriving." And she bustled off.

Jaxom liked Jancis. Not long ago, they had shared lessons at the Mastersmithcraft and he remembered that she had worked a lot harder than he had—and that she clearly had a talent for smithing. She deserved her Master's status. He had been a bit surprised when she and Piemur had come to an understanding, though Sharra had heartily approved. Wandering up and down the Southern coastline had turned Piemur strange there for a time, she had said. What he needed to set him right was a sound relationship. And certainly the impudent young harper would encourage Jancis to develop some needed assertiveness and maybe lose some of the inhibitions caused by growing up in the shadow of her awesome grandfather, Fandarel. Jaxom knew just how capable a draftsman she was.

Tired but unwilling to settle down to sleep, Jaxom wandered to the entrance, nodding to the two bored guards as he walked out into the cool night air and up the mound of excavated dirt, to stand on its summit. Ruth rumbled affectionately at him from the next hillock, and Jaxom sent the white dragon a caressing thought.

Though Jaxom hadn't even mentioned it to Sharra, he felt oddly proprietorial about this plateau, which he and Ruth had originally discovered, and in particular about this Aivas entity, which they had dug out. Having heard Aivas list the names of the first colonists, Jaxom wondered who his ancestors had been. He had never been comfortable with having Fax as his sire, which was the main reason why he so rarely made use of many of a Lord Holder's traditional privileges. Larad of Telgar was not a prideful man, but he must feel immensely proud of his heritage after hearing of his forebears, Sallah Telgar Andiyar and Tarvi Andiyar. Groghe was a sensible man, but knowing that his direct ancestor had been a universal hero would make the Fort Lord Holder inordinately proud. But why hadn't Fort Hold been named after the valiant Admiral Benden? Why was Benden Hold in the east? And why hadn't Aivas known more about the dragons? Fascinating. No doubt there would be more revelations.

I listened, Ruth said, gliding from his perch to the mound on which Jaxom stood, *to what this Aivas creature said. It is true that we were an experiment?* Ruth moved forward until he was close enough to touch

Jaxom and then leaned his head against his weyrmate. *What is an experiment?*

Jaxom heard the indignation in Ruth's tone and stifled a chuckle at his friend's reaction.

"A most felicitous happening, dear friend, not that it matters a lead mark how you and the other dragons came to be," Jaxom said stoutly. "Besides you've always known—better than anyone else on Pern—that dragons are cousins to the fire-lizards. So why should it bother you how you were created?"

I don't know, Ruth replied in a strangely subdued, uncertain tone. *Is this Aivas thing good?*

"I believe it is," Jaxom answered, briefly considering his reply. "I think it will depend on us, the use to which we put the information the Aivas can give us. If it rids Pern of Thread . . ."

If it can, that means dragons won't be needed anymore, doesn't it?

"Nonsense," Jaxom said more sharply than he had intended. He threw his arm around his dragon's neck in quick reassurance, caressing Ruth's cheek and leaning into his shoulder. "Pern will always need dragons. You could do a lot more useful and much less dangerous things than sear Thread out of the skies, believe you me! Don't you fret for a single moment about our future, my friend!"

Jaxom wondered if F'lar, Lessa, and F'nor had heard from their dragons on that score. But he knew that such a worry would not be the important issue to them. The dragonriders were totally committed to ridding Pern of Thread. Everyone knew that F'lar had set that as his life's task.

"No, Ruth, don't you worry your heart out over that. Threadless skies are, I fear, a long way off in Pern's future! Aivas may know a great deal more than we do about Oort Clouds and planets and things, but it is only a machine that speaks. Talk's cheap."

Still soothing Ruth's cheek, Jaxom looked out over the settlement that his ancestors had once inhabited. There were unsightly mounds in every direction where buildings had been greedily excavated only to prove disappointingly empty. How ironic that the real treasure should be nearly the last thing to be uncovered. Incredible that the treasure should prove to be the agency that unlocked the truth to their past. Would it be the key to their future? Despite his reassurances, Jaxom harbored some of the same doubts that made Ruth fretful.

Maybe it was wrong for F'lar to wish an end to Thread, if it inevitably meant an end to usefulness for dragons. And yet, to see the

ANNE MCCAFFREY

last of Thread, in his own lifetime . . . More importantly, to be able
to improve life on Pern with the vast store of knowledge Aivas said
it had—surely that was for the good of all?

Just then he saw lights coming up in some of the buildings that
the excavation teams were using as dormitories. It was not yet dawn,
but obviously there were many others who, like Jaxom, had slept
little that night, restless with all the history and incredible moving
images churning in their minds.

And what of Aivas's promise of help? It? He? Referring to this—
this entity—as an 'it' seemed impolite. The masculine voice was so
rich and lively. Yet Aivas called it/himself a machine, the product of
an advanced technological culture and, for all its knowledge, an inanimate device. Jaxom felt more comfortable thinking of Aivas as real,
as real as his own flesh-and-blood self.

It was then that Jaxom realized that he was going to have to revise
many previously accepted concepts. That could be hard to do. The
familiar was so comfortable. But the thought of the challenge brought
a thrill to Jaxom—the incredible excitement of a future he could not
have imagined just two days before, when he and Ruth had helped
Piemur and Jancis excavate this one building out of the hundreds
here. He didn't feel tired—he felt exhilarated.

"It's going to be exciting, Ruth. Think of it that way, as an exciting
challenge." He rubbed Ruth's eyeridge with his knuckles. "We could
both use a challenge, something new. Life's been getting dull."

You'd better not say that to Sharra, Ruth advised.

Jaxom grinned. "She'll be challenged, too, if I know my mate."

Ramoth, Mnementh, Canth, Lioth, Golanth, and Monarth are coming,
Ruth said, his tone brightening.

"Reinforcements, huh?" Jaxom gave the eyeridge one more stiff
drubbing. "Company for you certainly."

Ramoth is grumpy, Ruth said, his tone suddenly wary. *Canth said
that lights were burning all night in Lessa's weyr, and Ramoth had long
conversations with all the other queens.* He sounded anxious.

"Don't worry, Ruth, please. It's going to work out. This is just a
new beginning, just as our Impression was! Though nothing could
ever be better than *that* day was for me!"

Ruth raised his head, his eyes altering from a murky shade to a
happier blue-green.

The incoming dragons were circling, their faceted eyes vivid green
and blue points against the dawn-gray light. As they backwinged,
their hind legs poised to take the impact of landing, Jaxom was just

able to discern that each dragon carried extra passengers. Some of the dragons waited only long enough to let their passengers dismount before they launched themselves again, disappearing *between* when they had gained sufficient height. The others settled down to wait while their riders and passengers headed for the administration building.

Jaxom sighed and gave Ruth an affectionate farewell slap before slipping back down the dusty slope to greet the new arrivals. When F'lar, Lessa, and Master Fandarel reached him in the doorway, Jaxom informed them that Aivas was resting.

"Resting?" Lessa demanded, halting so abruptly in midstride that F'lar had to sidestep to avoid barging into his slender weyrmate.

"The solar panels run out of power," Jaxom replied.

Master Fandarel looked both aggrieved and incredulous. "But—but Aivas said that he could provide twelve different stations."

"Lower your voice, please, Master Fandarel. Master Robinton's still asleep." Jaxom kept his own voice low as a hint to the others. "I brought Sebell and Menolly and the Records Master Robinton wanted Aivas to see. Jancis and I got as far as the sixth Turn before Aivas turned off. He says he'll be all right again after a few hours of sunlight."

"So we get here in the middle of the night and it isn't working?" Lessa said, disgusted.

"Now, there is much we can do while we await his revival," Fandarel said soothingly.

"What?" Lessa demanded. "I don't want people bungling about in the dark caves, you know. And it's scarcely the time to start reassembling this facility. F'lar and I have questions for Aivas. It's one thing to be *promised* a miracle, quite another to produce it. In courtesy, we should allow the other Weyrleaders to see and hear this Aivas for themselves, for I assure you," she added at her drollest, "they didn't believe what had happened here. And if they come and there's nothing to see . . ." Her voice trailed off ominously.

"I hardly believe it myself," F'lar remarked with a wry grin at Jaxom. "So I can't fault others."

"There are more than enough glowbaskets to illuminate the caves," Master Fandarel said in his approximation of a whisper, "and the dawn is not far away now. My craftsmen can begin to assemble the items Aivas said it needs. Where are those sheets Aivas made? Bendarek is fascinated by my description of printed sheets emerging from a wall. He's just coming up the hill now." Clearly Master

Fandarel entertained no reservations about accepting the Aivas's offer to restore his Records to legibility.

"Where are Sebell and Menolly?" Lessa asked, peering down the
corridor toward the Aivas chamber.

Jaxom chuckled. "They're getting some rest. Aivas wouldn't even
talk in front of them."

"Why not?" Lessa asked, surprised. "We told him they were coming."

"But they're not on the list. And while I'm a Lord Holder, and
Piemur's a harper, we had no Weyrleader present."

Lessa frowned.

"That's exactly what we stipulated, Lessa," F'lar said. "I can trust
someone that is scrupulous about obeying orders. Particularly something as potent as this Aivas."

A bass rumble startled them, and it took a moment to realize that
the noise was Fandarel's chuckle. "It is the function of a machine to
do what it is designed to do. I approve."

"You approve of anything that's efficient," Lessa said. "Even if
that isn't always sensible."

"We've lived too long with dragons," F'lar said, grinning down
at his diminutive weyrmate, "who understand what we mean, even
when we haven't said it."

"Hmmm," Lessa replied in a testy mumble as she gave him a sour
glance.

"We all will have new things to learn, I think," Fandarel said.
"And it is time. Jaxom, I'll need those sheets Aivas made, so I can
give them to Bendarek."

Obediently, Jaxom collected them from the flat worktop where Piemur and Jancis had left them. "Jancis went to make fresh klah," he
told Lessa. "She should be back any time now."

"Then off you all go," Lessa said, flipping her hands at them in
dismissal. "Jaxom, if you're all determined to get a start on the caves,
take Fandarel on Ruth, will you? That way he won't break his neck
stumbling about in the dark. I'll wait for Jancis and Aivas."

2
▼▼▼▼▼▼▼▼

By the time the sun had risen, many had come to view Aivas—
the tale had spread as fast as Thread burrows. Curiosity and
disbelief are mighty movers, so men and women had come from every
Hall, Hold, and Weyr. To the disgust of some, most of the fervor was
prompted not by Aivas's vast store of new knowledge, but by the
chance to glimpse the miraculous moving pictures that this marvel
was purported to produce.

Fandarel, supervising the acquisition of the material on Aivas's
list, was busy in the Catherine Caves. Breide, overwhelmed with
helpers, was making great strides in carefully clearing the ash and
dirt from the roof to expose the remaining solar panels. Master Esselin was poring over Aivas's redesign plans, though he railed that
Breide's men were not working fast enough for him to begin his job.
Breide retorted that he hadn't even dismantled the buildings that
were to provide the material for the extensions, so what was Esselin
bleating about?

Lessa, hearing the argument, told them to stop behaving like apprentices and go about their duties. Then she, with Menolly and Jancis, found willing helpers among the women to do the drudge work
of washing down the walls of long-disused rooms and shoveling out
the dirty ash that had seeped in around windows and doors. The
largest room, which the women decided must have originally been
intended for conferences, was prepared for that purpose again. Re-

membering what she had seen stored in the cave, Lessa sent for enough furnishings to make the room useful: tables, desks, and as many chairs as could be easily reached without getting in Fandarel's way. All these were washed down, revealing bright colors that made cheerful accents in the otherwise bare rooms. The room farthest from all the activity was turned into a private retreat for the Masterharper, complete with a comfortable bed, a well-cushioned chair, and a table.

"The only problem will be in getting him to use it," Lessa said, giving the table a final swipe with her cleaning cloth. She had smudges on her cheeks, across her fine-bridged nose, and on her strong chin. Her long black hair was coming loose from its braids. Menolly and Jancis exchanged glances to decide who would tell her how dirty her face was. Jancis thought that the Weyrwoman's disarray, as well as her energetic cleaning, made her suddenly more accessible. The young Smithmaster had always been scared of the famous Weyrwoman.

"Somehow I never thought that I'd see the Weyrwoman of Pern working like a drudge," Jancis murmured to Menolly. "She does it with a vengeance."

"She had practice," Menolly said with a wry chuckle, "hiding herself away from Fax in Ruatha Hold before Impressing Ramoth."

"But she looks as if she was enjoying this," Jancis said in faint surprise. Actually, she was, too. It gave her a sense of achievement to return a dirty room to cleanliness and order.

The charts that Lessa had requisitioned from Esselin's archives arrived, and the Weyrwoman had the girls hold them up on the various walls to decide the best position.

"Is it really right to put such precious artifacts to such a . . ." Jancis struggled to find the appropriate word.

"Mundane use?" Menolly asked with a grin.

"Exactly."

"They were initially used in this way," Lessa said, quirking her lips and shrugging her shoulders. "So why not put them back up?"

Applying herself to the task had restored the Weyrwoman's equilibrium; the discovery of Aivas and its promise to help F'lar achieve his deepest ambition had shaken her. She desperately wanted what was promised, almost as much as F'lar did, but she was fearful of the consequences. The morning's scrubbing attack had allowed her to expend some of her anxiety. Now she felt herself peculiarly revived.

"Since the maps haven't deteriorated—amazing material the settlers used—I see no reason why we shouldn't use them for the purpose they were designed for," she went on briskly. She had decided that "settlers" was a less intimidating word than "ancestors." She studied one of the maps. "The Southern Continent certainly does spread out, doesn't it?" And she smiled, half to herself. "Lift your corner a trifle, Jancis. There! Now it's straight!"

She smoothed the map of the Southern Continent against the wall. Then, with considerable satisfaction, she sited a tack and hammered it in with a rectangular lump of rock she had found. Esselin had dithered so much about giving them two baskets and a shovel that she hadn't bothered to ask for a hammer. The rock did as well.

She stood back with the girls to survey her handiwork. The lettering on the maps still took her moments to decipher. It was familiar and yet different, and certainly larger. She wondered how Aivas had fared reading the crabbed tight script that Master Arnor had used in writing up the Records. Poor Master Arnor.

Not to mention poor Robinton, who had been so mortified to learn that there had been language shifts despite all the hard work that the Harper Hall had put into keeping it pure. Old Arnor's mind was notoriously inflexible, and the old fellow might have spasms when he heard that. Which was yet another aspect of this discovery: Its knowledge and its obvious intelligence put Aivas into the role of a Master of Masters in all disciplines—except, perhaps, the dragons. She might have been reading things into its tone, but had there been a note of excitement in that otherwise level voice when it mentioned the dragons?

"Yes, the maps are appropriate here, aren't they? Not merely decorative." She smiled at Jancis and Menolly. Working with Piemur's young woman had reassured her that the journeyman was well matched with Fandarel's granddaughter. Lessa had been dubious about including Jancis on Aivas's roster, but she had lost her reservations this morning. Jancis had earned a place, and not simply because she had been instrumental in finding the room and was proving to be a willing worker. She had the right attitude toward Aivas and the future.

Jancis's eyes glowed as she studied the map. "They produced so many wonderful things. Things that could last for centuries; materials impervious to Thread. Things that will enrich our lives, too."

"True enough, but how am I going to reduce this—" Menolly waved an arm in Aivas's direction. "—into a ballad that will explain these events to people?"

Lessa chuckled. "A change from your usual subjects, isn't it? You'll manage, Menolly dear. You always do, and splendidly. And don't bother to explain—I doubt even Master Robinton could 'explain' a phenomenon like Aivas. Present him as a challenge, to shake us all out of our mid-Pass doldrums." She pulled out a chair, absently gave it a flick of her rag, and sat down with a loud sigh. Then she cocked her head at the other two. "I don't know about you two, but I could certainly use a nice hot cup of klah."

Jancis sprang to her feet. "And fruit and meatrolls. The cook was up before dawn, complaining about hordes to feed on short notice—but he was making enough food to feed a Gather. I'll be right back."

Menolly turned to Lessa then, her expression serious. "Lessa, is Aivas going to be a good challenge? Jaxom told us such incredible things. Some people are simply not going to accept them, or even try to." She thought of her hidebound parents and others of similarly rigid minds whom she had not in her Turns as a harper.

Lessa gave a resigned flick of one hand. "It's been found. I don't want to deny it, even if its discovery means some painful reassessments. I found it fascinating to hear how the settlers got here—the pictures they had of Pern in the black heavens are truly awesome. I'd no idea it could look like that! And it was thrilling to hear how bravely our ancestors struggled to destroy Thread. We've been used to it—even if *some* thought we'd had our last Pass four hundred Turns ago." Her lips curled with remembered malice for those doubters. "But what a terrible shock it must have been for them." With an apologetic expression, she touched Menolly's hand lightly. "You are one of those who truly deserved to hear that history, Menolly, but we'd no idea what had been discovered when we were sent for. Maybe Aivas wouldn't mind repeating it for you, and the other Harper Masters, because that is something the Hall should circulate. It should be compulsory for children to learn our true origins. We'll need new Teaching Ballads. But that is for Sebell to decide, isn't it?" Then her expression altered again, first to a look of awe, and then to a grimace. "I can tell you that I had trouble believing my eyes and ears when Aivas said that the settlers actually created—'bi-o-en-gin-eered' was his word—our dragons." Her grin was tinged with rancor. "I'm almost relieved that there are so few Oldtimers left alive. They'd have found *that* very hard indeed to accept."

"Do you find it hard to accept that dragons were engineered from fire-lizards?" Menolly asked teasingly. Lessa had made her dislike of the small draconic cousins very plain over the Turns, and Menolly was always careful to keep hers out of the Weyrwoman's way.

Lessa made another face, more reflective than angry. "They *are* dreadful nuisances at times, Menolly. Did you leave yours behind in the Harper Hall today?"

"No." Menolly's sideways glance challenged Lessa. "Only Beauty, Rocky, and Diver came along this morning. They're keeping Ruth company. They've always adored him."

Lessa looked thoughtful. "Aivas commented on Ruth, but he appeared to be quite surprised by Ramoth, Mnementh, and Canth. I must ask him why when I get the chance. Well, at least we have something *we* can explain to Aivas." She let out a gusty sigh. "And if he can help us end Thread forever . . . I only hope that he can!"

To Menolly's fine-tuned harper's ear, she thought that there was an undertone of desperation in Lessa's voice. The Weyrwoman caught her expression and nodded slowly, her eyes sad. "At this point in a Pass, Menolly, we do very much need a hope that there could be a way to clear our skies of Thread. And get on with the sort of life the settlers had hoped to lead here."

"Jaxom told us that Aivas had said that there was a *possibility*."

"At least Jaxom repeats things accurately," Lessa said at her driest. "You should have heard some of the rumors in the Weyr this morning. The Weyr Harper is going to see that those are suppressed, and accurate information circulated. Hope is all very well, but it must be realistic."

"But Aivas did say it was possible?"

Lessa nodded. "Possible! But we'll have to work hard to achieve it. We'll have to learn a lot of new things."

"Even that could improve morale." Then Menolly added more briskly, "The wonder is that our ancestors managed to survive each new Pass losing so little of our culture."

"They had to, as we have had to. But we know that so much of our culture *was* lost. If that threat were removed, oh, what a wonderful future we could contemplate!"

Menolly caught Lessa's eye in a significant stare. "Wonderful for the dragons and the Weyrs, too?"

"Yes!" Lessa's explosive reply surprised the Harper Hall Master. "Yes, it will be even better for dragons and Weyrs." She took a deep breath and exhaled, jabbing her finger at the map. "We'll have a new world to explore again." She leaned forward, peering at the map. "I wonder what 'Honshu' was."

Just then Jancis returned, carrying a basket with a klah pitcher, cups, and food. She was also full of news.

"You should see what they've done while we've been cleaning," she said, a broad smile on her face. "You should also see the mob wanting to gawk at Aivas." When Lessa sprang to her feet, Jancis waved her back down. "F'lar, Sebell, and Master Robinton are in control. We'll be the better for something to eat. Here, Lessa, fresh redfruit and nice hot rolls. If you'd pour the klah, Menolly," she said, passing around the fruit and rolls.

"You're as efficient as your grandsire," Lessa remarked approvingly, settling back into her chair. The smell of warm bread and meat reminded her that it had been a long time since that hurried early-morning porridge at Benden Weyr. "Menolly, as soon as you've eaten, I want you on Aivas's roster." She turned to Jancis. "How long has Aivas been—" She searched for the appropriate word. "Available?"

Jancis grinned over the rim of her cup. "Long enough to approve or discard what Grandfather brought out of the caves for inspection. Masters Wansor and Terry are attempting to follow a diagram on how to assemble the—the components." She hesitated briefly over the unfamiliar word. "They've sent for Masterglassman Norist, because two of the screens were cracked. Aivas wants to discover if we have the skill, only he said 'technology,' to duplicate the material. He's very diplomatic, but he's certainly putting every one on their mettle. He—it—" Jancis shook her head, then appealed to Lessa. "What *do* we call the thing? Aivas says he/it is a machine, but with that beautiful voice, he sounds very human."

"Beautiful voice?" Menolly asked through a mouthful of redfruit, hastily stemming the juice from dripping down her chin.

Lessa chuckled. "Yes," she said with a grin at Menolly's reaction. "A beautiful voice. Almost as good as Master Robinton's."

"Really?" Menolly's thick eyebrows rose at that comparison to her beloved Master. "How clever of our ancestors," she added, not rising to Lessa's bait.

Lessa grinned more broadly. "Yes, it's only fair to warn you. The thing is rather awesome."

Menolly grinned back. "Too kind of you. I wonder if he knows anything about ancestral music forms?"

Lessa laughed. "I could hear that question coming."

"He said," Jancis put in, keeping her expression bland, "he had the Planetary Engineering and Colonial Kit in his memory banks, as well as what cultural and historical records were deemed relevant by the colonists. Surely music would be considered a cultural necessity?''

Lessa hid a smile, delighted by Jancis's subtle tease.

"If it isn't, it should be. It will be my first question of this Aivas," Menolly replied equably. She took a firm bite out of her meatroll.

"Aivas is a clever enough affair, but it's only got the one voice, however mellifluous," Lessa went on. "Only one voice to sing with, even if it does have ancient music in those formidable memory banks."

F'lar appeared in the doorway, looking harassed as he pushed a wayward lock off his forehead. "There you are, Lessa. Menolly, Robinton wants you and Lessa, and we have got to discuss the length of that sharding roster. *Everyone* has questions that require answers from Aivas. Piemur has the right of it, though. Most of them don't believe what they've been hearing." He perched on the table and broke off a piece of meatroll. "They probably won't believe even after they've seen Aivas."

"How can we fault them on that score?" Lessa asked. "But it's a waste of Aivas's valuable time to humor skeptics. And ours. We must have a conference."

Jancis jumped up, aware that her presence might be superfluous.

"No, child, don't disappear. A conference is not that imminent." Lessa gave a droll snort. "Not with everyone rushing around every which way this morning. But do get more cups, klah, and food. F'lar, eat something."

F'lar made a dismissive gesture. "I don't have time right now. There's too much to be done." But he crammed another bite of meatroll into his mouth.

"When did you intend to stop for food?" Lessa asked tartly. Rising, she pulled F'lar off the table and pushed him by the shoulders into the nearest chair. She put the rest of the meatroll in front of him and refilled her own cup for him, adding the amount of sweetener he preferred in his klah. "You didn't sleep last night, and if you don't eat, you'll be useless just when you're most needed. Now, who's importuning you? Do we have enough Lord Holders, Craftmasters, and Weyrleaders to constitute a majority?"

"Every single Lord Holder we didn't cram in yesterday is here, and every Mastercraftsman." F'lar flung up both hands in an extravagant gesture of impatience.

ANNE McCAFFREY

"Surely you've explained . . ."

"We've all been explaining," F'lar said irritably. "I know we've got touchy prides among our ranking personalities, but you'd think each one had been personally insulted by not being summoned yesterday." He bit into the meatroll and washed it down with a gulp of klah, scowling as he swallowed. "The worst complainers are those who haven't paid much attention to what's being done here at Landing. Different tune right now, I can tell you."

Lessa regarded him with astonishment. "How'd they all find out?"

F'lar flashed an ironic grin at Menolly. "Guess?"

The harper groaned and hid her face in her arms.

"Those dratted fire-lizards again!" Lessa's scowl was fierce. She shook her head. "And I suppose they came a-dragonback."

F'lar grimaced as he pushed hair off his forehead again. "I should never have given Hall and Hold resident dragonriders. They've taken to using the courtesy as if dragons were runnerbeasts."

"Oh, well, we have to take the bad with the good, and the courtesy certainly improved relations with Hold and Hall. It's just awkward at the moment. Nevertheless, it is essential that the Lords and Craftmasters experience Aivas for themselves. There'll be some hidebounds who will deny the evidence of their eyes and ears anyway. So, if they're here, they might well have a chance at Aivas."

"Oh, they're here," F'lar said airily, waving his second meatroll. "Sebell lets them in a few at a time and interrupts the session whenever Aivas is needed for the ongoing work. Most of the them go away shaking their heads and trying not to look bewildered. Very few of them have understood the significance of Aivas." He brought his fist down on the table. "When I think of what we once had, once were! What we can be again with Aivas's help!"

Lessa smiled at his intensity. "According to Aivas, even Landing wasn't built in one day." She began to knead the taut muscles about his neck and shoulders. "Eat, love. We've handled the skeptics before. We'll do it again in our own inimitable fashion." She leaned down and kissed his cheek.

F'lar gave her a rueful grin. "And you're handling me as you usually do, aren't you?"

Lessa gave him a look of mild indignation as she slipped back into her chair and picked up her half-eaten roll. "Reassuring you, dear heart."

From Mnementh, Lessa heard an incredulous mental snort.

Don't spoil the effect, she told the bronze dragon.

Not likely, Mnementh replied sleepily. *The sun is exceedingly warm here in this Landing place.*

Ramoth agreed.

Sebell appeared in the doorway then, nodding at the two Weyr-leaders as he beckoned to Menolly.

"Master Robinton wants to have Menolly added to the roster. N'ton's there as Weyrleader. And Fandarel snatched Jancis on her way to the kitchens. She's needed to do some drafting. Someone else is bringing more klah and food." Sebell helped himself to the remaining meatroll. "This'll make a good conference room." Then, draping one arm around Menolly's shoulders, he steered her out the door.

Lessa shot an intimate look at her own mate, and he grinned as he chewed the last of his meatroll and reached for a redfruit.

"Are you already on the list?" Menolly asked Sebell as they made their way down the corridor.

He gave her a mischievous grin, hugging her against his side. They fell easily into step. As he often did, Sebell wondered at his great good fortune to have won Menolly as his mate. He could not mind that part of her heart which was Master Robinton's. Part of his was the Harper's, too, along with his complete loyalty and respect; but Menolly was the joy of his life.

"How long must we wait?" Oterel, Lord Holder of Tillek demanded, scowling deeply as the two harpers passed him where he waited in the hallway.

"The room is small, Lord Oterel, and there is a great deal to be done today," Sebell said placatingly.

"Small or not, Fandarel and other very minor craftsmen have been in there for hours, and now he has hauled his granddaughter in, too," Oterel complained peevishly.

"If you were able to draw clear diagrams as she does, Lord Oterel," Menolly said, "you would doubtless be in there." She had disliked the testy old Lord of Tillek Hold ever since he had spoken out so vehemently against her attaining her Mastery.

Oterel glared fiercely back at her. Beyond him, Lord Toronas of Benden Hold covered a grin with his hand. "You're impudent, young woman, far too impudent! You dishonor your Hall."

Sebell gave him a long quelling look and then pulled Menolly into the small room. It was hot and stuffy, with stools crammed so closely together that she wondered how Jancis, Piemur, Terry, and another smith she didn't recognize could draw at all. Fandarel was hovering over them while N'ton leaned indolently against the far wall. Then she saw the screen and its display of unfamiliar objects as clearly defined as if the actual item had somehow gotten inside this Aivas and been magnified.

"Now, once the connections with the F-322RH have been made"— the rich, beautifully modulated voice made Menolly gasp in surprise; she glanced around and caught Sebell's grin at her reaction as she tried to locate the source of the voice—"the circuit will be completed. Add this board to those already installed and come back to me for the next step."

Obediently the four left, talking to one another in low tones. N'ton came forward then, and Fandarel cleared his throat.

"We three—Weyrlander N'ton; I, Craftmaster Fandarel; and Masterharper Sebell—request that you add Master Menolly of the Harper Hall to the roster."

"Will Master Menolly please speak so that a voiceprint may be taken?"

"A voiceprint?" Menolly asked, astonished.

"Yes, a human's voice is a more effective means of identification than physical appearance, which could be duplicated. Your voiceprint cannot. Therefore, it is necessary for you to speak so that a voiceprint ID can be registered to the roster file."

Menolly, rendered uncharacteristically speechless by the unusual request and the glorious voice, looked helplessly at Sebell. He flicked his fingers encouragingly, grinning cheerfully while N'ton mouthed words at her.

"I'm Menolly, once of Half Circle Sea Hold, and I'm better at singing than speaking," she said, stammering slightly in her confusion. Then she fretted that she was letting a stammer be registered.

Master Fandarel made a tumbling gesture with his hands, which she took to mean that she should continue talking.

"My rank is Master in the Harper Hall. I compose music and write lyrics. Master Sebell, here, is my mate, and we have three children. Have you heard enough?"

"That is sufficient for a voice with such a distinctive timbre," Aivas said. "Are copies of the music you write available? For the main files?"

"You want my music?" Menolly exclaimed in surprise.

"Music was very important to your ancestors."

"You have some of their music?" She could barely contain her excitement.

"There is an extensive file of music, spanning over two thousand years."

"But you're only one voice?"

There was a significant pause. "It would be inappropriate to use more than one in conversational mode. This system is, however, adapted to reproduce music in its varied instrumental forms."

"It is?" Menolly was aware of Sebell's chuckle and N'ton's grin.

"We'll get our turn, lovey," Sebell said softly. "I promise you that. Master Robinton is as eager as we are, but there are more urgent priorities."

Menolly gulped back disappointment and looked helplessly at Sebell.

"I must leave now," Fandarel said. "We are going to see how to reconstruct that power station, Aivas, and dragonriders have gone to bring my nickel-cadmium batteries, as you call them."

"Does Master Facenden understand how to connect them to the auxiliary power points shown to him?" Aivas asked.

"Yes, I made certain of his comprehension. He will also construct a cage to keep the unwary from touching the fluid or the wires. Come, N'ton, if you'd be so good as to assign dragonriders to take us up the river to the dam site." Fandarel wheeled about and strode down the corridor, N'ton beside him. Both ignored attempts by those waiting in the hall to stop and quiz them. Sebell gestured for Menolly to take one of the stools before he called Lords Oterel, Sigomal, Toronas, and Warbret to enter. Oterel pushed his way in first, wearing a triumphant expression that faded as he looked about him in bewilderment. When all four were in the room, Sebell introduced them to Aivas.

"It is a pleasure to make your acquaintances, my lords," Aivas replied courteously. Menolly noticed that his deep voice was subtly deferential. "Soon this facility will be enlarged so that larger audiences can be accommodated."

Sebell caught Menolly's eye and winked at her. Both appreciated Aivas's smooth tact.

"You can see us?" Oterel asked, still looking around for something, Menolly wagered, that he could recognize as eyes.

"The visual sensors are registering your individual presences. You will most certainly be recognized again whenever you return."

Menolly hastily covered her mouth. It wouldn't do for Oterel to see her grinning at his confusion. This Aivas was half-harper. How did it know just how to deal with the old bore? Had Sebell warned it?

"You don't have any eyes," Oterel said querulously.

"Optics are the eyes of a machine, Lord Oterel."

"I understand that you knew our ancestors, Aivas," Lord Sigomal said while Oterel floundered over the implication that eyes were somehow inferior. "Can you tell me who mine were?"

"Lord Sigomal," Aivas replied, sounding genuinely apologetic, "no input has been received on such specific details. A list of the names of those settlers who removed to Fort Hold is being prepared and will be made available to anyone who requests a copy. Your own Hold Records probably detail who established Bitra. However, you may be pleased to know that your province was named for one of the shuttle pilots, Avril Bitra."

Menolly wondered at the odd clipped delivery of that information. Aivas had an incredibly flexible voice, capable of amazing dynamics and nuances. Maybe Master Shonagar, the Hall's eccentric voice teacher, could be pried out of his domain to hear such a wonder.

"Lists of ancestors are the best you can do? That isn't going to be much use to us!" Oterel exclaimed in keen dissatisfaction.

"In your case, Lord Oterel, it is reasonable to assume that Tillek was either established by or named for Captain James Tillek, the captain of the *Bahrain*, a man of considerable acumen and talent as a seaman and explorer."

Oterel began to swell with importance.

"Regretfully, Lords Toronas and Warbret, your Holds were established long after input ceased. Would it be possible to add your Records to the information files of this time period? That would further the understanding of the structure of a Hold. There is so much that must be gathered before what you have created here on Pern can be fully appreciated."

Just then Master Wansor walked in and, mumbling over the page he was reading, stumbled into the seated Warbret. Profusely apologizing, he was confronted by a glaring Oterel, who accused him of barging in on Lord Holders.

"I've only one small question, but it is extremely urgent," Wansor said in his gentle, contrite voice. He took a breath to deliver the question.

"Master Wansor, you need only place the paper on the plate for it to be read and an answer given," Aivas reminded him most courteously.

Menolly raised her eyebrows. Few people paid Master Wansor the consideration his true abilities deserved.

"Oh, yes, I keep forgetting," Master Wansor said. Excusing himself, he wove a path past the stools to the control board. A round, little, unpretentious elderly man, he had to bend over to see with his weak eyes where to place the paper. The panel glowed more brightly. "Ah, yes. There!" And he patted the paper into position.

"Lord Toronas, your Hold was obviously named to honor the memory of Admiral Paul Benden," Aivas said, while several lightning flashes on the panel suggested to Menolly that Wansor's paper was being attended to simultaneously. Then, to the amazement of all, the main screen displayed the image of a fine-looking man, his face full of character. A man to trust, Menolly decided. Then she was stunned by the realization that Aivas had known and talked to that man, so long dead and so long remembered. "A fine man, Admiral Benden," Aivas went on. "Holding the settlers together, always encouraging, preserving them through considerable trials to establish a safer haven in the Northern Continent."

"And I'm related to the admiral?" Toronas asked, rather more humble in his request than Oterel. "Our earliest Records are impossible to decipher."

As the Lord Holders awaited Aivas's reply, Menolly noticed Wansor's discreet departure.

"It is entirely possible," Aivas said, "even likely that you are a direct descendant. Four children were recorded to the marriage of Paul Benden and Ju Adjai. Perhaps if you bring in your Records at some later date, they can be deciphered. A program is available that utilizes a special light which can often restore lost words and phrases."

Enthralled, Menolly listened as Aivas dealt with both Sigomal and Warbret, as cleverly and in as personal a fashion, catering to their self-images.

Then Jancis, Piemur, and Benelek hovered uncertainly in the doorway, each clutching several sheets. Piemur rattled his to get Sebell's attention; the Masterharper deferentially told the Lord Holders that Aivas must be consulted again and politely gestured for them to leave.

Oterel grumbled, but Sigomal rose readily enough and took the old Tillek Lord by the arm. "It's stifling in here, Oterel. Far too stuffy for comfort. I don't know about you, but I intend to search out those

Records and then see what this Aivas thing can tell me. Come along now.''

"He manipulates them like so many string-dolls," Menolly told her mate in an undertone after he had escorted the Lord Holders into the hallway.

"Master Robinson had advised that tact and flattery might be required," Aivas replied. "Especially for those who cannot be accommodated with a lengthy interview."

"How did you hear me?" Menolly asked, dismayed that Aivas had overheard her whisper.

"Master Menolly, you are sitting beside a receptor. Whispers are clearly audible."

She caught Sebell's amused glance. He might have warned her about that.

"Don't distract Aivas, Menolly," Piemur said, arranging his papers on the plate.

"Master Menolly is not a distraction," Aivas said mildly. "Next page please, Piemur."

"Could you really read those old moldy Records?" Menolly asked.

"The attempt should be made. The ink that was used to write the Records you were kind enough to bring last night is of an indelible type that will yield to certain techniques available to this facility. Outside manual assistance will be needed, however, to prepare the documents before they can be scanned. That is a project which has been put on hold."

"On hold?" Menolly was delighted by the unusual but descriptive phrase. "How explanatory!"

Then she heard the sounds of movement in the hall and saw a file of people, laden with cartons, striding purposefully toward her. She saw F'lessan and F'nor among them.

"I'd better leave," she said reluctantly.

"Hang about," Sebell told her.

"You seem to be bringing the cave here. Wouldn't it have been easier to move Aivas to the caves?" she asked.

"Negatory," Aivas said in as sharp a tone as Menolly had yet heard him utter. "This installation must remain in its present position, or it cannot access *Yokohama*."

"I was being facetious, Aivas," Menolly said penitently, and rolled her eyes at Sebell.

As the dragonriders came in, Menolly moved to N'ton's earlier position against the wall and watched as carton after carton was displayed to Aivas, to be either dismissed or sent into the rooms where others were attempting to construct the devices that would permit wider access to Aivas's facilities. None of the dragonriders seemed at all surprised to see her there, and F'lessan's grin had lost nothing of his usual impudence in the presence of Aivas. But then the son of F'lar and Lessa took nothing very seriously except his dragon, Golanth. Mirrim followed close on T'gellan's heels; the two from the Eastern Weyr were never far apart since they had declared themselves weyrmates. Mirrim had certainly bloomed and relaxed in the warmth of his preference, Menolly reflected.

"I didn't see you here earlier," Mirrim said in an aside to Menolly while waiting for her burden to be assessed by Aivas.

"Oh, I arrived here late last night with the Records of this Pass," Menolly replied. "Then Lessa grabbed me for some drudgery." She extended her strong hands, her calloused fingers still showing water-wrinkles.

Mirrim rolled her eyes. "I'm just as glad we got in on the fetch-and-carry end of things. Let's compare notes later, huh? I'd better go," she added with a smug grin, "T'gellan's waving at me." She hefted the carton over to Aivas's screen.

When Aivas had delivered a verdict and the riders had left, Sebell gestured for the Craftmasters to come in and be introduced. Again they were all courteously, if briefly, addressed, and Aivas issued the request to see their craft Records. When they had left, Menolly slipped over to Sebell.

"How on earth will Aivas find time to look at so many records?" she asked, whispering in his ear.

"He doesn't need sleep, only power," Sebell replied. "If we can supply that when the solar panels falter, he'll go on all day and night. You don't sleep, do you, Aivas?"

"This facility operates as long as it has sufficient power to do so. Sleep is a human requirement."

Sebell winked at Menolly.

"And you have none?" she demanded, jamming her fists into her belt as she faced the screen squarely.

"This facility is programmed to give optimum use at human convenience."

"Do I hear a tinge of apology in your tone, Aivas?" she asked.

"This facility is programmed not to give offense."

Menolly had to chuckle. Later she realized that that was when she began to accept Aivas as an individual entity and not as an awesome relic of her ancestors' contrivance.

"Menolly?" the Masterharper called from the far end of the corridor, which was, for the first time, empty of importunate visitors. "Is Sebell there with you?"

Sebell moved to where he could be seen.

"Take over from him, will you, Menolly?" Robinton asked. "We've got enough here for a conference."

Sebell put his hand on Menolly's upper arm, giving it a reassuring squeeze. "You saw how I conducted the encounters," he said. "If anyone else shows up, just introduce them."

"That didn't work last night when Piemur tried it," Menolly said.

Sebell grinned, squeezing her arm again. "Master Robinton and F'lar worked out a necessary alteration in the protocol."

"Another new word?"

"Aivas for convention or courtesy." He gave her a quick kiss on the cheek. "You won't be missing anything in the conference, you know."

"I do, and I'm relieved not to have to sit through another one," she called after him as he hurried down the hall to Master Robinton. Sebell knew how she hated formal ceremonies. Or would they now be called protocols? She smiled to herself, then realized that she was alone with Aivas.

"Aivas, would you be able to give me an example of ancestral music?"

"Vocal, instrumental, orchestral?"

"Vocal," Menolly replied without hesitation, promising herself that she would hear the other categories, too, when there was a chance.

"Classical, ancient, or modern; contemporary folk or popular; with or without instrumental accompaniment?"

"Anything, while we've got a free moment."

"Anything is too vague a category. Specify."

"Vocal, popular, with instruments."

"This was recorded at the Landing celebration." And suddenly the room was filled with music. Menolly immediately identified several of the instruments: a gitar, a fiddle, and something with a pipe-like sound; and then voices, untrained but enthusiastic and musical. The melody was hauntingly familiar to her; the words, though clearly sung, were not. The quality of the sound, however, was incredible. These voices and instruments had not been heard for centuries, and yet the sounds were as unblurred by time as if the musicians were present. When the song ended, she couldn't speak for the wonder of it.

"Was that not satisfactory, Master Menolly?"

She shook herself. "It was immensely and incredibly satisfying. I know that tune, too. What did the . . . settlers"—yes, she thought, Lessa was right to call them by that less intimidating noun—"call it?"

" 'Home on the Range.' It is classified as American Western folk music. Several variations were included when the music library was installed in the memory banks."

She would have asked for more, but Piemur came striding into the room carrying a strange contraption, a thin wide ribbon of colored strings hanging from one side. The front of it resembled part of the Aivas worktop, a series of depressions in five ordered ranks under a dark sheet of what looked to be more plastic.

"Kindly hold it over the view panel, Piemur. Level with your head, please." There was a long pause for assessment. "It seems to be correctly assembled. A final check will be its installation and activation, but that must wait on a power source and connections to this board. How is Master Terry progressing with the wiring?"

"I don't know. He's in another room. I'll just go and check for you. Here, Menolly, hang on to this. I don't want to risk dropping it." With an encouraging grin, Piemur deposited his load in her arms and half ran down the corridor.

"Why do you have that?" Jancis asked, arriving with a similar object in her hands.

Menolly told her and watched while Jancis repeated Piemur's antics. Right behind her came Benelek, Lord Groghe's clever son, who was now a smith journeyman. Fandarel had found him so extremely inventive that Menolly was not at all surprised to see him taking an active part here.

When Aivas had approved their efforts, Benelek wanted to know when they could hook up.

"When there is power available. So, Journeyman Benelek, you may as well assemble another keyboard while you're waiting," Aivas replied. "Ten are possible with the parts in hand. Two need replacement screens, if the Glassmaster will oblige."

"I really do not understand how you would be able to handle twelve people at once, Aivas," Menolly said.

"You play more than one instrument, do you not? That is, if this facility has properly understood the training practices of your Hall."

"I do, but not all at once."

"There is in this facility many parts, each of which can operate separately and simultaneously."

Silently Menolly considered that concept, unsure how to respond. Then, just when it would have begun to seem rude for her to remain quiet, Master Terry came trotting down the corridor, loops of material strung all over him.

3
▼▼▼▼▼▼▼▼

Down the hall, in the refurbished conference room, seven Lord Holders, eight Craftmasters, eight Weyrleaders, and four Weyrwomen were assembled in an extraordinary meeting. Harper Journeyman Tagetarl had been brought in to take full notes of the proceedings.

F'lar stood up to take charge, though everyone could see that Master Robinton would have been happy to officiate. There were those who thought the Harper had not looked so animated and vigorous in many a Turn, and assumed that the rumors of his decline must have been vastly exaggerated. Note was also taken that the Weyrleaders looked less haggard, almost cheerful—even optimistic.

"I believe you've all been introduced to Aivas," F'lar began.

Lord Corman of Igen snorted. "Introduced? To a talking wall?"

"It is much more than a talking wall," Robinton said tartly, glaring at Corman, who rolled his eyes at the Harper's unexpected vehemence and nudged Lord Bargen of High Reaches Hold beside him.

"Considerably more than just a wall," F'lar said. "Aivas is an intelligent entity, constructed by our ancestors who first settled this planet. It contains the information which our ancestors needed and used. Valuable knowledge which can teach us how to improve Hold, Hall, and Weyr." He took a deep breath. "And destroy Thread completely."

"That I'll believe when I see it," Corman replied with a disbelieving snort.

"I promised you that, Lord Corman, at the beginning of this Pass, and now I can fulfill that promise!"

"With a wall's help?"

"Yes, with this wall's help," Robinton replied, his voice intense with conviction as he glared angrily at the Holder.

"You wouldn't be so skeptical if you'd been here yesterday and heard Aivas!" Larad said, jumping to his feet, his tone trembling with controlled anger. Corman recoiled in surprise.

"With all due respect, F'lar, Robinton, Larad," Warbret said appeasingly, "we've been called down here so frequently to see useless hulks, empty buildings, and caves bulging with shards and artifacts that I personally didn't think anything could be that urgent this time. I do find it very odd in you, Weyrleader, to be taken in by talking walls spouting archaic legends."

Robinton rose up out of his seat, bellowing such a protest that Warbret regarded him with amazement. "Gullible? Warbret, I, Robinton of Cove Hold, may be old but I cannot be considered gullible . . ."

"Nor I," Fandarel added, also on his feet and looming over the incredulous Holders. "This is not a *wall*, Lord Corman." The scorn in the usually equable Mastersmith's manner made everyone stare at him. "This machine, this Aivas, was so efficiently and beautifully crafted by our ancestors that it has survived centuries and still functions. *That* is more than the best any present crafthall can do!" He jerked his big head to emphasize his respect. "Make no further insult on our intelligence or integrity, Lord Corman. You may not choose to believe in Aivas but most assuredly, I"—and he thumped his chest with his massive thumb—"Fandarel, Mastercraftsman, do!"

Corman subsided in bewilderment.

"So why have you called this session, then?" Warbret asked.

"Out of courtesy. So you'd all be made aware of the importance of this find as soon as possible," Lessa snapped. "I'm not letting the Weyrs open to any charge of duplicity or hiding away valuable artifacts."

"My dear Weyrwoman," Warbret began placatingly.

"Well, maybe not you, Warbret," Lord Groghe intervened, "but I could name some . . ." He left his words hanging. "You weren't here, so you didn't listen, as I did, and I'm no more gullible than

Robinton, F'lar, or Fandarel. But if this Aivas thing really can rid us of Thread, I'm all for giving it every assistance."

"If it can do that," Corman challenged, "then why didn't it do it for our ancestors?"

"Yes, why didn't it?" Toronas of Benden asked.

"Because two erupting volcanoes altered their plans," F'lar replied with great patience. "Landing—which is what our ancestors called this place—had to be evacuated. No one returned from the North to find out what Aivas might have learned."

"Oh." With that, Toronas subsided.

"I didn't mean offense, F'lar," Warbret said reasonably. "I just think you're all jumping to conclusions on very flimsy evidence that this Aivas apparatus can do the half of what you think it can."

"Aivas has already proved to me," Fandarel said, his rumbling voice overpowering the others, "that it can restore information that has been lost to my Craft over the last millennium: information that will improve not just my Craft but conditions throughout Pern. You know very well, Lord Warbret, that the depredations of time have rendered many Records illegible. And that many of the conveniences which were our heritage from our ancestors have begun to fail. Further, Aivas has given me plans for a far more efficient power system. One so efficient," the Mastersmith added, pointing a thick forefinger at the Igen Lord Holder, "that your Hold could be kept cool even at high noon at the height of the summer by the current of your river."

"Really? I can't say I'd mind that," Corman admitted, but his skepticism remained. "And just supposing," he added in a sly voice, glancing sideways at F'lar, "this Aivas *does* help you get rid of Thread, what will dragonriders do for occupation?"

"We'll worry about that when we have destroyed Thread."

"So you have some doubts yourself, Weyrleader?" Corman asked quickly.

"I said *when*, Lord Corman," F'lar said in a grating tone. "Are you arguing with our eagerness to dispense with accepting your tithes?" The Weyrleader's expression was sardonic.

"No, I mean, we've willingly tithed this Fall . . ." Corman floundered briefly and threw up his hands, recalling the time when he had not willingly supported Benden Weyr.

"And just how will this talking wall of yours destroy Thread, Weyrleader?" Masterglass-smith Norist demanded, his cheeks red with more than the broken capillaries from facing his hearths. "By blowing up the Red Star?"

Larad leaned across the table toward Norist, his eyes narrowed in anger. "Does it matter how it is achieved if it is, Master Norist, so long as there is never another Pass?"

"May I live to see that day," Corman said in a facetious tone.

"I intend to." F'lar's voice and expression were steely with determination. "Now, if we have settled the question as to why at least the dragonriders feel Aivas is important . . ."

"Dragonriders are *not* the only ones, F'lar," Fandarel said, bringing his heavy fist firmly down on the table, rattling everything on it.

"Nor Mastercraftsmen," Lord Asgenar added staunchly.

"I, too," Groghe said when Corman snorted. "Sometimes you can be sharding hard to convince, Corman. You'll change your mind when you've *heard* Aivas. You're not that much of a fool."

"Enough!" F'lar took charge again. "The purpose of this meeting is to apprise you of the discovery of Aivas and its inescapable value to Pern as a whole. Which we have done to those of you who bothered to come. Further, I trust you other Weyrleaders—" F'lar scanned the seven present. "—will join Benden in making full use of the Aivas."

"Now listen here, F'lar. You can't arbitrarily decide something that's going to effect Hold, Hall, and Weyr until everyone's had a chance to see for themselves," Corman began, glancing at Warbret and Bargen to support him. "I think this ought to be taken up at the Holders' quarterly meeting—which isn't that far off now."

"Holders may decide for themselves," F'lar said.

"And Craftmasters," Norist put in, his expression forbidding. His glare rested longest on Fandarel.

"Decisions on who uses the Aivas ought not to be delayed," F'lar said.

"C'mon, F'lar," Groghe said. "You haven't waited on anything. Scrambling about caves in the dark, hauling in apprentices and journeymen from all over the continent to resurrect bits and bobs of strange gear." He held up a hand when he saw F'lar's concerned expression. "Not that I, personally, don't agree with you, Weyrleader. Deciding anything at the Holders' Quarterlies can try the patience of a dragon. However, I did see and hear Aivas." He turned slightly in his seat toward the other Lord Holders. "The device is amazing, and I am convinced of its value!"

"There was a time, Corman," F'lar said, with a slight smile that reminded the Lord Holder of another occasion when the Benden Weyrleader had faced the massed and armed disapproval of the Lord

Holders and bested them, "when you and all the other Lord Holders urgently required me to put an end to Threadfall. Surely you want me to get on with that task as swiftly as possible?"

"You've done exactly as you ought," Groghe said, daring Corman to protest.

"Indeed you have, Weyrleader," Toronas agreed. F'lar found the new Benden Holder a vast improvement on the previous one, Lord Raid.

"However," the Weyrleader went on, "it is painfully obvious that we have lost most of the skills our ancestors had. We must relearn them, with Aivas's guidance, so that we can indeed remove forever from this planet the menace of Threadfall." F'lar looked from Norist to Corman to Warbret and then other Lord Holders, who had not taken part in the argument. "Isn't it sensible to start on the program as soon as possible? To restore what we have lost?"

"And you expect all of us to take our orders from this Aivas?" Norist asked sarcastically. He had been exceedingly reticent when Aivas had queried him about his Craft.

"Master Norist," Fandarel began in his slow deliberate way, "if there are opportunities to improve our Craft skills, surely it is incumbent on us to do so?"

"What that Aivas suggested I do in the Craft which I have Mastered, and efficiently, for the past thirty Turns, goes against every established procedure of my Hall!" Norist wasn't going to give an inch.

"Including the now illegible ones in your oldest Records?" Master Robinton asked gently. "And here is Master Fandarel, fretting to get on with the restoration of an ancestral power station, quite willing to accept new principles from Aivas."

Something akin to a sneer curled Norist's thick, scarred lip. "We all know that Master Fandarel is endlessly fiddling about with gadgets and gimmicks."

"Always efficient ones," Master Fandarel replied, ignoring the disparagement. "I can plainly see that every Craft can benefit from the knowledge stored in Aivas. This morning Bendarek was given invaluable advice on how to improve his paper, Aivas called it, and speed up its production. Very simple, but Bendarek immediately saw the possibilities and has gone back to Lemos to develop this much more efficient method. That's why he's not here."

"You and Bendarek," Norist said, a flick of his fingers dismissing the newest Mastercraftsman's products, "may exercise your prerog-

ANNE McCAFFREY

atives. I prefer to concentrate on maintaining the high standards of my Halls without dissipating effort on frivolous pursuits.''

''You don't, however,'' Lord Asgenar said, with a droll grin, ''object to making use of the frivolous pursuits of other crafthalls. Such as the load of sheets delivered to you last month. Bendarek expects to be able to increase production of paper''—Asgenar grinned more broadly—''so that no one will be kept waiting for supplies.''

''Glass is glass, made of sand, potash, and red lead,'' Norist stated stubbornly. ''You can't improve on it.''

''But Aivas suggested ways to do just that,'' Master Robinton said at his most reasonable and persuasive.

''I've wasted enough time here already.'' Norist stood up and stalked off down the hall.

''Damned fool,'' Asgenar muttered under his breath.

''Back to the important point, F'lar,'' Warbret said, leaning forward across the table to the Weyrleaders. ''The possibility of eliminating Thread. Just how does this Aivas propose to go about this? F'nor didn't have much luck when he tried.''

Remembering how close F'nor had come to dying in his attempt to go *between* to the Red Star itself, F'lar stared at him for a moment, then collected himself and went on. ''Lord Warbret, until you have first listened to and seen the history Aivas has to tell you, you will not appreciate how much we will have to learn before we can even understand his explanations of what we have to do.''

''And Aivas's showing and telling beggars my poor skill,'' Robinton said with unusual humility. ''For he was there! He knew our ancestors. He was created on the planet of our forebears! He witnessed and recorded events which have become our myths and legends.'' His voice rang with such feeling that there was a moment of respectful silence.

''Yes, you and Lord Corman should hear Aivas before you dismiss the gift we have been offered,'' Lessa added softly but just as fervently.

''Mind you, I'm not against going along with your course of action,'' Warbret said, after a moment, ''if it can help us eradicate Thread. And if you say, Weyrwoman, that we should hold our decision until we've heard this Aivas speak, when will that be possible?''

''Hopefully, later today,'' F'lar replied.

''The batteries should be in place now,'' Fandarel reminded him, ''but I must go. Aivas is going to need much more power. And I will

· 55 ·

see that he gets it.'' He rose and stood there for a moment, surveying the gathering. ''Some of us will be called upon to change the ways and patterns of a lifetime, which is not an easy thing to do, but the benefits will more than compensate for that effort. We have endured enough of Thread. Now we have the chance to eradicate this menace, and we must grasp it firmly in both hands and succeed! Facenden,'' he said, turning to his journeyman, ''stay in my stead and report to me later.''

Then he left, his heavy steps audible down the short corridor.

''I think this meeting has gone on long enough, too,'' Corman said. ''Do as you wish, Weyrleader. You generally do anyhow.'' But this time his comment held no rancor. ''Just see that there is a full report of these activities for the quarterly Convocation.''

He also got to his feet, nudging Bargen to join him. But the High Reaches Lord Holder only regarded him thoughtfully and did not rise.

''Will you not stay to hear the history, Corman?'' Robinton asked.

''In that stuffy little room?'' Corman asked indignantly. ''Have my harper learn it and I'll hear it in my own Hold, in comfort and at my own convenience.'' And with that he left.

''I will listen,'' Bargen said. ''I have come this far, though I am by no means certain that it is the wisest course to encourage this awesome Aivas thing.''

''At least you will listen,'' Robinton said, giving an approving nod. ''Sebell, how many can we comfortably accommodate in that stuffy little room?'' He said it blandly enough, but several of the Weyrleaders smiled.

''Certainly all here who wish to attend,'' Sebell said. ''There are now enough benches and stools, and if a few of us have to stand, I gather no one minded yesterday. I certainly won't.''

''We don't have to ask this creature's permission?'' Bargen asked.

''Aivas is nothing if not accommodating,'' Master Robinton said, grinning broadly.

They filed down the hall then, three Lord Holders, the Weyrleaders and Weyrwomen, and the Craftmasters. Terry was already there, looking mightily pleased with himself but warding people away from the bundle of cords that wound from Aivas and stretched along the left-hand wall and out into the adjacent room. A window had been inserted, high on the right-hand wall, allowing fresh air to circulate through the room. There turned out to be enough benches and stools to seat almost everyone, including Lord Groghe, who had decided to sit through Aivas's telling a second time. Menolly stood beside Se-bell. She groped and found his hand when the first vision of Pern in the blackness of space lit the screen.

"Now that's amazing," Bargen exclaimed, but he was the last to speak until Aivas ended its account with the final view of an airsled disappearing through the ashfall to the west. Then, slightly dazed, he muttered, "Corman's an old fool. Norist, too."

"Thank you, Aivas," Groghe of Fort Hold said, rising and shaking out stiffened limbs. "Of course, I saw it yesterday, but it's worth seeing again. And any time I can." He nodded emphatically at F'lar. "You know that I'll support you, dragonriders. You will, too, won't you, Warbret, Bargen?" His question was more of a demand, and he jutted his chin at his peers, ready to coerce them into agreement.

"I think we must, Warbret," Bargen said as he rose and turned, courteously inclining his body toward F'lar and then Master Robin-ton. "Good day. And good luck."

The other lords left with him.

"I don't mean to dash all this optimism," G'dened of Ista Weyr said, "but Aivas said nothing to the point of just *how* we're going to accomplish the elimination of Thread."

"No, he didn't exactly, did he?" R'mart agreed, shaking his head as if to clear it. "The ancestors had a lot more equipment and gadgets and those sleds. If they couldn't get rid of Thread, how shall we?"

"There is a time for all things to be accomplished," Aivas said. "As mentioned last night, several conclusions had been made. The most important, for you, is that in four years, ten months, and twenty-seven days, it will be possible to jolt the eccentric planet out of its present orbit, permanently. It will then be close to the orbit of your fifth planet, far from Rukbat—though, as you now know, the Thread swarms still follow it past Pern."

The Aivas had the stunned attention of everyone in the room as a diagram of Rukbat's planets blazed on the screen. They moved slowly around their primary, and the wanderer crossed at an angle to them.

F'lar gave a weak laugh. "The dragons of Pern are strong and willing, but I don't think they could move the Red Star."

"They will not," Aivas said. "For to attempt the feat would be to endanger their lives and their riders'. But the dragons are able to perform other, vital tasks that will allow you to alter that planet's course permanently."

Once again everyone was silent.

"That I might live to see the day," G'dened of Igen murmured fervently. "I'd go forward another four hundred Turns if we could do that!"

"If that could be done," R'mart asked, "why didn't our ancestors do it?"

"The conjunction of the planets was not then auspicious." The Aivas paused briefly, then went on with what Master Robinton heard as irony. "And by the time these calculations had been made, all had gone north, leaving this facility unable to inform its operators." Aivas paused again. "The dragons you have nourished to such size and strength will be critical to the success of the project. If you are willing."

"If we are willing!" T'gellan and T'bor cried in astonished chorus. All the dragonriders sprang to their feet. Mirrim hugged T'gellan's arm, her expression fierce with determination.

"F'lar's not the only one," N'ton added, "whose greatest wish is to exterminate Thread!"

D'ram, the oldest of the riders, had tears streaming down his cheeks. "We are nothing if not willing, Aivas. Even this old man and his ancient dragon!"

From outside came a chorus of dragons bugling, the rich bass of the bronzes, the thrilling sopranos of the queens, and the high piercing tone of Mirrim's green Path.

"It will not be an easy task," Aivas said, "and you will have to study assiduously in order to lay the necessary foundation to bring success to that day."

"Why must it be four years, ten months, and whatever days?" K'van, the youngest Weyrleader, asked.

"Twenty-seven days," Aivas corrected him. "Because that is the precise moment when a window will be open."

"A window?" Inadvertently K'van looked at the new one in the wall.

"As a rider, you always take your dragon to a precise place when you go *between*, do you not?" K'van was not the only rider to nod agreement. Aivas went on. "It is even more important to be precise when one is traveling in space."

"We're going to be traveling in space?" F'lar asked, gesturing toward the screen where they had briefly seen what space was like.

"In a manner of speaking," Aivas said. "You will come to understand, and correctly interpret, the terms that define the tasks before you. In the lexicon of space travel, a window is the interval that brackets the moment within which you have flexibility to achieve your objective, also traveling in space. If this is to succeed—"

"*If?*" R'mart almost yelled. "But you said it *could!*" He glared accusingly at F'lar.

"The plan is viable and has every chance of succeeding *if* the requisite effort is put into its implementation," Aivas said firmly. "But success will depend on the learning of new skills and disciplines. It is obvious that while all dragonriders are dedicated men, you also have little leisure at your command. But the dragons and the riders are requisites to the task, supported by Craftmasters and those Lord Holders who will lend men and women as support staff. It would be best if everyone on the planet could be involved in the project. As were your ancestors."

"I still don't see why our ancestors didn't take care of the problem when they had the chance to," R'mart said.

"Your ancestors did not have dragons the size and intelligence of yours. The species has evolved and exceeded the original genetic specifications. If you will observe . . . ." Images of two dragons flicked onto Aivas's screen. "The bronze is Carenath, Sean O'Connell is his rider, and the other is Faranth and Sorka Hanrahan." Two more dragons appeared on screen, three times the size of the first two. "Now, there are Ramoth and Mnementh. The scale of comparison is accurate."

"Why, that bronze isn't as big as Ruth," T'bor said, shooting an apologetic glance at the Benden Weyrleaders.

"No, he doesn't seem to be," F'lar replied equably. "You've made the point, Aivas. Now, how do we start this training you speak of?"

"Not today, certainly," Aivas said. "The first priority is a proper power source, which Master Fandarel has been good enough to undertake in his efficient fashion." Master Robinton swung to stare sharply at the screen. Aivas continued. "Second, the installation of the additional stations. Third, a supply of paper sufficient for hard copy for instruction and explanation. Fourth—"

F'lar waved both hands, grinning. "Enough, Aivas. When the craftsmen have done your bidding, we'll be ready to take instruction. That I promise you."

"Good," Master Terry said, rising from his stool and hitching his heavy tool belt to a more comfortable position. "Are you leaving here now?" he asked amiably. "Because I've got more connections to make to Aivas, and you're in my way."

"There'll be food and drink in the conference room by now," Lessa said, encouraging everyone to leave.

Master Robinton waited until all the others were well down the corridor. He glanced at Terry, busy laying out the cables and muttering to himself.

"Aivas?" the Masterharper said in a whisper, "do you have a sense of humor?"

There was a distinct pause before the reply came. "Master Robinton, this facility is not programmed for senses. It is programmed to interact with humans."

"That is not an answer."

"It is one kind of an explanation."

With that, Master Robinton had to be content.

The four Eastern Weyr dragonriders glided down in a spiral to the hillside above the dam. All interest in the ancients' settlement had been centered on Landing. No one had yet any occasion to wander about the nearby hills looking for evidence of the settlers' handiwork, so the presence of an obviously man-made lake—for Fandarel had dammed up a few useful streams in his Turns as apprentice and journeyman in the Smithcrafthall and recognized the configuration—was yet another surprise.

The lake stretched back, a glittering long finger contained between two high ridges. The dam had been built across the neck of the southeast end. Though the structure had been broached and two cascades fell gracefully from the height into the ravine below, it was still the biggest dam Fandarel had ever seen.

The marvelous thing, Master Fandarel realized, was not that it had been made, but that so much of it had survived for twenty-five centuries. As D'clan's brown Pranith skimmed the top, Fandarel could see that the passage of all that time had taken some toll on the dam. Grooves, like the bites of a creature larger even than a dragon, had been gouged in the top, creating openings for the falls to tumble through. Floods, no doubt, he decided, pushing large boulders or debris relentlessly against it. He pulled on D'clan's sleeve and pointed a thick forefinger vigorously downward. D'clan nodded, grinning, and in the next instant, Pranith tightened his spiral and glided to a neat landing on the left-hand side, the longer intact span.

With a grace and agility envied by many younger and fitter men,

Fandarel slid from the brown neck and landed lightly on his feet. In a moment he was down on his hands and knees, knife blade scraping aside mud and caked dirt to examine the material of the dam. He shook his head.

"Plascrete, Aivas said," he muttered to himself as the others in his party joined him. Evan, the journeyman who often translated his designs into solid reality, was a self-contained man who hadn't so much as blinked when he took instructions from "the talking wall." Belterac was nearly as grizzled as Fandarel; he was wise in his craft, and the steadiness of his work habits offset the apprentice Fosdak, who was erratic and troublesome but strong as a draft animal. The last was Silton, a useful and diligent young man who had shown some of Master Terry's dogged perseverance. "They built this of plascrete," Fandarel went on. "Stuff that will last for millennia. And it has. By the shell of the first Egg, it has!"

The three dragons were as interested in the dam as the humans were: they walked along the wide top, their wings folded to their backs, and suddenly V'line laughed and said aloud that his bronze Clarinath wanted to know if there would be time for a bath. The water looked so clear and clean.

"Later, please," Fandarel said, continuing his inspection of the edifice.

"Amazing construction," Evan murmured, scuffing the surface with his heavy boots on his way to the lake side of the structure. He peered over the edge. "Water levels are marked, Fandarel. Can't have been high in Turns, though it has been from time to time."

Then he walked to the ravine side and pointed downward and to his left. "There, Master, that's where the ancients had their power station."

Fandarel squinted, shielding his eyes with one huge hand, then nodded in satisfaction as he saw the remains of the building. Something had smashed into it from a height. Probably the same debris that had breached the dam, crashing down on the place with tremendous force.

"D'clan, if you and Pranith would be good enough to take us down there," Fandarel said, pointing. "Evan and I will go first to be sure it is safe enough."

D'clan and Pranith obliged, finding sufficient room to set down by the ruins. All that was left of the structure were the heavy girders that had supported the roof of the power station, and the inner wall, which looked to be cemented to the naked rock. But the floor, despite a thick carpet of pebble-encrusted dirt a full knife blade deep, had remained impervious to the passage of time.

"Those strong young backs can clear this, Evan," Fandarel said. "D'clan, can you wave the others down here? Then the dragons may have a swim."

"They spend more time in the water than in the air," D'clan complained. "They're more likely to wash the hide off 'em, if they're not careful. A hide-damaged dragon's no good *between*." But his tone was more affectionate than captious.

While the others started shoveling away the mud, Fandarel and Evan made careful measurements of the area to be enclosed, then calculated where the new power wheel would be situated. With deft lines, Evan made a preliminary sketch of what the finished installation would look like. Fandarel, watching over his shoulder, nodded approval. Then he looked about, squinting up at the high, smooth face of the dam and the hillsides.

"Now," he said, satisfied with his analysis of the site's needs, "we go back to Telgar, to assemble the components." He grinned at Evan. "It will be a novel thing, will it not, to work from proper plans?"

Evan merely raised his eyebrows. "Can't be but more efficient that way."

"My dear F'lar," Robinton said reassuringly to the Weyrleader, who was patently disappointed at his failure to gain the full backing of the Lord Holders, "Aivas impressed Larad, Asgenar, Groghe, Toronas, Bargen, and Warbret, plus Jaxom. Seven out of sixteen's not bad for a start. Oterel's doddering, and Corman always needs time to mull things over. If the various projects for which you will need workers here continue to clear out that beggars' cave of Laudey's, he'll back you." Robinton put one hand on F'lar's shoulder and gave it just a little shake. "F'lar, you so desperately *want* to eradicate Thread. That's your first responsibility. Managing their Holds is theirs, and sometimes, as we both know, they forget the wider view. Yes, K'van?" The Harper had been aware that the young Southern Weyrleader was hovering in the background. "Have I been monopolizing F'lar when you need a word with him?"

"If I might intrude . . ." K'van said.

"My glass is empty." With a raffish grin, Robinton took himself back to the food-laden table in search of a wineskin.

"Was Lord Toric asked?" K'van said hesitantly.

"Yes, indeed, he was, K'van." F'lar drew him to one corner of the room, where they were less likely to be drawn into the lively discussions of the other Weyrleaders. "I charged Breide in particular to let him know."

K'van managed a fleeting grin—they both knew that Breide's main function at Landing was to report to the Southern Lord Holder everything of interest. Breide's conscientiousness often served up such quantities of trivia that Toric obviously did not bother to read the reports.

"He's trying to get enough men over to the island to shift Denol and his kin." Everyone knew that Toric was furious about the attempt by a band of rebels to take over the island he claimed as part of his Hold.

"I'd've thought he'd accomplished that already," F'lar said in surprise. "Toric can be very determined."

K'van's grin was sour. "He's also determined to have the Weyr's help."

F'lar started angrily. "There's no way he's to have that, K'van!"

"And so I've told him, time and again. The Weyr is not there for his convenience."

"And?"

"He doesn't take my no as final, F'lar." K'van faltered and he gave a helpless shrug to his shoulders. "I know I'm young to be a Weyrleader . . ."

"Your youth is not a relevant factor, K'van. You're a good Weyrleader, and I've had that assurance from the older riders in your Weyr!"

K'van was young enough to flush with pleasure at hearing such praise. "Toric wouldn't agree," he replied, twitching his straight-held shoulders.

F'lar could not deny the fact that K'van's slim, youthful build would put him at a disadvantage in a confrontation with the tall and powerful Southern Lord Holder. At the time K'van's Heth had flown Adrea's queen, Toric had been enthusiastic about having a Benden-trained Weyrleader. But he had not had rank rebellion in his Hold at that point.

"At first," K'van went on, "he wanted the Weyr to take his soldiers to the island. When I refused, he said that he'd be satisfied that I'd done my duty to the Hold if I told him where the rebels had made their camp. His argument was that we overfly the island during a Pass so we'd see where they were, and that information would assist him in suppressing the rebellion. When I refused, he started to harass some of the older bronze riders, suggesting that I'm too young to know my duty to the Lord Holder.''

"I trust he's had no joy on that score," F'lar said sharply.

K'van shook his head. "No, they told him that such action was not a Weyr responsibility. Then—" The young Weyrleader hesitated.

"Then?" F'lar prompted grimly.

"He tried to bribe one of my blue riders with the promise of finding him a suitable friend.''

"That is enough!" F'lar's expression darkened, and he irritably pushed hair back from his forehead. "Lessa!" he called, beckoning urgently to her.

When F'lar explained K'van's problem, she was equally incensed.

"You'd think he'd know better by this time not to try to bully dragonriders," she said, her voice crisp with anger. When she saw K'van's apprehensive expression, she gave him a reassuring touch. "It's scarcely your fault Toric is as greedy as a Bitran.''

"Desperate, more like," K'van said with the hint of a smile. "Master Idarolan told me that Toric had offered him a small fortune in gems and a fine harbor if he'd sail a punitive force to the Island. But he wouldn't. And, furthermore, he's told all the other Shipmasters that they're not to help Toric in this matter. They won't, either.''

"Toric has ships of his own," Lessa said irritably.

K'van had relaxed enough to grin. "But none large enough to transport a sufficiently large force to be effective. His landing parties have been ambushed and either wounded severely enough to make them useless or imprisoned by the rebels.'' His grin grew broader. "I've got to hand it to Denol—he's clever. But I wanted to tell you what's been happening before lies or rumors got back to you—or other Lord Holders complained about our attitude.''

"Quite correct, K'van," F'lar said.

"We'll have to find time to visit Lord Toric," Lessa said, a steely look in her eyes. Then she smiled, a nasty smile that made K'van relieved that it was not directed against him. "Lord Toric *needs* a full report on Aivas and what's happening here at Landing. I think we'll inform him ourselves, F'lar?''

"I'm not sure when," F'lar said with a sigh. "But we'll make the time somehow. K'van, just keep your Weyr out of Toric's squabble."

"I shall!" And there was no doubt in the Benden Weyrleaders' minds that he would. K'van had been a determined and responsible youngster, and now that he was grown to manhood, those traits were refined. He would stand against Toric simply because Toric didn't think he could.

"**N**ow, place this plug," Aivas told Piemur, illustrating the appropriate one on the monitor, "in this female socket!" When Piemur had complied, Aivas went on. "There should be a green light on the base of the monitor."

"There isn't," Piemur said in a voice that was almost a wail. He sighed gustily, hanging on to his patience.

"Then there is a faulty connection. Remove the cover and check the boards, mother, input-output, and memory," Aivas said. It didn't help Piemur's temper that Aivas seemed totally unruffled by yet another failure. It simply wasn't normal for an entity to be so bloody methodically insensitive. "Machines must first be properly assembled before they can function as they were designed. That is the first step. Be patient. It is only a matter of discovering which is the faulty connection."

Piemur found that he was trying to bend the screwdriver in his hand. He took a deep breath and, not daring to look to either side of him, where Benelek and Jancis were concentrating on assembling their own devices, he removed the cover of his. Once more.

They had been at this tedious and exacting task ever since Terry had arranged all the wires and connecting cords to Aivas's satisfaction. It soothed Piemur only slightly that Benelek, who had always been mechanically inclined and good with his hands, was not faring any better. Nor was Jancis, though her current ineptitude distressed him for her sake. Piemur's shoulders ached with cramp, his fingers were thick with all the finicky little movements, and he was going sour on the whole project. It had seemed such a simple affair. Find the cartons in the caves with the stored units, dust 'em off, start 'em up, and that'd be that. But it wasn't. First Aivas had made them learn what each unit was—keyboard, liquid-crystal display, computer box, touch keyboard panel—and the codes for the various "boards" that activated the computer terminal. Fortunately, when it came to soldering broken connections, Jancis and Benelek were adept. Piemur burned his fingers once or twice in practice, but he caught on quickly enough. Fingers made dexterous by playing instruments easily adapted to the new task. But the initial enthusiasm that had motivated Piemur since before dawn had long since drained out of him. Only the fact that neither Jancis nor Benelek faltered kept him going.

"Let us begin again," the inexorable, calm Aivas voice continued, "by checking each panel to be sure there is no damage or break in the circuits or chips."

"I've done that twice already," Piemur said, setting his jaw.

"Then it must be done again. Make use of the magnifying glass. That is why our boards were all made to be visible, serviceable. On Earth it was not possible to check them visually like this. There it was done by facilities in factory outlets. Here we must just proceed patiently."

Holding his temper firmly in check, Piemur went over the chips, circuit by circuit, scrutinizing the resistors and capacitors. The beads and silvery lines that had once fascinated him had become anathema, called by stupid terms that meant nothing to him but trouble. He devoutly wished he had never seen the bloody things. Close scrutiny did not disclose any obvious breaks. So, exercising the greatest control on his fingers, he replaced each component as carefully as he could. They all slotted firmly into place.

"Be sure that each card is seated securely in the grooves," said the ever-calm Aivas.

"I just did, Aivas!" Piemur knew he sounded petulant, but in the face of Aivas's imperturbability, he found it even harder to be objective. Then his good humor reasserted itself. Machines, he reminded himself facetiously, did only what they were programmed to do. They did not have emotions to interfere with the smooth performance of their duties—once a smooth performance had been attained.

"Before you replace the cover, Piemur, blow gently across the unit to be sure there are no motes of dust clogging the connections."

Master Esselin had the reconstruction of the Aivas facility in hand, but the work roused clouds of dust, some of which sifted into the chamber despite all precautions.

Piemur blew carefully. Replaced the cover. Picked up the plug and inserted it. It took him a full moment to realize that a green light indeed shone on the panel just where it was supposed to, and that a letter had appeared on the liquid-crystal display. He let out a whoop, startling Jancis and Benelek.

"Don't do that, Piemur," the young journeyman exclaimed, scowling up at him. "I nearly soldered the wrong connection."

"It's really working, Piemur?" Jancis looked up hopefully.

"Green and go!" Piemur chortled, rubbing his hands together, ignoring Benelek's sour looks. "All right, Aivas, now what do I do?"

"Using the letters on the keys in front of you, tap out README."

Hunting out the various letters, Piemur tapped out the phrase. Instantly the screen in front of him blossomed with words, numbers, and letters.

"Hey, look, you two. Words! My own screen full of words!"

Benelek spared only an irritated glance, but Jancis rose to stand behind him and admire the result. She gave him an approving pat and then returned to her task.

"Read carefully and absorb the information on the screen," Aivas said, "and you will learn how to access the programs you need to reach the information you desire. First you must become familiar with the terms. Being comfortable with these terms increases your efficiency as an operator."

By the time Piemur had read through the instructions several times, he wasn't much wiser, for it appeared to him that familiar words no longer meant what they should. He sighed and started at the beginning of the page again. Words were a harper's profession, and he would learn these new interpretations if it took him a full Turn.

"I've got it, too!" Jancis cried elatedly. "I've got a green light, too!"

"That makes three of us then," Benelek said smugly. "And I tap out README, Aivas?"

"The initial lesson is the same for all, Benelek. You are to be congratulated! Have more students been enlisted in this project? There is much to be done."

"Patience, Aivas," Piemur said, imitating the machine's tone and grinning at Jancis. "They'll come in their fairs once word has got round."

"The rider of the white dragon, Lord Jaxom? Will he be one?"

"Jaxom?" Piemur asked, mildly surprised. "I wonder where he got to."

4

F or most of that day, Jaxom had been as thoroughly thwarted as
    Piemur could have wished. He and Ruth had transported five loads
of cartons from the caves to the Aivas building, then just when the
last had been off-loaded, Master Fandarel had urgently requested the
two of them to convey Bendarek back to Lemos and his crafthall.
The woodsmith couldn't wait to initiate Aivas's plans to redesign his
paper-making machinery and to improve the quality of the product
by adding a rag content to the wood pulp.

When Jaxom and Ruth returned to Landing, Master Terry had
needed help in locating cables and wires which, after much scrambling about, were found in an almost-overlooked alcove in the caves.
Jaxom and Ruth naturally obliged Master Terry by transporting him
and the coils back to the Aivas building. Jaxom tried not to care,
reminding himself that he was assisting the overall effort, except that
he had had rather different notions of how he and Ruth would spend
the day.

The white dragon had looked forward to basking in the hot
Southern sun. The winter in the North had been cold and clammy,
with little sunshine. And Jaxom had especially wanted to work on
Aivas's contraptions with Piemur, Jancis, and Benelek.

But Jaxom had made a habit of being accessible, amiable, and helpful. People found it much easier to ask him to oblige than they did
other dragons and riders. As Ruth never objected, Jaxom felt con-

strained to assist whenever they could. Sharra thought it was because he was so determined to be the opposite of his despotic sire, Fax. She felt Jaxom carried this second-generation atonement too far sometimes, and she was quick to interfere if she felt his willingness was being abused. But she was back in Ruatha, and this was rapidly becoming one of those times when amiability was a bloody nuisance.

By the time Terry had off-loaded his coils of wires, Jaxom became aware of a rumbling in his stomach—not surprising, since he had had nothing but klah and a meatroll with Menolly and Sebell in the early morning. Sharra always worried about him remembering to take time to eat, and Jaxom tried to remember her injunctions. He wished that her gravid condition had not prevented her from accompanying him here, but she couldn't risk going *between* right now. So he walked over to the kitchen building, unaware that F'lar was holding the extraordinary meeting, or he would have been there to lend his support. Jaxom had to help himself to food, because the cook and the drudges were busy dealing with an apprentice who had badly burned his hand on a hot spit—which reminded him that he had promised to convey Master Oldive to Landing. Maybe when that chore was done, he and Ruth could do as they wished.

When Jaxom and Ruth came out of *between* above the great courtyard of the combined Harper and Healer Halls in Fort Hold, Ruth was suddenly surrounded by a chittering fair of fire-lizards, their demands shrill with warning.

"What's the matter with them, Ruth?" Jaxom asked.

Master Oldive doesn't want you to land in the courtyard, Ruth replied. *He says the harpers will latch on to you and he'll never get to Landing.* Ruth sounded puzzled, but Jaxom laughed.

"I should've thought of that myself. So what does Master Oldive suggest we do?"

I don't know. They've gone to tell him we're here. Ruth glided to the far side of the big Harper Hall complex, where they would not be so easily seen from either the Hall or the adjacent Fort Hold.

He comes, Ruth said, just as they were once again surrounded by now happily chirping fairs of fire-lizards, doing one of their intricate aerial displays of delight. *They see us from the Hold,* he added, as another full fair of fire-lizards came zooming in on them, shrieking urgently. *No, we have more important things to do than stop at the Hold right now,* Ruth said, and added a warning bugle that sent the newcomers whizzing back, their voices thin with distress at his reprimand.

"Lord Groghe's at Landing," Jaxom said, trying not to feel guilty about ignoring the request. "He'll tell them all he wants them to know when he gets back."

His queen fire-lizard has been in and out of the Hold with messages. They know all they need to know about this Aivas, Ruth rumbled in subtle discontent.

Jaxom slapped the white dragon's neck affectionately. "You wouldn't fit in the room, dear friend. Piemur said his Farli went to sleep, totally uninterested in Aivas."

Ruth rumbled again. *Here comes the Masterhealer.* He veered sharply, descending at such an angle that Jaxom reflexively grabbed the riding straps and arched backward against the steep dive.

"You could have warned me," Jaxom remonstrated mildly. Ruth had a habit of sharpening up his rider's reflexes with unexpected maneuvers. The white dragon grunted with satisfaction at the success of his trick as he backwinged to land neatly a length from Master Oldive, who shambled up to them at a surprisingly rapid rate for a man with legs of unequal length and a humped back. He had a large satchel thumping behind his normal shoulder, but he waved a greeting, a huge grin on his face.

"Ho, there, Jaxom! I feared that you'd forgotten me in all the furor." He leaned against Ruth for a moment to recover his breath. "I'm not as fit as I think I am," he said. They both heard the shouts and saw folk in harper blue charging out of the courtyard archway. "Quickly. If they catch you, we'll never leave."

Ruth crouched down on his forequarters, crooking his left foreleg as a step for the Masterhealer. Jaxom leaned down to grasp Oldive's arm. Winded the man might be, but he exerted a powerful pull as he hauled himself to Ruth's back and settled behind Jaxom.

Immediately Ruth sprang aloft, his white wings taking the first important downstroke and beating upward so that the disappointed cries were quickly lost.

"When you're ready, Ruth," Jaxom said, picturing the Aivas building and being very careful to detail the alteration of the mounds in front of it so as not to have Ruth land out of time. Since the initial excavation, enough space had been cleared there for several dragons to land.

The cold of *between* sucked warmth from their bodies, and then they were suddenly in the bright, hot southern afternoon sun. A good-sized fair of fire-lizards swirled up to welcome Ruth, who was a particular favorite of theirs. As usual in the South, there were as many wild ones as those whose necks were banded in the colors of the people they were beholden to.

"By the first Egg, I don't recognize the place," Oldive said in an awed voice as Ruth glided in to land.

"I'm not sure I recognize it either," Jaxom said, grinning over his shoulder at Oldive. "Master Esselin has already got one annex up." He pointed to the swarm of men working furiously to erect walls on the right-hand side of the Aivas building.

"Oh, you're using parts of the old building!" Oldive exclaimed.

"F'lar suggested it! Makes sense, instead of having to haul in building materials when there are all those empty buildings."

"Oh, true, true." Oldive's tone did not indicate complete approval.

"And only from the smaller buildings—the family units, Aivas called them. There are several hundred of them," Jaxom went on reassuringly. During their rummaging in the Catherine Caves, Terry had given Jaxom an account of the morning's session with Aivas and the renovations planned.

"Is every Weyrleader here?" Oldive went on, suddenly aware of the long line of sunbathing dragons on the ridge above the settlement.

Jaxom laughed. "Since Aivas promises to help obliterate Thread, they wait on his every word." He held up a steadying hand as Oldive dismounted from Ruth's back.

"How?" The old man almost lost his footing in surprise. Jaxom braced him, catching the pack before it could swing around and totally unbalance the healer.

"I don't exactly know." Jaxom shrugged, experiencing another surge of annoyance at being out of things so far that day. "I was hoping to find out more this morning, but I've been otherwise occupied."

Oldive put a sympathetic hand on Jaxom's arm, his expression apologetic. "Conveying the curious to the new wonder?"

"Oh, I don't mind, Oldive." He grinned slyly at the healer. "If you will remember to ask Aivas about those two patients Sharra's so worried about."

"They are first on my list, I assure you, Jaxom. Marvelous woman, Sharra, always giving of her own energies and as selfless as you are yourself!"

Jaxom looked away, his embarrassment made all the more acute by the awareness that he would have preferred to have spent the morning learning new things from Aivas. But he was here at last, and he eagerly anticipated Master Oldive's reaction to Aivas.

Inside the building, Esselin's craftsmen were making an appalling amount of noise with their hammering. There was dust everywhere. Jaxom was amazed at how much had been accomplished. Walls had been washed clean, revealing bright, cheerful colors. He wondered how color had been impregnated into the material, for it didn't look like any painted surface he had ever seen. He could hear lively conversations off to the left; F'lar's voice was recognizable, as were T'gellan's and R'mart's. He guided Master Oldive to the right and relived the thrill of the previous day's discovery as they faced the closed door to Aivas's room.

Jaxom rapped on the door in a courteous warning and then opened it on a scene of great industry, which only served to reinforce his niggling resentment. Seated in front of a table made of a board supported by empty cartons, Piemur, Jancis, and Benelek were crouched over the units that he had helped resurrect from the Catherine Caves. And, adding insult to his sense of injury, the sharding things were working. His three friends were tapping away industriously at the keyboard units in front of them. He inhaled deeply through his nostrils to disperse his pique: a reaction he found unacceptable in himself.

Piemur craned his neck around to see who had entered. "Good day to you, Master Oldive. Welcome to the hallowed Aivas chamber. Where've you been all day, Jaxom?"

"I see you've made good use of *your* time," Jaxom replied, trying very hard to neutralize his ill feelings and not quite succeeding. He caught Oldive's sideways glance and made himself smile. "But I'm here now, and you can teach me what I need to know."

"No chance of that," Piemur replied with his usual impudence. "You have to start from the same point we did. Aivas's orders."

"I'm quite willing," Jaxom said, trying to see the writing on Jancis's screen, the closest to him.

She had stopped whatever she had been doing to smile at her old friend Master Oldive. Now she wrinkled her nose at Piemur. "You are the limit sometimes. The components are all carefully set out in the next room, Jaxom. I'll help you, even if he won't."

Benelek didn't look up from his work. "He's to muddle through all by himself, Jancis, or he doesn't learn."

She rolled her eyes at Benelek's uncompromising attitude. "Oh, he'll have to do it himself, but a wink is as good a nod at times. Besides, I think we'd all better move into the other room. I can't stand it when Master Oldive goes into gory details. And that's what he's here to do with Aivas." She winked at the healer. "Every Craft has its hazards, I suppose."

"Oh, yes, we certainly should allow him some privacy," Piemur agreed, rising from his stool.

"Interruptions, always interruptions," Benelek muttered sourly. But he got up, too, and carefully began to start the transfer.

"I heard the Weyrleaders back there," Jaxom began, wanting to effect the introduction protocol for Aivas. "Should I get one in here?"

"Won't be needed," Piemur said. "Special dispensation has already been recorded by Aivas. Just go ahead and introduce Master Oldive."

Which Jaxom did, exceedingly grateful that he would have no further delay in catching up with his friends.

"It is a pleasure to meet a man who is so highly praised by all," Aivas said.

The rich voice, so humanly inflected, caused Master Oldive to stare about in considerable consternation.

"Aivas is, so to speak, all around you in this room," Jaxom said encouragingly when he saw how disconcerted the healer was. "He's a bit much to get used to at first, I agree. Scared the lot of us."

Busy disassembling the makeshift table, Piemur shot Master Oldive an indulgent grin. "You'll get used to a disembodied voice real quick, the kind of sense Aivas talks."

"Go teach yourself to be sensible for me, young Piemur," Aivas said in a jocular tone that startled everyone.

"Yes, sir, good Master Aivas, yes, sir," Piemur quipped, bowing humbly as he backed out of the room, carrying the table board and nearly knocking himself down when he forgot to lower the board to get it through the door.

Jancis, following Piemur and Benelek, pulled the door shut behind her as she left.

"Please make yourself comfortable, Master Oldive," Aivas suggested. "Did you by any chance bring recent Records from your Hall? Those from the Harper, the Mastersmith, and the Woodsmith have already been assimilated, but for a proper assessment of your society's achievements, Records from every Hall, Hold, and Weyr are gratefully accepted."

Master Oldive had absently seated himself, and his satchel, heavy with the notes he had brought with him, began to slide from his shoulder. He caught the strap and, with a shake of his head, recalled his wits.

"Lord Groghe said that—" Master Oldive hesitated briefly, not knowing the appropriate form in which to address the entity, "—*you* know, well, everything."

"The memory banks of this facility contain the most comprehensive data available at the time the colony ships set out for their destination of the Rukbat system. That includes medical information."

"May I ask how that information is organized?"

"Basic anatomy, microanatomy, physiology, autocrinology, medical biochemistry, and many more categories, such as immunology and neuropathology—which, it is fair to suggest, may no longer be known to you."

"In that you are correct. For we have lost so much knowledge, so many techniques." Oldive had never been more keenly aware of the gaps in his Craft.

"You distress yourself unnecessarily, Master Oldive, for all those whom I have met so far are in excellent health and well above what was considered normal weight and height by the medical standards of your ancestors. There is much to be said for a nonindustrialized civilization."

"Industrialized? That term is unfamiliar to me, though I recognize the root word."

"*Industrialize*," Aivas intoned. "Transitive verb: to organize large industries in; as, to industrialize a community; to introduce the economic system of industrialization into; as, to industrialize a new nation. An industrialized society, in contrast to an agrarian one like yours."

"Thank you. Why would an industrialized society produce less healthy folk?"

"Pollution of the atmosphere and environment by industrial wastes, noxious fumes, chemical effluents, contamination of field-grown edibles, among other evils."

Master Oldive was speechless.

"Those who settled Pern wished to found an agrarian society. To that end they were receptive to many anti-industrial cultures, like the ancient gypsies, as well as retired military types. Their objective has been attained in this, your present," Aivas said.

"It has?" Master Oldive was surprised that Pern had succeeded in anything other than surviving nine Passes of Threadfall.

"In more ways than you might imagine, Master Oldive, being too close to have an objective view. Apart from the inconvenience of the organism, Thread, you have achieved much."

"Addressing you, Aivas, I perceive that we have also lost much."

"Perhaps not as much as you think, Masterhealer."

"In my Craft, I *know* that we have lost the capacity to alleviate much suffering, prevent the plagues which have all but decimated the population from time to time . . ."

"The strong survived, and your population was renewed."

"But so much knowledge was irretrievably lost, especially in my Craft."

"Those losses can be remedied."

Master Oldive was caught up short by what sounded very much like a pun to him. But surely a machine . . . He cleared his throat, but it was Aivas who continued speaking.

"Would it ease your mind to know that even the most astute medical practitioners among your ancestors sometimes felt themselves helpless against plague? That they constantly sought new methods of easing pain and correcting afflictions?"

"It should, but it doesn't. But, to urgent matters, if I may, Aivas?"

"Of course, Master Oldive"

"There are several patients, three suffering severe pain which we are unable to relieve, wasting in both flesh and spirit. If I tell you their symptoms, would that be sufficient for diagnosis?"

"Proceed with the symptoms. If they can be matched with cases on record, a diagnosis is possible. As there are three point two billion documented histories that can be consulted, a similarity may be found that would suggest suitable treatment."

With fingers fumbling with hope, Master Oldive opened his casebook to the first of Sharra's two patients. He owed Jaxom that courtesy.

"What're you doing?" Jaxom asked, mystified by the way the others were intently regarding their gray screens. Aivas's main screen was not at all like these smaller ones.

Benelek gave a snort of impatience and bent further over the board. He pecked about with his index fingers in no pattern that Jaxom could discern.

"We're becoming familiar with the keyboard configuration," Pie-

mur said, with a malicious grin at Jaxom's ignorance. "We're learning our way through the commands. Don't let us keep you from
contrapting your own. You're a half day behind us already."

"That's mean, Piemur," Jancis said. Taking Jaxom by the hand,
she pulled him over to the boxes and cartons that had only been
partially unpacked. "Take a keyboard, then one of those larger boxes.
Put them on the table, and take one of the liquid-crystal display
screens."

"The what?"

"One of those." She pointed. "And be careful. Aivas said they're
fragile, and we only have so many of them. Take off the plastic, and
you'll need your knife. That stuff is unbelievably tough. Then," she
continued, handing him a very small-headed screwdriver and a magnifying glass, "unscrew the big box. You'll have to check over all the
circuits to be sure none of them have come adrift. The glass will help
you quickly locate any breaks."

Benelek suddenly uttered a resounding oath and banged his fists
on the table. "I've lost it all. Everything!"

Piemur glanced up, surprised at Benelek's uncharacteristic out-
burst. "Well, reboot." The new word tripped easily from his Harper-
trained tongue.

"But you don't understand!" Benelek waved his hands wildly
above his head. "I lost all I had typed. And I had it almost done!"

"Did you save?" Jancis asked sympathetically.

"Yes, I did, up until just the last bits," Benelek said, his frustration
dissipating. Jaxom watched in fascination as the journeyman jabbed
at various places on the board in front of him and then *ahh*ed in
satisfaction at the result.

"Don't dally now, Jaxom," Piemur said with a wicked grin. "You
must join our jolly band, where one misused key can destroy a whole
hour's hard work."

"Aivas did say we'd have to learn many new skills," Jancis said
reasonably. "Oh, shards! I've done something wrong now, too." She
peered at the blank screen, then frowned down at the keyboard.
"Now what key did I press that I shouldn't have?"

As he drew his beltknife, Jaxom wondered just why he wanted
any part of what was obviously an occupation fraught with frustra-
tions.

The quick tropic evening caught them unawares. Piemur, cursing
under his breath at any interruption, darted around the room, opening the glowbaskets. But the light was not shining at the correct angle

to light up his screen so, still swearing, he altered his chair. Absently, still tapping away, Benelek followed his example. Jancis and Jaxom, seated at the right angle, continued with their lessons.

"Who's in here now?" Lessa's voice said from the hallway. The door opened and she stuck her head in. "So this is where you all got to. Jaxom, Master Oldive needs you and Ruth again, and I think it's high time you left here. Your eyes are burnt holes in your head. And the rest of you are no better."

Benelek glanced up only briefly. "This is no time to stop, Weyrwoman."

"This *is* the time to stop, Benelek," she replied in an uncontradictable tone.

"But, Weyrwoman, I've got to assimilate all these new terms and be able to—"

"Aivas!" Lessa raised her voice as she turned her head to the right. "Can you turn these things off? Your students are too diligent. Not that I don't approve—in theory—but they could all use a good night's rest."

"I didn't save—" Benelek shouted, spreading his hands in high indignation and staring in horror at a suddenly darkened and unresponsive screen.

"Your work has been saved," Aivas's voice assured him. "You have toiled without renewing yourself all day long, Journeyman Benelek. Even machines need maintenance. Your body can be considered a soft machine which also needs frequent sustenance. Refresh yourselves. Return tomorrow with energy and concentration renewed."

For a few seconds Benelek looked as if he might rebel. Then he sighed and pushed himself back from the table over which he had been bent for hours. He gave Lessa a sheepish grin. "I will eat and rest. And begin again tomorrow—but there is so much to be learned, so much more than I ever imagined."

"Indeed there is," Master Oldive said, emerging from the Aivas room, a thick sheaf of papers clutched in one hand and his satchel in the other. He looked from one to the other in bewilderment. "So much more than I dreamed." And then he sighed with great satisfaction, holding up the sheaf. "But this is a good start. A very good start."

"You will need some klah before Jaxom takes you anywhere, Master Oldive," Lessa said. She took the healer firmly by the arm and nodded to Jancis and Jaxom to take his encumbrances from him.

He relinquished the satchel readily enough but he clutched the sheaf to him.

"Let me at least tidy them up, Master Oldive," Jancis said earnestly. "I shan't disarrange their order."

"It wouldn't matter anyway," Oldive said with a weary flick of his long-fingered hand. "They're numbered and separated into categories." Jancis still had to gently pry his fingers loose. "I have learned so much, so much," he muttered with a bemused smile on his face as Lessa led him down the hall. The others followed, suddenly aware of their own fatigue.

You have been in there for six hours, Jaxom, and you had better eat something, or Sharra will blame me, Ruth said. *You're very tired, you know.*

Oh, I know I am. I know I am. Jaxom wondered if klah would be enough to revive him.

"Is it our turn now?" Terry asked as he and several eager-faced journeymen came around the corner from the entrance hall. When Lessa nodded, he urged his followers down the hall at a jog trot.

Their energy appeared almost obscene to Jaxom. No one had the right to have that much vitality at the end of a day. As they passed him, he noted that their shoulder knots identified them as coming from Tillek, far enough west that it was actually early in the day for them. He sighed.

Lessa installed Master Oldive in a chair at the table and gestured for the drudges to supply everyone with klah and plates of roast beast and tubers. Never had such a plain meal smelled so appetizing to Jaxom. He gobbled down the food, and when he was offered a second helping, he took as much again.

There was more color in Master Oldive's cheeks as he made inroads on his generous serving. Benelek ate with single-minded intensity, his eyes focused on some obscure distance, and occasionally he nodded his head as if approving his ruminations. Jaxom decided he hadn't the energy for thinking right then. He would think again the next morning. Sharra would understand. He hoped Brand would, since he would once again have to leave the Steward to cope with the details of running Ruatha Hold. Brand never seemed to mind. On the other hand, Lytol might, but surely Master Robinton would explain the importance of Aivas to Jaxom's old guardian.

"I must send a message to that young journeyman of Wansor's," Oldive told Lessa, his enthusiasm vivid on his long face. "I must have an apparatus similar to the one that was found in Benden Weyr.

ANNE MCCAFFREY

It will magnify blood and tissue so that we can identify disease and infection.'' He reached for the neat pile Jancis had made of his papers and started leafing through them. "Aivas states that the use of a microscope is essential to improve medical diagnosis and even treatment. He has given me the details of how to run other necessary diagnostic tests.''

"A microscope?'' Lessa asked indulgently. She thought highly of the Masterhealer, who had recently sent her a woman possessed of a miraculous talent for repairing even the most damaged wings or hideous Thread-scores.

"That's the word.'' Oldive put a hand to his forehead. "Aivas crammed so much into my poor head today that I wonder I can remember my name.''

"It's Oldive,'' Piemur said, putting on an innocently helpful expression. He rolled his eyes at the quelling glance Lessa threw him. Jancis poked him in the ribs, and he subsided meekly enough.

When they had finished their meal, Jaxom presented himself ready to convey Master Oldive back to the Harper Hall.

"Ah, no, Jaxom, I would like to go directly to Ruatha. I have advice for Sharra.'' There was a radiant smile of great satisfaction on the healer's face.

"Aivas knows a cure?'' Jaxom asked.

Master Oldive nodded toward his stack. "Cure? Perhaps. Certainly several avenues of investigation that may provide relief.'' Then he sighed. "There was so very much medical acumen lost over the centuries. He didn't say so, of course, but Aivas was clearly taken aback by our lack of remedial surgery. He was, however, most commendatory about our preventive measures and nonsurgical techniques. Ah . . . .'' He made a weary gesture with one hand. "I could go on and on.'' He smiled with self-deprecation. "With whom should I arrange additional time with Aivas? There are both Masters and journeymen who would benefit immensely by consultations with him.''

Lessa looked up to see a weary-looking F'lar standing in the doorway. He shrugged.

"I hadn't thought about apportioning Aivas's time,'' the Weyrleader said.

"As soon as we manage to set up these individual stations,'' Piemur said, "there'll be four more links to Aivas.''

"The Healer Hall should have priority,'' Lessa added with a frown, scrubbing at her face in fatigue.

"Those are to be teaching consoles," Benelek said, scowling.

"For us, maybe," Piemur said. "But if they access Aivas, then they can be used for other purposes. At least that's what I figure."

"You're a harper, not a journeyman mechanic."

"I'm a Mastersmith," Jancis put in, her tone edged, "and let me remind you that Piemur got his unit up and running before either of us did."

"Enough!" Lessa brought her hand down on the table with a slap of authority. "We're all tired." She rose abruptly. "Ramoth!" Outside, the golden queen dragon bugled a response. "You're all to leave this building *now*!" She leveled a stern look first at Benelek and then the others. "Including us." Her gaze settled on F'lar, who grinned and held up both hands as if to fend her off. "The two buildings to the left of this one have been set up as dormitories. Go!" She shooed them off with her hands, then glared at them until they started to move.

Master Oldive chuckled softly as he accompanied Jaxom out of the building. "Not that I think I will sleep tonight at all with so much to absorb and review. Why, Jaxom, even what I learned today is only the veriest crumb of the medical knowledge which Aivas had stored! He clarified my understanding of several perplexing conditions. I must have Master Ampris, our herbalist, bring him our pharmacopoeia." A weary smile lit Master Oldive's face. "He said we have made very good use of indigenous plants, and he recognized many as those brought by our ancestors from Earth. Earth!" And Oldive looked up at the star-spangled sky, turning his twisted body to scan the dark heavens above them. "Do we know where Earth is in relation to Pern?"

"I don't think so," Jaxom replied in mild surprise. "I don't remember that Aivas gave the direction. Maybe he didn't want to. Our ancestors came here to escape a war, a conflict of such scope and dimensions, waged against an evil far more destructive than Thread, that they wanted to forget Earth."

"Really? Could anything be more destructive than Thread?" The healer was both astonished and appalled.

"I find it hard to believe, too," Jaxom agreed.

Ruth glided in from his sunning spot to the cleared area in front of the Aivas building. He ducked his head to receive his weyrmate's affectionate slap.

"You must have baked yourself," Jaxom said, shaking his hand as if to cool it.

Yes. It was good. Ramoth and Mnementh are waiting for us to leave this space, Ruth said. *There's really enough room, but you know Ramoth. She likes to boss me.*

Jaxom chuckled as he mounted, aware that fatigue was making him clumsy. With no prompting needed, the white dragon crouched down to accommodate Master Oldive. Hauling the healer up only emphasized Jaxom's weariness. But they would be home soon. Inwardly he groaned: They would have to make yet another run later, to take Oldive back to his Hall.

Sharra will make him stay the night. He'll want to talk, so she won't let him go. Ruth said.

As Ruth rose from the ground, Jaxom and Oldive were able to appreciate just how busy Landing had become. Paths lit by glowbaskets spread like the spokes of a wheel radiating out from the Aivas building. Carpenters and joiners were working by glowlight to finish roofing the substantial annex. All of the housing immediately adjacent was lit, and the warm evening air was redolent with the aromas of roasting meats. On the mounds beyond, large, vivid, blue-faceted dragon eyes punctuated the darkness like immense jewels on a deep blue background. Two rose and glided beneath Ruth as he continued to rise.

All right, Ruth, let's go home to Ruatha. Jaxom gratefully focused his thoughts on the Hold, the big courtyard in front of the wide steps, and the smaller court that had been their quarters during their youth. The cold of *between* held a wicked bite on tired minds and bodies. It did not help to emerge into the weak afternoon sunlight and the chill of winter. Jaxom could feel Oldive shivering behind him. But Ruth had emerged only a few wing strokes above the Hold and glided effortlessly into the main courtyard, the Hold's fair of fire-lizards wheeling in raptures at his return.

Sharra, a thick furry cloak thrown over her shoulders, came running down the steps to them, effusive in her welcome, helping Master Oldive dismount, securing his satchel as it swung off his shoulder, smiling her delight up at Jaxom, and with her free hand giving Ruth an affectionate slap. Though she asked nothing, Jaxom knew his wife well enough to know that she was bursting with questions. He threw one arm across her shoulders and kissed her cheek; her smooth skin and the scent of her revived him as he guided Oldive up the steps and into the warmth of the Hold.

I'm going inside immediately, Ruth told his rider, *or I'll lose all the benefit of my sunning.* And he took himself off to his weyr in the old kitchen where, Jaxom knew, a fire would be waiting in the hearth.

Sharra ordered food and drink as she pushed the two men toward the small office where they would have some privacy from the many people eager to hear Jaxom's report of the ongoing events at Landing. "Later, later," she told them firmly, and closed the door.

Before Oldive joined Jaxom and Sharra at the fire, he carefully laid his satchel on the wide desk where Jaxom generally sat to manage the details of his Hold. A pile of messages and Records lay waiting for his attention. There was a scratch at the door, and then the Steward himself entered, carrying a laden tray.

"Oh, that's kind of you, Brand," Jaxom said. "Lessa made us eat before she'd let us leave, Sharra, but klah will go down well. With a lashing of that fortified wine I see you brought along." Jaxom grinned at the stocky man who had been his friend since his childhood and was now his most valued assistant. "No, stay, Brand. You've the right to hear what keeps me from my proper tasks."

Brand waved his hand in a disclaimer as he helped Sharra pass the hot drinks, the pungent wine masking the klah's fragrance. Jaxom took a judicious sip and felt the liquid rushing to restore warmth. Master Oldive, too, seemed to revive somewhat and sank into the chair that Brand placed close to the fire for him.

"My dear, your female patient is suffering a gall bladder malfunction," the old healer told Sharra. "Unfortunately, the man appears to have a cancerous growth, as we suspected. We can cure the one, for I have been given a specific medication for dissolving the gravel within the organ, but we can only ease the other from life." Master Oldive paused, his eyes wide and bright with excitement. "Aivas has the most extraordinary fund of medical information, which he is quite willing to impart to us. He can even help us revive corrective surgical procedures, which you know I have yearned to do. Our Craft may have been limited to repair surgeries for lack of proper training, but he can help us recover much of that lost skill."

"That would be wonderful, Master, but would we be able to overcome the prejudice in the Hall about intrusive measures?" Sharra exclaimed, her face mirroring her hope.

"Now that we have a mentor of unquestionable probity, I think that once we have proved the benefits to patients who will not mend without drastic measures, we can overcome those scruples." He drained his cup and resolutely rose to his feet. "A few moments in your infirmary, my dear Sharra, and we shall have the medication for your gall bladder sufferer. The other poor wight . . ." Oldive shrugged, his expression deeply compassionate.

"Come then, and you can tell me all the medical details that would bore Jaxom and Brand to tears," Sharra said, grinning fondly at her mate.

"You *never*—" Jaxom paused to give that adverb full emphasis. "—bore me, Sharra." The loving look that she gave him warmed as the klah had not.

"You look tired, Jaxom," Brand said when the door had closed.

"I am, Brand, and my head aches with what I've seen and heard in the last two days. But I feel—I feel—" Jaxom stopped, clenching one fist. "That this is most momentous thing that has happened to Pern since—" and he laughed. "—our ancestors landed here." His second laugh was not as easy. "Not that everyone will see it that way, I'm sure."

"There are always those who oppose change," Brand said with a resigned shrug. "Has the Aivas told you exactly how it proposes to eliminate Thread?"

"We are mere babes, Brand, and must put in much hard work and learn many new things before Aivas will give us any details. But you should have seen Fandarel." Jaxom's laugh was uninhibited. "And Benelek. They were spinning like tops to do everything at once. When Ruth and I got off transport duty, I was allowed to put together one of Aivas's gadgets." He examined the fingers of his right hand, the solder burn and the nicks where the screwdriver had slipped. "I'm learning to access knowledge. Tomorrow I may even get to read some of Aivas's stored wisdom. I tell you, Brand, the next few weeks are going to be fascinating."

"Another way of telling me you'll frequently be away from the Hold?" Brand asked, grinning.

"Well, apart from overseeing Falls, there's not much to do right now in the depths of winter, is there?" Jaxom replied defensively.

Brand laughed and, with the familiarity of their long and close relationship, clapped Jaxom on the shoulder. "That there isn't, lad. I'd be happy to learn if Aivas knows any way of heating stone-cold holds."

"I'll ask him!" Jaxom promised earnestly. "I'll ask him." And he leaned forward to warm his hands again.

5

Against his entreaties, F'lar took Master Robinton back to Cove Hold.

"You need the rest and the quiet, Robinton," F'lar told the Harper sternly. "You won't get that if you're allowed to stay at Landing again tonight. You're exhausted."

"But what a wonderful way to get tired, F'lar. And every time I turn around, I think of something else I must ask Aivas." Robinton chuckled. "It's rather like knowing you have the most fabulous vintage in your glass and being torn between drinking and admiring."

F'lar shot him an amused look. "That's apt enough, considering the source."

"I try! But surely you appreciate why I'm loath to leave?" And the Harper's expression was entreating.

"Oh, I do, Robinton." F'lar grinned as he handed the man down from Mnementh's great shoulder. "But it'd be worth my peace with Lessa if we let you overstretch yourself."

"But this is giving me new life, F'lar. A new hope that I never imagined to receive."

"Nor I," F'lar replied fervently. "Which is why we must take care of you all the more—to interpret for us."

"Interpret? He speaks in plain and simple terms."

"Not what Aivas says, Robinton, but how our people will see what he offers. For me, and all dragonriders, despite the future effects on

Weyrs and dragonkind, I cannot but accept Aivas's offer to rid us of Thread. But already there are those who are either frightened or feel threatened by what Aivas can tell us, or give us.''

"Yes, similar thoughts had crossed my mind," Robinton said solemnly, but then he flashed F'lar a roguish grin. "But I also cross them out. The good done us will far outweigh the bad."

"Get a good night's rest, Robinton. Benden flies Thread tomorrow, but D'ram will oblige, I'm sure, to get you back to Landing."

"Him!" Robinton was suddenly petulant. "He's worse than a milk mother, as it is." And he settled easily into D'ram's voice. " 'I wouldn't, if I were you, Robinton! Have you eaten enough, Robinton? Now would be a good time to rest in the sun.' Tsck! He fusses me!''

"Not tomorrow. D'ram's as eager to see and hear more of Aivas as you are, you know," F'lar said just before Mnementh launched himself upward.

I've told Tiroth to take you tomorrow only if you're well rested, the dragon said. Zair, bronze tail wrapped about the Harper's neck and talons lightly clasping his right ear, chirruped agreement.

"Oh, you!" Robinton was torn between irritation at their overprotectiveness and pleasure that Mnementh had a word for him. He could never forget how much he personally owed the dragons who had kept him alive when his labored heart had faltered that terrible day at Ista Weyr two Turns earlier.

When he arrived at Cove Hold, Robinton was forced to admit to himself that he was tired. Just walking the short distance to the steps of his lovely residence winded him. There were lights on in the main hall: D'ram and, doubtless, Lytol waiting up for him.

Zair chirped again, confirming his guess. Well, they would not tax him, and certainly they both deserved a brief report of the day's activities. Only how to be brief, considering all that had occurred since he had awakened early that morning? Only *that* morning? It was Turns away in knowledge and understanding.

But when he walked into the pleasant, well-lit room, D'ram, the venerable retired Weyrleader, and Lytol, former dragonrider and Jaxom's mentor, would listen to no explanations; they ushered him to his room with instructions that he was to rest first.

"Whatever momentous events occurred after I left can wait until morning," D'ram said.

"Drink your wine," Lytol added, holding out the Harper's beautiful blue glass goblet. "And yes, I've added something to make you sleep tonight, because just one look at your face tells me you need rest above all else."

Robinton closed his hand about the goblet. Norist might be a closed-minded Craftmaster, but he blew elegant glass when he had a mind to, *and* in the exact shade of harper blue. "But I've so much to tell you," the Harper objected after a sip of the wine.

"All the better told when you've had a good night's sleep," Lytol said. When he would have bent to undo Robinton's boots, the Harper became indignant and pushed him away.

"I'm not quite that tired, thank you, Lytol," he said with great dignity.

Laughing, the D'ram and Lytol left. Robinton took another sip of wine before loosening the fastenings of his boots. The third before he hauled his tunic over his head. And another as he loosened his belt with his free hand. That's enough, he told himself and, draining the cup, lay back. He had only sufficient energy to pull the light blanket over him against the possible chill of a morning sea breeze. He felt Zair nestle down on the next pillow—and that was all.

The next morning he awoke slowly, aware that the dream he had had during the night had been both satisfying and confusing, but its ephemeral details eluded a conscious effort at recall. He lay for a moment, orienting himself. Sometimes, of a morning, he had difficulty remembering what day it was, or the tasks he had mentally assigned himself to accomplish.

Today he experienced no such disorientation. He remembered everything that had happened the day before with amazing clarity. Ah, that was good. A challenge to stimulate his flagging faculties. Corman and his accusation of gullibility! Indeed! Zair rumbled reassuringly on the pillow and stroked his head against Robinton's cheek.

"Will you pass the word along that I'm now completely refreshed?" he asked the bronze fire-lizard.

Zair regarded him, tilting his head sideways, his eyes whirling ever so slightly with the green of contentment, and gave a chirp. Then he rose and stretched, his transparent wings arching over his head before he shook and folded them tightly along his spine.

"So, are Tiroth and D'ram awake to take me?"

Zair ignored him and began to groom his left hind claws.

"I gather that means I must bathe and eat first?" As he rose, Robinton realized that he had slept in his trousers—for the second night in a row. He shucked them off, snagged a large towel, and, opening the door from his corner room to the wide porch that sheltered Cove Hold from the intense sunlight, strode out. Descending the flight of steps with more vigor than he had climbed them the previous night, he jogged down the sandy track to the sea. Zair swirled overhead, crooning approval as Robinton dropped the towel on the white sand of the Cove and continued on into the pleasant waters. With Zair plunging into the next wave right beside him, Robinton emerged, propelling himself forward with a strong overarm stroke. A group of wild fire-lizards joined him and Zair, zipping just above the water alongside him or plunging in just in front of his face, missing body contact by inches. As often as they had seen humans bathing in the sea, they never ceased to be fascinated by swimmers.

Robinton turned back to shore, allowing the waves to carry his body forward. The sea was gentle this morning, but the exercise was still a fine toner. He dried himself off, then knotted the towel about his waist and strode off toward the house, where D'ram and Lytol were waiting on the porch. "Tell them, Zair, that I'm completely refreshed and in vigorous health."

"You're awake, are you?" D'ram called. "About time. It's well past noon."

"*Past* noon?" Robinton stopped in his tracks, appalled at having wasted so much time sleeping. Who knew what he had missed of Aivas's disclosures that morning? "You should have wakened me!" He did not attempt to keep the irritation out of his voice.

"Your body has more sense than you do," Lytol added, rising from the hammock hanging in the corner of the porch. "You got only the sleep you needed, Robinton. Pour him some klah, D'ram, while I finish preparing his breakfast—our lunch."

As Robinton came up the steps, the aroma of the klah that D'ram was pouring was enough to remind him that hunger was a need, too. He settled himself down, and between bites of the substantial breakfast that Lytol served him he brought them up to date.

"And so, the miracle begins," he said, finishing his account.

"You've no doubt in your mind, Robinton," Lytol said with his usual skepticism, "that this Aivas can effect the annihilation of Thread?"

"By the first Egg, Lytol, one cannot doubt it. The marvels we saw, the very fact that our ancestors made that incredible flight from the planet of our origin, lend credibility to his promise. We have only to relearn the skills we lost, and we can triumph over this ancient menace."

"Aye, but why didn't the ancients rid us of Thread then, with all their incredible crafts and their full knowledge of the technology lost to us?" Lytol asked.

"You're not the only one to query that, Lytol," Robinton said. "But Aivas explained that the volcanic eruptions came at a crucial time and the settlers went north to establish a safe base. So their plans to defeat Thread were interrupted."

"Why didn't they come back when Threadfall ceased?"

"That Aivas didn't know." Robinton had to recognize that there were gaps in Aivas's account. "And yet . . . a musical instrument can only do what it is constructed to do, or one of Fandarel's machines. Therefore, a machine, even as sophisticated as Aivas, could do only what it/he was designed to do. It/he"—I really must make up my mind how I consider the thing, Robinton thought—"is unlikely to tell lies. Though I suspect he," Robinton said, making up his mind, "does not reveal the whole truth. We've had enough trouble absorbing and understanding what he's already told us."

Lytol gave a snort, a cynical expression on his face which, Robinton was relieved to notice, was not mirrored by D'ram.

"I would like to believe that we can!" Robinton added.

"Who wouldn't?" Lytol said, relenting slightly.

"I believe Aivas," D'ram said. "He speaks with such authority. He explained that the time will be right in four years—that is, Turns—ten months and twenty-seven days. Twenty-six today. The time factor has to be correct to succeed."

"Succeed in what?" Lytol persisted.

"*That* is something we must also learn." Robinton laughed in self-disparagement. "Not to put too fine a point on it, Lytol, but we're plainly too ignorant to understand his explanation. He did try—something about windows, and leaving Pern at just the precise moment to intercept the Red Star, or rather the planet which appears red to us for so much of its orbit in our skies. He showed us the diagram." Noting his defensive tone, he shook himself. "If you wish to query him, Lytol, I'm sure you can."

Lytol cast Robinton a sardonic look. "There are others with greater reason to consult Aivas."

"But you *must* hear our history from Aivas, Lytol," D'ram said, leaning forward across the table. "You'll appreciate then why we can so unreservedly believe in Aivas and in his promise."

"He really has got to you, hasn't he?" Lytol shook his head at their credulousness.

"If you listen to what he says, you'll believe," Robinton said, rising. He had to clutch at the towel to keep it from slipping, which reduced the dignity of his pronouncement. "I'm dressing to return to Landing. D'ram, will you and Tiroth oblige me?"

"Since you are rested," D'ram said, giving his housemate a long and searching look, "we will, of course, oblige. Lytol, will you not join us?"

"Not today."

"Are you afraid of being won over despite your reservations?" Robinton asked.

Lytol shook his head slowly. "That's not likely. But go. Enjoy your dream of Threadfree skies."

"The last of the true skeptics," Robinton muttered under his breath, somewhat disturbed by Lytol's continued disbelief. Did Lytol think old age had dulled Robinton's wits or discriminatory faculties? Or did he believe, like Corman, that the Harper was gullible enough to be taken in by any plausible story?

"No," D'ram assured him when he voiced the question to the old Weyrleader as they walked toward bronze Tiroth, waiting for them on the strand. "He's too pragmatic. He told me yesterday that we were far too excited to think logically about the repercussions Aivas will have on our lives. Altering the basic structure of our society and its values and all that twaddle." D'ram's snort indicated that he did not agree. "He's been through several upheavals himself. He's unlikely to welcome another."

"But you do?"

D'ram smiled over his shoulder at the Harper as he settled himself between Tiroth's neck ridges. "I'm a dragonrider, Harper, and dedicated to the eradication of Thread. If there is even the slightest hope . . ." He shrugged. "Tiroth, take us to Landing!"

"Watch out, D'ram," the Harper cautioned. "It's undergone considerable alterations even since yesterday noontime when you left it."

So Monarth warns me. Although the Harper knew that Tiroth was speaking directly to D'ram, his chest swelled with the privilege of hearing. *I have the altered scene from him. It* has *changed.*

Was there a note of discontent in Tiroth's tone?

However, the great bronze dragon took them *between* and reentered on the hill west of the Aivas building, hovering in the air above the line of dragons sunning themselves on the promontory. Robinton looked up at the dragons on the hill, to see if he recognized any of the bronzes or the queens. Then he remembered that Benden Weyr would be involved in riding Threadfall today.

Gliding down toward the building, Robinton and D'ram could not see the alterations until the bronze veered to his right and back-winged to land on the wide yard.

"I'd no idea!" D'ram gasped, turning to stare at the Harper, who was no less surprised than he.

Robinton hid his own reaction behind a quick smile of reassurance. Obviously, Lytol was in the minority, to judge by the changes here: all designed to facilitate access to Aivas. The original wing had been tripled in size, with odd lean-to sheds, like skirts, along all three sides. As the Harper dismounted, he recognized more of Fandarel's batteries housed under the sheds—sufficient power, he assumed, to sustain the entity all the hours of the day and night until the new and more powerful water-turbines were finished.

In the broad new courtyard, several knots of folk were arguing vociferously with each other while, above their heads, fire-lizards made raucous sounds of agitation. Most of the people wore the shoulder knots of Masters and journeymen from various Crafts; their tunic devices told Robinton that they came from different Holds, as well.

"Free-for-all?" D'ram asked, dropping to the ground beside Robinton.

"That's what it certainly sounds like," Robinton did not recognize any of the dissenters, though he noted four of Master Esselin's biggest workmen standing in front of the closed doors of the building. He took a deep breath and strode forward.

"Now, just what seems to be the trouble here?" he asked loudly. It took only a moment for all the disputants to realize who was addressing them; immediately he was encircled, each plaintiff demanding his attention. "*Now wait just a moment!*" he bellowed. Behind him on the hill, bronze and gold dragons added their authoritative bugle, and silence fell. Then he pointed at one man wearing a Masterminer's knot and Crom's device.

"Master Esselin will not let us in," the man said belligerently.

"And my Lord Holder"—a man wearing the head-Steward knots of Boll pushed forward from the group—"insists that we be given the facts about this mysterious being."

"Deckter charged me to do the same," a Steward from Nabol said in the most aggrieved tone of the three. "We demand to know the truth about this Aivas. And I'm to see this marvel before I return to Nabol."

"Yes, you all have been unconscionably slighted," Robinton said soothingly. "And those of us who have been fortunate to hear Aivas *know* that seeing Aivas is the first step in believing what he can do for us all, Hold, Hall, and Weyr. Why, *I've* only just been allowed to return." He feigned indignation at such an omission. That the much respected Harper of Pern should be denied access, too, seemed to appease them. "Now, you must realize that the room where Aivas is installed is quite small, though I notice there have been attempts to enlarge the space." He craned his neck as if trying to see just how much larger it was. "Hmmm. Yes, working day and night from the look of it. Most commendable really. Now, if you'll just bide here, I'll see what can be done about your quite legitimate request to see Aivas."

"I don't want to just *see* it," the miner complained. "I want it to tell me how to get back to the main lode of a very rich vein of ore. The ancients located all the ores on Pern. I want it to tell me where to dig, since it knows everything about Pern."

"Not everything, my dear fellow," Robinton said, less than surprised that Aivas was already being considered an omniscient being. Should he emphasize that Aivas was only—only? he thought bemusedly—a machine, a device that had served their ancestors as the receptacle of information? No, their understanding of machinery, craftsmen though many of them were, was too rudimentary. They would not grasp the concept of so complex a mechanical apparatus, let alone the concept of an *artificial* intelligence. The Masterharper didn't understand that all too well himself. He sighed with resignation. "And he knows very little about Pern as it is today, though a great deal about Pern as it was twenty-five hundred Turns ago. I suppose none of you heard that you were supposed to bring Hall Records with you? Aivas particularly wants to bring himself up to current times with every Hall, Hold, and Weyr."

"No one said anything about Records," the miner said, taken aback. "We heard it knew everything."

"Aivas will be the first to inform you that while his knowledge extends to many subjects and skills, he is *not*, happily, all-knowing. He is . . . a talking Record, and far more accurate than ours, which tunnel snakes, time, and other perils have rendered illegible."

"We was told he knew everything!" the miner insisted stubbornly.

"Not even *I* know everything," Robinton responded gently. "Nor has Aivas even once suggested that he does. He knows a great more, however, than we do. And we shall all learn from him. Now, let me speak to Master Esselin on your behalf. There are, let's see, how many of you?" And he did a quick head count. "Thirty-four. Well, that's too many for one go. D'ram, choose by lots. You all know D'ram here as a fair man. You'll all have a turn—brief it may be, but Aivas you shall see."

Master Esselin was delighted to see the Harper but appalled at Robinton's solution to the matter of the plaintiffs.

"We can't send them away unhappy, Esselin. They have every bit as much of a right to see Aivas as a Lord Holder. More, even, because they'll be the *doing* of Aivas's grand plans over the next few years. Who's in there now?"

"Master Terry with Masters and journeymen from every Smithcrafthall in the world." Then his eyes went round with anxiety. "And Master Hamian from Southern Hold and two of his apprentices."

"Ah, Toric's finally sent an emissary?" Robinton wasn't sure if the news pleased or worried him. He had rather hoped not to have to contend with Toric's avarice yet.

"I don't think he comes on Lord Toric's behalf." Esselin shook his head, his eyes still wide with apprehension. "Master Hamian did say to Master Terry that his sister, the Lady Sharra of Ruatha, suggested that he drop everything and come here immediately."

"And so he should. So he should," Robinton agreed affably. Hamian would be an excellent man to have involved here. A clever innovator who had already put back to use what the ancients had left behind in a Southern mine. "I'll just see when it's convenient to interrupt them for a few moments. Believe me, Esselin, it's the better part of discretion to give those fellows out there the chance to see Aivas for themselves."

"But they're only Stewards and small miners . . ."

"There are more of those than of Lord Holders and Crafthallmasters and Weyrleaders, Esselin, and every single one of them has the right to approach Aivas."

"That wasn't what I was told," Master Esselin said, resorting to his usual obstructive attitude, thrusting his heavy chin belligerently forward.

Robinton eyed him pityingly for such a long moment that even the thick-skinned Esselin could not fail to notice that his behavior was unacceptable to the Harper.

"I think you will find before the day is out that you will be told differently, Master Esselin. Now, if you will excuse me . . .'' And with that Robinton strode down the hall to the Aivas chamber.

As he approached, he could hear Aivas's sonorous voice using the sort of penetrating tone that suggested he was addressing a large group. When Robinton quietly opened the door, he was first amazed at how many people were standing in the room, and then that even more occupied the new wings on either side of the Aivas facility. Two doors had been opened into the large annexes on either side. The two walls enclosing Aivas were intact, of course, but much more space had been made for larger audiences. This afternoon the group was composed of smiths who were, in general, possessed of large, powerful bodies. Master Nicat, the Masterminer, was seated at the front on a bench with Terry and two of his best Masters, who were all busily copying the diagrams on the main Aivas screen. Jancis was also there, in a corner, bent over a drawing board on her lap. Others in the room were doing their best to draw, too, some using the backs of others to steady their pads. Robinton could make no sense of the complicated design, but it was obvious from the rapt attention it was being given that it was of great importance to the Smithcrafters. Aivas was explaining, adding numbered specifications that also meant nothing to the Harper. The measured voice enjoined his listeners to ask questions on any point that was not clear.

"You have explained in such detail," Master Nicat said, his swarthy face wearing a most respectful expression, "that even the most simple-minded apprentice would understand."

"Ah, if you don't mind, Aivas . . .'' A Masterminer whom Robinton knew to be the Master of the works at one of the larger Telgar iron foundries raised his hand. "If faulty melts can be remedied up to standard, then can we repair the damage to ones long since discarded?"

"That is correct. The process can be applied to used metals. In fact, quite often the use of old metal improves the final product."

"Even metals made by the ancients?" Master Hamian asked. "We have found some in what I understand were the original workings at Andiyar's Stake in Dorado."

"Once in the crucible, the melt burns off impurities of all kinds." Then, to Robinton's astonishment, Aivas added, "Good afternoon, Master Robinton. What assistance do you need today?"

Robinton found himself embarrassed. "I do not intend to interrupt . . .''

"You aren't," Terry replied, rising and stretching. "Right, Nicat?" he added to the Masterminer, who looked like a man hoping that he had understood his orders.

The other craftsmen began low conversations with neighbors, and those nearest the door began to file out, carefully folding their drawings and notes.

As Robinton moved farther into the room, he caught the pungency of sweating bodies, laced with the taint of metal's acidity and the odd dank smell of deep mine shafts. As the room emptied, he could appreciate the size of the room that had been achieved overnight.

"Well, well!" he murmured, noticing the windows on either ends, opened to a breeze which began to circulate freely as the last of the craftsmen left. Jancis alone remained in her corner, furiously scribbling.

She looked up and smiled at the Harper. "We've accomplished so much today, Master Robinton."

"And did you get any sleep last night, young woman?"

Her cheeks dimpled in a mischievous smile. "Indeed we did!" And then she colored. "I mean, we both slept. I mean, Piemur fell asleep first—oh, blast!"

Robinton laughed heartily. "I won't misconstrue, Jancis, even if it mattered. You're not going to let all this fuss and fascination delay your formal announcement, are you?"

"No," she said firmly. "I want to bring the date forward." She blushed prettily but kept the eye contact. "It would make things easier." She gathered up her things. "The others are all in the computer room. You might want to take a crack at it, too."

"Me?" The Harper was dumbfounded. "That's for young resilient minds like yours and Piemur's and Jaxom's."

"Learning is not limited to the young, Master Robinton," Aivas said.

"Well, we'll see," the Harper replied, hedging and running his fingers nervously over his face. He was acutely conscious that he could no longer retain the words and notes of new music and had few doubts that the problem would extend to other areas. He did not think himself a vain man, or excessively proud, but he did not wish to show to disadvantage. "We'll see. Meantime, we have a minor problem . . ."

"With that lot out there, determined against all Master Esselin's prejudice on seeing Aivas?" Jancis asked.

"Hmm, a minor miner problem," Robinton heard himself saying, and groaned.

Jancis pleased him by chuckling. "It is apt," she said. "They *need* to see Aivas so that they can tell their lords and masters that they have?"

"That's about the size of it. Aivas, if you would agree, I shall waft them in and out, with just time enough to say that they've been here."

"Is that your true wish in this instance?"

Robinton cleared his throat. "I could wish that as many men and women as possible on this planet could be exposed to your fund of knowledge, but even with these enlarged accommodations, that is neither possible nor wise. The parochially minded tend to flog petty issues to a nubbin. The worried assume their problems are uniquely threatening, or that you are omniscient enough to solve any problem put to you."

"It has always been so, Master Robinton," Aivas said, as accepting as ever. "Mankind has always put great faith in oracles."

"Oracles?" The word was unfamiliar to the Harper.

"A full explanation of the phenomenon should be kept until you have forty-four hours free, for the file on religion is lengthy. At this moment in time, how do you propose to satisfy the petitioners outside?"

"By sending in small groups to see and question you, however briefly."

"Then permit them all to enter. The outside sensors indicate the exact numbers that this room can now accommodate."

While Master Esselin looked on in dismay and disapproval, the entire gaggle hurried down the corridor.

"Good afternoon, gentlemen," Aivas said, his mellifluous voice startling the newcomers into awed silence. "Within the walls you are currently facing, there is an Artificial Intelligence Voice-Address System that stores information for retrieval. Or Aivas, to use the appropriate acronym. It is seen that there are among you those of the miner craft. No doubt you noticed that Masterminers attended the previous lecture. It would be of considerable value to you to consult with these men on the new methods of smelting ores. It is hoped that you two Stewards from Crom and Nabol have brought with you the Records of your Holds. These will be vital in assessing the present, and future, productivity of the properties you so ably manage for your Lord

Holders. You glass-smiths and journeymen from the Halls at Igen and Ista have, in the sandpits and lead mines of your respective Holds, some of the best silicates in this world, which accounts for the fact that you produce the finest, most durable glass on the planet. If this facility may be of service in any way to your crafthalls, please ask Master Robinton to appoint a time for a longer discussion."

Most of the attendees simply gawked, trying to find the source of the disembodied voice. The Ista glass-smith took a hesitant step forward, swallowed hard, and spoke.

"Master Aivas, Master Oldive asked me to construct the lens of a microscope for him." The words came out in a rush.

"Yes, such an instrument is of vital importance to the Healer's Hall."

"I looked up our Records, Master Aivas." He pulled from his tunic some moldering sheets, stained, spotted, and full of holes. "But, as you see . . ." He held them out toward the screen.

"Place them over the lit panel on the worktop, Masterglass-smith."

Looking about for reassurance, the Istan hesitated, until the Harper shooed him forward. The others stared at the glass-smith for his audacity. Part of one page crumbled off even as he placed it over the lighted panel. His journeyman rushed forward and, with the air of a man greatly daring, shoved the missing corner up against the broken end.

Instantly the screen lit up with an image of the much damaged drawing. Magically an unseen point connected up the missing lines and while the watchers gasped in wonder, the diagram became entire. From the printer slot emerged a sheet, which the dazzled journeyman took at Aivas's suggestion.

"Look! Look! Finer than the best draftsman we have could render it!" the excited man exclaimed.

"Next page, please," Aivas said, and the glass-smith, with some fumbling, managed to comply.

Very shortly the missing notes and explanations had been restored, and everyone in the room had had a chance to see the reconstructed sheets.

"Have you any queries regarding the manufacture of barrel, focusing devices, or lenses?" Aivas asked politely.

There were one or two questions from the journeyman; his master was too dazed to be coherent.

"If some should arise during manufacture—" Aivas finished.

"During what?" the journeyman was startled into asking by the unfamiliar word.

"During the making, either send your question to Master Robinton or return for additional explanations or further demonstration."

It was easy then for Robinton to move the group out of the room and speed them on their way down the hall.

"That took ten minutes," Aivas said in a low tone. "A useful disposition of time."

"Have you been advised to appoint me your aide?" the Master-harper asked in an amused tone.

"Your impartiality is legend, Master Robinton, and your scrupulous sense of fair play has just been demonstrated. Master Esselin's definition of priority is noticeably skewed toward rank. The glass-smith's need of stored information was indeed a priority that ought to have been immediately scheduled when he arrived early this morning. Master Esselin ignored him."

"He did?" Robinton was annoyed.

"If you will see to it that he does not exceed his very limited authority, considerable future ill-feeling will be avoided."

"I will see to that immediately, Aivas."

"If you should be unwilling to act in this capacity, perhaps D'ram, the bronze dragonrider, would assist. He, also, is held in the highest regard by peer group, Hall, and Hold. Is it true that he came forward in time four hundred Turns to fight Thread? That he has already spent a good portion of his life in that onerous task?"

"That is correct, Aivas."

"This generation, and his, are amazing, Master Robinton." Though the words were spoken levelly, the tone of admiration was unmistakable, and Robinton squared his shoulders proudly.

"We are of one mind in that." Then, brusquely, Robinton added, "As your aide, Master Aivas, I'll just set Master Esselin straight on the matter of assigning priorities without consultation. You may be sure he will obey you as promptly as he does myself or the Weyr-leaders."

Back in the hall, Robinton cut short all of Master Esselin's tedious explanations and apologies. He found D'ram in the room where Piemur, Jancis, Jaxom, and Benelek were clattering away at their lessons on the small screens. They were each working on different projects, he could see; he recognized that Jancis was somehow replicating the diagram that Aivas had shown the miners.

"Come on, Master Robinton," Piemur said, looking up from his screen. "I fixed a station for you to experiment with."

Robinton held up his hands and backed away. "No, no, I've appointed myself aide to Master Aivas for the afternoon. You cannot believe how stupid Esselin is."

"Ha! Yes, I can!" Piemur said emphatically.

"He's as thick as two short planks," Benelek grumbled. "And he doesn't like any of us coming and going as we need to."

"I don't have any trouble," Jancis said, but her eyes danced with mischief. "All I have to do is give him a cup of klah or something to eat from the tray when I bring it in."

"And that's another score I'm going to settle with ol' Master fuddy-duddy Esselin," Piemur said heatedly. "You are *not* a kitchen drudge. Does he never see the Master tab on your collar? Doesn't he know you're Fandarel's granddaughter and top of your own Craft?"

"Oh, I think he will," Jaxom remarked without looking up from his board, his fingers flying across it. "I caught his paternal act this morning, and I reminded him that the proper form of address for Jancis is Mastersmith. You know, I don't think he had noticed the collar tabs."

"That's no excuse," Piemur retorted, likely to fume until he himself had settled the score with the old man.

"Perhaps Master Esselin should go back to his archives," D'ram said. "That's what he's supposed to be doing."

"And about all he's good for," Piemur muttered.

"However, since someone must take over his current responsibility, I think I shall appoint myself in his place."

"A marvelous notion, D'ram," Robinton said while the others let out a cheer. "Actually, Aivas had already recommended you in that capacity. He's heard that you are a well-respected and scrupulously honest character. He doesn't know you as well as I do, of course." When D'ram glanced apprehensively at him, Robinton broke into a teasing grin. "In fact, I think we should inveigle Lytol up here, too. Or would three honest men be too much for the job?"

"There can never be enough honest men," Jaxom said firmly, looking up from his screen. "I think the challenge would be good for Lytol." His expression reflected a deep concern for his aging guardian. "The pair of you already look the better for some proper use of your long experience. And there *ought* to be someone in charge who's got the sense he was born with."

"I second that," a voice said from the doorway. In walked Mastersmith Hamian. "I had to elbow the old fool aside to get back in here. I see what Sharra meant when she said you were all wrapped up in this, Jaxom," he added, tolerantly grinning at his sister's mate before he nodded courteously to the others in the room. "I didn't want to cause undue consternation among my peers earlier, Master Robinton, but would Master Aivas be able to tell any of us—me, because I'm dead keen to know—how the ancestors made their durable plastics?"

"Hurrah!" Piemur and Jancis cheered together. And Piemur jumped from his stool and thumped Hamian's back.

The big smith from Southern Hold was not as tall or as massive as Master Fandarel, but he was solid enough to absorb Piemur's hearty pounding without giving an inch. He grinned at his friend, his large and even teeth white in his tanned face. "Glad someone approves. Do you?" He looked directly at the Harper.

Robinton looked inquiringly at D'ram. "And thus we make the first test of our authority?"

"I'd say Hamian is exactly the right man to try something so new—new to us at least," D'ram said, nodding.

"So it's now up to him who knows," Robinton said, and jerked his head towards Aivas's room. "Let's ask."

All but Benelek traipsed along to hear what Aivas would say. Robinton beckoned for Hamian to stand squarely in front of the screen, then had to prod him when the big smith suddenly found it difficult to frame the question.

"Ask him. He hasn't bitten anyone," Robinton said.

"Yet," Piemur added, pretending to be worried.

"Ahem, Master Aivas . . ." Hamian faltered again.

"You are volunteering to learn how to make silicate-based plastics such as your ancestors used in building materials, Master Hamian?"

Hamian just nodded, his eyebrows raised in comical surprise. "How'd he know that?" he asked in a low aside to the Harper.

"He's got long ears," Robinton replied, amused.

"Incorrect, Master Robinton," Aivas said. "This facility has far more sensitive receptors than ears, Master Hamian, and since the door to the adjacent room was open, the conversation was audible. To reiterate, you wish, Master Hamian, to learn how to produce the plastics your ancestors used."

Hamian squared himself in front of the screen, throwing his head up. "Yes, Master Aivas, that is my wish. There are sufficient of my peers eager to improve the quality of iron, steel, brass, and copper, but, having seen the durability of the ancients' plastic materials, I would like to specialize in them. It is my belief that this could be as important a material to us as it was to our ancestors."

"The manufacture of plastics was a highly refined skill in your ancestors' time. Different polymers produced different end products that could be pliable, semimalleable, or rigid, depending on the chemical formulae. As surface petroleum was discovered near Drake's Lake, there is no reason you cannot revive organic plastic manufacture. However, you will have to understand considerably more chemistry than is currently part of your Mastery training. The manufacture itself can be defined as a continuous mass-solution process. Two units were left in the Catherine Caves by Joel Lilienkamp."

"Lilienkamp?" Piemur cried, pivoting to point both forefingers at Jancis, who also cried, "Lilcamp?"

"Who *was* Joel Lilienkamp?" Piemur asked Aivas.

"The Expedition's supply officer: the person who preserved so many artifacts in the Catherine Caves."

"Jayge just *has* to be a descendant," Piemur crowed, and then abruptly apologized for his interruption.

"The two large polymerizing units are not marked as having been protectively packaged. Therefore they will have suffered decay and are unlikely to be operative. But they can be used as templates. You will learn much in the reconstruction, Master Hamian, and have more to learn in the chemistry and physics experiments that you will be set."

Hamian's grin stretched from ear to ear. "My pleasure, Master Aivas, my pleasure." He rubbed his big callused hands together in eagerness. "When do I start?"

"First, you must find the prototype models in the cave." Aivas's screen lit up with the pictures of two thick cubes with a variety of curious extrusions. "These are what you must find. They will be heavy and cumbersome to move."

"I've moved odder and heavier objects, Master Aivas."

A paper illustrating the necessary objects extruded from the slot, and Piemur handed it to the Southern smith.

"You will require a workshop in which to disassemble them and decide what materials you have readily available with which to assemble a modern model. It is advisable that you not be the only one to study these basic sciences: The manufacture of suitable polymers will require a considerable team of workers trained in chemistry and physics."

Hamian smiled ruefully. "Study will obviously be necessary, just to understand the unfamiliar words you're using."

"I think it's safe to say," Master Robinton put in, glancing pointedly at Piemur and Jancis, "that you will have at least three or four more students in your class, Aivas. I'm sure, Hamian, that you will want some members of your own Hall trained, as well."

"I've one or two likely fellows in mind, that's certain," Hamian replied. He drew in a deep breath and exhaled. "My thanks, Master Aivas."

"Acknowledged, Master Hamian."

"How'd you escape Toric?" Piemur asked softly, masking his words behind one hand.

"Escape doesn't enter into this, Piemur." Again Hamian said with a droll grimace, "I'm my own master. I've organized Southern's mines to produce with or without me leaning on anyone. Now I shall broaden my own horizons, as Toric did his. My thanks, Master Robinton, D'ram. I know where the caves are. I'll start right away." And he strode purposefully out of the room and down the hall.

As soon as the smith had turned the corner, Master Esselin ducked out of one of the sleeping rooms on the corridor, his expression aggrieved.

"Master Robinton, I told that smith he wasn't to—"

"Master Esselin . . ." Robinton adopted his most charming manner as he put an arm around the man's fleshy shoulders and turned him around. D'ram closed in on the other side, so that Esselin was inexorably led toward the entrance hall. "I do believe that you have been most shamefully treated lately."

"I?" Esselin's fretful look turned to surprise as he laid one plump hand on his chest. "Yes, Master Robinton, when bullies like that Southern smith pay absolutely no attention to my orders . . ."

"You're quite right, Master Esselin. Most shameful, and I think your good nature in suspending your invaluable archival contributions to this site has been woefully abused. Therefore, it has been decided that Weyrleader D'ram, Lord Warder Lytol, and myself should relieve you of this onerous duty and let you get back to your own responsibilities."

"Oh, but, Master Robinton . . ." Esselin would have slowed his pace if the other two had let him. "I didn't mean to imply that I was *unwilling* . . ."

"You have been willingness itself," D'ram said, shaking his head.

"And all to your credit, Master Esselin, but fair's fair, and you've been more than kind to officiate. We will now take over from you."

Master Esselin continued his protests all the way out the door and down the walk to the path that led to the Archive complex. Gently but firmly Weyrleader and Harper gave him a final push, smiling and nodding and totally ignoring his repeated demurrals.

"There!" D'ram said once they were back in the building. He brushed his hands together in satisfaction. "I'll take the first watch, Robinton." He turned to one of the guards. "I'm in charge now. What's your name?"

"Gayton, sir."

"I'd take it kindly, Gayton, if you'd fetch something cool to drink from the kitchens. Bring enough for all of us here. And no, Robinton, he is not going to bring you any wine quite yet. You'll have to have a cool head when you stand your watch, you know."

"Why, you old coot!" Robinton exclaimed. "My head remains cool no matter how much wine I take. The very notion."

"Take yourself off, Robinton." Grinning, D'ram shooed him away. "Get into mischief somewhere else."

"Mischief?" The Harper grumbled with mock indignation, but just then they both heard a triumphant shout from Piemur, so he hurried along to see what had occurred.

"I did it! I did it!" Piemur was still carrying on when the Harper arrived. Jancis and Jaxom both looked slightly envious; Benelek adopted a distant attitude.

"Did what?"

"Made a program all by myself."

The Harper peered at the enigmatic words and letters on the screen and then at his journeyman. "That . . . is a program?"

"Sure is. Dead easy once you get the hang of it!" Piemur's elation was infectious.

"Piemur," the Harper found himself saying, "I have a few hours to spare right now while D'ram's on duty. Did you or did you not mention that there was a spare one of these contraptions?"

"Indeed there is, Master." With considerable satisfaction on his face and not a trace of his usual impudence, Piemur spun out of his seat and went over to the shelf where the components were neatly stacked.

"I think I may regret this," the Robinton said to himself.

"It is to be hoped that you will not, Master Robinton" was Aivas's low reassurance.

Zair nipping his ear roused Robinton from a doze. He had been leaning back in his chair, head resting on the support, legs propped up on the desk, and as he woke the first thing he was aware of was the crick in his neck. His knees wouldn't at first bend as he lowered his legs. When he groaned, Zair nipped him again, eyes flaming red-orange.

Instantly the Masterharper was alert. Down the hall, he could hear Aivas's voice explaining something and the lighter voice of one of the students querying. That was as it should be. He looked up at Zair, who was staring out the door into the night. It was then he caught the faint noise of something cracking, and the even fainter splashing of liquid.

He rose, silently swearing at the recalcitrance of aging joints that no longer functioned smoothly. As stealthily as he could, he moved across the entrance hall and out into the night. He knew it was near dawn; the insect sounds that had lulled him to sleep on his post had ceased and daytime noises had not yet begun. He crept forward, hearing that soft cracking noise again. To his left, where the banks of Fandarel's batteries had been installed against the wall, he saw darker shadows. Two men. Two men busily smashing the glass tanks that held the battery fluid.

"Now, just what do you think you're doing?" he demanded, out-raged. "Zair! Grab them! Pie . . . *mur! Jancis! Someone!*" He ran forward, determined to prevent any further damage to Aivas's power supply.

Later, he wondered what he had thought he was doing, an un-armed elderly man attacking vandals. Even as the pair came at him with upraised clubs or iron bars or whatever they had been using to smash the battery tanks, he wasn't afraid: just purely and simply furious.

Fortunately Zair had weapons, twenty sharp talons, and as the little bronze swooped to tear at the eyes of the first man, Piemur's Farli, Jancis's Trig, and half a dozen other fire-lizards joined the bat-tle. Robinton caught a handful of tunic and tried to drag the man to the ground, but with a savage jerk, accompanied by an anguished squeal as fire-lizard claws racked facial skin, the man broke free and took to his heels. His companion swatted viciously at the aerial at-tackers and then ran off as well. The fire-lizards followed, dividing into two groups to follow the separating fugitives.

By the time human assistance arrived, even the sound of the van-dals' retreat was lost to listening ears.

"Don't worry, Robinton," Piemur said. "We've only to check who got clawed. We'll find them! Are you all right, Master?"

Robinton was clutching at his chest and panting from his exertions, and although he gestured fiercely for Piemur and the others to follow the fugitives, he became their first concern.

"I'm all right, I'm all right," he cried, trying to avoid their solicitude. "Go after them!" And he fell into a fit of coughing, caused more by frustration than by exercise.

By the time he had convinced them of his well-being, the fire-lizards had returned, looking exceedingly pleased with themselves for having chased the intruders. Disgusted at the vandals' escape, Robinton grabbed up a glowbasket and led the way to the point of attack.

"Five smashed, and if you hadn't heard—" Piemur began.

"I didn't hear. Zair did." Robinton was furious with himself for having dozed off.

"Same thing," Piemur replied with an impish grin. "And they didn't break enough tanks to jeopardize the power supply. Don't fret now, Master. There're spares in Stores."

"I'm fretting because it happened at all!" Robinton heard his voice rise in angry stress.

"We'll find the vandals," Piemur assured his master. Guiding the old Harper back to his chair, he poured him a cup of wine.

"We'd better," Robinton said savagely. He knew there was growing antagonism to Aivas, but he had not really considered, even for a moment, that someone would actually attack the facility.

But who? he wondered, sipping at the wine and feeling its usual efficacious soothing. Esselin? He doubted the fat old fool would dare, no matter how upset he might have been over losing his sinecure. Had any of Norist's glassmen been at Landing that day?

"Don't fret yourself," Piemur repeated, regarding his master with continued anxiety. "See? Zair's bloodied one of them. We'll find them, never fear."

The men were not found the next morning, although Piemur organized a discreet search of the entire complement at Landing. He even went so far as to rouse Esselin well before the indolent man was apt to be awake, but the round, fat face was blemish-free.

"They must have just kept running," he reported to the worried Harper, who was overseeing the replacement of the battery tanks.

"We must build a barrier across these," Robinton said. "We must mount a watch at all times. Aivas cannot be jeopardized."

"Have you decided who's the most likely suspect?" Piemur asked, watching his master's tired face.

"Suspect? I've a variety of choices. Proof, no!"

Piemur shrugged. "Then we watch harder." Then, as an afterthought, he asked, "Why didn't Aivas sound an alarm? He usually sees what's going on, night or day."

When queried on that point, Aivas replied that the vandals had been operating under the level of the exterior visuals, and the only sound the audio sensors had picked up had been consistent enough with usual nocturnal activity.

"What about in here?" Robinton asked.

"This facility is safe. Do not fear vandalism in here."

Robinton was not all that reassured but could not argue the point, as the first of the new day's students were arriving.

"We'll keep this to ourselves for the time being, Piemur," Robinton said in a tone that brooked no argument.

"What about a message to all harpers to watch out for claw-marked faces?"

Robinton lifted his shoulders briefly. "I doubt they'll appear in public until they're healed, but send the message."

6

As events over the next few weeks proved, the self-appointment of the Harper, the old Weyrleader, and the retired Lord Warder as Aivas's custodians was providential. The management by three men who already enjoyed reputations for probity and impartiality went unchallenged. Certainly the accumulated knowledge of Harper, Weyrleader, and Lord Warder was utilized to its fullest in the rebirth and administration of Landing.

Some visitors—the merely curious—became disenchanted when they discovered that Aivas ignored foolish or egocentric questions. Those willing to be enlightened and to work hard to acquire the new disciplines stayed on and profited.

Until ten secondary stations were up and running, the three custodians arranged appointments for Aivas, deftly slotting in emergency consultations without offending anyone. And, because Aivas needed no rest, concentrated lessons, such as those for Master Oldive and other healers, were scheduled for the early hours of Landing's day.

The major crafthalls were not the only ones to send representatives; it became prestigious for the Lord Holders to send promising sons and daughters, as well as likely candidates from minor holds. There were so many at first, some of whom were obviously ill-equipped to deal with radical new concepts, that it was kinder and less bothersome to set each applicant a basic test: an aptitude test,

Aivas called it. It certainly weeded out the idlers and those without true scholarship.

Lessa and F'lar never became proficient in their use of a console, mostly because, in the Harper's estimation, they had little time to spend learning the essentials; but they did grasp the fundamentals of accessing information. F'nor didn't even try, but his mate, Brekke, joined the Masterhealer's dedicated group in their striving to regain the lost medical techniques. Mirrim, determined to keep up with T'gellan, struggled on despite a most distressing start and succeeded. K'van became as adept as Jaxom and Piemur.

To the surprise and delight of his close associates, the taciturn Lytol became an avid user, accessing files from the widest range of topics. He insisted on taking the late shift, as he never required more than four hours of sleep anyway.

"Lytol's always been a deep person, with unexpected reserves—or he wouldn't have survived as long as he has," Jaxom replied to those who commented on Lytol's new obsession. "Though I don't understand his fascination with all that dry historical stuff when there's so much more that we can apply to *living* and working here and now."

"On the contrary, Jaxom," the Harper replied. "Lytol's investigations may be the most significant of all."

"Even more significant than Fandarel's new water-turbine power stations?"

The Mastersmith had taken great satisfaction in demonstrating how a model of the proposed generator worked, as his foundry labored day and night to complete the components of the full-scale machinery.

"That is certainly significant now," the Harper replied, choosing his words carefully. "But there's the problem of general acceptance."

Various study rooms had been set up, each dedicated to a different subject. Two of the larger rooms became laboratories to teach the basic sciences that Aivas felt were required as foundation courses, as he termed them: chemistry, physics, and biology. One room had been set aside for short consultations, and another for general teaching; a fairly large room was set aside for the healers, and its walls covered with various diagrams "of the most gruesome sort," in Jancis's estimation. Aivas also requested that a room be reserved for special students, those who were taking concentrated courses in a variety of subjects: Jaxom, Piemur, Jancis, K'van, T'gellan, N'ton, Mirrim, Hamian, three journeymen, an apprentice of Hamian's, four other young bronze riders, two brown, four blue, and three green riders. Other riders would follow when there was space in the classes, since the Weyrs were the most eager to take advantage of Aivas.

Occasionally Robinton liked to walk down the hall and listen in on the instructions. One day when he peered in on a lesson including Jaxom, Piemur, Jancis, and two Smithcraft journeymen, he saw an astonishing sight.

A ring of dull metal hovered about two inches above the high worktop in front of them. As they reached forward to touch it, it slipped along the bench as if it were on invisible rollers. Aivas continued his explanation.

"The lines of magnetic force in the ring are induced in such a way that they exactly oppose the electromagnets that are generating the field."

Robinton made himself small against the doorjamb, so as not to disturb the fascinated students.

"This is far more dramatic at very low temperatures, where there is no electrical resistance, the rings are superconducting, and the current passes without any loss. There are not the facilities here to show you this, but you will be ready for the superconductivity lesson in three or four weeks. Jaxom will be ready for it sooner; Piemur must do more on winding electromagnets with proper toroidal windings. Journeyman Manotti, your metal formers were not up to the standard required, but you have a week in which to improve."

Robinton tiptoed quietly away, not wishing to embarrass the students. But he was smiling as he sauntered back to the entrance hall: a good teacher should give praise, encouragement, and admonition as required.

There were auxiliary workshops for smith, glass, and wood crafts in the larger of the excavated structures at Landing, staffed with masters, journeymen, and apprentices.

One morning, Lytol and Robinton were startled to hear a loud explosion and rushed to the source of the sound, which had come from Master Morilton's glass forge. There they found Master Morilton helping Jancis to blot the blood from a mosaic of cuts on the face of Caselon, one of the Glass-smith's apprentices. There were tiny bits of mirrored glass everywhere.

"Now," Master Morilton was saying calmly, addressing his remarks to the others in the forge, "you appreciate why protective goggles are so important. Caselon could well have lost his eyesight when that thermos glass exploded. As it is . . ." Morilton glanced inquiringly at Jancis.

"As it is," she said, with a wry grin, "Caselon's going to have the most interesting pattern of scars. Oh, don't worry," she added as the youth cringed. "They'll heal to nothing. Don't grimace. You'll only bleed until I've got you properly annointed with numbweed."

As Lytol turned to deal with the press of curious people who had rushed over, Robinton looked about the place. Master Morilton had certainly set up quite a crafthall here. A pump was going *tapockety-tapockety* in the corner. A tube reaching up to the apparatus had a leather collar at the top, on which were the remains of a mirrored bottle neck. The rest of the glass was everywhere in the room, a myriad of tiny glinting pieces.

"Shards," Caselon muttered, trying not to flinch from Jancis's ministrations. "That was my twentieth!"

Robinton then noticed that nineteen vacuum flasks were neatly racked on Caselon's half of the worktable; another twelve stood on the other side, where another apprentice, Vandentine, was working. How they had escaped the flying glass splinters, he didn't know.

"We are not in competition mode here, Caselon," Master Morilton said, wagging a stern finger at the boy. "What exactly happened? I was concentrating on Bengel's wand work."

"I dunno," Caselon said, shrugging one shoulder.

"Aivas?" Master Morilton asked. The glasswork facility included a direct connection to Aivas.

"When he molded the glass, he didn't ultrasonicate it or even tap it as you have taught him, to get the bubbles out of the mix. He was too busy trying to outproduce his partner. There were bubbles in the glass, so that under vacuum it imploded. But you may now use two of his vessels to demonstrate the properties of liquefied gases."

Numbweed had stemmed the bloodflow from Caselon's face, so Master Morilton gestured for him and Vandentine to follow him to an adjacent room. Robinton trailed behind. In this room, there was a different kind of pump; from a frost-covered nozzle, drops of a faintly blue liquid dripped to fall into a thick, mirrored catch-pot every second.

"The blue liquid is the air itself, the air in this room," Aivas continued, "which we are compressing and then rapidly expanding so that it cools again and again, further and further, until a tiny fraction of it liquefies."

Master Morilton said, "Don't touch the radiator vanes—they'll blister your fingers. This, Master Robinton," he added, smiling at their guest, "is a multistage refrigerator, quite different from the one you've been using in Cove Hold to chill fruit juice and foodstuffs."

Robinton nodded wisely.

"This last stage is the most difficult," Aivas said as Master Morilton gestured for Caselon to fill his flask. The room was filled with mist as the liquid air seethed until it had cooled Caselon's flask. Robinton moved his feet away as some of the pearly drops ran across the floor toward him. "Now, Caselon," Aivas instructed, "return to your workspace and observe the antics of liquid air."

Caselon was already doing so as he left the room.

"Play with air?" Robinton asked, perplexed, and he noticed Master Morilton's knowing smile.

"This liquid helium," Aivas went on, "or rather, these liquids can flow in opposite directions at the same time; they will creep out of the top of a tall vessel and leave none in the bottom, and will even creep faster, much faster, through tiny holes than through large ones. You may fill a flask with liquid air yourself, Master Robinton, and experiment on your own. This is one of the most dangerous, and therefore educational, exercises for the students to do. Jancis, Sharra, there are flasks for you, too; this experiment is an important one for both of you." The way the two girls smirked at each other suggested to Robinton that they didn't know why it would be. "When you have become familiar with liquid air, we can begin to learn about the special properties of liquid hydrogen, and especially of liquid helium."

"If it's dangerous, should we be doing it?" the Harper asked.

"Danger can be quite educational," Aivas replied. "It is unlikely, for instance, that Caselon will forget to tap his mix no matter how many glass inserts he blows from now on."

It was an hour before Robinton and Lytol, whom the Masterharper had interested in the liquid-gas experiments, returned to their usual duties.

More and more of the dwellings at Landing became occupied. Many of the artifacts so long stored in the Catherine Caves had been put to use, though the custodians had decreed that samples of each be retained to exhibit in Master Esselin's Archive building. Abandoned Landing once again became a bustling community. Where the walks and small yards had been cleared, there were even signs of renewed grass and weed growth.

"Are we a bit mad to reestablish this settlement?" Lessa asked one evening when she and F'lar had taken an evening meal in the Aivas building with Jaxom, Robinton, D'ram, Lytol, Piemur, and Jancis. "Those volcanoes could erupt again."

"I did mention that to Aivas," Lytol said, "and he replied that he is naturally monitoring seismic activity. Some of the instruments which the settlers' vulcanist installed are still functioning. He also assured me that there is little activity in the chain."

"And that is a positive thing?" Lessa asked, still skeptical.

"So Aivas assured me," Lytol replied.

"I'd hate to lose all we've rebuilt here," F'lar said.

"Unfortunately," Lytol commented, with an ironic half smile, "Aivas can't be moved."

"Then let's not worry about something that may not develop into a problem," Robinton said firmly. "We have sufficient immediate ones. Such as how we're going to handle Master Norist. As you know, he had threatened to disavow Master Morilton's Mastery and to disown all journeymen and apprentices who have produced glass according to the, ahem, spurious methods and techniques of Aivas."

"He calls Aivas 'the Abomination'!" Piemur said with a malicious chuckle. "Aivas said—"

"You didn't *tell* Aivas that?" Jancis was aghast at Piemur's tactlessness.

"He didn't mind. I got the feeling it amused him."

Master Robinton gave Piemur a long look. "Do you—any of you— ever get the feeling that Aivas is amused by us?"

"Sure," Piemur replied blithely. "He may be a machine and all that, and while I know a great deal more about machinery than I used to, certainly, he's a Master machine that interacts with humans, so he must have criteria by which he recognizes levity. He may not guffaw as some do at my jokes and anecdotes, but he certainly enjoys listening to them."

"Hmmm" was the Harper's noncommittal response. "About Norist . . . As the duly elected Mastercraftsman, guiding his Halls, he can be replaced only at a convocation of all Masters. Unfortunately, the Glass-smithcraft is not a large one, and most of the Crafthallmasters are as dogmatic as Norist. On the other hand, I won't sit by and see Master Morilton disavowed or harassed or humiliated because he has learned something Norist didn't teach him. He's certainly proved adept at the new skills."

"Norist has also been leaning heavily on poor old Wansor," Lytol said. "Fortunately, Wansor appears oblivious both to the criticism and the fact that he might suffer the same discipline as Morilton. In spite of Norist's declaration, Morilton has managed to recruit quite a few journeymen and apprentices who have felt restricted by Norist's rigid adherence to Recorded techniques."

"If Norist is leaning on Wansor, why don't we lean on him?" Jaxom asked.

"I will," Lytol replied with a ghost of a smile. "And I would be happy to. A man who will not see beyond his nose has no right to be Craftmaster!" His smile was replaced by censure.

"Hear! Hear!" the Harper cheered.

"I also heard that Norist is denying Morilton the use of the best sandpits," Lytol went on, frowning.

"That's no problem at all. We've sand aplenty on this coastline," Piemur responded.

"Dimwit. Beach sand isn't what's used for glass," Jaxom said with some disdain. "It's the pits at Igen and Ista that have fine stuff."

"And those are the ones that Norist has denied Morilton," Lytol explained.

"He hasn't denied Lord Jaxom of Ruatha Hold!"

"Nor D'ram," the aged bronze rider said as firmly as the young Lord Holder.

Even Lytol grinned at that solution to Norist's intransigence. "Microscopes require a very high quality glass, you know."

"In any case, I don't see that as a major difficulty," D'ram said, glancing over to Jaxom. "Ruth and Tiroth won't mind a little excursion, I'm sure." Jaxom nodded obligingly. "You take Ista, and I'll get some from Igen."

"There's nothing on the settlers' map to indicate closer deposits, to reduce transportation time?" F'lar asked.

Robinton held up one finger. "We'll ask." And he pecked out the query with considerable speed on the keyboard of the unit in the room.

Immediately a list of locations scrolled out, with the type of sand to be found at each. Those sands that could be used for medical glass were starred, but Aivas recommended in particular the sands found at Paradise River and in an inland sandpit near the site of old Cardiff.

D'ram said he would go to the Cardiff site, as he knew that Jaxom would prefer a chance to see Jayge and Aramina, who were holding at Paradise River.

"Hmmm," the Harper said, studying his screen. "Aivas reminds me that he wants more green and bronze riders for training."

"Would he take a big brown or two?" F'lar asked. "I've several riders who've offered. Seems like Aivas is biased against the medium sizes."

"I asked him about that," D'ram said, "for I thought it odd that he'd want only the largest and the smallest. He says the operation requires them, but he won't elaborate beyond stating that he must have enough candidates to allow him to pick the most likely to succeed in the venture and to have sufficient trained backup personnel." D'ram shrugged at his inability to explain further.

"I *wish*," Lessa said, "that occasionally he would be specific. Then we would have something to tell those we must disappoint. I don't want any resentful dragonriders. Though, in general, I'd say that morale has improved in all the Weyrs. And," she added, making a face, "all the Weyrs want to participate."

"Aivas did remark that it was easier to teach the younger dragonriders," D'ram went on, "since there were fewer set mental patterns. Of course, there are naturally some few exceptions," he added smugly, rather pleased that he was one of them.

"Is that all right now?" Jaxom asked. "I'd better get back to Ruatha." His grin was abashed. "I'll bring in Paradise River sands tomorrow, but I'd better spend some time at home."

"In danger of being disowned?" Piemur asked with an impudent grin.

Jaxom disdained to reply, while Jancis elbowed the young journeyman harper in the ribs.

"Go on, then," F'lar said, with a bland sideways glance at Lessa.

"I'll just ask Aivas to print out the location of the sandpit," D'ram said, rising to leave with the young Lord Holder.

There was a slight frown on Lytol's face as the two left.

"Don't fret, Lytol," Lessa said reassuringly. "Sharra's got every right to be annoyed at the amount of time Jaxom's spending here."

"Especially when I'm sure she's dying to take the healer lessons," Jancis said. "But Piemur, have you noticed it, too? That whenever Jaxom misses a day, Aivas particularly asks why?"

"Hmm, yes, I had at that," Piemur replied, momentarily thoughtful. Then he assumed a careless pose. "But Aivas sure works Jaxom harder than any of the rest of us, bar Mirrim and S'len."

"S'len?" F'lar asked. "Isn't he that young green rider from Fort?"

"That's the one. And Aivas insisted on drilling Mirrim to bring her up to a level with the rest of us," Piemur added.

"*Why* would the green dragons be so important to Aivas?" Lessa asked.

"They're small, that's why," Piemur said.

"Small?"

"Well, that's my hunch, and Ruth's the smallest of them all," Piemur went on. "There's no doubt in my mind that those two will play a special part in Aivas's Great Scheme."

Lessa and Lytol both looked concerned.

"Oh, don't worry about Jaxom," Piemur said airily. "He's the best of us all. Has a real grasp of all that navigational mathematics Aivas throws at us, and the spatial relationships."

"Has he suggested *anything* yet?" Lessa asked Robinton and Lytol. Both men shook their heads.

Then Robinton grinned. "I get literary quotations, such as: 'There's a time for some things, and a time for all things: a time for great things, and a time for small things.' I am forced to assume that this is the time for small things, like assimilating all those foundation courses from Aivas; while the time for great things is still four Turns, seven months, and however many days away from us."

"Literary quotations?" F'lar asked, surprised. His lessons with Aivas tended to the practical: tactics, mathematical projections of Threadfall, and draconic healing—though he practiced none of the latter, he kept himself informed of Aivas's innovations.

"Oh, yes. And though Aivas admits he is choosing what he thinks might appeal to my tastes, our ancestors had fascinating and complex literatures from ever so many cultures that put ours to shame. Some of our epic sagas he has identified as paraphrases of Terran originals. Fascinating."

"Indeed, my studies have been equally absorbing," Lytol said, leaning forward on the table, his face lighting with his own enthusiasm. "I don't think any of us realized that our present political structure was handed down from the very Charter our ancestors brought with them. That is historically very unusual, Aivas told me."

"Why should it be?" F'lar asked, mildly surprised. "It allows Weyr, Hold, and Hall to function without interference."

"Ah, but interference was a major factor in Terran politics," Lytol replied. "Spurred by territorial imperatives and, all too often, sheer greed."

Adroitly interrupting another of Lytol's historical perorations, Lessa rose, nodding to Robinton and the two young journeymen.

"We must get back to the Weyr now. Aivas gave me another healing compound to try on Lisath's wing. It simply isn't mending as it should."

I told *Aramina that we're coming,* Ruth said as Jaxom mounted him. *She likes to know, you know,* he added in a confidential tone.

Jaxom rather wished that Ruth hadn't committed them to paying a call on Aramina and Jayge. He really ought to get right back to Ruatha, and go to Paradise River in the morning, as he had said he would.

"Well, we won't stay long, mind," Jaxom said, giving Ruth an indulgent slap.

The white dragon was very fond of the young woman who, as a girl, had heard dragons so easily—and so incessantly—that she had inveigled Jayge of the Lilcamp Traders to take her as far away from dragons as he could to preserve her sanity. Shipwrecked on their way to the Southern Continent, they had been rescued by shipfish and set ashore. There they had discovered and restored ancient buildings, not realizing the significance of their find. Located by Piemur on his coastline survey, they had been officially named as Holders of Paradise River and had increased their numbers to a sizable Hold, including a Fisher Hall. The former trader had been immensely surprised when Piemur and Jancis told him that a paternal ancestor named Lilienkamp had been instrumental in saving so much useful material in the Catherine Caves.

Following Aivas's directions, Jaxom and Ruth emerged over rather anonymous grassland. It wasn't until they had overflown the alleged site several times that Jaxom noticed the declivity well overgrown with grass and shrubs, with the suspicion of white glinting through the vegetation. They landed, and by kicking and gouging, Jaxom peeled back the obscuring greenery and lifted a handful of sand so fine it was nearly powder. Working up quite a sweat, he filled the large sacks he had brought with him. Finally, hot and tired, he remounted his dragon.

He had cooled off by the time Ruth glided to a gentle, faultless halt in front of the gracious ancient residence of the Paradise River Hold.

"And a good day to you, Lord Jaxom and Ruth!" Jayge said, coming down the stairs from the wide porch. "Ara started squeezing fresh juice the moment Ruth told her you were coming. And I'm glad you did, because something's come up!"

I'm going swimming. The fire-lizards said they'll scrub my back, Ruth told Jaxom, his eyes whirling with green delight. At Jaxom's approval, the white dragon hop-glided right into the river, several full fairs of fire-lizards, both wild and banded, circling ecstatically above him.

"Off for a scrub, is he?" Jayge asked. He was of medium height, his bare chest burned a fine deep brown, his legs not quite as dark. His oddly flecked green eyes stood out in a tanned face that reflected a hint of a strong personality and a basic tranquility, even though a slight frown crossed his face as he led Jaxom up to the coolness of the porch. "I'm glad you stopped by, Jaxom. How did you work up such a sweat in *between*?"

"Stealing sand."

"Indeed?" Jayge regarded him thoughtfully. "Now what would you need Paradise River sand for? As I'm sure you're going to tell me anyway." He gestured for Jaxom to take the hammock while he leaned against the porch banister, arms folded across his chest.

"The settlers had a sandpit back in that scrubland of yours. They thought highly of Paradise River sands—for glass making."

"There's enough certainly. Did Piemur and Jancis find those whatchamacallums . . ."

"Chips?" Jaxom supplied with a grin.

"Chips, then, useful after all?"

"Well, we managed to salvage the usable transistors and capacitors, but they haven't actually been put onto a board yet."

Jayge gave him a long, hard, suspicious look before grinning. "As you say!"

Just then young Readis, clad only in a clout, came out onto the porch, rubbing sleep out of his eyes. He eyed Jaxom steadily. "Ruth?"

Jaxom pointed to where the white dragon, surrounded by industrious fire-lizards, was wallowing in the shallow water.

"He's enough of a guardian, isn't he?" Readis asked his father, tilting his head back in a stance that reminded Jaxom of Jayge.

"Ruth's bathing right now, and besides, I'd like you to tell Jaxom what happened to you and Alemi the other day," Jayge said.

"Did you come just to hear?" There was a certain element of vanity in young Readis's grin. Jaxom was suddenly aware of how much he missed his own son, Jarrol, an engaging two Turns old.

"Well, that was one reason," Jaxom replied mendaciously. "So what did happen to you and Alemi the other day?"

Aramina emerged from the house, carrying her squirming daughter under one arm and a tray in her free hand. Jayge sprang quickly to relieve her of the tray, but she gave him two-Turn-old Aranya instead and served Jaxom a tall, cool drink and some freshly baked sweet biscuits. It took a few more minutes until Readis had been sat in a chair, his small glass and two biscuits to hand. As Aramina settled herself, Readis looked to his father for his cue to begin.

"Uncle Alemi took me fishing three days ago in the skiff. The big reds were schooling out there." Readis's brown arm indicated a general northerly direction. "We was to have a beach meal 'cos it was Swacky's nameday and we needed big 'uns to grill. There was only little squids on the edges of the school. Then, all o' sudden, a big one got Uncle's hook and it dragged us, boat and all"—Readis's eyes were shining with remembered excitement—"right into the current. But Uncle Alemi, he wrestled it aboard and it was this"—he held his arms as wide as they could go—"big. No funning!" He glared briefly at his father, who was hiding his laughter in his hand. "It was big! You ask Alemi! But he hung on, and I helped him gaff it aboard. Then my reel started spinning, and Uncle Alemi and I had to put our backs into landing that one. That's why we didn't notice the squall coming up."

Jaxom glanced anxiously at Jayge and Aramina. Alemi knew his Craft, and he would never endanger anyone.

"It was some squall, I can tell you," Readis said, jerking his chin to emphasize the details, in the manner of any good storyteller. "We got tossed and spun about 'cos there was no way the sail would have lasted in a blow like that. And then a big wave overturned the skiff and I came up coughing and sputtering, Uncle Alemi hanging on to my arm fit to break it." The little brown face regarded Jaxom seriously. "I'm not afraid to admit I was some scared. The sky around us was black and the rain coming down so heavy we couldn't see the shore. But I'm a good swimmer and I can see now why Uncle Alemi always makes me wear my deep-water vest even if it is hot most times and rubs my back. See?" He swiveled his torso, raising one arm over his head, to show Jaxom where the underarm skin had been abraded. "Then it happened!"

"What happened?" Jaxom asked as if on cue.

"I had my arms out, trying to keep my head up, when suddenly something came smack-dab into my right hand. *And* started pulling me. Uncle Alemi yelled at me that it was all right. We were safe. I was to hang on tight, just as he was doing.''

"Shipfish?'' Jaxom asked with an incredulous glance at Readis's parents. He knew that Jayge and Aramina owed their lives to shipfish; even Master Idarolan swore that the sleek big sea creatures would rescue humans in stormy areas.

"A whole pod of 'em,'' Readis said proudly. "And every time my hand slipped off, there was another one right behind to hang on to. Uncle Alemi says there must have been twenty or thirty. They pulled us far enough in for us to see the beach and reach safety on our own. *And*,'' he added, pausing to give emphasis to his final words, "the next morning the skiff was found beached up by the Fishhold, like they knew exactly where it belonged.''

"That is some tale, young Readis. You're a harper born. An amazing rescue. Truly amazing,'' Jaxom said with genuine feeling. He glanced at Jayge, who nodded supportively. "The redfish weren't by any chance returned with the skiff?'' he asked.

"Nah.'' Readis dismissed that with a flick of his wrist. "They drownded. So we had to eat ol' stringy wherry 'stead of good juicy redfish steaks. And you know something else?''

"No, what?'' Jaxom asked politely.

"The shipfish kept talking to us all the time they was saving us. Uncle Alemi heard them, too.''

"What did they say?''

Readis frowned deeply in concentration. "I don't 'xactly remember the words. The wind was shrieking, but I know they were shouting at us. Encouraging us like.''

Until Jaxom caught Jayge's eye, he thought it was a youthful embellishment on a hectic rescue story, but Jayge nodded in confirmation.

"Readis, why don't you run down and see if the fire-lizards are giving Ruth a proper scrubbing?'' Jayge suggested.

The sturdy little boy jumped to his feet. "Can I? Really?'' He flashed a radiant grin at Jaxom.

"Really, you can,'' Jaxom assured him, wondering if Jarrol would be as enchanting as Readis when he was five.

"Yahoo,'' Readis cried, tearing off down to shore where Ruth was afloat.

"That's exactly what happened to him and Alemi?'' Jaxom asked.

"With no invention,'' Aramina said, obviously proud of her son.

"Alemi said that Readis didn't panic and obeyed him instantly. Otherwise—" She broke off, her face paling under her warm tan.

Jayge leaned toward Jaxom. "I wondered if you'd mind asking this Aivas thing of yours what he knows about the shipfish. Alemi also swears that they were speaking words, though over the wind and sea noises, he couldn't distinguish exactly what they were saying. He thinks they were giving them directions or reassurances. Piemur mentioned a passing reference to the big fish—doll-fins—which Aivas said were brought here from Terra. I asked him to inquire, but I guess it slipped his mind."

These days Jaxom always carried a small pad and pencil in his belt pouch. He made a notation. "I won't forget," he assured them, patting his pouch when he had replaced pad and pencil.

As soon as Ruth had had time to dry off in the sun, Jaxom called him up from the beach. Readis was squealing with rapture, for Ruth had allowed the lad to climb up on his back for the short walk back. Aramina gave Jaxom a full net of fresh fruit to bring Sharra and Jarrol, and he thanked her profusely.

As Ruth ascended to a safe height, Jaxom came to a conclusion, based on the guilt he experienced in being so long away from Ruatha—yet again!

Ruth, let's shave three hours off our return. That's safe enough, and we'll be back in Ruatha just as everyone's getting up.

You know Lessa doesn't like us timing it.

We haven't in Turns, Ruth.

Sharra will know.

I'm hoping she'll be so glad to see me she won't mind—this once. Jaxom stroked Ruth's neck urgently. *Let me handle my mate.* Ruth didn't like to deceive either Sharra or Lessa. *It's not deceiving Sharra. It's getting home early for a change. Not a big thing to ask.*

Oh, I suppose it won't matter this once. I always know when we are.

However, as soon as they came out of *between* above Ruatha Hold, Jaxom had cause to regret coming home at all. A wild blizzard blowing down from the mountains all but obscured the Hold.

A good thing I always know where I am, too, Ruth remarked, craning his neck and blinking windblown particles out of his faceted eyes.

Can you see to land, Ruth? I never thought to check on the weather conditions. Jaxom covered his cheeks with his gloved hands, feeling the chill entering his bones despite the heavy riding jacket. His legs, clad in trousers appropriate to Southern's summer, felt like lengths of ice.

I didn't either, Ruth replied forgivingly. *Only a moment or two longer. I'm right above the courtyard.*

Suddenly he backwinged, and Jaxom felt the jar as the white dragon landed with an uncharacteristic thud.

Sorry. Snowdrift.

Jaxom wasted no time sliding off his dragon, but his path to the big doors that opened into Ruth's weyr at Ruatha Hold was impeded by the heavy drifts. He had to scoop snow away to get one leaf of the door open wide enough that Ruth could find purchase for his forepaws. Then dragon strength hauled the stout metal door back through the drifts.

Get inside. Go on, Ruth ordered his rider, and Jaxom was all too willing to obey.

Once inside the weyr, which was only warmer by virtue of being out of the chill and gusting wind, both dragon and rider struggled to pull the door shut. Rubbing his legs fiercely to restore feeling, Jaxom half ran across the stone floor of the chamber to the capacious hearth, where a fresh fire had been laid. His fingers fumbled with the fire-maker before he got it lit, but at last the flames were eating hungrily at the dry wood, and Jaxom was able to warm himself.

"I don't usually *mind* the cold," Jaxom said, removing his jacket and shaking off the snow. "It's just coming from all that lovely weather . . ."

Meer says that Jarrol has a bad cold and Sharra's not feeling good with being up all night, Ruth told his weyrmate, his eyes tinged with the yellow of worry.

"Young children often have colds this time of year," Jaxom replied, though he knew that Jarrol had had far too many sniffles that winter. And poor Sharra was exhausted from nursing him, for she refused to allow anyone else to tend their firstborn. "Sometimes, Ruth, I'm very stupid," he exclaimed abruptly. "There's no reason in the world Sharra can't come south, enjoy decent weather, and study with Aivas!"

How? She can't go between *carrying a baby.*

"She can come by ship. We'll just find out from Master Idarolan when he can accommodate her on a trip south. They make the journey often enough. Yes, that's what we'll do. We'll all go south. There's nothing here at this season that Brand can't manage without me."

Suddenly Jaxom felt a great deal better. And not long after, when he found Sharra rocking their cold-fussy son in the warmth of their apartment, her instant enthusiasm for the removal was as keen as his. The subject of his unusual arrival did not come up at all. As soon as Jarrol was lulled back to sleep and laid down in his cot, Sharra proved to Jaxom's delight just how glad she was to have him home and in bed.

His face screwed in an anxious grimace, Harper Journeyman Tagetarl came striding out of the Aivas complex toward Robinton's desk in the foyer. "Aivas would like to speak to you and Sebell when it's convenient," he announced.

"Oh? What's he stewing up now?" the Harper asked, noting how uncharacteristically perturbed the journeyman appeared to be.

"He wants the Harper Hall to build a printing press." Tagetarl agitatedly ran his hair back from his face with both hands and heaved an exasperated groan.

"A printing press!" Robinton gave a gusty sigh, then reached up to nudge his bronze fire-lizard awake. "Zair, please find Sebell and ask him to join us?"

Zair chirruped sleepily but obediently unwound his tail from the Harper's neck. He walked down Robinton's arm and onto the table, stretching himself as he did so, and then leaped away and flew out the open door.

"Sebell can't be far if Zair's not bothering to go *between*," Robinton remarked. "Have some klah while we wait. You look as if you need some. Why did Aivas suddenly decide the Harper Hall needs a printing press?"

Tagetarl gratefully poured himself a cup, hooking a chair to Robinton's desk and, once again, smoothing back his long black hair, less urgently this time.

"I asked could we please have copies of the string-instrument quartets he played the other evening. Domick particularly wanted to have a transcript. He said he's tired of hearing us rave about ancestral music. Domick added,"—Tagetarl smiled ruefully—"that with so many masters and journeymen working here, he's not able to come and hear for himself."

Robinton grinned, knowing that Tagetarl had probably edited the Composition Master's acerbic comments.

"Aivas said that he's got to conserve the paper he has left and he has to consider music to be a nonessential in view of the demands on his resources. He's down to the last two rolls. He feels we ought to have our own replication machines." Tagetarl grinned expectantly.

"Hmmm. That's certainly reasonable." Robinton tried to sound enthusiastic, since Tagetarl was evidently much taken by the idea. But he was considerably concerned over just how much more could be added to the "essential" mechanizations already being undertaken. There were so many people from so many Halls already working full tilt on half a dozen critical projects. "Undeniably a great deal of information ought to be circulated. Especially for distant Halls and Holds that cannot send representatives here."

Zair returned, chirping in the tone that said his errand had been successful. He had only just settled himself again across Robinton's shoulders when Sebell came running. He had obviously dressed in a hurry, and his hair was still wet.

"Easy, Sebell. There's no urgency," Robinton said, raising a hand to slow the Masterharper down. "I hope Zair didn't misinform you."

Catching his breath, Sebell gave his mentor a salute and a wry grin. "Obedience to any summons from you, Master, is too deeply engrained to change now."

"Even when you're Masterharper of Pern?" Robinton's grin was sly. "Especially now that you are Masterharper of Pern, you should be allowed to finish your morning ablutions."

"Klah?" Tagetarl suggested, and when Sebell nodded appreciatively, the journeyman poured him a cup.

"I'd just finished showering," Sebell replied, accepting the klah. "So now that I'm here, how can I assist you?"

Robinton gestured to Tagetarl.

"It's really Aivas who wants to talk to you and Master Robinton," the journeyman said. "He needs a printing press, and he says that according to his understanding of our present structure, that should be the responsibility of the Harper Hall."

Sebell nodded, accepting the information. Robinton recognized the mannerism as a habit of his own, which Sebell adopted when he, too, was absorbing unexpected requests.

"Any form of communication is indeed a Harper Hall function. What exactly *is* a printing press?" Sebell asked after taking several thoughtful sips of his klah.

"An improvement on Master Arnor's crabbed script, I devoutly hope," Robinton remarked in a bland tone. The other two harpers rolled their eyes. "Something approximating the readable print which Aivas produces would be an enormous help."

"Aivas is apparently the only one in the world who easily reads Arnor's script. What's the problem?" Sebell asked Tagetarl.

"Domick's been after me to get copies of some of the splendid music Aivas has been playing for us."

Sebell nodded understandingly. "That was inevitable. And certainly the request is only fair, when he's had to take over so much Hall management to keep us here."

"Don't let Domick pressure you with insidious suggestion," Robinton said, wagging a finger at his colleagues. "Though he will certainly find the string music utterly fascinating."

"We all do," Sebell said as he rose. "Let's see exactly what this printing-press project entails. We are certainly not a mechanically inclined Hall, even if we produce our instruments." And all three harpers went to consult with Aivas.

"Harpers may not be mechanically inclined," Aivas replied when Sebell expressed his concerns, "but they are not without skill or intelligence, Master Sebell. Replicating or duplicating written material can be achieved by a variety of methods, of which the current laborious hand copying is the most prone to error. Using the relics of machinery and parts still available in the Catherine Caves, it will be possible to assemble a more efficient method of reproducing multiple copies of essential information, and the musical scores requested by your colleague in the Hall."

Sheets spewed from the print slot into Tagetarl's agile hands.

"The drawings itemize the parts you should be able to find in the caves, and the few that Master Fandarel will need to fabricate for you. It will be in his interests, also, to cooperate." There followed one of those pauses that Robinton liked to interpret as indicative of the various humors of Aivas. This one, he was sure, was a pointed reminder of how much the Smithcrafthall had already benefited by Aivas's assistance. "With the intelligence that appears to mark even apprentices in your Hall, you should be able to assemble the apparatus by the time Master Fandarel has finished installing the water-turbine station. There will then be sufficient power to run the printing press, as well. Master Bendarek has succeeded admirably in producing continuous rolls of paper, which are also essential to the process.

"The manufacture of the individual letters and numbers to comprise a legible type font, and the musical and scientific signs, should be relatively simple for those with good manual dexterity." Another page came out, illustrating a highly readable type font. "Journeyman Tagetarl is a dexterous carver." His remark astonished Tagetarl, who could not imagine how Aivas had learned about his handiwork. "There may be others with similar artistic talent who might assist."

"There isn't a printing press in the Catherine Caves?" Sebell asked, his tone slightly wistful.

"Unfortunately, no. Replication and data storage had developed well past such cumbersome processes. This method will, however, be sufficient for your needs for some time to come."

Sebell had taken the type-font sheet from Tagetarl. "It'll be nice not to have to squint or use a magnifying glass to read." He gave his head a shake. "Master Arnor won't like it."

Robinton grimaced and then sighed with regret. "Perhaps it is time. He's almost blind right now, you know. And those wretched apprentices take terrible advantage of him. Menolly was telling me about an incident only last week. One impertinent youngster handed in a scurrilous verse in place of the ballad he had been assigned—and poor Master Arnor approved it."

Tagetarl masked a grin. "That's not the first time Master Arnor's had that trick played on him."

"This printing press would help conserve your supplies, Aivas?"

"It will, but that was not the basic reason to suggest that you extend your activities to include such a fundamental improvement in data handling. You will find that eventually you will need more than one press, so it would be prudent to learn the principle and improve on it in your own time."

"I think—" Robinton paused to glance at Sebell, aware that he was encroaching on the new Masterharper's authority with the suggestion. "—that this first printing press should be constructed here in Landing."

Sebell nodded, guessing the real reason for his mentor's suggestion. "That would certainly be less of an affront to Master Arnor." He examined the sheets with Tagetarl. "Dulkan's already here, and he's done some fine brasswork for harp plates. There're four more of the older apprentices, waiting for their hour on the General Science Course. We could use them until their appointment."

Robinton beamed at the two men, pleased to see the alacrity with which they were already moving forward on the project.

"Terry's down at the Catherine Caves right now, in fact. If we hurry, we can get advice from him, too," Tagetarl said eagerly.

With the briefest but still most courteous of farewells to Robinton, the two young men strode out of the room and down the hall, exchanging ideas on how to proceed.

Sometimes, Robinton thought as he slowly eased himself down into the nearest chair, such energy exhausted rather than revived him. Not that he wouldn't be delighted with this printing press. Able to run off as many copies as needed? What a concept!

It truly amazed him that there were now so many devices that had never before been required. The effects on Hall, Hold, and Weyr, only beginning to filter through, would be profound. Lytol, having delved into the history and politics of their ancestors, had already worried about what he called the erosion of values and the subversion of tradition by new demands. The promise of the eradication of Thread—the possibility, Robinton sternly corrected himself—motivated all but a few dissenters. Even the most conservative of the surviving Oldtimers had come around to support the Benden Weyrleaders.

And how *were* dragons and their riders to occupy themselves when Thread was no longer the rationale for the Weyrs? Robinton knew, though the notion was not widely discussed, that F'lar and Lessa wanted to lay claim to considerable lands here in the Southern Continent. But would the Lord Holders, who themselves looked greedily toward the open space of the vast Southern Continent, be complacent about such claims? Toric's realization that he had settled for such a small portion of the southern lands still rankled in that ambitious man's mind. In Robinton's estimation, the Weyrs deserved whatever they requested after centuries of service, but would the Lord Holders, and the Halls, agree? That concerned him the most. Yet it seemed to worry the Weyrleaders least. And what if, in the four Turns ten months, and three days specified by Aivas, the attempt should fail? What then?

Perhaps, and he brightened suddenly, all this new technology would absorb both Hold and Hall, to the exclusion of the Weyrs. Hold and Hall had always managed quite nicely to ignore the Weyrs between Passes. Perhaps things like power stations and printing presses were indeed valuable, but for more abstruse reasons, as well as the obvious ones.

"Aivas," Robinton said in greeting, carefully closing the door behind him. "A word with you." He cleared his throat, wondering why Aivas could sometimes reduce him to the nervousness of an apprentice. "About this printing press . . ."

"You do not concur with the necessity of such a machine?"

"On the contrary, I most certainly do."

"Then what troubles you? For your voice betrays a note of uncertainty."

"Aivas, when we first realized what you represented in terms of knowledge, we had little idea of the scope of all that had been lost over the centuries. Yet now, rarely does a day go by but some new device is suddenly on the essential list. Our skilled craftsmen have enough lined up to keep them busy for the entire Pass. Tell me, truly, *are* all these machines and devices really necessary?"

"Not to the way of life you had, Master Robinton. But to accomplish what is apparently the desire of the majority of Pern, the destruction of Thread, improvements are essential. Your ancestors did not employ the highest technology available to them: They preferred to use the lowest level necessary to perform the function. That is the level that is presently being reestablished. As you yourself requested in the initial interview."

Robinton wondered if he had imagined the tone of mild reproof. "Water-driven power . . ." he began.

"Which you already had available to you."

"Printing presses?"

"Your Records were printed, but in a laborious and time-consuming fashion that, unfortunately, permitted errors to be made and perpetuated."

"The teaching consoles?"

"You have harpers who instruct by set lessons. You had even managed to rediscover papermaking before accessing this facility. Most papermaking techniques, Masterharper, are refinements of techniques you already employ, made easier by some basic machinery and of no higher level than your ancestors brought with them. It is little more than correcting long-standing errors and misconceptions. The spirit of the original colonists is still intact. Even the technology that must be utilized to thwart the return of the wanderer planet will be of the same level as your ancestors'. There may be other scientifically advanced methods now available to Earth scientists that could be utilized if there were still communication between this planet and Earth. Great strides in cosmology were being announced at the time the colony ships left Earth's system. These were not, however, incorporated into the memory banks of this facility. Once you have regained the appropriate level of understanding, you may progress, or not, as you choose."

Robinton pensively rubbed his chin. He could scarcely fault Aivas for doing what had been specifically requested, that Pern be brought back to the level of knowledge it had originally enjoyed. It was also obvious that Aivas was obeying the initial request that only what was really needed be revived. It was just stunning to realize how much *had* been lost.

"This world has survived, Master Robinton, with more dignity and honor than you would imagine—as Lord Warder Lytol is discovering in his exploration of history."

"Perhaps I have not paid as much attention to his studies as I ought."

"That statement was a private analysis of achievement, Master Robinton. It is for Lord Warder Lytol to arrive at his own conclusion based on his studies."

"I wonder if his conclusion will parallel your impartial one."

"You should delve into history and arrive at your own, Master Robinton." There was one of the interesting pauses that Aivas tended to affect. "Printed books would make that much easier for you."

Robinton glared at the green light on the face of the Aivas facility and wondered, once again, what constituted "artificial intelligence." The several times he had asked that direct question, the reply had been a repetition of a translation of the acronym. Robinton now understood that there were explanations which Aivas either could not, or was programmed not to, make.

"Yes, printed books would be much easier," the Harper agreed at last. "But according to what you've shown us, the settlers had other devices, much more compact."

"That technology is too advanced to be considered at the present time and would involve processes that are presently beyond your abilities or needs."

"Well, then, I'll settle for books."

"That would be prudent of you."

"And you will remain prudent in what you ask us to re-create?"

"That is a corollary to the prime goal of this facility."

Robinton was content with that answer. But just as he had his hand on the door pull, he turned. "Would this printing press be able to print musical scores, as well?"

"Yes."

"That would be much, much easier for the entire Hall," he said. He felt so buoyant as he retraced his steps down the hall that he began to whistle.

7
▼▼▼▼▼▼▼▼

PRESENT PASS 21

Lessa roused abruptly, opening her eyes to a darkness which suggested that daylight was still hours away. F'lar lay sprawled beside her, his forehead touching her shoulder, one arm thrown across her, one leg pinning hers down. Their bed was oversized, but he invariably managed to occupy more of it than she did. In fact, there were only finger lengths between her and the edge. She must have told herself to wake up at this barbarous hour—she had always had that ability. But why? Her mind was too sleep-fogged to provide an immediate answer.

Ramoth was sound asleep, too. And Mnementh! All of Benden Weyr was asleep, including, she discovered with irritation, the dragon and rider supposedly on watch on the Rim. She would blast him as soon as she figured out why she was awake at this appallingly early hour.

Then she saw the lighted clock face on the bedside locker. Three bloody of the clock! Progress was a two-edged dagger. Having a reliable timepiece that was visible in the dark only made the darkness and this early rising harder to endure. But seeing the clock reminded her of why she had to get up early that morning. She pushed at F'lar, who was never easy to wake up unless Mnementh called him.

"F'lar, wake up! We've got to get up." *Ramoth, dear, wake up! We've got to be at Landing. Aivas particularly wants us there.* She prodded F'lar's shoulder more urgently and, struggling to pull her legs out from under his, reluctantly rose from the comfortable, warm bed.

"We've got to get down to Landing early this morning. Early *their* morning."

There were moments, and this was one of them, when Lessa's enthusiasm for the Project faltered. If, however, this was the morning when Aivas would set in train the results of two Turns of hard studying and work, the early rising would be a minor sacrifice.

In the bigger chamber of the queen's weyr, she could hear Ramoth mumbling and grunting, denying the summons just as F'lar was doing.

"Well, if I have to get up, you will, too," she said, and callously hauled the sleeping-fur off her weyrmate.

"What the—" F'lar tried to grab the fur, but Lessa, with a chuckle, snatched it from his hand.

"You've got to get up."

"It's the middle of the bloody night, Lessa," he complained. "We don't have Fall for another day and a half."

"Aivas wants us there at five of the clock Landing time."

"Aivas!" He sat bolt upright, wide-eyed, pushing his tumbled hair back from his face.

Lessa snorted at F'lar's response to that name.

"My shirt!—" he cried, shivering convulsively in the predawn cold. "Heartless woman!"

She snatched shirt and pants up from the chair and tossed them to him. "I am not at all heartless!"

Then she opened a glowbasket to find fresh clothes for herself. F'lar made a quick stop in the bathing room while she poured klah for them both. With her cup in her hand, she passed F'lar on her way in; then she washed quickly and replaited the ends of her braids.

"Watch rider's asleep," she told him when she got back into the weyr, where he was stamping into his boots and shrugging on his riding jacket.

"I know. I've sent Mnementh to scare the living lights out of both of them." He cocked his head then as they both heard a reverberating roar and a startled squeal. "That'll teach them."

"One day Mnementh's going to startle one or both of a watchpair off the Rim!" she replied.

He grinned at her. "Haven't yet! Here!" And he held out her flying jacket and cap. As she stuck her arms in the sleeves, he bent and kissed the back of her neck. F'lar was often amorous when he first woke.

"That makes me shiver!" But she didn't pull away, so he kissed her again and hugged her affectionately. Leaving one arm across her shoulders, he guided her out to Ramoth's weyr.

The gold queen's tail was still in the weyr; the rest of her was out on the ledge. And, as F'lar and Lessa joined her there, Mnementh lowered his head from the level above the queen's weyr, his eyes gleaming brilliant blue-green in the darkness.

Who did you scare awake on watch up there, Mnementh? Lessa asked.

B'fol and green Gereth. They won't sleep on watch again. The bronze dragon's tone was particularly severe, an attitude with which Lessa had no quarrel, for both B'fol and Gereth were well enough on in Turns not to be delinquent.

"Next Fall, B'fol and Gereth will handle firestone sacks," F'lar remarked, having followed the exchange. This was no time for Benden Weyr to get slipshod. "Have we time for porridge?" he asked hopefully.

Considering that days at Landing were apt to be spent in nonstop work, Lessa thought a good breakfast was only prudent, even if they were already behind the appointed hour. "We'll make time," she said, a ripple of mischievousness in her voice.

"Now, now, Lessa," he began in a tone of mock reproof, "if we don't let anyone else time it . . ."

"Rank has some privileges, and I'll think the better for a decent breakfast in my guts," she said. "So we'll make a little time. Especially since you're so hard to wake up." She laughed softly when he sputtered a protest. "If you please, Ramoth!" And the queen crouched to allow her rider to mount. "You won't mind giving F'lar a lift, will you, dearest? I don't want him falling off that upper ledge, trying to mount Mnementh in the dark."

Ramoth turned her head toward F'lar and blinked. *Of course.*

Mnementh waited until both riders were settled on the queen's neck before pushing off from the upper ledge and gliding down beside them to the floor of the Bowl. As soon as they had landed, the night lights in the Lower Caverns were visible, as well as the banked fire on the small hearth where a big kettle of porridge was simmering. The huge klah pot was pulled slightly to one side so that the contents would not become too strong to be palatable.

As Lessa filled two bowls with the steaming cereal, she was glad that they had the place to themselves. The bakers must just have left—for the big table near the main hearth was full of cloth-covered breadpans. F'lar brought over two cups of klah, spooning an almost indecent amount of sweetener into his, and then sprinkling as much again over the porridge Lessa set in front of him.

"It's a miracle you don't gain weight with all that sweetener," she began.

"Or lose my teeth," he said, adding the second half of that long-standing complaint. He gave her his widest grin and tapped his teeth with his spoon. "But I don't and I haven't." He dug into his breakfast.

Lessa sipped at her klah first, wanting to clear the last of sleep from her wits.

"Do you suppose that Aivas is going to start the Project this morning?"

F'lar shrugged as the question caught him with a hot mouthful. He swallowed. "I can't think why else he called a meeting of such a group at such an hour. According to the original schedule he gave us, we should be ready to start. Despite what some critics imply," he added with a grimace that had nothing to do with the piping-hot porridge on his spoon, "he keeps his promises."

"So far," Lessa said in a dour tone.

"Well, he has!" Then F'lar looked at his weyrmate. "You don't really believe he can keep his promise about Thread, do you?"

"I just can't figure out how he can contrive to have us do what the settlers couldn't!" She glared at him, both relieved and sorry that she had come out with the doubt that had been increasingly bothering her.

F'lar covered her hand with his. "He's done everything he's promised to do. And I believe him, not just because I, as a dragonrider, want to, but because he sounds so very sure."

"But, F'lar, every time he's been asked, he hasn't *promised* that we will be able to destroy Thread. He's said it is *possible*. That's not quite the same thing."

"Let's just see what today brings, huh, love?"

F'lar gave her that knowing look of his which sometimes she wanted to scratch off his face. She took a deep breath and held back a scathing retort. Today could prove much, and as deeply as she wanted it to prove that F'lar was right to place so much confidence in Aivas, she had to prepare him for possible disappointment.

"But if today is a disaster, that's going to reduce our effectiveness at next week's Conference at Tillek Hold to choose Oterel's successor."

F'lar frowned. "I recognize that danger. I'm reasonably sure that Aivas also does. I'd say that's why he scheduled this meeting. His timing so far has been nothing sort of phenomenal."

"He and Lytol are really into the political aspects, aren't they? I could almost wish that Lytol was still Ruathan Lord Warder. That'd give Groghe the support he needs. Even I have heard the grumbling about Ruatha's young Lord Holder spending so much time down here instead of in his Hold."

"At least Ranrel can't be considered too young to be a Lord Holder, Lessa," F'lar reminded her. "He's in his mid-thirties, with five children. And he's certainly the only one of Oterel's sons who's shown any initiative at all. That port-renewal project of his was inspired." F'lar chuckled. "Even if he did add insult to injury by insisting on using Hamian's stuff to build the new wharfs and reinforce the piers."

Lessa had to grin, remembering the fuss Ranrel's innovative engineering had caused among those who derided or downright rejected any useful products of "the Abomination." F'lar scratched sleepily at his scalp and yawned.

"And when the other brothers tried to belittle Ranrel's project, along comes Master Idarolan, raving about the facilities," she said.

"That's not going to hurt when the Lord Holders convene. His mate's a Masterweaver. *She's* interested in having a power loom. I don't know where she found out that such things were possible."

Lessa threw up her hands. "*Everyone's* gone 'power' mad."

"It sure reduces sheer drudgery."

"Hmm. Yes. Well, eat up. We'll be late."

F'lar grinned before he upended his klah mug. "We already are, you know. It's as well you're permitting us to time it." He laughed at the wicked glare she gave him.

After putting their crockery in the main sink to soak, they fastened jackets and caps and left the cavern.

"We were supposed to be there half an hour ago, Ramoth," Lessa told her queen as she mounted. "We need to be there on time."

If you insist, Ramoth replied disapprovingly.

The others were already assembled in the main hall when the Benden Weyrleaders arrived. Robinton looked sleepy, but Jaxom, Mirrim, Piemur—with gold Farli curled about his shoulders—and the three male green riders all appeared very wide-awake indeed.

Jaxom straightened his shoulders and pulled at the lightweight sleeveless tunic he wore, to free it from his sweaty back. Irrepressibly, Piemur grinned at that evidence of his friend's nervousness. Mirrim was equally nervous. The other three green riders, L'zal, G'rannat, and S'len, were shifting from one foot to another.

"All present and accounted for, so let's see what Aivas wants with such an ill-assorted crew," F'lar said, nodding at Lessa to lead the way. As he strode forward, he tossed a reassuring smile over his shoulder at Jaxom and the others.

When Aivas had asked for this predawn meeting two days earlier, his special students had been excited by the prospect that he intended to launch *the* plan. They had been careful to contain that excitement to prevent even more rumor circulating. Not even Piemur had been brash enough to ask Aivas for confirmation.

Certainly all these young folk had studied diligently over the past two Turns, even if their lessons and drills seemed to be irrelevant or endlessly repetitious until, as Jaxom had remarked to Piemur, he could do them in his sleep.

"That may be what Aivas wants," Piemur had said with a shrug. "They make about as much sense as the drills he gives me for Farli."

Jaxom saw him stroking Farli's back as they marched down the hall and into Aivas's room. The lights brightened, and Piemur grinned to himself: Master Morilton's "light bulbs" worked just as the original ones had. Yet another minor triumph for the Masterglass-smith, working from plans of the "Abomination." The thought of that epithet caused Jaxom to frown—Master Norist was not the only one who had come to refer to Aivas in that manner. Of course, if today *was* truly the beginning of the assault on Thread, that tune could easily change before there was more cause to worry about the growing number of dissidents.

"Good morning," Aivas said at his most polite and noncommittal. "If you will seat yourselves, I shall explain today's project." He waited until they had taken their places and their excited murmurs had dwindled into respectful silence.

Then the screen displayed a clear picture of the view with which they had all become familiar: the bridge of the *Yokohama*. Only this time there was an addition: a space-suited figure slumped over one of the control panels. There was an almost simultaneous intake of breath at the realization that the body was that of Sallah Telgar, who had died so valiantly to save the colony. This, then, was the actual bridge of the *Yokohama*—not the image that Aivas had supplied during their training. Then the focus of the picture slid across the consoles beyond the figure to rest on the board marked LIFE-SUPPORT SYSTEM.

Jaxom saw Piemur reach up to stroke Farli, whose gaze was fixed on the screen. She gave a little chirp, for she, too, recognized the board. She had been working for a month on a mock-up, pushing at two toggles and depressing three keys in a certain sequence. She could now perform those movements in less than thirty seconds.

Over the past two Turns, Aivas had subtly collected many facts about both fire-lizards and dragons. The most relevant fact was that both creatures were able to maintain the oxygen levels in their systems for almost ten minutes without suffering undue discomfort or harm. That time could be pushed to fifteen minutes, but after that amount of time, both fire-lizards and dragons would need several hours to recover from the effects of oxygen deprivation.

One of the exercises with fire-lizards and dragons in which there had been no success had been getting them to take an object from one place and bring it to another. Telekinesis, Aivas had called it, but the concept—patiently explained—confused the dragons as thoroughly as it did the fire-lizards. They would go *between* to get the required object, but they could not bring it without physically collecting it. Aivas had explained that if the dragons and fire-lizards could transport themselves telekinetically, it logically followed that they ought to be able to use their abilities to *lift* distant items to them.

"Today, Piemur, you are asked to send Farli to the *Yokohama* to manipulate the switches as she had been taught to do. There is no oxygen at present on the bridge, and it is essential that the life-support system be activated before we can take the next step. Another of the toggles will transmit a report on the general condition of the *Yokohama*.

"Oh!" Piemur murmured very softly, then sighed gustily. He stroked Farli, who chirped again, her unblinking eyes still on the screen. "Somehow I thought that's what you'd say."

"She has been an excellent pupil, Piemur. There should be no problem, as she is well accustomed to obeying you."

Piemur took a deep breath. "All right, Farli," he said. He unwrapped her tail from his neck and held up his arm in the position that indicated she was to take a message.

Carefully walking along his bare arm with her talons sheathed, Farli reached his forearm and turned about to face him, her eyes whirling alertly.

"Now—" Piemur held up his right hand. "This is going to be slightly different, Farli. I want you to go up in the sky, to the place you see in my mind." He closed his eyes and focused his thoughts tightly on the scene of the bridge and the particular console she was to activate.

Farli chirruped queryingly, looked over her shoulder at the picture on the screen, and burbled once, reclosing her wings on her back.

"*No*, Farli, not into the screen. Get the 'where' from my mind." Piemur closed his eyes again, concentrating on the exact place he wanted her to go, emphasizing the life-support console next to the slumped corpse. When she chirruped again, this time almost impatiently, he sighed and turned to the others in defeat.

"She just doesn't understand," he said, trying not to let his disappointment color his voice. Not that he blamed *her*. She had *been* to most of the places he sent her. How could he get across the difference between traveling around the planet and going into space above it? Especially as he could not quite grasp the concept himself.

Farli emphasized this by flitting from his arm to the room in which she had been trained, moments later coming back and trying to fly into the picture on the screen.

Piemur's grin was weak. "What do you bet she's gone and done her exercises again? That much she understands!"

Disappointment was palpable in the room. Piemur kept his eyes straight ahead, on the tantalizingly unreachable view on the screen.

"So?" F'lar asked. "What do we do now, Aivas?"

There was a long pause before Aivas spoke. "The mind of the fire-lizard does not function in recorded animal behavioral patterns."

"That's not surprising. Your records only cover Terran types," Piemur remarked, trying not to feel so depressed about his little queen's failure. She was the best of the whole fair, better even than Menolly's Beauty, who was certainly very well trained. But he had hoped that she would be able to make this strange variation of flight. "It's also a long way to ask her to go when no one's been there before."

Another silence hung on the room.

"There's only one dragon in fact," F'lar said slowly and thoughtfully, breaking the pause, "who's ever been off the planet."

"Canth!" Lessa exclaimed.

"F'nor's brown Canth is too large," Aivas said.

"It wasn't his size I was thinking of," Lessa replied. "It's his experience in going above this planet. He's done it, so perhaps he can explain to Farli so that she'll understand what's wanted of her." Her eyes lost their focus as she sought for Canth.

Yes, we can come immediately, Canth replied to Lessa's request.

There was a stir of anticipation among those waiting in Aivas's room. Piemur kept stroking Farli, who had returned to her position on his arm. He murmured softly that she was a marvelous fire-lizard, the best in the world, but that the toggles she was to pull and the buttons she was to press were really not the ones in the next room but, rather, identical ones up on the *Yokohama*, far above their heads in the dark sky. She kept cocking her head this way and that, her throat pulsing as she tried her very best to understand what was wanted of her.

"Ah, they're here," Lessa said. "F'nor's on his way in."

Looking as if he had dressed in a hurry, F'nor came running into the room. "Canth said it was important," he said. After a puzzled glance around the room, he regarded Lessa expectantly.

"Aivas needs Farli to get to the bridge on the *Yokohama*," she explained. "Farli doesn't understand her directions. You and Canth are the only two on Pern who have left the planet. We thought Canth might be able to clarify the instructions so Farli will know what she is expected to do."

As she spoke, F'nor pulled off his flight cap and shucked off his heavy riding gear. When she had finished, his expression turned humorously quizzical.

"Well, now, Lessa, that's a problem. I've never been exactly sure how Canth and I managed that abortive flight in the first place."

"Do you remember what you were thinking?" F'lar asked.

F'nor chuckled. "I was thinking I had to do something to keep you from trying to get to the Red Star." Then he frowned. "Come to think of it, Meron was there, and he tried to make his fire-lizard go. She disappeared in a flash, and I don't know if she ever returned to him."

"Farli's not afraid," Piemur said staunchly. "She just doesn't understand where she's supposed to perform what she's been trained to do."

F'nor spread his hands in a gesture of appeal. "If Farli can't get the hang of it, I don't think any of them could."

"But could Canth explain to her that he went off the planet? Into space?" Lessa asked.

Could you, Canth? F'nor asked the brown dragon. Canth was in the process of draping himself on the ridge above Landing where the rising sun would warm him.

You showed me where you wanted me to go. I went.

F'nor repeated Canth's answer. "A planet is a bigger target than a spaceship we can't see."

Farli does not understand, Canth added. *She has done the things she was asked to do in the place where she has always done them.*

Canth, Lessa asked the dragon directly, *do you understand what we're asking Farli to do?*

Yes, you want her to go up to the ship and do the things she has been trained to do there! She doesn't understand where she is to go. She's never been there.

Jaxom squirmed a little on the chair. Considering how hard Piemur had worked with Farli, it was a crying shame that the little creature couldn't grasp the essential point.

Ruth, do you understand? he asked the white dragon. Sometimes fire-lizards listened to Ruth when they ignored everyone else.

Yes, but it is a cold, long way for a fire-lizard to go if she hasn't been there before. She's trying very hard to understand.

A lot of thoughts crowded Jaxom's mind just then. But the main one was that Ruth was *not* too big to fit on the bridge—if his wings were folded back and he landed precisely on the floor just in front of the lift door. He would also have to remain very still, for Aivas had said there was no gravity on the bridge. Ruth would be in free-fall. Aivas did not see that as a problem for a dragon or a fire-lizard, accustomed as they were to being airborne. Jaxom had known that that was one reason Aivas had grilled him so long and so hard on the layout of the bridge and lectured him on null-gravity conditions. But until Farli had done her exercise on board the *Yokohama*, turning on the bridge's life-support system, Ruth and Jaxom could not go.

Aivas had had crews searching the Catherine Caves assiduously for "space suits." They had found two—or, rather, the perished scraps of fabric and the bright plastic shapes that had once serviced it. Oxygen cylinders had been manufactured, being not dissimilar to agenothree tanks. HNO_3, Jaxom reminded himself, now that he knew the precise chemical constituents of the flame-producing mixture. But there was no protection for a frail human body in the absolute cold and airless vacuum of the *Yokohama*'s bridge in its present state.

Jaxom thought that manufacturing proper equipment would prove to be Aivas's alternative. He had already had several long discussions with Masterweaver Zurg. But alternatives would take time, not to mention more experimentation on the part of both Zurg and Hamian's innovative crew—more time in which the disenchanted Lord Holders could steadily withdraw their support from Landing.

If only Farli could understand, Jaxom thought, searching his own mind for any clues that he, or Ruth, might be able to give her. Ruth had perceived the difference, but he was much smarter than Farli. He understood so much—as much as I do, Jaxom thought with great pride.

As you understand, so do I. Ruth's tone was almost accusatory. *It is not really a very long way* between *but it* is *up far.*

Although Jaxom leaped to his feet, shouting "No, Ruth, no!" he was too late. For Ruth had already gone *between.*

"Jaxom!" Lessa exclaimed, her face white. "You didn't send him?"

"I most certainly did not. He just went." Jaxom was aghast, and Farli began shrieking protests, her wings extended, her eyes whirling with startled, angry red.

Outside, Ramoth and Mnementh bugled their own warnings.

Don't, Ramoth! Mnementh! Lessa cried. "We'll rouse everyone in Landing and they'll know something's gone wrong." Then she turned into F'lar, clutching at him in her fear for Ruth—and for Jaxom.

"*Jaxom?*" F'lar bellowed seeing the shock on Jaxom's face. Mirrim, her tanned cheeks bleached white, had leaped to Jaxom's side, as had the other green riders, their expressions anxious, ready to support him. Robinton and F'nor were too stunned to react, so there was only Jancis to watch the screen and count.

"He's all right," Jaxom managed to say, though his mouth had gone terribly dry. The strong link with Ruth had attenuated to just a faint touch. "He's still with me."

"Did you tell him to go?" F'lar demanded, his expression so fierce that even Lessa recoiled.

Jaxom gave the Benden Weyrleader an inscrutable glare. "He bloody just went and did it! Ruth's got a mind of his own!"

Then Jancis leaped to her feet, gesticulating at the screen. "There! There! He's there! On the count of ten."

There, undeniably on the bridge, wings tucked tight, his whole body flattened, was Ruth. Before their eyes, he drifted upward, peering about him with an expression of astonishment, until his head touched the ceiling.

"Ah! Well done, Ruth! Jaxom!" Aivas's bellow of triumph cut across the racket of astonishment and surprise that reverberated around the room. "Jaxom, tell Ruth not to be surprised to float. He is in free-fall, with no gravity for up and down. Warn him not to make any energetic movements. Does he understand, Jaxom?"

"I am, I did. He understands," Jaxom said, staring in fascination at the screen.

"See, Farli!" Piemur pointed excitedly. "Ruth's led the way for you." But Farli was so confused by the sudden cheering and shouting in the room that Piemur had to grab her by the cheeks and turn her head toward the screen and Ruth! "Go to Ruth!" The little queen gave a squawk and, launching herself from Piemur's arm, disappeared.

"Jaxom, you tell Ruth to get back here right now!" Lessa shouted, recovering from her shock. "Mind of his own, indeed! I'll give him a mind to obey!"

"Restore yourselves to calm observation!" Aivas's voice once again cut through the furor. "Ruth is unharmed. And . . . Farli has found her way."

Piemur let out a yelp of surprise, plainly audible in a room suddenly gone very quiet. For Farli had indeed found her way to the bridge of *Yokohama* and, with one talon firmly hooked on the edge of the console, was diligently pulling toggles and pressing buttons. Lights appeared on the board.

"Mission accomplished," Aivas said. "They may return."

Farli came and has done her job, Ruth said, not realizing that Jaxom could see him. *I'm floating. Let go, Farli. It's not at all like being* between. *A most unusual sensation. Not like swimming, either.*

It was also a most unusual sight for those observing Ruth as he drifted gently across the bridge, a handspan above the arc of consoles, ducking his head to keep from scraping the ceiling.

As Farli released her grip, she, too, began to float. Startled, she extended her wings and gently revolved end over end, colliding with Ruth. He reached out to steady her, and both were propelled farther away from their original locations, toward the great plasglas window on the bow of the bridge complex. Suddenly Jancis began to giggle, and the tension in the room evaporated.

I think that's quite enough clowning about now, Ruth, Jaxom said, trying to sound stern. But he couldn't help grinning along with everyone else over the antics of the two creatures. *You scared the life out of me! Now get back down here.*

I knew exactly where to go. I showed Farli. I had no problem at all doing it, and this is fun. With a negligent shove of one wing, Ruth executed a complete turn in the air and began floating back toward the lift. *Will we get to come back again?*

Only if you and Farli get your bodies back on Pern this instant!
Oh, all right. If you say so.

Laughing with a mixture of amusement, sheer relief, and fury, Jaxom dashed down the corridor and outside. The others were close on his heels, full of triumph and the laughter of relief. Lessa, however, was raging at the risk Ruth had taken, and she knew from the set expression on F'lar's face that he felt the same.

Halfway down the corridor, F'lar caught Lessa by the arm. "You may be furious, Lessa, but we can't intervene in this. And I probably lost as many seconds of my life as you did over Ruth's leap."

"Ruth cannot be allowed to be so irresponsible," she said, fuming. "Jaxom isn't. I don't understand how Ruth gets away with such disobedience. Ramoth wouldn't."

"Ruth and Jaxom were not Weyr-trained. But don't think Ruth's going to get off easily for this escapade." He managed a droll grin. "Judging by the look on Jaxom's face, he's had a fright he won't forget. That will inhibit Ruth far more surely than threats from you and me." He gave her one of his little shakes. "More important, the less furor there is right now, the fewer rumors will abound."

Lessa let out a heavy sigh, glared at him, and then gave herself a shake, releasing herself from his grasp.

"Yes, we don't want this bruited about—at least, not quite yet. But I tell you, and I'll tell Jaxom, too, I don't want to live through another few seconds like that again. All I could think about was how under the heavens would we explain to Lytol."

F'lar grinned wryly. "As it's turned out, Lytol can print this up as a turning point in the modern history of Pern."

"And just won't he!"

Discretion muted the congratulations for the brave venturers, but everyone patted Ruth and scrubbed at his eyeridges until his eyes were whirling with delight. When Farli finally settled down again on Piemur's shoulder, she also received extravagant caresses. False dawn was just lightening the eastern horizon, so there was a good chance that few were awake to wonder at the fuss being made of Ruth.

"I think," Robinton began when the elation abated, "that we'd better return to Aivas. I, for one, would like to know what's next."

"Well, that depends on what Aivas learns from the instrumentation that Farli just turned on," Jaxom replied. "If the bridge is intact, warms up, and there's enough oxygen left in the tanks that supply that area, Ruth and I go up—together." He grinned. "That's when we initiate the telescopic sequences that will reaffirm the position of the system's planets—most particularly, our old enemy, the Red Star.''

That was, however, not quite all that Aivas had in mind when, late the next day, the bridge atmospheric conditions were found to be satisfactory.

''Piemur, I would like you to accompany Jaxom,'' Aivas said when the group reassembled.

''I'm not supposed to go with him this trip,'' Piemur exclaimed.

''Originally, no. Two men will be needed for what should now be the first project. To demonstrate proper respect for Sallah Telgar, it is fitting that her mortal remains be brought back to Pern and properly interred. No doubt, Lord Larad would like to attend to whatever burial rituals are currently practiced.''

A profound silence prevailed until Robinton cleared his throat.

''Yes, that would be not only respectful and appropriate, but a long-overdue honor for such a valiant lady. I'll inform Lord Larad immediately.''

''Would her space suit be usable after all this time?'' Piemur asked, curious. When he saw the shocked expression on Jancis's face, he belatedly realized how callous that sounded and, groaning, hid his face against his arm. Farli curled her tail consolingly around his throat.

''With some minor repairs, it is to be hoped that the space suit is usable,'' Aivas replied so calmly that Robinton was certain that recovery of both body and suit had been planned from the start. ''You are both to dress as warmly as possible, as the bridge temperature currently reads ten degrees below zero.''

Jaxom was unmoved by that information, since he was used to the absolute cold of *between*, but Piemur gave a dramatic shudder and hunched his shoulders as if already warding off the chill.

''Can Farli come, too?'' he asked.

''That would be advisable,'' Aivas said. ''If Jancis's Trig will accompany Farli, there would then be two fire-lizards who understand this sort of *between* transfer.''

Despite an obvious reluctance, Jancis instructed her young bronze Trig to settle himself on Piemur's right shoulder. Jaxom and Piemur left the buildings by themselves so as not to suggest to anyone outside their small group that this journey was anything unusual. The bulky tanks of oxygen, which Aivas had insisted they bring in case of emergency, had already been secured to Ruth's back, but Jaxom checked the ropes before he and Piemur mounted.

''Ready, Piemur?'' Jaxom asked over his shoulder.

"As ready as I'll ever be," the harper replied, resettling his grip on Jaxom's wide belt. "But I'm awfully glad Ruth's already been there."

Tell Piemur not to worry. It's fun to float! Ruth remarked as he launched himself.

As Jaxom passed on that encouraging message, he felt Piemur's spasmodic tug on his belt and knew that the harper was also nervous. Not that he didn't trust Ruth to get them there. It was just such a long way!

Between never seemed so cold nor the transfer so long, yet Jaxom, counting silently, reached ten seconds just as they emerged onto the bridge deck of the *Yokohama*.

"Are we there yet?" Piemur asked. His hands were rigid on Jaxom's belt. As Jaxom looked over his shoulder to reassure the harper, he realized that Piemur had his eyes squeezed shut.

Rather than laugh at his friend, he cleared his throat and turned his head forward—and began to slide sideways off Ruth's neck.

"Shards! What's happening?" Piemur exclaimed, opening his eyes as he and Jaxom continued to slide to their right until they came up against the cold wall.

Don't make sudden moves, Ruth warned both of them.

"I heard you, I heard you," Piemur replied. The freezing wall seemed to burn through the leather of his helmet and his jacket. "It is *cold* up here!"

Jaxom only nodded. "I'm going to pull us back up on Ruth, Piemur," he said. Carefully grabbing a neck ridge, he slowly righted them. Farli unwrapped her tail and peered up at Jaxom, chirping encouragingly.

"That's all I need," Piemur said wryly. "My fire-lizard telling me how to handle free-fall!" Farli pushed off from his shoulder and floated upward. Trig squeaked; when Farli answered him in an encouraging tone, he let go of his perch and, following her example, also drifted away. The two came to rest on the ceiling, chittering animatedly.

"That's enough, the pair of you," Piemur said, disgusted.

"They're not coming to any harm," Jaxom said, "and Ruth says if we move slowly enough, we'll be all right. We've got a lot to do. Look, Piemur, I'll dismount—carefully—and then you can untie the oxygen tanks. Ruth says the tanks are bulky and he doesn't move until we've untied them. *He* wants to look out the window."

"*He* would!"

Jaxom heard the note of self-disparagement in Piemur's voice and grinned. "They did have some practice, you know."

"Hmmmm! The air here smells peculiar, sort of dead."

"It'll probably improve with the fresh tanks," Piemur said cheerfully.

Cautiously, Jaxom dismounted on the right-hand side of the white dragon. Keeping between Ruth and the wall might prevent him from floating about.

Your placement is perfect, Ruth, he told his weyrmate approvingly, hanging on to a neck ridge as he judiciously lowered himself.

It's the only place I'd fit, Ruth remarked, slowly turning his head to his right to observe the margin. *I'll hook my tail so I won't drift when you unload me.*

Now I know why dragons have tails! Jaxom replied, giving a nervous chuckle.

"Don't laugh," Piemur warned. He had just swung his leg over and had to clutch at Ruth's wing joint to keep from floating upward.

"I wasn't laughing at you, Piemur. Ruth's just found out how to anchor himself. Watch his tail. And dismount to the right, not the left. Don't grab that wing joint so hard. Wings are fragile."

"I know, I know. Sorry, Ruth." But as Jaxom watched anxiously, he could see that Piemur had to make a considerable effort to relax his grip. "I've done some crazy things in my life, stealing fire-lizard eggs, crawling into carry-sacks, scrambling along shorelines—but this is undoubtedly the craziest," Piemur muttered to himself as he eased off Ruth's back, following Jaxom's example. At last his feet touched the deck. "Made it!" he exclaimed.

Wedged between the wall and his dragon, Jaxom began to untie the ropes that secured the oxygen tanks to Ruth's back.

"Huh!" Jaxom exclaimed in surprise as the tiniest push sent the first tank drifting toward the deck. "Well, easier off than on! As Aivas said." He grinned at the young harper, who was gaping in surprise. "No weight at all." With one finger, he pushed the second tank after the first.

"Hey, I could get to like a place where work is play," Piemur said with a grin as he began to relax.

"Here—let's stack them against the wall. By the first Egg!" Jaxom inadvertently used more force than necessary to lift the tank and nearly launched it over Ruth.

"Wow!" Piemur stretched out to restrain the tank and found himself rising. But he was quick enough to grab Ruth's wing and correct the reaction. "Yeah, this free-fall stuff has distinct advantages! I'll tend to the others."

While Jaxom watched in surprise, Piemur took a firm hold of Ruth's shoulder neck ridge and executed an effortless flip over the white dragon's back.

"Whee!" The exclamation was part laugh and part surprise that his unorthodox maneuver succeeded in guiding him neatly into the narrow space between the dragon and the railing around the upper level of the bridge. "This is fun!"

"Watch it, Piemur. We don't want those tanks crashing into anything."

"I'll just tie these down."

"It is safest to secure any loose object on board a spacegoing vessel," Aivas agreed, as calm as ever. "You are doing well. Bridge temperature is still rising, and all proximity alarms are quiescent."

"Proximity alarms?" Piemur asked, his voice rising in surprise.

"Yes, this facility is now receiving function reports and damage analysis," Aivas went on. "Considering its length of time in space, the fabric of the *Yokohama* has not had a significant breach. The solar-powered deflector shields display no operational damage. As you will remember from your studies, these panels provide power to the small thrusters that keep the ship in its geosynchronous orbit. There has been minor penetration of some of the outermost sectors of the main sphere, but these were automatically sealed off. None of those sections are now required. The doors on the cargo bay are still open, and a malfunction light is on. However, your assigned tasks take precedence. Please proceed. Oxygen remains at a normal level, but you will shortly feel the effects of the low temperature, decreasing manual dexterity. Gymnastic displays should be curtailed."

Jaxom smothered a laugh and hoped that only he had heard Piemur's insolent mutter about all work and no play.

Moving carefully, Jaxom ducked under Ruth's neck and took a firm hold on the railing. To his surprise, he saw that Piemur was hovering motionless on the wide steps down to the command level of the bridge. Looking up from his circumspect movements, Jaxom, too, was transfixed by what had stunned the harper: Below them lay Pern, its blue seas glistening to port, while to starboard was visible the coastline and vivid greens, browns, and beiges of the Southern Continent.

"By the Egg, it's just like the pictures Aivas showed us," Piemur murmured reverently. "Magnificent!"

Unexpected tears pricked his eyes, and Jaxom swallowed hard as he viewed his world as his ancestors had once seen it at journey's end! That must have been a triumphant moment, he thought.

"It's big!" Piemur added, daunted by the prospect.

"It *is* a whole world," Jaxom replied softly, trying to reorient himself to the incredible size of it.

With great majesty, the scene was imperceptibly altering as the planet swung toward the dusk line.

"Jaxom? Piemur?" Aivas recalled them to their duties.

"Just admiring the view from the bridge," Piemur said briskly. "Seeing's believing." His eyes still on the wide window, he floated over to the flight of stairs and pulled himself hand over hand along the railing down to the flight deck. From there he used every available handhold to make his way to the console he was scheduled to program. At last he wrenched his gaze from the spectacular view and studied the job at hand.

"I got more red lights than I like," he told Avias as he strapped himself into his seat.

Jaxom, making his way around the upper level to the science positions, could see the red lights on those boards, as well. He pulled himself into a seat and strapped in.

"I've got them, too!" he said. "But not on the telescope settings."

"Jaxom, Piemur, key in the override commands and then go to manual."

Jaxom's board was immediately cleared of over half of the red dysfunction lights. Three remained, along with two orange lights. But none of those would interfere with the program he was to initiate. A quick glance told him that Piemur was already tapping away at his assigned keyboard.

Jaxom set to work, stopping now and then to flex his fingers and gaze wonderingly at the fantastic view of Pern. Nothing could detract from that spectacle, not even the comical antics of two fire-lizards cavorting in the weightlessness. Oddly enough, their excited squeakings and chitterings as Farli dared Trig to more and more outrageous maneuvers helped dispel the unreality of this bizarre environment.

Once Jaxom began to concentrate on setting the program for the telescopes, Ruth released his tail anchor and drifted with great dignity toward the wide bridge windows, where he could indulge his fascination in Pern and the starlit blackness. The fire-lizards continued their chittering conversation.

I don't know what they are, either, Ruth said. *But they're pretty.*

What's pretty? Jaxom asked, looking up. *Can you see the other two ships?*

No. There are things flowing past us.

Things? Jaxom craned across his console to see what Ruth was seeing. However, his view was blocked by the bodies of the dragon and fire-lizards, who had their faces pressed against the far right of the bridge viewport.

Suddenly all three creatures flung themselves back, away from the window, the motion sending them careening toward Piemur and Jaxom.

"Hey, watch out!" Jaxom ducked as Ruth zoomed overhead. At the same moment, there was a distinct rattling sound.

"Something's hitting us!" Piemur cried. Unstrapping quickly, he pushed himself off to the viewscreen.

"What is hitting you?" Aivas demanded.

Piemur bumped against the viewscreen, looking right and left. "Jaxom, ask Ruth what he saw. I can't see anything." Pressing his left cheek to the plasglas, he tried to see beyond the thick curve of the window.

Things—like fire-lizard eggs—coming straight at us, Ruth replied.

"Well, there's nothing out there now," Piemur said. He headed back to his station, grabbing the back of his chair just as he was about to overshoot it.

"Aivas?" Jaxom asked.

"The pinging indicated the screens deflecting a small shower of objects," Aivas replied calmly. "No damage is reported. As you will have learned from your studies, space is not a barren void. Minute particles are in constant motion through space. Doubtless a shower of some sort startled Ruth and the fire-lizards. You would be wise to continue your tasks before you become incapacitated by the severe temperatures."

Jaxom noticed that Piemur, too, was not completely reassured by that explanation. But it was true that the icy cold was seeping through their layers of clothing and so, as Ruth and the fire-lizards cautiously, with much chirping and twittering, returned to their positions at the window, the men returned their attention to their consoles.

Jaxom worked as fast as he could, but still the cold increasingly penetrated the down-lined gloves that had always kept him warm through hours of Threadfall. Maybe space *was* colder than *between*, he thought, flexing frozen fingers.

"Aivas, didn't you say there'd be heat on the bridge?" he complained. "My hands are getting numb with cold."

"Readings indicate that the bridge heating is not working as efficiently as possible. It is probable that the resistive ceramic of the units has crystalized. This can be repaired later."

"That's good news," Jaxom said as he double-checked his entries. Then he straightened up. "Mine's done—program ready."

"Activate," Aivas ordered.

Jaxom punched that key with some trepidation—though the Egg knew how he could have gotten it wrong with the endless drills Aivas had put him through in learning the sequences of attitude, exposure, and sectors. With considerable personal satisfaction, he watched the fast-forward scroll of the display as it confirmed his plotting.

"This board's much faster than the ones we've been using," he remarked.

"The equipment on the *Yokohama* was state-of-the-art when the ship was commissioned by the Pern Charter Group," Aivas said. "High-speed computations would have been essential in astronavigation."

"I told you we were using baby stuff," Piemur murmured.

"Before the infant walks, it must learn to crawl," Aivas said.

"Is everyone hearing all this?" the harper demanded with some indignation.

"No."

"I thank your mercy for that! And my program's up and running, too, by the way."

"That is correct. You must now begin phase two of the schedule. You will find the auxiliary oxygen storage behind Bulwark B-8802-A, -B, and -C," Aivas instructed.

Piemur was shaking the fingers of his gloved hands. "My fingers have never been this cold! I'll give you Bitran odds this bridge is colder than *between*."

"In point of fact," Aivas remarked, "it is not. But you have been in that very cold temperature far longer than you have ever remained *between*."

"A point," Jaxom reminded Piemur as they pulled themselves up along stair rail. "Remarkable feeling, this weightlessness," he said with a comradely grin at the harper.

Piemur gave him a happy grimace of agreement. Just then Farli and Trig came tumbling end over end above their heads, making them duck—which sent them bouncing off the steps.

"Careful!" Jaxom cried, reaching for the railing as smoothly as he could.

"Ohohohohoh!" Piemur continued to float on up to the ceiling.

By the time Jaxom, securely holding on to the rail with one hand, had grabbed the floating Piemur by the ankle and hauled him down, neither was sure whether to laugh or swear at their clumsiness. However, the slight mishap made them all the more circumspect in their motions. They located, opened, and examined the auxiliary oxygen compartment, then carefully removed the one empty tank, maneuvered the four they had brought with them into the space available, and made the necessary connections to bring the replacements into the system.

"Phase three may now be initiated," Aivas told them once the connections had been checked.

Jaxom caught Piemur's gaze, and the young harper gave him a wry grin, shrugged, and turned back to the space-suited figure they had both been avoiding.

Ruth, we need you back on the landing, please, Jaxom said as he and Piemur solemnly converged on Sallah's body. He swallowed.

As they lifted it from the chair it had occupied for 2,500 Turns, the rigid space-suited body retained the position in which it had originally collapsed across the console. Jaxom tried to feel reverence for the personality that had once inhabited the frozen shell they were handling. Sallah Telgar had given her life to prevent the defector, Avril Bitra, from draining the *Yokohama*'s fuel tanks in her bid to escape the Rukbat system. Sallah had even managed to repair the console Bitra had wrecked in her fury at being thwarted. Odd that a Hold had been named after such a woman, but then, Bitrans had always been an odd lot. Jaxom chided himself for such thoughts. There were some very honest, worthy Bitrans—a few, anyway—who were not given to gambling and the other forms of gaming that fascinated so many of that Hold. Lord Sigomal kept to himself, but that was far preferable to the late Lord Sifer's well-known unsavory appetites.

With the ropes that had held the tanks in place, Jaxom and Piemur strapped the bent body between Ruth's wings. Sensing their mood alteration, Farli and Trig had ceased their cavorting, and when Piemur again mounted the white dragon, they quietly settled to his shoulders.

When Jaxom slid astride Ruth, he could no longer control his jaw, and his teeth began to chatter. Had Sallah felt this creeping cold as she died? Was that what had killed her, abandoned so far above the planet? His chilled fingers could barely feel Ruth's neck ridge.

Let's get back to Landing before we freeze solid, too, Ruth, he said.

"Can we go before we freeze solid?" Piemur asked wistfully, unaware that he was echoing Jaxom's silent request to Ruth.

Now! Jaxom longingly projected a vivid scene of warm, balmy Landing to his dragon.

As they entered the chill blackness of *between*, he was still not sure which was colder.

Much later in the evening of that momentous day, when Lessa had a chance to sit down and think about it all, she wondered just how Aivas—quite likely with Lytol's connivance—had contrived such an extraordinary and timely event as the return of Sallah's body. This would have considerable impact on the entire population, both North and South, both doubters and believers. Sallah Telgar's heroism and self-sacrifice had, in the past two years, become a favorite harper ballad, repeatedly requested at all Gathers and evening entertainments of any consequence. To be able to bring her back from her lonely crypt should be considered a significant vindication of the Landing effort.

Lord Larad was absolutely dumbfounded when Robinson, conveyed by Mnementh and F'lar to Telgar Hold, apprised him of the retrieval of his ancestress's remains.

"Yes, yes, indeed, Sallah must be honored. There must, of course, be some ceremony fitting such an occasion." Larad looked helplessly at Robinson.

Burial services were usually brief, even for the most honored being. The deeds and goodness of unusual persons were perpetuated in song and harper tales, which were considered the most fitting of memorials.

"A performance of the Ballad of Sallah Telgar would certainly be appropriate," Robinson said. "Full instrumental accompaniment to chorus and solo voices. I'll speak to Sebell."

"I never thought to have the chance to honor our brave ancestress," Larad said, and floundered once again.

Fortunately Lady Jissamy, Larad's astute and capable wife, stepped to his side. "There is that small cave, just to the north of the main court, the one which that recent rockslide revealed. It is just large enough—" She faltered and then recovered. "And certainly accessible, easy to reseal."

Larad patted her hand gratefully. "Yes, the very place. Ah . . . when?" he added tentatively.

"The day after tomorrow?" Robinton suggested, resisting an urge to grin in triumph. The day after next would be just the day before the Lord Holders convened about the matter of the late Oterel's successor.

Larad shot him a quick glance. "You couldn't possibly have planned it this way, could you, Masterharper?"

"Me?" Years of practice made it possible for Robinton to affect genuine surprise. He waggled his hand in denial.

F'lar came to his assistance with a disgusted snort. "Hardly, Larad. We knew she was there. So did you. Aivas included her sacrifice in his historical narrative. Today was the first chance to actually get to her. And it just doesn't seem proper to—well, just to leave her remains there."

"To give her rest after all that long time in cold space," Jissamy said with a delicate shudder. "It's time and past it. Should we make it an open ceremony?"

"I think that only proper. Telgar, of course, should have the honor, but many will wish to be respectful," Robinton said with a properly grave mien, hoping that the occasion would spark considerable interest through Hold and Hall. Even those who were not curious about Sallah could be expected to come, if only to see who else attended.

When Jaxom, Piemur, and Ruth arrived back at Landing, they had gratefully turned their burden over to Masterhealer Oldive and two of his Masters. Now the mortal remains of Sallah Telgar rested in a finely joined coffin of Master Bendarek's best wooden panels.

Shown the cleansed space suit, Aivas assured all that the heel of the suit and the other small tears could be mended. Aivas remarked to Lytol that since someone would be expected to wear that suit, it was fortunate indeed that superstition was not a facet of Pernese culture. Lytol disagreed. He and Aivas immediately became involved in a discussion of primitive religions and arcane beliefs, so that Robinton was just as glad that he was free to leave for Telgar Weyr with F'lar. The Harper wondered fleetingly if he would have done better to have stayed to listen to what was certain to be a fascinating debate; but he was deriving too much satisfaction in being the bearer of such remarkable tidings.

One of the older Telgar sons brought in a tray with wineglasses and a fine crystal decanter, which Robinton decided must be one of the new designs Glassmaster Morilton had produced. The next son arrived with a tray of piping-hot little pastries and some good Telgar mountain cheeses. With a glass of white Benden in his hand, Robinton was definitely pleased that he had come.

"You said, did you not," Larad began, "that someone had actually been on the old ship? Was that judicious?"

"Necessary," F'lar said. "No danger involved. Piemur's little fire-lizard did exactly as Aivas taught her. So there's air on the bridge, and it's warmed up. Ruth will take Jaxom back again tomorrow to find out why the cargo-bay doors have remained open. Probably a trivial malfunction, according to Aivas. All in all—" F'lar paused to sip his wine. "—a most auspicious beginning. Most auspicious."

"I'm glad to hear that, F'lar," Larad said, nodding, his expression solemn. "I'm very glad to hear that."

"Not half as glad as I am to be able to report it," the Benden Weyrleader replied.

8

▼▼▼▼▼▼▼▼

Keep a grip on me, will you, Ruth? Jaxom said as he carefully swung his right leg over the white dragon's neck ridge. Maneuvering in free-fall had been easier the previous day, when he and Piemur had had each other to hold on to. He had gotten the hang of slow, controlled movements, then, but today the bulky suit impeded him, and he felt ungainly. The heavy magnetic-soled boots made his feet especially clumsy. He clutched at Ruth's neck suddenly as he felt his body moving in a direction other than *down*. Ruth caught him by the ankle, and suddenly he was right side up, the boots anchoring him safely to the deck.

Knowing that his fellow students were observing him made him hope devoutly that he didn't look as ridiculous as he felt. Sharra had told him repeatedly that he had not looked at all foolish coping with weightlessness the day before. He should relax in satisfaction that both he and Piemur had handled themselves most creditably. She only wished that she could somehow have seen the view of Pern which had so transfixed them.

"I've never seen that particular look on Piemur's face before. Jancis was impressed."

"So how did I look?"

"Dumbstruck, just like Piemur," she replied, giving him a mischievous grin. "About the same way you looked when you saw Jarrol for the first time."

At least today, Jaxom knew he had some control over his movements—as long as he kept his feet on the deck. He took the first step forward, wrenching the heavy boot's grip off the floor and stamping it down in front of him. Ruth had landed in the same spot as before, right by the lift door. Jaxom had only to duck under the dragon's neck to reach the control panel, which Aivas had assured him was in working order.

I'll move out of your way, Ruth said obligingly. Picking up his hind legs, he flipped over and over backward, coasting toward the window. *It's better than the view from the Star Stones on Benden or the fireheights at Ruatha.* By the time Jaxom had pressed one thick-gloved finger on the pressure panel, Ruth had his nose against the plasglas and was staring out into space.

Jaxom still could not dispel the sense of being an intruder which he had felt keenly the day before, walking where his ancestors had, manipulating switches, toggles, and keyboards just as they had once done. He had told himself that that was partly because of the gruesome errand he and Piemur had been on, retrieving Sallah Telgar. He had hoped the feeling would have altered now that he was here on another errand, but it had not.

Though he and Piemur had, miraculously, been able to log into their respective consoles and complete their tasks, Aivas had not been able to discover why the cargo-bay doors remained open. Today, after a brisk tutorial session from Aivas, Jaxom's assignment was to descend to the Cargo level and attempt to use the control console or the manual override there.

"It is to be hoped that one of those two systems is operational," Aivas said.

"Why?"

"Otherwise, you would have to venture outside the ship to discover what was keeping the doors from closing."

"Oh!" Jaxom had seen enough footage of Aivas's training tapes to wonder if he would have the nerve to space walk.

The lift opened and he stepped in. The door shut. Once again consulting the diagram in his hand—though he had memorized it— he punched the button marked CB for cargo bay before he noticed how many levels the lift served. Although Aivas had assured him that the solar panels of the *Yokohama* contained sufficient power to operate the bridge lift, he had a nervous moment before the long-unused mechanism rumbled into action.

"The lift is operational," Jaxom told Aivas in what he hoped was a casual tone. "I'm descending." He had also been instructed to keep up a running commentary. Jaxom was not by nature garrulous; it seemed inane to keep reporting simple actions, even if they were not taking place under normal conditions. Aivas had merely repeated that this was normal procedure for a single operative in what was to be considered a hostile environment.

"Proceed," Aivas said.

The descent seemed to take both a long time and no time at all. A warning note sounded, and a red sign—DANGER: VACUUM!—appeared on the door of the lift.

"What do I do now, Aivas?"

"Press the PUMP DOWN button on the right of the sign and wait for the danger lights to go out."

Jaxom did as he was instructed. He noticed that his suit puffed out and seemed slightly less wieldy. He was just growing accustomed to that alteration when there was a melodious ding and the door slid silently aside—and Jaxom looked out at a vast blackness that framed an even blacker area that was punctuated by star lights. There was no reassuring sight of sunlit Pern below him. He didn't move a muscle.

Don't be nervous. I'd come after you if you fell out, Ruth said encouragingly.

"I've reached the cargo bay," Jaxom said belatedly. "There's insufficient light." And that, Jaxom said to himself, must be the single most stupid understatement he had ever made!

"Feel to the left of the door. There will be a panel." Aivas's voice in Jaxom's ear was steady and reassuring, and he let out his breath, only just realizing that he had been holding it in. "Wave your hand across the panel, and emergency lights will come on."

We hope, Jaxom said to himself. Moving with extreme care, he obeyed and was unutterably relieved to see a line of lights come up all around the immense cargo bay. The effect did heighten the blackness of space, but he felt better with the partial illumination. "Yes, I now have light." *It's bigger even than Fort's Hatching Ground,* he told Ruth, looking about in awe.

"There is a handrail all around the inside wall of the cargo bay," Aivas went on conversationally. "To your left you will see a bank of lights, and the console should be visible under them."

"It is."

"It will be faster to go hand over hand, Jaxom," Aivas went on, "and quite safe. Otherwise you would exhaust yourself needlessly."

Jaxom wondered if Aivas knew just how scared he was. But how could he? So Jaxom took a deep breath and, lifting his left foot, reached out and caught hold of the handrail. It was round and firm in his grip and amazingly reassuring for a mere thin rail of metal. "I've got it. I'm proceeding as directed."

Holding very tightly with both hands, he kicked off his right foot, balanced the reaction against the solid rail, and began to move hand over hand, hauling his weightless body after him.

"How did my ancestors manage to load ships working like this?" he asked, unable to think of anything else to say.

"Your ancestors worked in half gravity in this area during loading, but the rest of the ship was on normal gravity."

"They could do that? Amazing," Jaxom replied dutifully. He was nearly halfway to the console. The curve of the bay now hid the unnerving sight of star-studded space. He wanted to increase his pace but sternly held himself to a rhythm that would prevent sudden, unexpected reactions. He could feel the sweat on his forehead, and then the little suction fan in his helmet turned on and the moisture was evacuated. That phenomenon occupied his mind until he was actually at the lighted console.

He activated it, and a range of red and orange lights flickered into being. Jaxom experienced a slight shock and then began reading the dials. Some of the red lights were perfectly in order, indicating, as they were meant to, that the cargo-bay doors were open. He sighed in relief and applied his lessons to deciphering the rest. When he was sure of what sequence to use, he entered the appropriate code. The orange light began to flicker. The legend above it said: RTC. He reported that to Aivas.

"That explains why the cargo-bay doors remained open. They were on a remote time control, which must have malfunctioned. The simplest method now is to use the manual release, Jaxom," Aivas told him. "It is found under the terminal. Open the glass lid and pull."

Grabbing the handle of the manual release, Jaxom gave a yank. When nothing happened, he gave a second, more forceful yank. Fortunately he was still holding on to the handle, for the force of the yank sent him dangling above the deck, hanging on by one outstretched arm. A strange gargling noise echoed in his ears.

"What has happened, Jaxom?" Aivas asked, his voice as calm as ever.

Jaxom's momentary panic subsided. In chagrin, he explained.

"Pull yourself toward the deck by exerting a downward pressure on the handle, and very slowly tuck your feet forward," Aivas instructed.

Jaxom obeyed and was relieved to feel his soles restored to a firm contact with the deck. Engrossed in recovering from his hasty action. he did not at first notice the alteration in the light on the deck. The motion caught his peripheral vision to the right; he turned his head, remembering to move slowly, and saw the great cargo-bay doors folding slowly inward, wrapping him in more complete safety.

The door lights on the panel turned from red to green, and suddenly the aggravating orange light winked out.

"Operation completed," Jaxom said, wanting to shout in relief.

"That is enough for today. Retrace your steps and return to base."

Later that afternoon, when Robinton, Lytol, and D'ram arrived for a private meeting, Aivas had further interesting disclosures to make.

"Your wandering planet is flagrantly erratic," he told them. "There has been time to study most of the Records presented to this facility. Even the most illegible ones have been deciphered, using available restoration techniques. The Red Star, as it is inaccurately called, has an aberrant course and does *not* cross Pern's path every two hundred and fifty years. The orbit varies by almost ten years in four Passes— three were two hundred fifty-eight, and one was two hundred forty. Thread Passes alter from forty-six years in the Second Pass to fifty-two in the Fifth and forty-eight in the Seventh. The two intervals of four hundred years each appear to suggest that the planet did not, in fact, orbit as far as the Oort Cloud, or was, in some inexplicable fashion, diverted from its usual orbit. The former theory is more acceptable than the latter. Another possibility"—and the resonant tone indicated that this was most unlikely—"is that it passed through attenuated portions of this cometary reservoir. Of more importance, and based on calculations from the *Yokohama*'s bridge, this Pass will be short by three years."

"Now *that* is very good news indeed," D'ram said. "But I don't understand how such inaccuracies could have slipped into the Records."

"That is not at issue," Aivas replied. "Though the method of dating on this planet promotes error."

"Then that would account for the need to position the Eye Rocks, wouldn't it?'' Lytol asked. "Because no matter if dating was faulty, the Weyrs would always know exactly when a Pass was imminent.''

"An ingenious method of ascertaining the correct position of a planet, though by no means original,'' Aivas replied.

"Yes, yes,'' Lytol said hastily. "You told me about Stonehenge and the Triangles of Eridani. Do the inaccuracies have any other importance?''

"That information is still being correlated and updated. Optimistically, it augurs well for the success of the Plan.''

"And we can reassure Holds and Halls on that account?'' Robinton asked, his voice buoyant with hope.

"You can indeed.''

"This briefing, then, is to decide what information can be made public.''

"Yes.''

"What else can we tell them?''

"As much as you know.''

Robinton chuckled. "Which is very little.''

"But significant,'' Aivas replied. "The two expeditions to the *Yokohama* have been extremely successful. You may also report that the next exercise will extend to the four green riders. It is vital for them to make bridge transfers and continue the research that Jaxom and Piemur initiated. Each will have an objective during his time on board.''

"*Why* did Jaxom have to close the cargo-bay doors today? Especially when you said that that area will not be used for some time,'' D'ram asked, curious.

"It is necessary for someone to get practice in working in free-fall and to become accustomed to using the space suit. Jaxom is the most adept computer operator, and Ruth is the most courageous of the dragons.''

Robinton noticed that Lytol perceptibly preened himself on hearing such praise of his ward.

"Does the fact that he is also a Lord Holder and can report on his expedition come into consideration?'' Robinton asked, amused.

"That did figure in the choice; but competence, and being a dragonrider, were more important.''

Robinton chuckled. "So who goes next?''

"Now that Ruth has led the way, the green dragons will feel compelled to follow where the littlest one of them has gone before. They will be sent in pairs: Mirrim and Path, G'rannat and Sulath. They have complementary temperaments and skills."

Robinton chuckled. "You are indeed well versed in manipulating people."

"It is not manipulation, Master Robinton. It is understanding the basic personalities of those who are being trained."

"The cargo area is large enough for bronze dragons to transfer," D'ram suggested.

"Not until there is also sufficient air for them to breathe. They will play a major role in future steps, D'ram," Aivas said. "But the next step will be to reestablish oxygen-producing algae in the hydroponics area to purify the air of the few usable areas on the *Yokohama*. The telescope will have to be adjusted periodically. There is one probe left that may or may not be operational. It could be useful. Failing that, it would be helpful if perhaps a bronze dragon and his rider could venture to obtain samples from the Oort debris."

"What?" The exclamation came in a chorus from all three startled men.

"A sample of pre-Fall Thread was never obtained by the colonists, though several attempts were made. An analysis," Aivas insisted, raising its voice over renewed protests from the three custodians, "would be carried out in the one remaining operational laboratory on the *Yokohama* in the cold-sleep facility. The rewards of a proper scientific analysis of the Thread material far outweigh any risk. From what I have seen of the abilities and intelligence of the bronze dragons and their riders, the risk would be minimal—once, of course, they have the exact directions for such a flight, and when protective gear is available for the rider."

The three regarded the screen with varying degrees of stunned amazement.

"Thread in its nodular form is not dangerous," Aivas continued, as if oblivious to the effect of that statement on the custodians. "It is only when it finds a hospitable environment that it alters. For the purpose of analysis, it can be kept safely contained in one of the sleep capsules. Seven of the most promising biology students are already sufficiently trained to handle such investigations, Lady Sharra being the best of them. Much equipment for the investigation of frozen human and animal tissue is still up there. Even an electron microscope is in place in the cryogenic laboratory—making it an ideal site for our purpose."

Aivas sounded perfectly reasonable, his suggestions as logical and forthright as always, but Robinton instinctively balked at the mere notion of such an undertaking. He didn't dare glance at D'ram, or Lytol.

"To destroy a menace, one must perceive it as a whole and in its separate manifestations," Aivas continued.

"How can we possibly destroy Thread, if what you have told us about this Oort Cloud that surrounds our system is true?" the Harper asked.

"What you have been told is fact."

"Fact is not the only truth," Lytol reminded them all.

"Now, let's not deviate from the subject at hand," Robinton said, eyeing Lytol sternly. The former dragonrider and Aivas could indulge in semantics and philosophy on their own time.

"One alters the facts," Aivas went on as if Lytol had not interrupted. "That is the plan."

"I wish," Robinton said, leaning forward earnestly, "that you would tell us the whole of this plan of yours."

"Master Robinton, to use an analogy, you would not expect a new student to read a score of music perfectly on his first try, would you?" When Robinton agreed, Aivas continued. "Nor would you expect that same student, no matter how talented, to be able to perform to a high level of competence, playing intricate passages, on an unfamiliar instrument, would you?"

"I take the analogy," Robinton said, raising both hands in surrender.

"Then be reassured by the successes already achieved: the lessons learned and understood. Progress toward the high level that must be achieved is being made, but it would be harmful to overwhelm your valiant people before they are properly prepared by education and experience."

"You are right, completely right, Aivas," Robinton agreed, shaking his head at the folly of his impetuous demand.

"How critical to Pern, and to this project, is this Lord Holders Convocation, Master Robinton?" Aivas asked.

Robinton gave a wry smile. "That's the debatable point. But when all the Lord Holders assemble, minor irritations have a habit of flaring up into roaring debates. We—Sebell, Lytol, D'ram, and I—have good reason to believe that Landing, and this project, may be called to question by some of the dissatisfied and conservative elements. We'll be better able to gauge reactions after Sallah Telgar's interment tomorrow."

"Will many attend that ceremony?"

Robinton's grin turned broad and slightly malicious. "Anybody who is anybody on Pern will be there! Master Shonagar has been relentlessly rehearsing apprentices and journeymen; Domick has been killing himself to produce suitable music, including a splendid fanfare of trumpets. Dragons will fill the sky to do her honor." Robinton felt an unexpected closure of his throat at the thought of the tributes arranged for this fabled ancestress. "Perschar, among others, will be on hand to illustrate."

"Such scenes would be an unusual addition to the archives of present-day Pern," Aivas remarked.

"You shall have them, of course," Robinton promised earnestly.

"As well as your individual verbal accounts of the proceedings."

"All of us?" D'ram asked surprised.

"Different perspectives often supply the full dimensions of an event."

B y the next evening, Robinton was not certain if the *full* dimensions of Sallah Telgar's interment would ever be properly recorded. It had been quite a day, and for once he admitted that he was very, very tired.

Larad and his lady had organized a splendid occasion, with master instrumentalists, under the direction of Domick himself, and singers from all over the continent to sing the Ballad of Sallah Telgar. The large Telgar Gather pits had been utilized to feed those who had begun arriving the day before. Most had thoughtfully brought their own rations, but Telgar stinted no one, and anyone of consequence was accommodated in the portions of the great Hold that had not been tenanted since the last plague. Robinton rather thought that every holder in Telgar had been drafted to clean; Lady Jissamy was by no means lax in her duties, even the farthest corner of her domain enduring inspection once every Turn, but the place sparkled and shone as never before.

The interment had been set for midafternoon. Every dragon came laden with as many passengers as it was safe to carry. Toric himself arrived on K'van's Heth; his seldom-seen wife, Ramala, accompanied him. He immediately began to solicit the other Lord Holders for guards to help him with his rebels. From the expression on the big Southerner's face, Robinton surmised that he was meeting with little success. When the Harper had a chance to compare notes with Sebell, it appeared that the Lord Holders, without exception, felt that this was an inappropriate time to recruit a punitive force—which meant that Toric would air that problem at the Conference. That was another debate sure to be heated. Robinton was of two minds about attending: he was no longer obliged to, but the invitation had been made to him, and though he trusted Sebell to report accurately, he preferred to make his own observations whenever possible.

However, all minor rifts and major controversies faded into insignificance as the interment ceremonies commenced. The Ballad was magnificently performed. Then, cued by Ruth and Jaxom, the massed Weyrs appeared in the skies above Telgar. Robinton felt tears well up in his eyes, tears not only in reaction to the honor the massed Weyrs did Sallah Telgar, but in remembrance for the previous occasion, nearly twenty Turns before, when the five Lost Weyrs had reappeared in the Telgar skies to meet Threadfall with Benden's valiant wings. Today, Lessa's Ramoth and Telgar's senior queen dragon Solth carried between them the hammock containing Sallah's coffin. The sun glinted off the gold plate, trim, and handles, giving the impression that Rukbat itself was honoring the gallant woman and causing the throng to gasp in awe. Ranged above the two queens, the Weyrs formed seven sections in a close formation, wingtip to wingtip, that was a feat of wingmanship in itself.

The entire mass followed the two queens down, hovering as Ramoth and Solth delicately placed their burden on the bier, the hammock falling gracefully to either side. An honor escort of Holders stepped forward to bear the coffin the last few lengths to its final resting place.

The massed dragonriders swirled, each keeping its Weyr formation, and came to rest either on Telgar's fireheights or as a border to the assembled. Then Larad stepped forward, his sons behind him, as Aivas had confirmed that they were, indeed, the direct descendants of Sallah Telgar and Tarvi Andiyar.

"Let this be a day of rejoicing that this valiant lady has returned to the world she gave her life to protect. Let her rest now with others of the Blood in the Hold that bears her name and honors her above all its ancestors."

With those simple words, Larad stepped aside, and the coffin was lifted to the shoulders of the escort and carried in measured step toward the tomb. As the coffin was placed inside, the dragons, one and all, lifted their heads to keen. A heart-tearing sound on any oc-

casion, but to Robinton, tears streaming down his face, the notes had
an oddly triumphant ring. As if in response to that, an immense
flurry of wings was heard, and what must have been every fire-lizard
in the North and South, wild and tame, swooped down in a deep,
wide aerial veil just above the heads of the escort, across the still
open tomb, adding their high voices in counterpoint to the dragons'
deeper tones. Then they swept up and, at the top of Telgar's preci-
pice, abruptly disappeared.

Robinton had wondered where Zair had gone to, and only now
realized that those around him who were usually adorned by a fire-
lizard had had empty shoulders from the moment the massed dragon
wings had appeared in the sky.

The escort, somewhat stunned by that final flourish to the solemn
event, stepped back, and the Telgar masons, their Gather-best clothes
protected by new aprons, moved forward to seal the opening.

In respectful silence—for even the youngest had been awed by
dragon and fire-lizard displays—the assembled waited until the tomb
was completely closed and the masons stood aside. Larad and Jissamy moved together to face the tomb and bowed deeply, as did the
escort. The obeisance was repeated by everyone present.

Then Larad, his lady, and the escort stepped back and proceeded
toward the broad court of Telgar Hold. Domick's musicians began to
play a solemn and majestic piece to signal the end of the ceremonies.
They followed behind the last of the crowd dispersing to enjoy the
hospitality of Telgar Hold.

Robinton was looking forward with great anticipation to tasting
one of the roast beasts turning on the great spits, not to mention a
fine vintage of Benden wine that he was certain Larad would provide
him, when he felt a touch on his elbow.

"Robinton!" Jaxom said in a low voice, his eyes sparking with
fury. "They tried to attack Aivas. Come!"

"Tried?" Robinton repeated, shocked. He simply couldn't comprehend what Jaxom had just said.

"Tried!" Jaxom repeated grimly, guiding Robinton by the elbow
toward the edge of those sauntering along toward the court. "Farli
brought just a scribble, so I know no more than that, but I for one
can't stand about *here*."

"Nor I!" Nothing would settle Robinton's pounding heart until he
saw with his own eyes that Aivas had suffered no damage. The very
thought of being deprived of the knowledge they were daily gaining
from the facility was enough to give him another heart attack. He

also decided not to spread the information until he had reassured himself. Shards! He was getting old. Why had he not realized that today would be the perfect time to make a direct attack—when Landing was nearly deserted. Everyone who could come was up here in Telgar.

"Edge over further, Master Robinton. We're almost to Ruth now. We'll just get to Landing and see for ourselves. I don't think anyone should ruin this," Jaxom said, gesturing to indicate the festivities.

"Properly said, Lord Holder." Robinton moved with more alacrity to where Ruth had been edging toward them as inconspicuously as possible. No one would think it odd that Jaxom and the white dragon would offer to save Robinton the walk back to Telgar Hold court. So they mounted and Ruth, swinging upward and over Telgar cliff, abruptly went *between*.

The white dragon came out right above a clearing in front of the Aivas building. As Robinton and Jaxom made their way to the door, those crowding the entrance parted to let them through. Noting their expressions, the Harper was puzzled: anger would have been understandable; amusement was not.

Lytol was on duty that day—someone had to see that the students appeared for their scheduled courses—permitting D'ram and Robinton to attend the Telgar ceremony. He was sitting in his customary seat, but he wore a bandage on his head and his clothing was torn. Jancis and the Landing healer were in attendance, but she grinned reassuringly at the new arrivals.

"Don't worry! His skull's too hard to crack," she said gaily. With an expansive wave, she directed their attention down the corridor to Aivas. "And *he*'s got a few tricks he never bothered to mention."

"Go look," Lytol said with a most uncharacteristic grin of pleased malice.

Robinton was first down the corridor; he stepped two strides in and stopped, causing Jaxom to bump into him. Standing guard were Piemur and six of the sturdiest students, hefty clubs held at the ready. Two of them wore head bandages. On the floor were the unconscious bodies of the attackers, the heavy axes or metal bars with which they had intended to wreak havoc on Aivas piled beyond reach.

"Aivas protects himself," Piemur said with a grin, swinging his club in a circle on its thong.

"What happened?" Robinton demanded.

"We were taking a meal break," Piemur said as Jancis joined him, "when we heard the most awful noise. We rushed back and found

Lytol, Ker, and Miskin knocked down, and then this lot acting as if their brains were on fire. Which, from the residual sound *we* heard, is a fair description.''

''But what—''

''This facility was provided with resources to prevent tampering,'' Aivas said, his voice reaching down the corridor. As matter-of-fact as the tone was, Robinton also sensed a faint note of satisfaction, certainly permissible, he thought, given the circumstances. ''There are sounds that, emitted at volume, can render humans unconscious. When the intruders attacked Lytol, Ker, and Miskin, it seemed advisable to initiate this defensive measure. Regrettably, some permanent aural damage may result, but most should regain consciousness within a few hours. They took more sonics than is—was—normally required in dissuasion.''

''I—we—had no idea you had defenses,'' Robinton said, struggling with both relief and surprise.

''A built-in feature of any Aivas, Master Robinton, though seldom required. These units are programmed with industrially and politically valuable information, which dissidents would find useful. Unauthorized access and/or destructive actions must, therefore, be actively discouraged, and this has always been a minor function of an Aivas facility.''

''Well, I must say, I do feel better knowing that, but why didn't you tell us?''

''The question didn't arise.''

''But you knew there'd been that attempt to ruin your battery power,'' Jaxom began.

''The facility was not in any danger from such crude vandalism. You were quick to provide effective measures against a repeat of such sabotage.''

''But why didn't you do whatever you did today then?'' Jaxom asked.

''Such measures are best invoked during a direct assault, when they are most effective.''

''What exactly did you do?'' Jaxom gestured to the limp bodies.

''Sonic barrage,'' Piemur said, grinning. ''Pure and penetrating sound. Must have hurt.'' He gestured to one man who lay faceup wearing a contorted expression that suggested the pain he had endured before unconsciousness had relieved it. Piemur gave the body a contemptuous push with his toe. ''I don't know where Norist got them.''

"Norist?" Robinton exclaimed.

Piemur shrugged. "Has to be Norist. He's the one who's most vocal about destroying the 'Abomination.' And look . . ." He bent and lifted the limp hand of one of the attackers. "Those look like glass-pipe calluses, and he's certainly got old burn scars on his arms. He's the only one who has them. But once they wake up, we can ask a few questions. And get answers!" Piemur's voice took on a harsh edge.

"Who knows about this?" the Masterharper asked.

"Everyone presently in Landing," Piemur said with a shrug, and then grinned impishly. "Which isn't many, since everyone who could grabbed a dragonride to Telgar. How'd that go?"

"Impressively," Robinton said almost absently as he moved to check the other would-be vandals. "The dragons *and* the fire-lizards accorded her their own tribute."

"Ruth didn't even warn me," Jaxom added with a wry grin.

It was fitting. The dragons were in agreement. The fire-lizards imitated them, but that was fitting, too, Ruth told Jaxom, who told the others.

Robinton didn't recognize a single face among the attackers. Gloomily he wondered if Norist had indeed planned and organized the assault. "Lytol's truly all right?" he asked in a low voice, glancing back toward the front entrance.

"He's got a terrible bump," Jancis said, "and the healer says he cracked a rib, falling on the edge of the desk, but his pride's more injured than his skull. You should have heard him complaining that Ker and Miskin were too slow on their feet to be of any assistance."

"Against eight men armed with axes and bars?" Robinton said, appalled at the possible harm such implements could have done to his friend, much less to Aivas. He found himself swaying a bit on his feet.

Immediately Piemur grabbed him, roaring at Jaxom to take the other side and ordering Jancis to get the healer and some wine, and they helped him into the nearest room and into a chair. Protestingly, he flailed at their hands, but even to his own ears his voice held a quaver of weakness that appalled him.

"It's time to bespeak Lessa and F'lar," Jaxom said, "and I don't bloody care what excuse they give Larad. Ruth!"

As Robinton lifted a hand to object, Jaxom's expression told him that he had already given Ruth the message to forward. Jancis arrived with a huge mug of wine, which Robinton sipped gratefully while the healer fussed at him.

"The Masterharper has taken no harm; his vital signs are restored to acceptable levels," Aivas said. "Do not distress yourself, Master Robinton, for there has been no lasting harm done to humans and none to this facility."

"That is not the point, Aivas," Jaxom said, whirling around. "No harm should have been considered, much less attempted."

"The winds of change create a climate of resistance. That is to be expected."

"By you?" Jaxom asked, irritated by Aivas's imperturbability. Why hadn't they realized how ideal this day was to dissidents like Norist, who would have known that Robinton and D'ram would attend the honors done Sallah Telgar, that anyone who could grab a ride a-dragonback would be gone from Landing?

"And me. Ease up, lad," Lytol said, entering the room just then. "I figured an attempt might be made. That's why I made Ker and Miskin stay back. But I didn't think there'd be so many of 'em. Rushed us, and we'd no chance." He looked keenly at Robinton. "Humpf. You look much the way I feel, Robinton." He lowered himself carefully into the nearest chair. "Master Esselin was with me at the time, but he fainted when that gang barged in. I hadn't thought to arm the students. They were nearby, and fifteen of 'em should have been sufficient deterrent."

Just then two of Esselin's young apprentice archivists came running down the corridor, shouting for Piemur.

"Quietly!" Piemur bellowed, then grimaced in apology.

"Harper, we found their runners, tied up in a copse just off the old sea road," the older lad reported. "Silfar and I rode a pair back after we'd moved 'em from where they was in case someone escaped. Trestan and Rona stayed 'cos Rona has a fire-lizard." His eyes were big in his flushed young face, and he was panting from excitement, as well as exertion. The eyes of the bronze fire-lizard clinging to his shoulder were whirling in violent patterns of red and orange.

"Well done, Deegan," Piemur said. "Have you winded your runners?"

"No, sir, Harper." Deegan's expression became indignant at the thought of injuring a valuable beast. "They're sweet movers. Cost a pouch or two for that sort of runner, sir."

"Send your bronze to reassure Rona and go back and bring in the others. We might find something interesting in their gear."

"All they had in their saddle packs was food, sir," Deegan added apologetically. "I looked, 'cos I thought there might be some clues."

Again Piemur nodded approval. "Off you go, then." He turned grimly to the others. "There're more in on this than Norist and his cranks. How'd expensive runners get south? Who put up the marks to buy eight and send 'em here?"

"Meaning a dissident Masterfisher is also involved?" Jaxom asked.

"That's the one craft that has not benefited very much from Aivas's stored information," Piemur said, frowning.

Robinton shook his head, but it was Lytol who spoke. "Not at all, Piemur. Master Idarolan was exceedingly grateful to Aivas for the detailed charts of depths and currents that Captain Tillek compiled. The overviews from space are truly astounding." Lytol paused in respectful awe, then shrugged. "Of course, there have been alterations in coastlines since then, but the accuracy of the charts makes it all that much easier to update them. Every master has been given copies, and specific area charts are being supplied to every fisherman. What Master Idarolan approves is accepted by every master of his craft."

"True enough," Piemur replied, but added in a sardonic tone, "though I can think of one or two extremely conservative and hidebound Masterfishers, without naming any names, who might sympathize with Norist's discontent. Look at how many people made it to Southern who weren't supposed to."

"A full purse can close many a mouth," Lytol added cynically.

"Let us not make rash assumptions," Robinton said.

"Lessa says it's impossible for either herself or F'lar to come," Jaxom reported at that point. "But F'nor can. The Weyrleaders're both livid and want to know how such an attack could occur."

One of the assault group stirred, moaning.

"We'll find out!" Jaxom and Piemur said simultaneously, and exchanged grimly determined glances.

"Might I suggest we tie these fellows up before they regain their wits?" Robinton asked, eyeing the sizes and comparing them to the slighter frames of the student guards.

"Yes, and we've just the thing to hand." Piemur reached for a coil of thick flex, a savage grin on his face. "C'mon, you lot," he said, turning to the students, "let's truss these sharding dimwits up properly."

Once restraints were in place, each man's clothing was searched, but the exercise proved fruitless. Old scars, thick ears, and broken noses suggested that five of the eight had fought often. Only the one bore marks of the glass-smith craft, but the remaining two were equally rough livers.

"Swacky might know some of 'em," Piemur suggested. "He's been sergeant at arms in enough Holds over the Turns to know a lot of the regulars."

"They'd hardly pick men we'd recognize, now would they?" Robinton said. "But if Swacky could identify any one of them, that might give us a direction for inquiry. Aivas, how long will they remain unconscious?"

Aivas said that the period was variable. "The duller the subject, the more sonic barrage is required. As you see, they survived to the very threshold."

"I don't like that at all," Robinton said explosively.

"However, they would not have passed the threshold," Aivas assured him.

Robinton shuddered and drank down the rest of his wine. "Let's get them out of the hall. Surely we have some secure building to hold them in. It's almost—almost obscene leaving them sprawled in the hallway like this."

"Assistance just arrived," Jaxom said.

They heard the bugling challenge of many dragons—F'nor, T'gellan, Mirrim, and nearly a full wing of Eastern Weyr riders.

"From now on there will be full dragon surveillance for Aivas," F'nor said when he had heard Lytol's concise report.

"Eastern insists on the honor," T'gellan said.

"I just wish it hadn't come to this," Robinton said, shaking his head wearily.

"My dear friend," Lytol said, placing a consoling hand on the Harper's shoulder, "it was bound to happen. You should have taken time to read the histories as I did. You would then have been better prepared for the cultural upheaval which is occurring in every Hold, Hall, and Weyr."

"I had hoped that Aivas would insure a bright future for us all . . ." Robinton began, raising his arms in an expansive gesture before letting them fall limply to his knees.

"That's because you're the eternal optimist," Lytol said with a sad smile.

"That's no bad way to be," Piemur said firmly, shooting Lytol a quelling glare. It pained the young journeyman to see his master so depressed and listless. The warder shrugged and turned away to hide his cynicism.

T'gellan dispatched a rider to bring Swacky from Paradise River Hold in the hope that he might recognize one of the intruders. Jayge, reckoning that he, too, might be of some help since he had seen so much of the Eastern Holds during his trading days, arrived with Swacky.

"Yeah, I recognize this pair," Swacky said, reaching out to turn one lolling head from side to side. "Bitrans, if I remember rightly. Bitrans'll do anything if you give 'em enough marks."

"Any name come to mind, Swacky?" F'nor asked, frowning.

Swacky gave a shrug of his thick shoulders. "No. Bitrans aren't friendly, and I don't think you're going to get much out of this lot. They're too stubborn to give in and too stupid to give up. They do stay bought," he added with grudging respect.

Jayge, kneeling by another man, shook his head. "I know him. I don't know where I know him from. I'll tell you one thing, though— he's worked fishnets. Look at these three-corner tears on his fingers and palms. That's net damage."

Robinton heaved a long sigh, and Lytol looked grimmer than ever.

When the first of them finally regained consciousness late that evening, he stared around with bleak panic in his face; it soon became obvious that he had lost his hearing. To written questions he merely shook his head. Consultations between Aivas and the healer about a return of hearing produced no helpful results.

"As a consequence to the extreme deterrent required to prevent their entry, regrettably permanent damage may have been inflicted," Aivas said.

When the vandals' animals were brought in, none of the gear identified its source. The saddles were new but bore no leatherman's stamp; the runners were not ear-notched or branded and betrayed the nervousness of very green animals.

"Probably stolen from Keroon or Telgar herds before spring culls" was the opinion of Masterherder Briaret, who came the next day to assist in the inquiry. "Whoever chose them knew his runners and picked those that don't show any particular characteristics from sire or dam. They was rough broke," he added, looking into the mouth of one and pointing out biting scars, "never been shod, and came by sea." He indicated the marks on hips, rumps, and shoulders that had been caused by rubbing against the sides of the narrow stalls used to transport animals by ship. "Don't think we'll find out where they was stolen from, but I'll put the word out to my Halls."

The tack, he said, was all apprentice-made, pointing out the flaws that would have made them unsalable at any reputable Tannerhall.

"These could have been picked up from various Halls over the course of a Turn or two, from 'prentices needing Gather marks. I'd say that whoever planned this has planned long and well," the Masterherder stated.

The sturdy but worn clothing was of a style and fabric available all across the continent, and the camping equipment had seen considerable use.

"Could've staked out here for a spell, just waiting for a good opportunity," Briaret guessed. "Like the ceremony at Telgar."

In one saddlebag the searchers found a small collapsible telescope of the sort used by fishermen, but it bore no other mark than the usual Telgar Smith stamp on the metal rim of the eyepiece.

When Master Idarolan was asked his opinion, he was outraged that any of his Craft could have been involved. He promised to investigate, admitting that there were some who were, unfortunately, no credit to their calling and were not above making a clandestine voyage for a full purse of marks after a bad season. He would name no one as yet, but he knew whom to watch, he assured everyone.

Swacky volunteered to stay at Landing as warder of the invaders, hoping that he might yet get one of them to confide in him.

Jayge lingered, too, finally admitting to Piemur and Jancis that he would very much like an interview with Aivas, if that was at all possible.

"No problem, Jayge," Piemur reassured him. He grinned broadly. "Beginning to think all this new technology has some use?"

Jayge gave a wry chuckle. "I need to know if Readis and Alemi are both losing their wits. They swear they've had more conversations with shipfish—dolphins. The dolphins say they came with the original settlers." Jayge set his jaw as if waiting for derision.

"Dolphins did come with the settlers, Jayge," Piemur reassured him. Jancis nodded, as well. Then the young harper's expression turned rueful. "We've been so busy with space that we really still haven't caught up on other important details. C'mon. Everyone else's busy with the intruders right now, so Aivas is free."

"The dolphins are indeed capable of communicating with humans," Aivas told Jayge when he asked. "Mentasynth enhancement is genetically transmitted, so that the ability would have survived through any number of generations. They were the most successful of the mentasynth experiments. It is good to know that the species has survived. Are they numerous? It would appear from the question, Holder Jayge, that contact has not been maintained. Is that so?''

"No, it has not," Jayge admitted apologetically. "Though my wife and myself, as well as my son and Masterfisherman Alemi, owe our lives to them.''

"The species has always been considerate of humankind.''

"And they do speak a language we humans could learn?''

"Since humans taught them the language, yes. But it would be the language of your ancestors, not that which is in current usage. This facility was able to make linguistic adjustments that would not be available to the dolphins, despite their great intelligence.''

"The shipfish have great intelligence?'' Piemur asked in surprise.

"They possess an intelligence measurably equal to, if not surpassing, most human intellects.''

"I find that hard to believe,'' Piemur muttered.

"Believe it,'' Aivas replied. "Holder Jayge, if you are interested in reviving the communications link with dolphins, this facility would be glad to assist you.''

Jayge grimaced. "It's not me, Aivas. I was just here and wanted to know. It's my son, Readis, and our Masterfisherman Alemi, who thought the dolphins were speaking.''

"The resumption of that link could be of great value to fishermen and all who use the seaways. Time can be allotted to that study.''

"I'll tell Alemi. He'll be delighted to hear it.''

"Your son?''

"Oh, Readis is a child.''

"A child has fewer inhibitions in learning new languages, Holder Jayge.''

Jayge's eyes bulged in surprise. "But he's only five!''

"A most receptive age. This facility would take great pleasure in instructing young Readis.''

"I'd really thought you all were embellishing your accounts of that Aivas of yours,'' Jayge said in a low voice to the grinning pair who escorted him out of the room, "but you were harper-true this time.''

"Aivas doesn't need embellishments,'' Piemur assured him smugly.

"You will bring Readis, won't you?'' Jancis asked. "Tell Ara that I'd take very good care of him while he's here.'' She giggled. "I think it's the best thing I've heard yet. Shipfish are smarter than us humans!''

"I think we better keep quiet on that score,'' Piemur said, his expression solemn. "We've got enough trouble as it is. That opinion'd really start a snake hunt. Even with folks who've got a lot of common sense."

"I think it's marvelous," Jancis repeated, grinning in broad malice. "It's perfect. Alemi'll be over the moons."

Jayge looked chagrined. "Ara'll beat him there. She swore blind that the dolphins talked to her when they saved us from drowning."

"Then bring Ara, too," Piemur suggested. "There ought to be more than just two to learn dolphin talk. Say, you know it might be smart to teach more kids than just Readis. Not meaning to detract from him, Jayge, but if, say, we put it about that Aivas was teaching mainly *kids*, no adults would get suspicious. Because I'm serious, people. I don't think we ought to spread this intelligence thing about."

"I agree," Jancis said.

Jayge shrugged. "I'll accept that judgment. And I'll bring Readis, Alemi, and whoever else he thinks we should include. Talking to ship-fish! Wow! That's a real stunner." And he shook his head slowly as his friends escorted him back to where V'line and bronze Clarinath waited to convey him back to Paradise River Hold.

T he day before the Lord Holders Conference, the Benden Weyrlead-ers held a short meeting at Cove Hold to decide whether to bring up the matter of the attempt to disable Aivas.

By then all eight men had recovered from the sonic coma: two would never be of use to anyone; none had recovered their hearing. Three wrote messages asking for relief from unbearable head pains, which finally abated after considerable dosing with fellis juice. Since none of them were willing to divulge any information about those who had hired them to attack Aivas, his guardians had no recourse but to have them all transported to the mines of Crom to work underground with other incorrigibles.

"Why do we have to bring the subject up at all? Let's just let rumor work for us," Master Robinton suggested with a devious smile. "Let them ask us for explanations. That is, if any are required."

"Seeing it my way for a change?" Lytol asked sardonically.

"The rumors are alive and exploding with inventiveness," Jaxom said, grinning at Piemur.

"I'm not sure that's altogether the wisest course," Lessa said, scowl-ing.

"Who has ever controlled rumor?" Robinton demanded.

"You!" Lessa retorted promptly, her scowl disappearing into a wide smile for the person who had so often deliberately spread rumors.

"Not really," Robinton replied smugly. "Not after I sent off the original version."

"Well, then, what's being bruited about right now?" F'lar asked.

"That Aivas perceives the motives of anyone approaching him and has withered the unworthy," Piemur answered eagerly, ticking off the variations of his fingers. "That he horribly maimed some innocent petitioners who had the audacity to approach him early one morning because they overheard him plotting with Lord Jaxom." Jaxom had apparently heard that variation and only snorted. "That we installed a squadron of Gather champions to defend the place and they'll beat up anyone they didn't like the look of; that there is a full wing of dragons constantly on guard and that they are somehow under Aivas's complete control; that fire-lizards are afraid of their lives to come near Landing anymore; that the Aivas has deadly and powerful weapons that can paralyze anyone not totally committed to his intentions for Pern's future. That Aivas has control of all Weyrleaders and Lord Holders—" Piemur had to wait until the indignation of the attending Weyrleaders subsided. "—and was going to take over the running of the planet, and that all too soon the three Dawn Sisters were going to come crashing down on Pern, causing irreparable damage to any Hold or Hall that won't support Aivas. And if the Dawn Sisters lose their position in the sky, all the other stars will go out of control, so that's how Aivas will prevent any further Threadfall, because Pern will be totally destroyed and not even Thread will find it hospitable." Piemur took a deep breath and, his eyes glinting with amusement, asked, "Heard enough?"

"All I care to, certainly," Lessa said with considerable asperity. "Absolute twaddle!"

"Is anyone taking any of it seriously?" F'lar asked, leaning forward.

Lytol sucked in his breath. "Some of that foolishness would account for the extreme tenseness of that delegation from Nerat, that group who applied for advice on how to counteract a blight. Masterfarmer Losacot had to chivvy them to enter the room. I mentioned the fact in my day report."

"Did Aivas notice their reluctance?" Lessa asked.

"I certainly wouldn't ask Aivas a question like that. Totally irrelevant," Lytol said, somewhat surprised and indignant. He gave Lessa a sharp look. "The important point is that they apparently received a positive answer, for they were discussing the ways to implement his advice when they left. Master Losacot stopped to thank me for slotting them in so promptly. I thought the matter quite urgent.''

"I still maintain that the more people who encounter Aivas," Robinton said, "the more support any plan of his will receive.''

"Not always," Lytol disagreed in a low voice.

Then he smiled at the Harper. "But you and I have agreed to differ on that score, haven't we?''

"We have," the Harper replied affably, but there was a sad shadow in his eyes as he gazed on the old warder.

"So, what attitude do we take at the Conference tomorrow?'' Lessa demanded. "Presuming, of course, the Weyrleaders will be allowed into the meeting.''

"Oh, you will be," Jaxom said. "Larad, Groghe, Asgenar, Toronas, and Deckter wouldn't permit exclusion of Benden and High Reaches Weyrleaders!" He grinned. "I think we ought to wait until *they* bring up the subject.''

"Tomorrow's a solemn occasion, Jaxom," Lytol said, favoring his former charge with a stern look.

"Not all of it, and I really can keep countenance when I need to, old friend." Jaxom grinned engagingly at Lytol and ignored Piemur's snort. "Since so many of us should be in attendance, T'gellan and K'van have doubled the dragon guard here.''

"D'ram's in charge," Robinton added. "Insisted, since both Lytol and myself ought to attend the Conference.''

"As if you'd miss it," Lessa replied, her eyebrows raised.

"This one least of all," Robinton remarked affably.

9
▼▼▼▼▼▼▼▼

In the spring of the year, Tillek Hold was at its most attractive, for the vivid blue skies seemed to brighten the Hold's granite cliffs and the sun often glinted off surfaces that were momentarily silver-gilt. From its position on the heights, the uppermost level of the Hold provided north and south views; on clear days, as today, one could see across the promontory to the southern coastline where the terrain fell away from the Hold height. Today banners flew from every window, brilliant panels in audacious colors bright against the gray stone.

Below the Hold, the natural deep harbor and the smaller holds and cots on the terraces that made up the large Tillek settlement were also decorated with banners, streamers, and even garlands of the various yellow blooms of spring. Ranrel's recent labors to improve docking facilities were being put to the test. Many people had elected to sail up the western coast to attend the Conference and the festivities following the confirmation of a new Lord Holder. But so spacious was the anchorage that not even the mass of craft, small and large, strained its capacity.

To Jaxom's surprise, Ruth came out of *between* over the harbor waters, giving him and Sharra an excellent view of the activity below them. It would appear that every small craft that could be paddled or rowed had been drafted to do lighter duty between the visitors' ships and the new wharf. There was even a line of crafts bobbing at each landing stair waiting to discharge passengers, gay in their festival attire.

Then Jaxom appreciated why Ruth had elected to bring them out over the water, for the congestion of dragons above the Hold itself would have taxed even the white dragon's vaunted ability to avoid collision.

"We really should have brought Jarrol and Shawan to this, Jax," Sharra yelled in his ear. "They would have adored all the color and excitement."

Jaxom shrugged; actually he was glad that Sharra had been dissuaded from that notion. The day was going to be full enough without his having to worry about the antics of two active and inventive little boys. And he wanted Sharra at his side without an incumbrance.

"There'll be other investitures, love, when they're old enough to appreciate it more," he shouted over his shoulder.

Ruth descended, moving with more decorum than usual in order to prevent Sharra's heavy formal skirts from billowing out.

"The unexpected perils of dragonriding," Sharra muttered, gathering the fabric in as much as she could while Ruth circled slowly to find a place to land in the crowded forecourt. Then, continuing the conversation that they had broken off to go *between*, she added, "Am I really to go up to the *Yokohama* with you the day after tomorrow?"

"Yes, indeed." Jaxom was pleased by the excitement in her voice. "Aivas says we've got to have the oxygen recycling to spend our time aboard efficiently, even in the few areas we'll be using. Putting breathable atmosphere in the cargo bay and the engine room is going to take a lot of oxygen, and we can't keep lugging tanks up and down. You and Mirrim will do just fine setting it up. You know the programs, and the instructions for starting the algae by heart. I heard you muttering the steps in your sleep." He grinned back at her, thrilled that he would have a chance to share with her the incredible experience of viewing Pern from space and happy for her to have a part in the project that absorbed him almost, he admitted with private candor, to the exclusion of everything else. "Besides, Aivas says the whole program is foolproof but we need the computer-controlled porous-technology $Co_2/0_2$ to supply sufficient oxygen. The system just wants starting and then regular checks. Once you and Mirrim understand the system, you'll teach other green riders. And with Path and Mirrim, and you and Ruth, there'll be proper control on the system. Meanwhile, the greens'll be hauling oxygen in tanks to tide us over until the system's fully operational again."

"Ruth would take anyone you asked him to," she reminded him. She wanted more than anything to be the one to join her mate on the *Yokohama*, but she was also very much aware that the mission could be dangerous. After all, she had two children to think of now, not just herself.

But I like taking you better, Sharra, Ruth put in. *Maynooth says it's my turn in the forecourt, but you're to dismount as quickly as you can,* he added. *Maynooth's rider is terrified of having a collision while he's on duty.* Ruth added a contemptuous snort for that possibility.

Jaxom helped Sharra unclip the riding straps and dismount, careful to keep the full skirts of her brand-new gown from becoming entangled in the harness or getting excessively rumpled. The color was an amazingly vibrant blend of green and blue, and the fabric was cut to a pattern that had been found by Masterweaver Zurg in Aivas's files. Jaxom, stunned anew by her subtle beauty, was torn between pride in his beloved and anxiety that others might monopolize her when the dancing began. With a smile, he helped her shrug out of the equally fetching jacket, its leather dyed a slightly darker shade than her dress, its fur lining too warm to wear in Tillek's sun. Then he offered his lady his arm, leaving Ruth free to find himself a spot on the sun-warmed heights, and the tall, handsome couple made their way across the crowded forecourt to the Hold entrance, smiling and nodding at friends and acquaintances.

Sharra chuckled softly. "I see that everyone who could afford it has been spilling marks into the Weavercraft coffers."

"I thought Master Zurg looked excessively smug when we passed him."

"He should be. Everyone, including that wretched dandy Blesserel, is wearing new clothes, either tailored by or made from fabrics bought from good Master Zurg. Except you." Sharra said that with a sniff of disapproval. "It wouldn't have taken much time to have a new outfit for today."

"Why? I'm not exactly threadbare or colorless," Jaxom replied. He was fond of the deep brown and russet he wore; he thought those colors went well with Sharra's azure. "And these clothes aren't all that old. They were new for our last Gather day."

Sharra sniffed again. "Half a Turn ago. You don't care what you wear so long as it's comfortable. Just look at the variety of style and hue others are wearing."

Jaxom closed his right hand over hers on his arm and gave it a squeeze. "You look grand enough for both of us."

Sharra gave him a droll sideways glance. "If you'd ever taken the time to be fitted for what I wanted you to wear, we'd outshine everyone else, love," She gave a resigned sigh. "As it is, it's just too bad the Craftmasters can't vote on the succession."

"They should, you know," Jaxom replied. "They're as vital to the smooth management of Pern as any Lord Holder."

"Sshhh," Sharra said, though her eyes twinkled at his heresy. "You upset sufficient Lord Holders without suggesting *that* innovation."

"It'll come! It'll come," Jaxom said. "Once the conservative element among the Holders are replaced."

"What if Ranrel doesn't make it? Brand did say that there would be protest over his use of the 'Abomination's' materials."

Jaxom snorted. "With bloody near everyone else wearing them? Besides, Ranrel's the only one of Oterel's issue who's ever worked. And he's improved the Hold's facilities. That has to count heavily in his favor."

"Yes, but he's also a journeyman, which men like Nessel and Corman take as an admission that he himself knows he's not Holder material."

"And Blesserel and Terentel, with their soft hands and steep debts, are? A journeyman's knot in the Fisherman's Craft at least says a man has skill, strength, and endurance. And he's had more of managing *men* than either of that useless pair," Jaxom said.

"Brand mentioned that Blesserel's been actively striving to get support from Corman of Keroon, Sangel, and Begamon—and even went to see Toric."

"Well, if he's promised to help Toric with Denol's island rebels, he'll be working against himself," Jaxom said scornfully.

"I don't know about that, Jax, I really don't," Sharra said, frowning slightly. "My brother's devious, as well as plain contrary at times." Then she smiled as she saw Toronas and his wife heading in their direction.

"Four votes wouldn't be enough anyway," Jaxom murmured with a reassurance he didn't really believe before the young Benden Holders joined them.

Robinton had wanted to arrive early at Tillek, to have a stroll around and get the feel of the assemblage. Somehow or other, Lytol had managed to delay their departure so that T'gellan deposited them only just before the actual Conference was due to start. Lytol secured him an oversized goblet of Benden white and insisted that he be seated on one of the few wall benches on the forecourt "for an overall view." Granted he had that, but he would have preferred to mingle with the crowd and sense the general mood.

"You're fussing over me, Lytol!" Robinton said querulously.

"You'll have enough excitement . . ."

"There are people I wish to speak with down there!"

"You can't alter the outcome of today's proceedings a half hour before they start, Robinton," Lytol replied.

"But you can!" Robinton knew that he was being testy with his old friend, and jealous.

"I will do as common sense dictates, Harper, and when that will be most effective." Lytol caught sight of Blesserel, Oterel's firstborn son, clad in uncharacteristically sober dark colors in a conservatively cut outfit. "As if that garb is going to counteract his years as a gaudy guy!" Lytol muttered contemptuously.

"I don't see Ranrel," Robinton complained.

"To your left, on the third riser, speaking to Sigomal," Lytol said, pointing.

"Well, good for him. He's not afraid to parade his accomplishments," Robinton said after a moment's regard. The youngest of Oterel's eligible sons had dressed in Fishcraft colors and wore his journeyman's knot fastened to his Tillek rank cord. "Ista and High Reaches will appreciate the compliment. And Master Idarolan."

"For all the good it does."

"Now, if only Craftmasters were allowed in on the voting . . ." Robinton said, half to tease Lytol and half in wishful thinking. Lytol merely grunted, a surprising reaction since, in previous times, he had been dead set against such an innovation. Was Jaxom having some effect on his former guardian after all? Robinton wondered.

"Idarolan's a sound man and manages to keep most of a very wayward lot in line—most of the time," Lytol said. "But inlanders would not be swayed by his opinions."

"Sangel of Boll is scarcely an inlander," Robinton protested.

"That doesn't mean he thinks with his wits," Lytol replied. "And it's the undecided Holders that must be swayed one way or another: Sigomal, Nessel, and Deckter."

"Deckter will appreciate Ranrel's harbor reconstruction. He's got a merchant's mind on such matters. Blesserel and Terentel have done nothing to improve Tillek Hold."

"Sigomal will side with Blesserel, if only to recoup the boy's gambling losses. You know the way Bitra always turns: markward."

The Hold bugler appeared at the massive entrance and blew the ten-minute warning. The babble of the crowd briefly abated, then increased with excitement as the fifteen Lord Holders began to make their way toward the steps. Lytol watched for Jaxom, Sharra on his arm, to emerge from the throng and unobtrusively beckoned him over. Jaxom's face lit with a big smile as he saw the Harper beside his former warder.

"My dear Lady Holder, you outshine the day," Robinton said, rising to take Sharra's hand warmly in his. "Has everyone here made Zurg markedly richer today?"

Sharra laughed at his outrageous compliment. Though she was a tall girl, she had to stand on tiptoe to plant a kiss on his cheek. "Even Master Norist," she whispered in his ear, giggling as she indicated with a nod of her head where the Glassmaster could be seen in the crowd, resplendent in red and yellow. "Did anyone have the nerve to tell him how much Zurg's Craft has been enhanced by the 'Abomination's' data?"

Robinton let out a bellow of laughter, beginning to let go of his annoyance with Lytol.

Sharra took an admiring pinch of his gracefully belled deep blue sleeve. "I see you endured the fittings and pinnings, too."

"I was excused them," Robinton said loftily. "Master Zurg has had my measurements all these years and presented me these glad rags as a token of his Hall's appreciation for time well spent with Aivas."

Sharra affected a shocked expression. "And here I thought you were Pern's most honest man."

"Not even Lytol is." Robinton gestured at the former Ruathan Warder's back, for Lytol was just entering Tillek's Great Hall with Jaxom. "But then Lytol, as a former weaver, has always been particular in matters of dress."

"I wish he'd managed to install that particularity in Jaxom." Sharra sniffed. "I'd chosen such a beautiful fabric, one of the new brocades in marvelous dark blue-green, and he never managed a single fitting."

"I fear he fit in other things," Robinton replied, unable to forgo the wordplay.

"Oh, you!" Sharra rolled her eyes dramatically, laughing.

A singularly lovely ripple of laughter, Robinton thought, grinning back at her. Zair, perched on the Harper's shoulder, chirped agreement.

ANNE MCCAFFREY

Just then the Tillek steward pulled shut the great Hold doors with a finality that echoed across the forecourt. The Harper and Sharra were close enough to hear the clang as the lock was spun shut. Conversation was momentarily stilled, and the kitchen doors opened. Drudges streamed out, carrying trays of klah, chilled fruit juices, and finger foods to ease the tedium of awaiting the decision.

The clang signaled the Lord Holders within the Great Hall to take their places at the round table. Before them, their places were set with fine glassware and small pitchers of klah, wine beakers, and bowls of succulent fruits.

The night before, Jaxom had been present at a special meeting— the subject of which had been himself—that included the Benden Weyrleaders, Lytol, Master Robinton, D'ram, and Sebell. He was the youngest Lord Holder, and while he was as capable as any of the much older men, perhaps more so than some, many had not yet forgiven his age.

"Especially," Sebell continued, holding Jaxom's eyes with an apologetic glance, "as you're working so closely with Aivas."

"That figures," Jaxom said with deep contempt. "And just how many of the oldsters refer to Aivas as the Abomination?"

Grinning at the epithet, Sebell winked at him. "The ones you'd expect: Corman, Sangel, Nessel, Sigomal, Begamon."

"Five, huh?" Jaxom replied. "That means no clear mandate for Ranrel, and I'll be stuck all day in Council."

"With little to say," Lytol added grimly.

Jaxom threw up his hands and, jumping from his chair, began to pace the room. "And how much longer do I have to play the idiot before my opinions"—he jabbed a thumb into his chest—"bear any weight?"

"It's what you don't say that will bear weight on this occasion," Lytol replied crisply.

"Lytol!" Robinton said warningly, raising an eyebrow at the old Warder. "His actions speak louder than words."

"Even if they do get me deeper into trouble with those hidebound relics," Jaxom said bitterly. "All right, all right." He spread his hands to pacify the others before he received another lecture. "I *appreciate* the circumstances. I'll content myself with voting as I see fit. I'll be polite when they cast aspersions on Aivas and all we're doing, but by the first Egg, I know more about Hold precedents and procedures than they've forgotten."

Although he had not mentioned that meeting to Sharra, it still rankled—all the more because the climate against Aivas, and himself, was so changeable.

With suitable dignified reserve, Jaxom seated himself between Lord Groghe of Fort and Asgenar of Lemos. He was not of a temperament to hold a grudge or keep a sulk, so he was amused that the known pro-Ranrel group had ranged themselves together in one quadrant of the table. Predictably, the supporters of Blesserel and Terentel had also seated themselves in blocks, though he wasn't sure how many supported which older son.

He nodded pleasantly to those opposite him—Sangel of Boll, Nessel of Crom, Laudey of Igen, Sigomal of Bitra, and Warbret of Ista, the ones reputed to favor Blesserel, the eldest son of Oterel. Begamon of Nerat, Corman of Keroon, and, surprisingly, Toric of Southern were said to prefer Terentel. Toric was probably being perverse, since he didn't know any of Oterel's sons well enough to have made an educated choice. It was enough for Toric that his sister's husband, along with Benden, Nerat, Telgar, and Lemos, was for Ranrel.

Jaxom took a deep breath, determined to be on his best behavior no matter how sorely he was tempted to "explain" matters to some of the old idiots. He picked up the klah pitcher, glancing courteously at Groghe with an offer to pour, which Groghe declined with a brief shake of his head. The portly Lord Holder was pulling at his pursed lips as he looked about the table, though his glance, Jaxom noticed, seemed again and again to veer back to Toric.

Skin bronzed and hair bleached almost blond by the Southern sun, Toric was quite a contrast to the older lords on either side of him. By comparison, Sangel looked more wizened than ever, and Nessel downright desiccated. On Nessel's other side, Laudey of Igen, his face as tanned as Toric's, looked the healthiest of the older group.

"D'you think Toric'll support Ranrel?" Groghe asked, shielding his mouth as he bent toward Jaxom.

Jaxom gave a slight shake of his head and replied with equal discretion. "Toric's been in a perverse state of mind ever since Denol went to the Big Island two Turns back. Then, too, Ranrel used Hamian's material, and Toric's annoyed with his brother and furious with the dragonriders for not assisting him in ousting Denol from the Big Island. So, since I've made no bones about preferring Ranrel *and* I'm a dragonrider, Toric is making his protest public."

Groghe gave a snort. "He's making too much of this Denol affair."

"You tell him, then, Lord Groghe. As I understand the tradition of Holding, he doesn't lose the island no matter who's improving it— it remains incontrovertibly his as part of his Hold grant. No one can usurp his title to it. Especially not someone like Denol."

Groghe swiveled around in his chair to gaze with some astonishment at Jaxom. "Are you sure of that? I mean, about the Holding? That no one can supersede his claim?"

"Of course I am." Jaxom grinned slyly. "That sort of irrevocable grant is mentioned in the settlers' Charter. And, remarkably enough, Pern still operates, and enforces, the rules and restrictions of that Charter, even if half the world doesn't know it. So, once given, a grant can't be rescinded. It can't even be ceded out of the Bloodline of the original grantee. When the last of the Bloodline dies, challenge decides the new Holder."

Groghe smiled grimly at that reminder of how F'lar and Fax had dueled to make Jaxom the heir to Ruatha Hold.

"Toric was awarded those specific Southern lands in compensation for Holding during the Oldtimers' incumbency of Southern Weyr," Jaxom went on. "If you'll remember, the Big Island is within the borders of that grant. No act of Denol's can alter Toric's title to the Island."

"Even if Toric's not put his own holders there?"

Jaxom grinned. "When Denol first came South, he agreed to hold for Toric. He can't disavow that. I'm sure he thought that because others have been granted the right to hold in their own names, he could simply cross the water and claim the Big Island. It doesn't work that way." Jaxom was rather pleased to note the respect in Groghe's eyes as he explained the ramifications. He had always been lucky to have the Fort Holder's good opinion, but he felt that he had reinforced that today. He valued Groghe's approval over that of any of the others, so this conversation was doing much to restore his pride. "Meantime, Denol's been improving the place with every cot and shed he's built, every crop he's planted. In fact," Jaxom said with a slightly wicked grin, "if Toric gave Idarolan the word, Denol's marketable goods could be collected and sold north, and the profit credited to Toric!"

"Well, that would solve that problem, surely."

"Yes, but Toric's not listening, and certainly not reading any messages from Landing," Jaxom said ruefully.

"Hmmm, yes." Groghe pensively fingered his full lower lip.

"Well, he'll listen to me, by the first Egg! Best thing about getting old is that you've got the authority to make people listen to you." He nodded sharply, emphasizing his remark.

Jaxom did not grin, nor did he add that getting older did not always give a person something worth listening to. But Groghe was more open-minded than some of his contemporaries, for which Jaxom was thankful.

"Heard you went upstairs again yesterday," Groghe commented, changing the subject. "What'd you do this time?"

"Closed some doors," Jaxom said with a diffident shrug. He had also spent a long time, Ruth beside him, looking down at the splendor of Pern as seen from space. Not even Piemur, harper-trained as he was, had been able to describe the scene adequately or convey how deeply it had affected him. Nor had Jaxom, though he had tried to tell Sharra something of the grandeur he had seen and the awe he had felt. He kept the vision solidly in one bedazzled corner of his mind. If only more of the Lord Holders would see, he thought, they would stop their petty bickering.

"Closed doors? Was that all?" Groghe asked in surprise.

"There's a lot to be done to set the *Yokohama* to rights. It's dangerous up there," Jaxom replied. That was a slight exaggeration, but Aivas had steadily repeated the fact that space was a hostile environment and humans must learn the necessary cautions to prevent accidents. "When the safety measures do check out, it would be our pleasure, Ruth's and mine, to take you up there."

Groghe, clearly astonished, hemmed and hawed nervously. "We'll see, lad, we'll see," he said finally.

Jaxom merely nodded and asked amiably, "Do you think this will take all morning?"

"Likely to." Groghe gave a snort, then covered his mouth so that only Jaxom would hear his next comment. "Sigomal needs Blesserel to be confirmed or he'll never get his money. That young fellow was gambling on succeeding and having the Hold's mark-coffers at his disposal."

Jaxom had already suspected that Oterel's oldest son was heavily in debt to the Bitran Holder.

"Does Terentel have any support?" Jaxom found it hard to imagine who would back Oterel's middle son. Some people seemed to be born losers: Terentel was such a one.

"Actually," Groghe said, his eyebrows going up in surprise, "I believe Begamon will. Corman, too, but probably only because he dislikes Blesserel and is feeling testy about the amount of interest in the Landing projects. He's still not convinced.''

''No one from Keroon Hold itself is involved, but there're enough from the minor holds so that no one at Landing's worried overmuch about his opposition,'' Jaxom replied. ''Keroon's more agriculturally oriented anyway.''

''And Corman's a stubborn old fool,'' Groghe added, eyeing Jaxom critically.

Jaxom contented himself with a grin. Then Asgenar touched his arm, and he turned to his right.

''Larad says that we have Deckter of Nabol, who of us all appreciates Ranrel's harbor repairs, ourselves, you, and Toronas,'' the Lemos Holder said. ''Which way will Lytol go?''

Jaxom shrugged. ''Where his conscience leads him.''

''Then he'll be for Ranrel,'' Asgenar said smoothly. ''We think Bargen of High Reaches is with us, too.''

''Really? I'd've thought he'd go with the other, ah, older Lord Holders.''

''He was impressed with Aivas, remember. He's got an odd twist of mind and wouldn't hold with Blesserel's profligacy or Terentel's apathy.''

''That gives Ranrel eight votes on the first ballot. Not bad. Maybe it won't take too long after all.''

''How did yesterday go for you?''

''Easy enough,'' Jaxom replied diffidently. ''Just had to close the cargo-bay doors.''

''Doors, huh?'' Then Asgenar leaned closer and spoke for Jaxom's ears alone. ''What was it like, Jaxom, bringing Sallah Telgar back?''

Jaxom felt himself go rigid in surprise. He hadn't thought Asgenar had a penchant for the macabre. ''I've been sent on some odd errands now and then, Asgenar,'' he replied, ''but that was the most unusual.''

''Aivas said she'd've been frozen as she died. Could you see her face? What did she look like?''

''We could see nothing,'' Jaxom lied. Even from Larad, Sallah's descendant, such morbid curiosity would have been unacceptable to him. ''The faceplate of the helmet was clouded.''

Asgenar seemed disappointed. ''I just wondered if she looked anything like we do.''

Jaxom gave a snort. ''Of course she did. All the settlers were humans, just like us. What were you expecting her to be?''

"I don't know—but I—" Asgenar faltered.

Jaxom was exceedingly glad that Lytol took that moment to call the meeting to order. In his position as the retired Lord Warder of Ruatha, Lytol had been chosen as the meeting's arbiter. He was also still entitled to vote, as a mark of respect for his probity and integrity in raising Ruatha's heir to his majority.

"We know why we're here and that the accession to this Hold has been challenged by the legitimate sons of the late Oterel. Proposing themselves, as is their right, are Blesserel, the eldest, Terentel, and Ranrel."

"Get on with it, Lytol," Groghe said, testily flapping his fingers at the man. "Put it to a vote and let's see where we stand."

Lytol regarded Groghe a moment. "There are procedures, and we will adhere to them."

"Thought you'd plunged headlong into all the new ways," Sangel said sarcastically.

Lytol regarded the Boll Holder with narrowed eyes and expressionless face until Sangel stirred restlessly and glanced at Nessel for support. With a slight smile, Nessel turned to his right-hand neighbor, Laudey, and murmured something.

Imperturbably, Lytol continued. "You might be interested to note that the manner in which this Council conducts the business at hand has not changed since it was first instituted twenty-five hundred Turns ago. The Charter was carefully promulgated and every contingency addressed. We will go on as usual."

Warbret of Ista looked surprised and leaned to Laudey to make a comment. Laudey's disapproving expression did not alter.

"If there are no further comments," Lytol said, having scanned the faces around the table, "let us cast the first vote. I do not need to remind anyone at this table that a majority of twelve is required to confirm a candidate. Signify your choice by number: one for Blesserel, two for Terentel, and three for Ranrel."

When he resumed his seat, he picked up the ink pen and, shielding the pad with one hand, made a brief inscription. Folding the sheet, he tore it from its glued backing.

Jaxom noted that everyone at the table was similarly employed and wondered if any of them realized that they were using new products to exercise their traditional franchise.

The votes were passed around to Lytol, who shuffled them as he received them so that the order in which he finally opened them would not indicate the origin. As he read them, he sorted them in three neat piles, one much thicker than the others. Meticulously he counted each pile before annoucing the result.

"For Blesserel, five votes; for Terentel, three; for Ranrel, seven. No clear majority."

Jaxom inhaled a long breath. The voting had gone as he had expected, but even so, seven on the first ballot was a minor triumph for Ranrel. Lytol made a wad of the voting papers and, putting them in the brazier, watched them burn before he again rose to his feet.

"Who will speak for Blesserel, the eldest?" Lytol asked as required.

Jaxom slumped down into the heavy chair, glad of the cushions that gave him a small measure of comfort. He hated this tedious part of the proceedings. The older lords would go on and on, given an opportunity. Then he remembered his covert role.

Ruth, please tell Master Robinton that the vote went seven to Ranrel, five to Blesserel, and three to Terentel, and I'm reasonably sure Toric voted for Terentel. He can't be serious, but he can be a nuisance, Jaxom told his weyrmate.

I told the Harper. He expected this outcome.

We both did, but it's going to be a long day. Are you comfortable in the sun?

I am! It is a fine day.

For you!

There will be time for feasting and dancing later. Now you must be Lord Holder.

Hastily Jaxom turned his inadvertent chuckle into a cough and reached for his cup, displaying an innocent expression when frowns were directed at him. He nodded apologetically at Sangel for interrupting his measured remarks supporting Blesserel's claim. Then Begamon rose and, with a series of rather disjointed comments, tried to sway votes in favor of Terentel. Privately Jaxom thought anyone else would have done better for Terentel than the Nerat Holder.

With the second vote, Terentel lost two supporters to Blesserel. The eldest son acquired seven votes, while Ranrel received eight. As before, Lytol burned the papers. Too close, and Jaxom tried to control the nervous jiggling of his leg.

Groghe signaled that he wished to speak, and Lytol consented.

"I'm not the oldest of you, but I have held Fort for longer than any of you others, bar Sangel." Groghe accorded the Boll Holder a bow and a smile. "Tillek was the third Hold to be established—"

"Word of the Abomination?" Sangel asked slyly.

"Aivas has now seen, and restored, the Records of every Hold, which can scarcely be called an abominable duty—boring, probably, if your ancestors inscribed as much trivia as mine did—"

"What's your point, Groghe?" Laudey asked testily.

"My point is that James Tillek, who founded this Hold, was a forward-looking man who charted the coastline and started the first Fishercrafthall. Tillek has always been the safest harbor on the western coast, with the biggest fleet and more Masters sailing 'em; its Lord Holders have always encouraged and assisted our fishermen. Ranrel thought enough of his heritage to take a Master's knot from the Fishercrafthall—"

"He did that because Oterel threw him out of Hold," Sangel retaliated.

"Order!" Lytol's voice boomed out with unaccustomed force, and Sangel subsided.

"Be that as it may," Lord Groghe continued, "he's certainly the only one of Oterel's sons who's ever done a day's hard work. I think he deserves to Hold now. Fort'll support him as Tillek's Holder in every way it can, so we will!"

Murmurs of "well said" caused Groghe to flush with pleasure as he seated himself.

Larad then asked to speak and did so concisely, adding that in his last months Oterel had been too ill to attend to many matters, and that the only one of his sons to take an interest in Hold management had been Ranrel. If Blesserel, however, or Terentel had done anything to take Hold in their father's name, he would like to hear of it.

"Clever point," Jaxom murmured to Asgenar.

Sigomal asked to be recognized.

"Blesserel had the onerous task of caring for his ailing father," he said, "and was scrupulous in all duties to ease Oterel in his last illness. He is a man of integrity . . ."

"He paid his gambling debts," Asgenar whispered to Jaxom, "when he could squeeze the marks out of Oterel's purse."

". . . with four fine strong sons and a fine woman to be his Lady Holder . . ."

"Ranrel's wife is not only a Masterweaver but considerably easier to get on with than Lady Esrella," Asgenar added quietly.

"Put in your mark's worth, Asgenar," Jaxom said.

"Why don't you speak?"

"And ruin Ranrel's chances altogether?" Jaxom tried to sound as if he didn't mind.

Asgenar inclined his head, accepting what Jaxom had implied: that as the youngest of the Lord Holders, his opinion was not much sought by others.

Meanwhile Sigomal wound up his peroration and sat down, glaring at Jaxom, who turned his head to regard Asgenar as the Lemos lord stood to speak for Ranrel.

"When a man does not wait for honors to be given him but works with his hands and achieves a mastery in a Hall, he has learned many of the skills needed to make a prudent and resourceful Holder under whose guidance Tillek will prosper. We can ask for no better-qualified a man than Ranrel. On all counts."

"I'd heard," Toric began, standing without Lytol's permission, "that Ranrel had quarreled with Oterel and was told never to show himself in Tillek Hold again. Can a father's express wishes be so totally disregarded by this Council?"

Bargen jumped to his feet, glancing belatedly at Lytol for permission.

"In my presence, Oterel retracted that statement two sevendays before he expired," he announced after Lytol nodded to him. "Ranrel is the only one of the legitimate male heirs who has achieved merit on his own cognizance. At the last, Oterel was proud of the boy, which is why Ranrel has my complete support."

"But he did not name him successor?" Toric continued, an enigmatic half smile on his face.

"Do you doubt *my* word?" Bargen demanded, scowling at the Southern Holder.

"Doubt doesn't enter into it, Bargen. The incident is recorded fact."

"Which is why the succession has been challenged," Lytol said. "And the right of any male descendant to challenge the succession, no matter what bad feeling existed between father and son, has been upheld on numerous occasions."

Groghe leaned across the table toward Toric and spoke in the blandest possible tone. "I'm sure Lord Toric appreciates that fathers and sons may agree to disagree."

Toric stared at the Fort Holder hard enough, Jaxom thought, for his gaze to burn holes through the man. Groghe shrugged. How had Groghe known that Toric had stormed out of his family's fishhold in Ista? That wasn't generally known, nor would Sharra have been so disloyal to her brother as to mention it.

"But it is as Lord Toric has said," Sigomal said, rubbing his hands together nervously, his expression one of specious regret. "Oterel disavowed Ranrel, and that should be noted. His challenge should be nullified."

"Blesserel must owe Sigomal a great deal," Asgenar murmured to Jaxom, his expression bland.

"Does anyone support Terentel's claim?" Lytol asked into the pause. When Begamon did not respond, he added, "Then let us vote between the two remaining candidates: Blesserel and Ranrel."

This ballot raised Ranrel's support to ten, but with Blesserel still polling five, the requisite majority had still not been attained.

"I am calling a brief adjournment, my Lord Holders, for private discussions," Lytol said and, rising, moved away from the table.

The others followed his example.

"We need two more votes," Groghe murmured to Jaxom, Asgenar, and Larad as they made their way to the tables where food was available.

"Toric has to have been the third vote for Terentel. I know Corman and Begamon espouse him," Larad said. "Is Toric hoping that loon Terentel will give him guards for that armed assault he wants to make on the Big Island?"

"Something like that, but I've a word for his ear alone," Groghe said, winking at Jaxom and grinning broadly.

"C'mon, Asgenar." Larad hauled the Lemos Holder after him. "We'll bear you out, Groghe."

Jaxom made a plateful of the spice cakes he knew Lytol liked and served his old guardian, all the while surreptitiously watching the three in close conversation with Toric. He looked quickly away when Toric suddenly swiveled in his direction, an indecipherable stare on his broad, tanned face. Jaxom wondered if Groghe had identified the source of his information. Toric then asked Larad a sharp question. Groghe responded, and Larad added a few words, while Asgenar nodded, one corner of his mouth slightly upraised.

"I think we just obtained one more vote for Ranrel," Jaxom murmured to Lytol, being careful to keep his face blank.

Larad and Asgenar stayed talking to Toric while Groghe made his way back to the Ruathans.

"That seemed to go down with no trouble, Jaxom. Clever of you. Though I don't think Denol should attempt to have a meeting with Toric when he finds out he can't make any profit for himself. Who else can we approach?"

"I'm not approaching anyone, remember? I'm deeply involved

with the Abomination," Jaxom said with a disgusted snort. "I'm not about to ruin Ranrel's chances by speaking up."

"You do yourself a disservice, lad," Groghe said kindly.

"I'd rather not do Ranrel one, Lord Groghe."

As Groghe turned away, Jaxom took the opportunity to inform Ruth of what was happening, asking him to tell Sharra.

Master Robinton thought it would go that way, Ruth replied. *He asked have you told Toric? He didn't say what.*

Groghe did, with Larad and Asgenar backing him up, Jaxom replied. *Certainly it's giving Toric something to think about. More'n I could get him to do. There's a recess on right now. The west coast contingent needs more klah to wake up enough to listen. I'll keep you all informed.*

Shortly thereafter, Lytol called the Lord Holders to order again and asked if anyone wished to add anything or supply new information to the Council.

"Another vote, Lytol," Deckter said. "There is other business to be discussed."

Jaxom had noticed Deckter in deep discussion with Warbret and hoped for success in that area. Two votes were all that was needed— unless Toric decided to be more difficult than usual.

This time everyone appeared to be counting as Lytol sorted, so all knew before the formal announcement that Ranrel had won. Sigomal looked ready to spit nails, glowering at Toric and Warbret, who had abandoned his cause.

"Ranrel has polled the requisite majority of twelve votes and is duly elected to succeed to his father's honor as Lord Holder of Tillek." Lytol gave Jaxom a warning sideways glance that the young Ruathan had no trouble understanding: He was not to make any premature announcement through Ruth.

"There are two other important reports to discuss in this Council. I now call upon Lord Jaxom of Ruatha Hold to inform us of any progress made toward the end of destroying Thread." Lytol inclined his head courteously to his former ward and sat down.

Jaxom stood abruptly, catching the attention of the entire table. The phrases he had rehearsed so often piled out of his mouth and continued even when he heard someone mumbling imprecations about the "Abomination's corruptions."

"Having received extensive training from the Aivas, Journeyman Harper Piemur and myself rode Ruth safely *between* and landed on the bridge of the *Yokohama*. We completed the programming of the telescope for use by Aivas from the Landing facility and initiated a damage report on the space vessel. We retrieved the remains of Sallah Telgar, which have since been suitably interred at Telgar Hold." He bowed deeply to Larad. "The next day Ruth transported me back to the bridge. I then proceeded to the cargo-bay area to close the outer doors, which had not shut due to a malfunction in the remote-closure program. Once the doors closed, I returned to the bridge and from there to Landing. Additional journeys to the *Yokohama* will be necessitated to improve the basic life-support systems, namely to replant the algae tanks. Additional personnel must become acclimated to free-fall conditions, and there will be several missions composed of different teams, using green dragons, in order to alter the telescope to maximize its use."

"And just what does that all mean when translated into normal speech?" Corman demanded.

"That the *Yokohama* can be used as a base from which to attack Thread in space, Lord Corman."

"So all the dragons are going up to the spaceship and attack Thread at a distance from the planet?" His sarcastic remark must have seemed as silly to himself as it did to the others, for he flushed and looked away from Jaxom.

"No, that is not the plan, Lord Corman. The plan is to divert Thread from ever falling to the surface."

"And how far are you toward that desired end?" Laudey asked, not quite as contemptuous as Corman had been.

"There are still two Turns, five months, and seven days before that end is achieved, Lord Laudey."

"And I suppose that you're here to ask our permission to draft more journeymen from our halls, more drudges from our holds?"

"No, sir, we don't 'draft' anyone," Jaxom replied. He couldn't help grinning—the problem was turning unsuitable people away from Landing without giving offense.

"And I suppose you're unhappy that those lower caverns of yours are pretty much empty of beggars and layabouts?" Groghe asked pointedly.

"And will they all stay usefully employed two Turns, five months, and however many days from now?" Laudey demanded.

"Do you, or do you not, wish to be rid of Thread, Lord Laudey? Lord Corman?" Jaxom demanded. "Admittedly, in two hundred and fifty Turns, *you* won't have to care whether or not we succeed. But your descendants will!"

"Are you speaking as a Lord Holder or a dragonrider, Jaxom?" Nessel asked snidely.

"Both, Lord Nessel!"

"Then we won't need dragonriders anymore!" Sigomal roared. "What're you dragonriders going to do then?"

Jaxom grinned back. "I think you will find, Lord Sigomal, that you will always *want* to have dragonriders on Pern."

"And how do you arrive at that?" Sigomal demanded.

"They do a lot more for you, and everyone here, than rid the skies of Thread. Think on it, Lord Sigomal." Jaxom smiled enigmatically. Let them cudgel their brains over that one. "Lord Toric knows what I mean, I'm sure."

Startled, Toric swung his piercing gaze to his sister's husband and began to frown.

"I don't get what you mean, young man," Sangel said in some agitation.

"My Lord Sangel, I would have thought that was too obvious to require explanation. May I continue, Lord Lytol?" When he had received the nod, Jaxom went on. "I will also tell you that Harper Piemur and I have seen this lovely world of ours, turning in space, from day toward night. It is the most incredible sight!" He knew his voice trembled slightly, but he was not ashamed. "Once we are certain that the life-support systems—oxygen and heat—are stable, I will take it upon Ruth and myself to bring any Lord Holder who wishes to the bridge of the *Yokohama* to see for himself what a splendid world we live on and how essential it is for us to rid ourselves of Thread forever."

Jaxom looked around, inviting someone to take up his offer. When his first round of the startled faces produced no other responses than nervous throat clearings and foot shiftings, he fixed his audience with a look that dared them to volunteer.

"I'd like to go," Larad said quietly, and Asgenar held up his hand, as well.

"And I," Lytol added.

"One doesn't see too much of the north from the *Yokohama*'s bridge," Jaxom admitted, "but Aivas is hoping to repair the damaged port-side viewers. That should make some of the east coast visible from space." He looked pointedly at Toronas who, after visible hesitation, raised his hand.

"How much of the Southern Continent is visible?" Toric asked in a hoarse bark.

"More, if we can repair the stern viewers," Jaxom replied, delighted that Toric had responded.

"I don't see what good'll come from all this," Begamon began querulously. "Risking lives on foolish sundreams of destroying Thread. It's been with us for hundreds of Turns. And I say again, if the ancients knew so much, why didn't they get rid of the stuff in *their* time? Huh? Why didn't they?"

"Aivas has answered that to my satisfaction," Lytol said firmly. "And don't forget that every task we have undertaken since his discovery has benefited everyone on this planet."

"How? Tell me, how?" Begamon demanded.

Lytol held up the pad, the ink pen, and a sheet of the weather reports that Aivas had been producing for the past two Turns to the delight and relief of holders, major and minor. Then he pointed to the ornate clock on the wall, ticking away the minutes of the meeting, and to the new clothing in which Begamon was dressed, made from one of Master Zurg's latest fine fabrics.

"I also heard that you've new power to irrigate your fields and portable stoves to heat your orchards during frosts," Lytol replied. "Not to mention the fact that your youngest granddaughter owes her life to Master Oldive's new surgical techniques."

"They're things we can use, see, touch, Lytol." Begamon waved his hand over his head. "Not something beyond our reach and our ken."

"Then let the things you can use, see, and touch reassure you that there is more to be learned, more to be explored, more to be understood to improve our lives, to insure our lives," Jaxom said, speaking so earnestly that even the oldest, most hidebound Holders listened with something akin to respect for his sudden authority.

"Thank you for your report, Lord Jaxom," Lytol said, smoothly breaking the long pause. "Let us now address the subject of—" At the murmur of disagreement, he held up his hand. "You will all have plenty of time to speak to Lord Jaxom after the business of this Council is over. The second matter to be brought to your attention is a notification from the Mastercraftsmen of Pern."

"Not *all* the Mastercraftsmen," Corman said, jutting his chin out belligerently.

Lytol neither glared nor stared, but his look succeeded in making Corman feel abashed at having interrupted so rudely. "The Mastercraftsmen of Pern, with one exception, that of Master Norist of the Glass-smithcraft, notify this Council of their intention to form two new Halls: Printer Hall, to be loosely allied with the Harper Hall but independent and autonomous, with three main crafthalls: the main Hall to be at Landing, with additional installations at Ruatha, which currently harbors no Crafthall, and at Lemos, in conjunction with the paper industry of Masterwoodsmith Bendarek. The second new Hall is to be Technicians Hall, loosely allied with the Smithcrafthall, to deal with problems arising from the new equipment—"

"I'll say no to that one immediately," Sigomal said, jumping to his feet. "That's catering to the Abomination and—"

"There will be no vulgar epithets at this table, Lord Sigomal," Lytol said at his most censorious. "Nor should I have to repeat that the Mastercraftsmen have no need of your permission. You have only to abstain from the purchase of any materials produced by a Crafthall which distresses you. Since it comes to my notice that certain projects of yours have benefited from new gadgetry of which only Aivas could be the source, you would be wiser to refrain from uttering such arrant hypocrisies in the Council."

Gaping, Sigomal sank back.

Jaxom managed not to smile at the Bitran Lord Holder's discomfiture. One of the men who had tried to attack Aivas had been a Bitran, but that was scarcely proof that the Lord Holder had been connected with the attack. Bitrans hired out to anyone who would pay them enough to make the job worth their while. Still, this was the first time Sigomal had publicly labeled Aivas an abomination.

"We will be duly informed when the new Mastercraftsmen are chosen and the parameters of their professional spheres decided. Let me further remind the Lord Holders that such additions to the Crafthalls require no ratification by this Council since the Halls have, by long custom, been autonomous. This is a formal notification of intent."

"Is that in the original Charter, too, Lytol?" Sangel asked nastily.

"No," Lytol replied, not the least bit perturbed. "The Crafthall scheme was originated shortly before the end of the First Pass by Fort, Ruatha, and Benden Holds to preserve skills and educate young men and women in the various urgently needed crafts. Originally," Lytol added, smiling slightly as he glanced toward Corman, "Ruatha Hold played host to the Masterbeastman and Masterfarmer until the wide plains of Keroon were explored and found more suitable to animal husbandry."

Larad rose to address the Council. "It is also worth noting that both Mastersmith Fandarel and Masterharper Sebell are completely within their rights to propose additional, separate Halls without even consulting other Mastercraftsmen. But they have done so and received full support—"

"It isn't full if one Mastercraftsman abstains!" Nessel took up the complaint in his peevish whine of a voice.

"Master Norist did not attend the meeting, though he was duly notified," Larad said. "Both the Printer and Technicians Halls will supply the special training now required and unavailable elsewhere. We have all benefited by the new machineries, especially clearly printed instruction books and records. For more people to enjoy these benefits, additional craftsmen must be trained in the skills."

"Why can't the printers work under Master Sebell and the repairers under Master Fandarel?" Corman demanded. "Why all this fuss to create new crafthalls?"

"Master Fandarel is working all the hours of the day already, filling orders for new equipment," Larad said. "He does not have the time, or the personnel, to oversee a new Craft."

"Well, this printing could be handled by your Masterwoodsmith, Asgenar," Corman replied. "He's not overworked."

Asgenar laughed. "He is, I am, and we still can't keep up with the demand from every single Hall and Hold for paper in the sizes, qualities, and styles you all seem to feel you must have." He shook his head. "Master Bendarek has a hall full of apprentices, only two journeymen, and no other master yet. He needs every pair of hands he can employ, but he can't oversee the printing, as well. Papermaking takes all his time and energy."

"Master Fandarel wished me to explain that specialist technicians will be required to keep all the new machinery operating at peak efficiency," Larad continued. "Right now we have machinery only a few people can understand or repair, while others are able to operate but not repair them. Eventually, we'll have men and women who can do both, but not right now."

"Then why don't you walk before you start running?" Corman demanded with a snort. "In my experience you can't race a yearling runner or force an immature herdbeast to breed or lactate."

Jaxom started to rise but felt Groghe lay a warning hand on his arm. It took a great deal of self-control for Jaxom to obey that tacit command. He fervently wished that he could speak for himself but grimly recognized that the older Lord Holders were not going to accept him as a peer. When he really had helped destroy Thread, would they consider him an equal then? Or would he still be classed as Holder by default?

"Machines *are* slightly different, Corman," Groghe replied, grinning patronizingly at the Keroon Lord Holder. "Once a machine is built, it does what it was designed to do. When it breaks down, you replace the worn part. You can't do that with livestock."

"No, damaged livestock can be slaughtered and eaten. Whaddya do with worn-out machinery? First thing you know we'll have piles of rusting scrap in every Hold and Hall. And probably the Weyrs, too, since this is all their fault."

"Lord Corman!" Trembling with outrage, Jaxom wrenched his arm from Groghe's grip and sprang to his feet, his fists clenched. "You may not disparage the Weyrs in my presence!"

He was only barely aware that Lord Groghe has risen beside him and clamped both hands on his left arm, while Asgenar, also on his feet, was restraining him on the other side. Larad was loud in his protest, as were Toronas, Deckter, Warbret, Bargen, and, to Jaxom's immense surprise, Toric.

"Lord Corman, you will immediately apologize to this Council for that remark!" Lytol roared.

With ten Lord Holders on their feet in protest, Corman had no option but to apologize. When he mumbled a phrase, Lytol icily demanded that he speak loud enough to be heard. Then Lytol stared at each of the standing Lord Holders until they sank back into their chairs.

"If we are to eliminate the menace of Thread, it will be necessary to have the equipment—equipment we are able to manufacture, operate, and service—with which to achieve that elimination. That has already been the ambition of every Weyr since Fort was first established. It is the end to which every Hold and Hall has worked. If to destroy Thread completely causes some reevaluation of ways and means, a displacement of useless or archaic traditions, the price is not too high for the reward of Thread-free skies." Lytol paused a moment, as if surprised by the vehemence of his own rhetoric. "There will be no mention of this incident when the Council is adjourned.

"Now," he continued briskly, "let us show some unanimity of purpose and encourage the two new Halls. How say you, Lords? Write 'yea' or 'nay.' "

Corman sat hunched in on himself, glowering, and his was probably the one blank sheet turned in to Lytol. There were two boldly printed "nays," but the "yeas" signified the approval that would be passed on to the two Mastercraftsmen involved.

"Who decides who're to be Craftmasters and pay for the establishment of these Halls?" Nessel asked.

"Craftsmasters have not yet been chosen, but there are suitable candidates. Empty buildings at Landing have already been altered for both new Crafts," Lytol went on, consulting his notes, "and the additional Halls will be built by those seeking to apprentice themselves to the new Crafts. Anyone wishing to transfer to either the Printer Hall or the Technicians Hall will need the permission of their Mastercraftsman and the Master of their present Hall."

"What about those working without their Mastercraftsman's permission?" Sangel asked disparagingly. Everyone knew he meant Morilton.

"That is an internal Craft matter," Lytol said, "and will be resolved by the parties involved, not by this Council."

"But what if we can't get glass—"

"There's no shortage of glass," Groghe said, curtly. "We buy what we choose from whom we choose. Simple as that! And there's many of us who patronize one Hall in preference to another. Always have, always will. It's only sensible, human nature being what it is."

Master Robinton wants to know what's delaying the announcement, Ruth said to Jaxom.

Talk. The choice has been made, but Lytol'll peel me if I usurp his prerogative. Just hearing Ruth's voice helped to soothe Jaxom, who was seething at the subtle, and not so subtle, currents. At least he now knew which Holders to watch: Corman, Nessel, Sangel, and Begamon. Corman was blunt enough to speak his mind, but the others had been nursing their resentment and grievances, and that wasn't healthy. Did their intransigence stem more from fear of Aivas, or from a stubborn intractable resistance to change?

"Is there any other business before the Council?" Lytol asked as procedure dictated.

"I have a question," Toric said, rising.

"Yes, Lord Toric?"

"Who is to be Lord Holder of Landing?"

For once even Lytol lost his composure and gawked at the Southern Holder.

Toric gave a faint smile of satisfaction. "Certainly a place as important as Landing cannot be left without proper supervision." He sounded eminently reasonable, but Jaxom almost guffawed at the shock registered on the faces of the other Holders. The expressions were even more indicative of which Lord Holders felt Landing was important; Jaxom noted those who did not, confirming his guesses: Sangel, Nessel, Sigomal, Corman, Begamon, and Laudey, though the Igen Holder seemed more diffident than antagonistic.

"You've not been keeping up with such minor details in the east," Jaxom heard himself saying in an amused drawl. "Lord Warder Lytol, Masterharper Robinton, and D'ram, Tiroth's rider, jointly administer Landing and equably represent the interests of Hold, Hall, and Weyr. The shared authority works well. You have always been welcome at Landing, Lord Toric."

"The moment the discovery of the Aivas was made," Lytol said, firmly taking charge, "a meeting was called on the site. The eight Lord Holders, eight Craftmasters, and seven Weyrleaders unanimously decided that, in view of its historical significance and its current educational status, Landing would remain an uncontested area."

Corman growled irritably to Nessel, but when Lytol gestured for him to speak up, he morosely subsided.

"How much of an area?" Toric all but pounced on Lytol with the question.

Lytol regarded him in subtle rebuke before answering. "The same area that was encompassed by the Landing site on the settlers' maps, of course."

Toric flicked a grimace at Lytol and sat down, his enigmatic stare checking the expressions of the others at the round table. Jaxom, scrutinizing him under cover of a hand on his brow, could not guess what thoughts might be going through the Southerner's covetous mind. Surely the man knew that further territorial acquisitions would be met with resistance from Hall, Hold, and Weyr—especially the Weyrs. Jaxom began to regret that he had given Toric a solution to the problem of the Big Island: *that* problem had kept the man from looking eastward for over two full Turns. Jaxom sighed. Sometimes one solved a problem only to create a half-dozen more.

He was considerably relieved when, with no more ado, Lytol called the Council meeting adjourned. There were protests and reproaches from certain quarters, but Lytol chose to ignore them, as was his right. However much Jaxom would have liked to storm out of the Great Hall, first he had to endure one more ceremony.

We're adjourned, he told Ruth.

Lytol led the procession, Jaxom deftly inserting himself between Larad and Asgenar and ahead of the Fort Holder. He grinned an apology at Groghe. Lytol gave the traditional three pounds of his fist on the door, which was opened immediately by the Tillek Hold head Steward. Privately Jaxom decided that all Stewards shared some arcane instinct that allowed them to sense the ending of a meeting. Lytol nodded, and the men at either side of the great doors wrestled to turn the metal lockwheel and hauled the halves apart. The bright sunlight was almost as dazzling as the finery on the people crowding the steps. Foremost of those were the three contenders: Blesserel, commanding a position in the exact center and looking far too smug; Terentel, standing a length to his left and wearing an almost imbecilic expression; and Ranrel, standing quietly at the far right. Behind him stood Master Robinton, Sharra, Sebell, Menolly, and the Benden Weyrleaders.

Jaxom lifted his lips in the merest of smiles and saw the relief on their faces even as Lytol began his formal annoucement.

"On the third vote, a majority of twelve was achieved," he said when the crowd's babble had died sufficiently for his voice to be audible. "The Council has elected a new Lord Holder. Lord Ranrel, may I be the first to offer my congratulations on your succession to the honor."

While jubilant cheers echoed off Tillek's granite walls, Ranrel looked genuinely stunned and none too sure he believed what he had heard. Blesserel looked murderous, and Terentel merely shrugged and, turning on his heel, pushed his way through the crowd to the nearest wine keg. From the fireheights, the dragons bugled their congratulations, and the air overhead was made hazardous by fire-lizards, zipping and darting and singing their high descants to dragon sound.

Lord Ranrel was immediately surrounded by well-wishers thumping his back, pumping his arms, and shouting congratulations. Blesserel was surrounded, too, by Sigomal, Sangel, Nessel, and Begamon. Jaxom didn't bother to check Blesserel's reactions. Sigomal's face was frozen with displeasure and a cunning that boded no good for anyone crossing him that day.

"Was it very bad?" Sharra asked as she embraced Jaxom. "Ruth said you were angry and upset, but he didn't know why."

"I was and I am. Give me your cup," he said, needing a steadying draught. "Let's get to Sebell and Master Robinton. There're things they should hear, as well. Your brother wanted to know who'd be made Lord Holder of Landing."

Sharra rolled her eyes in dismay. "He'll never learn, will he? So what was he told?"

"The truth," Jaxom replied. "You'll remember we asked Breide to be sure Toric knew Aivas was an important discovery."

Sharra wrinkled her nose, a mannerism Jaxom still found engaging. "He was so livid over Denol occupying his island that he could think of nothing else." Then she cast a sharp look at her husband. "You told him about the irrevocable grant?"

"I didn't. Groghe did. We needed his vote cast for Ranrel."

"He wasn't voting for Blesserel, was he?" Sharra was aghast.

Jaxom gave her a flash of a grin. "What happens in Council is not to become public knowledge!"

"Since when is your wife public?"

They made their way through the crowd and on to the quiet corner where Robinton and the others were waiting.

"My harpers, too, report resentment from those Holders, Jaxom," Sebell said when Jaxom had finished summarizing the proceedings. "I told Master Robinton and Lytol as much earlier today. And I've every apprentice with any wit whatever keeping his or her ears open here today."

"It's almost a relief to have the dissenters identified," Master Robinton said.

"Is it?" Jaxom asked skeptically. The retelling had depressed him. They had so much to hope for in the future—if only they could get over the pitfalls and trivial mechinations of the present.

Sensing his mood, Sharra leaned against her tall husband, and he allowed himself to be comforted. After all, they had voted Ranrel in despite the opposition. The dissenters were few in number, and all of them old.

10

M aster Idarolan became legless before anyone else on Lord Ranrel's celebratory day. He rarely imbibed, but having stood to lose the most if Ranrel was not elected, he had been under great stress and evidently had started drinking at his Hall over breakfast and continued all through the long morning until the result of the convocation was announced. Since the Masterfisher was also extremely popular, his uncharacteristic inebriety was kindly ignored. When he lurched over to the courtyard corner where Jaxom, Sharra, Robinton, Sebell, Menolly, and Tagetarl were seated, his gaiety was a welcome change from their gloomy conversation.

"There was no way," Idarolan announced in drunken joviality, "that we fisherfolk would have been happy to keep our Hall here with Blesserel Holding. He'd mortgage us mast, spar, hull, and anchor when we wasn't looking!" His exuberance was so infectious that Jaxom was not the only one to grin at his antics. "I'd've moved me, Hall, Master, journeyman, and apprentice, down to that fine harbor the old maps call Monaco. Yessur, that's what I'd've done had anyone but Ranrel become Holder."

"But Ranrel is Lord Holder, so you don't need to worry now," Robinton assured the Masterfisher. The Harper gestured for Sebell and Jaxom to find the man a stool before his legs buckled. Menolly and Sharra offered him choice portions to eat in the hope of counteracting the wine.

"I won't waste time eating what'll doubtless return on me all too soon," Idarolan said, waving aside the plates. Then he belched and apologized. "Don't mind me, ladies. I'm a relieved man, and I think that's what I'd better do, if you'll pardon the expression. Lord Jaxom . . ." He leaned at a dangerous angle toward the young Holder, his eyes unfocused. "Before I continue my drinking, would you be good enough to indicate the proper direction?"

Jaxom signaled to Sebell to help, and with both lending Idarolan support, they steered him toward the nearest head, just past the busy kitchens.

"I was fearful worried, I was, my ol' friends, that that Blesserel would take the honors. We'd be done for then, we would, we decent hardworking fisherfolk," Idarolan rambled on. "I couldn't've borne the waiting sober, could I? So I'd had to take a heartener, or three or four," he added, grinning with a fine appreciation of his present state. "But you know me, lads, I never drink on board. Never. Nor do any of my Masters—them as are on the Crafthall rolls, that is."

Jaxom got him into a stall, Sebell deftly adjusting his clothing. Then they both politely looked away. Idarolan began to sing some sort of a sea song, but though his speech was clear for a man well gone in wine, he couldn't do more than mouth the lyrics in a hoarse bass voice. He took his relief for such a long time that, despite themselves, the two old friends locked eyes in amazement at the older man's bladder capacity. Jaxom's grin became a chuckle, and then Sebell started to laugh. Oblivious to them, Idarolan continued his wild garble.

Then abruptly, the Masterfisher completed his business and sagged between them.

"Oops! Hang on to him," Jaxom said urgently, just managing to throw Idarolan's limp arm across his shoulders as the man started to slide to the paving.

"He is gone, Jaxom, gone," Sebell said, grinning broadly and shaking his head. "It might be kinder to just leave him here to sleep it off."

"Master Robinton would never forgive us. Slip into the kitchen, Sebell, and grab a pot of klah. We'll sober him up. Why should he celebrate only half a day? The best part's still to come." Closing the lid, he eased Idarolan onto the stool, one hand on the Masterfisher's chest to keep the flaccid body from falling.

"Be right back." Sebell slipped out of the stall, carefully closing the door behind him. Jaxom heard his boot scraping on the stone floor, and then the second door opened and closed.

Jaxom rearranged Idarolan into what he felt would be a more comfortable, or at least more manageable, posture, but the man was as slippery as a fish on a deck.

Jaxom adjusted boneless arms and hands on the man's lap, all the while holding his torso upright on the stool. The knees were together and the toes pointing in. Even in the soft court leather boots, Idarolan had big feet, Jaxom noticed for the first time.

Just then the outside door slammed inward, and the brush of footsteps on the flagging indicated the arrival of several men; men shod in leather shoes, not workboots, Jaxom decided, pleased with his power of observation. Wishing to spare Idarolan embarrassment, he quickly leaned forward to slip the bolt of the stall door shut.

"Well, he's not the only heir. He's not even the direct heir," one man was saying.

"We know that," a second man said in a gravelly voice. "His dam was only a third cousin, once removed, of the Blood. But the second cousin's alive, known to be of the Blood, and it's her son we'd support in his place. The lad'd be dead easy to manipulate. Fancies himself as a true Blood."

"Which he is," a lighter voice said.

"Don't forget her son has sons who're in the direct line, even if his mother disqualified him to the succession," the gravel voice said.

Jaxom couldn't figure out who they meant, for there had been no question of Ranrel's lineage. He had his father's light eyes and the rugged features of his maternal grandfather. But the tone of their discussion about this facile rearrangement of sons and true Bloods was distinctly unsettling.

"That doesn't disqualify him," the first man said in disgust.

"He's weyrbred, not holdbred, and a dragonrider, so he can't hold."

"His sons are too young to be considered, even with a warder. No, this local lad will suit the purpose. He only needs encouragement."

"So all we have to do is arrange a convenient accident to bring the Hold into contention again?"

"That's all," the gravel voice said.

"Yes, but how?" the light voice asked.

"He flies Thread, doesn't he? And he goes up to the Dawn Sisters, doesn't he? That's dangerous. We just wait for the right moment and . . .'' He had no need to finish his grisly premise.

Incredulous, Jaxom shook his head. He was aware of a paralytic chill oozing from his guts to his gorge as he realized that the men had to be referring to himself, Lessa, and F'lessan. The ''local lad'' could only be Pell, for his mother, Barla, was of the direct Ruathan Bloodline.

''I'm not going off good solid earth, I'm not,'' the second man exclaimed. They were moving away, their business completed.

''You won't have to,'' the first man said with an icy chuckle. ''We've . . .'' And the closing of the door cut off the rest of his sentence.

Jaxom realized that he had been holding his breath and expelled it. He was shaking. Lack of oxygen, he told himself, drawing in deep breaths. Idarolan groaned and began to slide out of a grip Jaxom had inadvertently relaxed.

''C'mon, Sebell. Hurry up!'' If only Sebell arrived just at that moment, he would see who had left the head. ''C'mon, Sebell!''

I'll tell his fire-lizard, Ruth said suddenly, his tone anxious. *What's worrying you? I can feel it. Is the fisherman ill?*

No, Ruth, he's only very drunk. Ask Kimi to tell Sebell to get a move on. Though I think it's too late now, he added glumly. He had not recognized any of the voices, and none of them had betrayed any particular twang that might have identified which Hold or Hall they came from.

He heard the door crash open. ''Jaxom? What's wrong?''

''You didn't happen to see three men leaving here, did you?'' Jaxom called anxiously.

''What's wrong? Kimi said it was urgent. Which three men? Everyone and his cousin is packed into the courtyard.''

Sebell fumbled with the stall door until Jaxom threw the latch over. Anxiously the Masterharper looked down at the comatose Masterfisher and then in astonishment at Jaxom. He had a pitcher in one hand and a mug tucked under his arm.

''Never mind, too late now,'' Jaxom said, feeling defeated. He decided not to worry Sebell by reporting a conversation that might well have been just disgruntled speculation. Talking was harmless, he told himself though the conversation he had overheard had sounded anything *but* harmless. He sighed in fateful resignation.

''What happened?''

Sebell's harper instincts were very good, Jaxom thought grimly. But then the man was trained to observe, to hear the unsaid.

Jaxom managed a detached manner. "I suppose one has to expect that not everyone is happy about Ranrel's Holding."

Sebell gave him a shrewd look. "No, but here's one who is. Hold his head up. Maybe the aroma of klah will revive him. And we've got reinforcements coming."

"I don't mind . . ." Jaxom began. He hated people to think him pretentious and unwilling to cope with an inebriated friend.

Sebell grinned as he passed the full cup of klah back and forth under Idarolan's nose. The man began to stir. "Yes, you're good about such things, Jax, but his people are worried about him, so let them handle it discreetly."

Once again the door crashed open and several men entered in haste. "Master Sebell?"

Sebell swung the stall door open. "In here!"

The switchover of attendants was quickly made, and just as Sebell and Jaxom swung out of the place they heard the unmistakable sounds that Idarolan had foretold and grinned at each other.

"My timing has always been excellent," Sebell said. "Even Master Shonagar agreed. Ah, the music has begun."

In the doorway, Jaxom hesitated, seeing very well why Sebell would not have noticed three men emerging from the heads. In just the short time that they had been assisting Idarolan, the courtyard had filled up with celebrants, all merry with wine and stuffing themselves on whatever was on the trays the drudges were carrying.

"When are you and Menolly doing a turn?"

Sebell winked. "Whenever the good Lord Ranrel asks us to!"

"A new song?"

"What else for a Lording!"

Jaxom took heart from Sebell's merriment. No use borrowing trouble. It had probably just been talk. But he would keep his eyes open.

Jaxom was feeling decidedly better by the time he and Sharra reluctantly retired from the dancing square. But duty called: Threadfall was scheduled to begin over water but creep forward over the southern border of Ruatha Hold. Jaxom never missed flying against Thread, no matter how involved he was with Aivas at Landing, and obligingly joined the wings of T'gellan's Eastern Weyr when Thread fell there.

It wasn't simply a point of honor with Jaxom; both he and Ruth were stimulated by the implicit danger of Fall and reveled in being part of a fighting Weyr.

"Look, Jaxom," Sharra said as they readied themselves to leave the Hold. She pointed upward, to the mass of dragon bellies just visible in the glow of the myriad lights that had blossomed at sundown on every wall, hold, cot, and ship. "I'll bet that's all of Fort Weyr going home!"

Jaxom was trying to adjust the riding straps so as not to damage Sharra's gown and spared only a glance. "You'd be right about that."

"Don't worry about my skirts, Jax, not after all the dust they've picked up from the dance square."

Jaxom humphed and felt Sharra's hand ruffling his hair. Then he grinned. He had worried that she had worn herself out with the dancing, but if she was still so playful, she wasn't too tired. They would get back to Ruatha in good time. *Ruth?*

I'll time it for you for good reason, but that isn't.

Oh, and isn't it? Jaxom swung up on the white dragon with a huge smile on his face. Sharra smiled back as she wrapped both arms tightly about him, trying to work her fingers up under his flying jacket to his bare skin.

You've time enough in hand. And Ruth sprang lightly from the ground, his wings making that crucial downward sweep.

"It's so beautiful!" Sharra shouted in Jaxom's ear. "Ask Ruth to hover. We'll never see Tillek look so beautiful again."

Ruth considerately began to glide in a wide slow circle, head down so that he, too, could enjoy the sight. Jaxom could see that the white dragon's eyes were sparklingly blue; each of the many facets of his eyes reflected tiny points of the bright lights of Tillek. The Hold, all the cots, and every ship in the harbor were outlined in radiance. There couldn't be a glowbasket left indoors.

Jaxom felt Ruth's sigh through his buttocks and, replacing this with a vision of Ruatha's unadorned heights, told Ruth to take them there.

It was not easy to climb out of bed the next morning, even though Sharra had already left it to comfort young Shawan, who had cried fretfully about dawn. Fall was not due until early afternoon, so Jaxom allowed himself a few more moments to savor the first morning cup of klah. Sharra came in with Shawan, once more a cheerful child. Jarrol appeared the moment he heard his father's voice and bounced across the bed, demanding a tickle, his cheeks still rosy with sleep and his curly hair mashed on one side of his head. The tickle duly administered, Jarrol followed his father as he washed and dressed. By then, breakfast was ready in the main room of their apartment.

Jaxom sent Jarrol to request Brand's company. Now was a good time to clear up any urgent Hold business that might have come up in the past sevendays of his latest absence from Ruatha. With Sharra and Jarrol planning to accompany him back to Landing the next day, there were other details to be arranged, as well.

It was while Sharra took the boys off on her own rounds that Jaxom remembered the strange conversation in the Tillek head.

"Tell me, Brand, what's young Pell, Barla and Dowell's son, doing with himself these days?"

"Learning his Craft from his father, but he'd rather be in Landing."

"Like half the Northern youngsters," Jaxom replied, leaning back in the fine wooden chair that Dowell had carved for him. "Has he any ability as a joiner?"

"He's capable enough when he gets into a task." Brand shrugged carelessly. "Why do you ask?"

"In the head at Tillek, I heard a rather odd conversation. It could be no more than disgruntled supporters spouting disappointment with the decision, I suppose. Pell would have a good claim to Ruatha, wouldn't he?"

Brand sat up, a look of consternation on his face. "What are you talking about, Jaxom?" he scolded, in the tone he had used to scold the erring boy that Jaxom had once been. "There's not a thing wrong with you, and you've two fine sons and probably more to come." He scowled. "What exactly was said? Have you told Lytol?"

"No, and you're not to either. This is between us, Holder to Steward, as well as friend to friend, Brand. I want that understood."

"Yes, of course," Brand hastily assured him, then waggled a finger. "But only if you tell me what you heard."

It was a relief to unburden himself, for Jaxom trusted Brand completely. He had hoped that, in the telling, the sentences would lose their burden of dread, but Brand took the implications quite seriously.

"Could anyone plan an accident for you or Ruth up there?" Brand asked.

Jaxom gave a snort. "I assure you that from now on, I intend to pick my companions carefully. But I don't think an accident could be easily contrived."

"The two trips you've already made were not without dangers."

Jaxom shook his head vigorously. "Not with Ruth so close at hand. Not with Aivas in constant communication with me. Piemur, and Farli and Trig, as well, were with us the first time. Sharra's to go up tomorrow—you knew that? Good. Mirrim and S'len are scheduled for the day after. None of them would conspire against me. Besides which, Ruth wouldn't let anything happen to me."

You may be very sure of that!

Jaxom grinned, and Brand, recognizing the signs of a Ruth-Jaxom exchange, began to relax and even allowed himself a slight smile.

"Clearly they underestimate both you and Ruth, and now that you're forewarned . . ." Brand frowned, his eyes narrowing into slits. "I'll have a word or two with young Pell. And young he is, proud of his heritage but not so foolish as to wish to become Holder by way of your demise. Besides you and your sons, there're also those three lads of F'lessan's. Their claim to Ruatha is direct through Lessa, even if she did defer to you at your birth. I can't see the older Lord Holders denying their claim because F'lessan's a dragonrider. The Bloodline would be the important aspect, so I don't think Pell would have a chance. At least not with the present composition of the Council. Not that the circumstance will ever arrive!" Brand's conviction did much to assuage the niggling anxiety in Jaxom's mind.

Then Brand squared his shoulders the way he always did when he was about to change the topic. "That was quite an inauguration," he commented. As Chief Steward of Ruatha, he had also attended the festivities at Tillek Hold. "Can't say as how Tillek Hold ever looked as inviting. We'll see some grand changes now Ranrel's Lord Holder. Good for you to have another Holder nearer your age."

Jaxom grimaced. "Yes, maybe then I can speak now and again at these Councils."

Brand smiled broadly. "I heard that Toric finally got your message."

"Hmm, yes, even if it was Groghe who delivered it. Now, what have you for me? I've Fall after the noon meal."

"More or less minor details to be discussed, Lord Jaxom. Let's see." Brand lifted the top sheet from the pile he had brought with him.

As Jaxom and Ruth circled down to Fort Weyr, Jaxom once again wondered what it had been like for the first dragonriders who had inhabited the old crater. Had they ranged themselves in preparation for their leader's commands as this century's dragons did, along the rim from the Star Stones to where Fort Weyr's bowl had crumbled in an ancient landslide? How many dragonriders had there been before they had needed to expand into Benden Weyr? There was no way of knowing—and Jaxom felt a pang of regret for the lost history, a regret made all the more bittersweet for the history they *had* been able to reclaim through Aivas. Still, whatever the glory of the past, the sight of the Weyr displayed was as breathtaking as ever. And Fort was right now at full strength, with this Turn's young riders taking their places in the wings. Green, blue, brown ranked in their wings beyond the bronze Wingseconds, every hide glistening with health in the midday sun.

Bronze Lioth, carrying N'ton, stood statuesquely in front of the Star Stones. Ruth answered Lioth's bugle of welcome and neatly took his customary position to the right of the Fort Weyrleader. N'ton gave Jaxom a salute and pointed down to the Bowl, where four queenriders were being accoutered with flamethrowers.

A blue rider, returning from a preliminary sweep, emerged abruptly into the air, giving the ancient two-armed signal that Thread was imminent. N'ton acknowledged that even as the assembled dragons, almost simultaneously, turned their heads to receive firestone from their riders. The queens bellowed their readiness and one by one lifted from the floor of the Bowl and spiraled up to take their positions to the left of N'ton and Lioth. The big bronze was carefully masticating the first of the many lumps of firestone that he would chew before the end of the Fall. Jaxom offered Ruth his hunk and listened, awed as ever to the sound of draconic teeth chomping on the phosphine-bearing rock. Knowing as he did now the scientific explanation for the process by which dragons digested the rock in their second stomach and belched the phosphine gas forth in flame did not in the least destroy his reverence for dragonkind.

Jaxom carefully watched Ruth chew, for now and then every dragon bit his own tongue or cheeks, a minor accident that nevertheless would disqualify him from flying that Fall.

When Lioth had finished his chewing, he let out another roar, and N'ton pumped his arm in the age-old signal to take to the skies. With a powerful upward lunge, Lioth left the Rim, Ruth a breath behind him. The queens with effortless grace were airborne the next second.

Making height, Lioth veered to the southeast, and one by one the wings rose into the air, maneuvering into their fighting positions: three on the level above, three just behind N'ton and Ruth, and the third carefully on a lower level with the queens' wing just below them.

All human eyes were trained on N'ton; all dragons listened for Lioth's word. As often as Jaxom had seen the flights of dragons go *between*, as often as he had himself been a part of that transfer, it never ceased to thrill him.

Between is *colder than space*, he told Ruth. A breath later they were above Ruatha's southern border, the expanse of the river a silver snake below them. And to the east was the silver rain they had come to destroy.

The wings met Thread, breathing fire on the thick strands and watching them curl and twist in flame and drop harmlessly as ash on the ground far below. The upper wings streaked across the sky, and at the lowest level, the queenriders sent flaring gouts of liquid fire after those few Threads that escaped the upper wings.

Once again, Jaxom and Ruth were part of the ancient defense of Pern, falling into its rhythm, escaping its hazards, flicking in and out of *between*, weaving across the breadth of Thread, flaming swathes through the deadly rainfall. Together they acted by reflex born of long practice, quite apart from conscious direction of either partner.

They had done at least eight traverses of the Fall, drifting farther and farther south and east, when a blue dragon just ahead of them screamed and ducked *between*. Jaxom tensed and waited a heartbeat, scanning for the blue's return. The blue reentered hundreds of lengths below his point of exit. His left wingsail was dotted with Threadchar.

He's badly hit, Ruth told Jaxom as the blue winked out again, no doubt to return to the Weyr and the waiting weyrfolk who would drench his injury in numbweed, ending his pain. *One of the new young riders. There's always one who doesn't keep his eyes open.*

Jaxom wasn't sure if Ruth meant the rider or the dragon. Suddenly Ruth veered, the riding straps cutting into Jaxom's left thigh as the white dragon evaded a thick clump. He did a reverse turn, almost on his tail, and flung himself down at the receding cluster, blowing mightily. Righting himself, he turned his head peremptorily to his rider, and Jaxom obediently offered more firestone. Chomping as he rose to see where his flame would next be useful, Ruth swerved to his right, once again throwing Jaxom's weight against the riding straps. Abruptly Jaxom felt the front strap stretch, leaving him far too loose in the saddle. Quickly he grabbed a neck ridge with his right hand, clamped his legs tight to the saddle, and hung on tight to the left-hand straps.

Ruth reacted on the instant, halting midair to allow Jaxom to regain his balance. A dribble of flame escaped his lips as he turned wondering eyes on his rider.

The strap broke? Ruth's query was laced with astonishment.

Jaxom felt along the length of it with gloved fingers. The worn spot was easy to locate, right below the belt clip, the leather stretched but not parted. It had been a very near thing. A little more pressure, and the strap would have snapped, flinging the rider dangerously out of the saddle.

All too clearly now, Jaxom remembered the ominous conversation he had overheard. Surely they could not have implemented their plan overnight? "An accident," they had said. What would be less suspicious than a rider's faulty harness?

A dragonman maintained his own riding straps, renewing them frequently, testing them every Fall for signs of wear or strain. Jaxom cursed himself. He hadn't actually looked at his harness that morning, merely lifted it from its peg in Ruth's weyr, a place open to anyone in Ruatha. And to any casual visitor.

One thing was colder than *between* or space. Fear!

It's not broken, Ruth. But the leather is badly stretched. Let's get back to Fort, and I'll cadge a replacement from the Weyrlingmaster. Tell Lioth why we're leaving. We won't be long.

Jaxom endured a well-deserved scolding from H'nalt, the Weyrlingmaster, for when they examined the leather strap, they found it to be plainly cold-hardened, brittle enough to stretch and crack. At least the metalwork of the toggles was bright enough to pass old H'nalt's scrutiny. Relieved that in this instance the problem had been caused by ordinary wear and tear, Jaxom and Ruth rejoined the Weyr and fought till the end of the Fall.

The first thing Jaxom did when he reached Ruatha was to cut new straps from the thick well-tanned leather made in his own Hold. That evening, with Jarrol's assistance, he oiled and sewed the straps onto the turnbuckles. He said nothing about the close call to Sharra, who, fortunately, was accustomed to seeing Jaxom spending an evening mending riding straps. Later, when he saw that Ruth was comfortably bedded down in his weyr, Jaxom put the mended harness on the peg, but thereafter he concealed the one he was using, as well as the double harness he and Sharra shared. Forewarned is forearmed, he told himself.

Waking hours before dawn in Ruatha for the trip to Landing, Jaxom helped Sharra wrap a sleeping Jarrol in his warm flying gear. Shawan was far too young to be exposed to the cold of *between* and would be tended by his nurse during his mother's absence. There were enough enticements on this trip to pry Sharra from her maternal duties: she would see firsthand why Jaxom was so preoccupied with this venture; she would have a chance to practice her profession; and she would see her dearest friends; Jancis had agreed to mind Jarrol along with her own Pierjan while Sharra was on the *Yokohama*. Her two fire-lizards, bronze Meer and brown Talla, were even more excited than she was and were rebuked for their agitation by Ruth as he launched himself from the dark courtyard at Ruatha.

The weather at Landing was chilly, as the Southern Continent was in its winter season, but the land was never as bleakly brown and bare as Ruatha in winter. Sharra loved Ruatha—it was Jaxom's home and where her children had been born—but Southern was where she had spent her youth.

As soon as they entered the Aivas building, Mirrim, who had been chatting with D'ram, ran to greet them.

"I'm ready when you are," she announced.

"Easy, girl!" Jaxom laughed. Her association with T'gellan had calmed her considerably, but she still tended to become a bit overzealous in her enthusiasms. Not necessarily a bad trait, Jaxom realized, but it could be wearing on her companions.

"Well I *am* ready, with only the two barrels and tanks to be positioned on my green Path. And if we don't know what we're supposed to do by now"—she shot a glance at Sharra—"we never will. It's so simple. Open the packets, add water, and stir."

"Not quite," Sharra said with a grin. "It's the setting of the mirrors that'll take time, and their positioning is crucial to the success of the algae propagation."

"I know, I know." Mirrim impatiently dismissed that with a flick of her fingers.

"Is S'len ready, too?" Jaxom asked.

"Him!" Mirrim gave an amused grunt. "He's studying the photos of the bridge area in spite of the fact that we're supposed to get our placement directly from Ruth."

"Who's to carry the water barrels?" Sharra asked. Taking Mirrim by the hand, she led her away to check on that detail.

"Heard you told Toric what to do," D'ram commented to Jaxom, his eyes sparkling with mischief.

"No," Jaxom replied smoothly. "Lord Groghe told Toric. Anything else I should know about Landing?" he asked pointedly.

"Aivas will tell you what you need to know about Landing." D'ram shooed him down the corridor. "He's expecting you."

Just as if Jaxom had not been absent for several days, Aivas outlined the schedule.

"There is sufficient oxygen in the Environment Sector now, but the duties are nevertheless to be carried out as expeditiously as possible. The fire-lizards are to accompany Lady Sharra and Greenrider Mirrim, as they would be sensitive to any sudden drop in pressure or in oxygen level. It is also an integral part of these exercises to accustom as many fire-lizards as possible to the act of transferring from the planet to the *Yokohama*."

"When will you explain *that* particular wrinkle in your master plan?" Jaxom asked. Silently he mouthed the response he had come to expect.

"In due time. If you knew the answer, why did you ask, Jaxom?"

Jaxom batted both hands at the Aivas. Little escaped that entity—even silent flippancy.

"Just checking," he replied amiably. "In case due time had arrived while I was gone."

"There is a great deal to be prepared before that time is accomplished. Surely you, of all people, who have been on the *Yokohama*, should realize that."

"Two more Turns?"

"Five months, and twelve days, with respect to the position of the eccentric planet. Meanwhile the fire-lizards can become messengers even as they are here on the surface, transporting items required on the *Yokohama* which are within the scope of their abilities."

Jaxom kept his resignation to himself. They had no option but to proceed at the pace Aivas set. But what—eventually—did Aivas intend the fire-lizards to transport? Jaxom couldn't imagine.

Aware that further questioning of Aivas would be futile, he joined the others to prepare for the day's exercise. There were plenty of willing hands to help them load Ruth, Path, and S'len's Bigath with oxygen tanks and water barrels, although Mirrim fussed inordinately about how the tanks were situated on her beloved Path.

"You're wasting time, Mirrim," Jaxom said finally, when she insisted on padding the knots across Path's back. "The load sits fine and we're not flying straight, you know." Privately he wondered if Mirrim was covering up a case of nerves. Sharra was composed enough, and so was S'len, though his face was flushed with excitement.

"I just don't want them shifting," Mirrim replied stiffly.

"Shift they will. All the way to the *Yokohama*," S'len remarked, grinning at her.

"Enough. We go! Now, Ruth!" Jaxom said, and felt Sharra's hands work tighter onto his belt. Then he gave Ruth the mental vision of the bridge and heard the white dragon pass the instructions on to Path and Bigath.

If there were many things Jaxom did not understand about Aivas, the artificial intelligence had some problem understanding dragon capabilities. For instance, how much weight could a dragon carry? For which the answer was: How much weight did the dragon *think* he could carry? An answer Aivas found specious—and certainly not helpful when what was needed was hard numbers.

Then there was the question, How do dragons know where to go? "Their riders tell them," did nothing to explain the actual process to Aivas. While Aivas did accept teleportation, it could not understand why telekinesis was so impossible a concept to explain to the dragons and the fire-lizards. Especially when Ruth had indeed understood what Farli had not: to go to the *Yokohama*.

In checking the details of this joint trip to the spaceship, Jaxom had asked Ruth if he could carry two riders, as well as two padded barrels, one of pure water and one of carbonated water. Ruth's reply had been affirmative although, as Aivas saw the load, it was more than the dragon's slight frame ought to be able to bear.

"If Ruth thinks he can, he can," Jaxom could only reply. "And it's not that far."

It might be easier, the white dragon remarked to his rider as he launched himself into the air, *to just go* between *from the ground instead of lifting*.

Is the load too much for you after all? Jaxom asked, teasing.

Of course not. Just bulky! Everyone's set. Here we go!

There was a squawk from the five escorting fire-lizards, and the next moment the tanks clanked against the bridge walls. Exclamations of surprise from the three newcomers punctuated their arrival.

Jaxom heard Sharra inhale in astonishment. Grinning, he skewed about on Ruth's neck and saw the expression of wide-eyed awe on her lovely face as she viewed the incredible vista of Pern spread out beneath them, framed by the vast blackness of space beyond. Meer and Talla, her fire-lizards, plus Mirrim's three, Reppa, Lok, and Tolly, had made the successful transfer and were tumbling about, shrieking with delight at the experience of free-fall.

"Oh!" she said, her eyes luminous with the dazzle she beheld. "Now I understand, dear heart, why you're so involved with this! Pern is so beautiful, so serene from up here. If only some of those contentious sour old men could see our world from this vantage point . . . Isn't it incredible, Mirrim?" There was a pause. "Mirrim?"

Jaxom turned to the green rider, who was staring out the wide window with bulging eyes.

"That's Pern?" Mirrim asked in a cracked voice. "Down there?" A limp hand pointed a finger to the deck.

"That's Pern! Isn't the view great!" Jaxom tried to sound reassuring—Mirrim was patently overwhelmed. "S'len? You all right there?"

"I th-think—ssso," the other green rider said with little confidence.

Jaxom grinned back at Sharra. "It is awesome," he agreed with the nonchalance of one who has overcome astonishment. "But stir yourselves. Remember how Aivas keeps reminding us we can't waste oxygen."

"Why not?" Mirrim demanded in her usual assertive way. "All we have to do is haul more tanks up here." With crisp motions, she unbuckled her riding straps.

"Careful now, Mirrim. You're in—ah—oops." Jaxom broke off; Mirrim had indeed forgotten how she was supposed to move in free-fall and was drifting ceilingward. "Just hold out one hand, and very carefully push away from the roof. That's right."

Mirrim had been too startled to cry out; also, she had no great wish to show to disadvantage. Now she did as directed and managed a weak grin as she grabbed Path's helpfully extended muzzle. Fortunately, the green was wedged fairly tightly between guardrail and wall and thus was not susceptible to the whimsies of free-fall.

"Make every motion slow and easy, S'len, when you're dismounting. Hang on to a neck ridge or something," Jaxom advised. Before he detached his riding straps he nodded to Sharra to follow the same advice.

Keeping up a running line of encouragement and advice, he su
pervised the unloading. S'len crowed in delight when he realized
that the heavy tanks could be shifted by the judicious prod of one
finger.

"They're still awkward," Mirrim said, poking one of the tanks
toward the storage area. Then she grinned. "T'gellan should see me
now. But I understand why Aivas specified green dragons."

"For once greens get the best assignments," S'len added proudly.

"Green dragons are far more versatile than anyone knows," Mirrim added staunchly. "Can't say the same for green fire-lizards," she
went on, sourly observing the absurd antics of Reppa and Lok, who
were tumbling end over end overhead, chittering ecstatically. Meer,
Talla, and her own brown Tolly had abandoned such nonsense and
were plastered against the window, their wings limp in their utter
fascination with the view.

As soon as the dragons had been unloaded, Ruth encouraged Path
and Bigath to join him at the window. While the white dragon floated
serenely from the upper level, Path and Bigath had a few problems
that the human observers found hilarious.

"They get the hang of it quickly enough," Jaxom said, watching
approvingly. "After all, they're used to flying."

Once the oxygen tanks had been secured, the others had a chance
to view the magnificence of the vast planet beneath them.

"Does the view stay the same?" Mirrim asked. "I can't see Benden
from here."

"Or Ruatha," Sharra added.

"I can barely make out Eastern Weyr," S'len put in, "and I thought
it was pretty big!"

"That's what a geosynchronous orbit means, my friends, the ship
stays in the same position relative to the surface of the planet," Jaxom
said. "However, if you'll move over to that first console—easy does
it!" He grabbed Mirrim before she could propel herself too forcefully
away from the window. "We can see the coast of Nerat and something of Benden on the rear screen, but," he added with a nod to
Sharra, "Southern Hold's over the horizon."

"Then don't let Toric up here, because all he wants to see is
Southern spread out before him," she replied with a wry smile.

They all managed to transfer without incident to the navigation
console, where Jaxom activated the rear screen.

"That's nothing," Mirrim said bluntly. "Too small."

"Just a minute," Jaxom replied, holding up one hand as he mentally rehearsed the procedure for altering the view on the main screen. He tapped it out and was gratified to see the screen alter.

"By the Egg, that's incredible!" S'len sighed, eyes round with amazement. "How'd you do that, Jaxom?"

Jaxom recited the sequences, and S'len nodded, repeating them in a mutter.

"Now, I'll help the girls get the barrels to Environment. If you'd rather Ruth and I accompanied you to the *Bahrain* . . ."

"No, no, that's hardly necessary," S'len said, affronted, and started to fasten his jacket.

S'len mounted Bigath.

Ruth, check their direction, would you? Jaxom asked his dragon.

Bigath knows exactly where he's going. Be easy, Ruth replied without turning his head from the window.

When Bigath and S'len had departed, Jaxom clapped his hands briskly.

"All right, girls, let's get these barrels down to Environment," Jaxom said, beckoning to them. "The section we're using is only one level down. It would keep the bridge supplied in case of emergency."

They got the barrels into the lift and down to the next level.

"I thought you said Aivas warmed this place for us," Sharra exclaimed, rubbing her arms vigorously.

Jaxom grinned. "It's warmer than it was, believe me."

Mirrim's teeth started to chatter, and she rolled her eyes and hurried to palm open the double doors just in front of the lift. "Wow! This is bigger than I thought it would be," she said as she entered the white room, glancing at the cabinets that lined one wall and the huge spirals of trays that would slowly revolve on their posts to allow each section the required amount of deflected light to propagate the algae.

"Come back here, Mirrim," Jaxom said as he gently kicked a barrel out of the lift.

It didn't take the three long to set up the supplies. Jaxom offered to help prepare the trays with the wet padding that would moisturize the algal spores, but the girls shooed him away. He watched while they found the supplies they needed, the packages of algae and nutrients that had to be added carefully to the fluid.

"Where's the con—" Sharra began, and then spotted the console that had been meticulously covered by whoever had decommissioned the facility. "All right, dear," she said, smiling absently at her be-mused mate and flicking her fingers at him to leave, "we've all we need. You'd best get on with your chores."

Jaxom made no move to leave. Mirrim, hunkered down by the shelves, glowered at him. "Git!"

Back on the bridge, Ruth and the five fire-lizards were still plas-tered to the window. Jaxom activated the link between the two ships and located S'len as he was painstakingly soaking the padding in a tray, holding one hand to prevent water from flowing out of the bar-rel.

Reassured that the others were doing fine on their own, Jaxom at last settled himself at the navigation board and activated the telescope to begin his own chore. He opened the channel to Aivas and received the new sequences for the telescope, which he was programming to scan the visible stars above Pern. By the time he and Aivas had double-checked the installation of the program, Sharra and Mirrim had returned to the bridge, moving with considerably more confi-dence in the weightlessness.

"S'len's working away?" Mirrim asked. "Time for us to do the *Buenos Aires*, then." She buckled up her jacket, nodding at Sharra to do the same. "Aivas, Farli has turned on the life-support systems there, hasn't she?"

"Yes. There is now oxygen in the relevant areas of the *Buenos Aires*."

Sharra gave Jaxom a look that was tolerant of Mirrim's predilection to take charge.

Ruth, Jaxom began, for although he did really trust Mirrim and Path, it was Sharra they would be taking to the *Buenos Aires*.

If Path caught me looking in, Mirrim'd never forgive you, the white dragon replied, giving his rider a doleful stare.

All right, all right. I trust her or I don't. And I do. I'll restrain myself.

So will I! And the white dragon dropped his jaw in a draconic grin.

When the girls were mounted on Path, Mirrim gave him a salute. "Don't wait for us. We'll go straight back to Landing."

Before he could protest, Path disappeared, along with the fire-lizards. Jaxom's fingers flew on the console, calling up the link to the *Buenos Aires* just as Path, with the girls and the fire-lizards, arrived.

Ruth gave such a scornful snort that he blew himself slightly away from the window.

"All right then, big eyes," Jaxom said, closing down the console. "Since my work's finished, we can go back to Landing."

W hen Sharra and Mirrim returned to Landing, Brekke and Master Oldive were there. Brekke, F'nor's introverted wife, had agreed to learn more about the treatment of wounds, since she often worked as an aide to Benden Weyr's healers.

"Master Morilton delivered the petri dishes today," she told them. "Aivas says that if you are not too tired, he can elaborate on his last lecture about bacteria and how to overcome them with what he calls an-tee-bi-ah-tics."

Sharra and Mirrim exchanged glances, but they were more exhilarated by their morning's work than tired. Sharra had been fascinated with the concept of isolating certain bacteria and finding ways to combat infection by developing special bacteriophages. So they filed into the laboratory room—and exclaimed in pleasure at the sight of sufficient microscopes for all. Brekke smiled quietly.

"We won't have to take turns!" Mirrim cried. "For my eye only!" Slipping onto the high stool, she peered through the eyepiece. "Hmmm. If you're looking at nothing, that's what you see."

"Please take positions at the microscopes," Aivas told them in a tone that meant they should listen carefully. "Not only has Master Morilton been able to deliver the petri dishes in which you may culture the bacteria of your choice, and the microscopes so that each of you may progress at your own speed, but Master Fandarel has contrived an ultrasound device by which we can break the bacteria up so that we may examine their structures chemically. Master Fandarel has put to good use his studies in electromagnetics. This is but one application—but, for you, a very important one.

"The bacteria collected for today's lesson come from wounds," Aivas went on, oblivious to or ignoring the grotesque face that Mirrim made. "Wounds that you will have seen in your independent areas. Wounds that become infected. By separating the bacteria, it is possible to discover the parasites—mostly symbiotic—which exist in the bacteria. By altering these symbiotic little parasites into pathogenic forms, making them like predators—you do recall the lesson on determining which is a predator and which is a parasite?"

"Yes, indeed, Aivas," Mirrim said, grinning. "Whether you admire them or they disgust you."

"You can always be counted on to remember such distinctions, Mirrim. It is to be hoped that this skill will extend into this area of your studies." Mirrim wrinkled her nose impudently, but Aivas continued. "So, one can disimprove a symbiotic parasite, turning it into a predator, and have a useful organism to destroy that particular

ANNE McCAFFREY

bacterium. This is often more useful than using antibiotics, as you will see.''

''How many bacteria are there?'' Brekke asked.

''More than there are grains of sand on all your beaches.''

''And we have to find every one of them?'' Mirrim was not the only one aghast at that prospect.

''You will have ample chance for independent study to do so if you desire. This is, however, one step to take along the road toward the reduction of bacterial infections. Now you will begin by culturing the effluent from a wound or a blood-containing medium, then isolating one kind of bacterium.''

11
▼▼▼▼▼▼▼

PRESENT PASS 20

"I suppose we should be grateful that there are still so many youngsters who'd prefer to be dragonriders in spite of the competition from Landing," Lessa said wryly as she looked out over the sixty-two candidates standing in the Hatching Ground.

F'lar looked down at his diminutive weyrmate and grinned. "*Any-one* is available for Ramoth's clutches. Groghe was almost dancing when his youngest daughter was chosen on Search."

"He'll be insufferable if she Impresses the queen," Lessa said with a chuckle. "Such a pretty child. Wonder where she got her looks."

"Lessa!" F'lar said, pretending shock. "Groghe shouldn't expect a clean sweep of the honors. After all, Benelek was elected first Master of the Technical Hall, and Groghe's got another son and a daughter doing very well in Aivas's study group."

"At least Groghe keeps his sense of proportion. Here he comes now." She pointed to Lord Groghe, who was leading the Fort Hold contingent into the Hatching Ground. His attire was almost sober in the midst of the other gaudily dressed folk. Lessa nodded approval. "And he's sensibly wearing boots," she went on as she watched the sturdy Lord Holder striding out across the hot sands while others in his party minced, lifting their feet high in an effort to cool their leather soles. "The Dance of The Hatching Ground Sands," she added, stifling a laugh.

"Come, we'd better get to our seats," F'lar said, extending his arm to her. "And see if the insoles Master Ligand's so proud of really do insulate the foot against heat, as well as the cold of *between*."

Lessa spared a critically admiring look at her new red boots before she took his arm. "It's the plant fiber he used for the felt that provides the insulation for either extreme."

She had a complete new outfit in a deep wine-red for this Hatching—Ramoth's thirty-fifth—especially as this clutch included a queen egg, the first in twelve seasons. The great queen rarely laid fewer than twenty eggs; this clutch, appropriately, numbered thirty-five.

The eight Weyleaders had already agreed on the necessity of the foundation of a ninth Weyr. The existing eight were completely full, with some two-year-old dragons still living in the Weyrling cavern for lack of space. While Weyrleaders were proud to be flying at strength, dragon dignity required independent quartering. Not only were there no more suitable sites in the North, but since so many people were taking up holdings in the South, it was agreed that a new Weyr should be located in the vast Southern Continent, preferably equidistant between K'van's Southern Weyr and T'gellan's Eastern. The grubs might protect the land and vegetation, but dragons were still needed to repel Thread from human habitations and beastholds. A little reshuffling among the existing Weyrs and there would be plenty of older dragonriders to balance out the young ones: dragons and riders who would appreciate quarters in the South, where the climate was kind to aging bones and the stiffness of old injuries.

Lessa experienced a flush of pride for what had been achieved over the past Turns by an ex-drudge from Ruatha Hold and the bronze Benden rider whom no one had wanted to believe. She glanced up at her mate, noticing that even more silver strands had appeared in F'lar's crisp black hair. The sun creases around his eyes had deepened, additional touches of aging, though he seemed to have lost not a jot of his vitality. Maybe they should resign Benden to the energy of younger riders, she mused. With fewer responsibilities, they could devote more time to all the splendid projects at Landing. Not that she thought she had a chance of coaxing F'lar away from Benden until he had eradicated Thread from the skies forever.

F'lessan had spent some time explaining to her that once there was a breathable atmosphere in the cargo bay on the *Yokohama*, even as big a dragon as Ramoth would be able to jump *between* to view Pern from space. Lessa wasn't sure either of them wanted to go that far, though she was more than pleased to find her ebullient son becoming a responsible and dedicated part of the Aivas team. She was genuinely fond of the only child she had been able to bear F'lar, but she had no illusions about him.

"Gone *between* in thought, love?" F'lar murmured, leaning down to her, amusement in his amber eyes. "Groghe's waving at us."

Spreading her best welcoming smile on her face as she stepped off the hot sands, Lessa located the Fort Holder and acknowledged his salute. The tiers were already packed with folk who had come to see a son or daughter Impress a dragon, or merely to attend what was invariably a magnificent occasion.

"Those new insoles work," F'lar said as he handed her up the stairs.

"Hmmm, don't they?" Then she noticed Larad and Asgenar with their wives and their older children on the second tier and waved cheerfully to them. Master Bendarek was on the same row as they were, but deep in a private dialogue with the recently appointed Masterprinter Tagetarl, he didn't see her.

She surveyed the ranks behind her, looking for Master Robinton and D'ram, a pair who rarely missed an Impression. Her eye picked them out easily, resplendent as they were in their Gather finery. Becoming so involved with the Aivas project had given them both, and Lytol, stimulation and new purpose. Why was it that these older men thrived on the challenge, while others, like Sangel, Norist, Corman, Nessel, and Begamon, rejected all that the new information provided Pern? No, not new: retrieved information. And just at the time of a Pass, when everyone needed such an infusion of hope.

Absently she responded to several other salutes before taking her place in the first tier.

It's almost time, Ramoth told her driver, swinging her head possessively over the queen egg.

Now don't scare the girls, dear.

Ramoth's eyes glittered in a rainbow gamut as she looked straight at her rider. *If they scare, they're not worthy of my daughter.*

You liked them well enough yesterday.

Today it is different.

Yes, Lessa agreed affably, versed in her dragon's whimsies. *Today your daughter Impresses.*

The humming had already begun as the massed dragons of Benden chanted their welcome. Feeling the sound vibrating through her bones, Lessa turned to smile softly at F'lar, who smiled back and took her right hand in his. This moving overture had become a special moment for them, an affirmation of their own love and a rededication to their own dragons.

An abrupt hush rippled down the tiers as the audience became aware of the distinctive sounds. Fire-lizards darted in to seek roosts on the topmost ridges, and though Ramoth followed their progress with her brilliant eyes, she no longer bellowed a warning if the creatures entered the Hatching Ground. After Lessa had heard Aivas's account of the fire-lizards' reception of their huge cousins at the first Hatching, she had told Ramoth, and both of them had felt more charitable since.

Some of the eggs in the main group were rocking slightly, and the fifty-seven boys closed in about them, hope and eagerness mirrored on their clean, shining faces. The five girls moved slowly but resolutely toward Ramoth, whose immense form covered the mottled queen egg.

Move back, dear, Lessa said gently.

Not quite growling, Ramoth took one backward step, flicking her tongue over her egg.

Ramoth!

"Up to her usual tricks?" F'lar asked.

"Hmmm." *Two more steps, please, dear, and do keep your tongue in your head. Such an undignified posture.* Lessa spoke firmly, and though Ramoth swung her head in a last show of reluctance, she did move back—five steps, deliberately more than requested—before she crouched down, glaring with orange-red flashing eyes.

Then Lessa cast an appraising glance over the five young women confronting the queen egg. Groghe's daughter, barely fifteen Turns old, was the smallest, a daintily made child. She had already Impressed two bronze fire-lizards, and Lessa hoped that they would contain themselves until after Impression was over. Ramoth might tolerate the creatures in the Hatching Ground, but not flying about her head. Still, Nataly had been sensibly raised, and her two fire-lizards had behaved themselves admirably since arriving at Benden.

Breda, the wraithlike blonde, came from Crom. Odd that Nessel did not object to Search, for all he opposed the Weyrs' energetic support of Aivas. She was very quiet, a journeyman weaver and, at twenty-two, the oldest candidate.

Cona was Neratian, and Manora had reported that in the sevenday that the girl had been at Benden Weyr, she had already been in the weyrs of three bronze riders. That was not a bad trait in a queen's rider; it was certainly preferable to a lack of sensuality.

Why the dragons had chosen Silga was a bit of a puzzle, for the girl had been terrified by her first flight *between*, and that was not a good omen.

The final girl, Tumara, was a cousin of Sharra's and so delighted to leave the isolated fisher's island off the Istan coast that Manora had commented the girl was wearing her out in her efforts to be useful.

Compliancy was a good trait, but too much became subservience, and that was not one of the more desirable qualities. A Weyrwoman had to be firm, fair, and sympathetic with her queen. Not that this pairing was certain to become senior in any Weyr.

Much had to be done, besides finding a suitable place for the new Weyr. Then, whichever junior queen—in whatever Weyr—next rose to mate would be flown by all unattached bronzes. The triumphant pair would be temporary Weyrleaders only until they had proved themselves. As fully three-quarters of the other queens on Pern were likely to come into season over the next few months, this was as fair a method as any to determine the leadership of the new Weyr.

The humming had increased to a frantic pitch. The first egg—Lessa breathed a sigh of relief when she saw a bronze head and wing emerge—had split cleanly, and the hatchling was up and out. A fine strong bronze, unsteady on its feet, of course, but able to extend its wet wings and swivel its head to and fro, trying to focus its bleary eyes on the figures before it.

With a shriek of triumph, it made a tremendous leap and landed in front of a stocky lad—from a Smithhall in Igen, if she recalled accurately. Sometimes the eager young faces seemed to blend into memories of all the candidates from the many Impressions held in this Hatching Ground over the past twenty-three Turns she had been Weyrwoman. Holding her breath, she watched that magical moment when the boy realized that the dragon had chosen him: ecstasy wreathed his face as he knelt to caress the imperious creature butting at him. Tears of joy streamed down his cheeks as he threw his arms about the damp bronze neck.

"Oh, Braneth, you are the most beautiful bronze in all the world!"

The audience let out a cheer and applauded while the dragons interrupted their hum to bugle a welcome.

After the initial Impression, other eggs cracked or split or crumbled to tip their inhabitants onto the warm sands, and brown, blue, and green dragonets were matched with compatible personalities.

"Good, twelve bronzes," F'lar said, keeping track of the pairings. "We could do with more browns—only four—but the distribution of blues and greens is exactly right."

Lessa had not been paying that much attention past the first three, for the queen egg was beginning to rock. Tentatively at first, and then with considerable energy. No cracks showed on the shell yet, a fact that was beginning to worry Lessa. Usually the queens were impetuous in their arrivals. Then the tip of the nose broke through, both wing claws appeared, and—as if the little queen had given a tremendous shrug—the shell parted vertically and she stood there, framed by the casing, looking about with great dignity.

"Oh, she's a darling, that one," F'lar murmured to Lessa. "Just look at her, queen of all she surveys."

With the unusual suppleness of a hatchling, the little queen tilted her head backward almost to her spine and gave Ramoth one long look before she swung her head forward again to regard the five girls facing her. Daintily, she stepped away from her shell. With a calm arrogance she swept her coruscating glance once more over those awaiting her decision. Lessa wondered if any of the girls were actually breathing at that crucial moment.

"I'll wager you a mark on Cona," F'lar said.

Lessa shook her head. "You'll lose. It's Nataly. The two are perfectly matched."

However, the little queen was quite an individual. She stalked to one end of the semicircle of girls, giving each a close scrutiny as she passed. She never even made it to Cona and Nataly—she paused at Breda, extending her neck and pushing her head very gently against the tall girl's body.

"That," F'lar said with a snap of his fingers, "for our choices."

Lessa chuckled. "The dragon always knows." Then she gave a little gasp. As Breda knelt to clasp the little queen's head to her breast, her rather plain face had taken on a beatific glow that transformed her into a radiant beauty.

Eyes luminous, Breda looked up at Lessa. "She says her name is Amaranth!"

"Well done, Breda. Felicitations!" Lessa called, having to shout above the applause that greeted the queen's Impression. *Are you satisfied?* she asked Ramoth, who was staring dourly at the pairing.

The girl wouldn't have been Searched if she wasn't suitable. We'll see how she copes with Amaranth. This one is a true daughter to me. From his high perch, Mnementh added a stunning triple-noted bugle. Ramoth craned her head up at him, her eyes dazzling with pulsating color. *You flew me well.*

F'lar grinned at Lessa, for they had both heard the remark. "We'd better get on with our day's duties, love," he said, using that excuse to put an arm about Lessa's slender waist and guide her down the stairs and out onto the Hatching Ground sands.

In an unusual display of maternal approval, Ramoth followed Lessa and F'lar as the Weyrleaders helped Breda escort Amaranth out of the immense cavern.

"Never for a moment did I think I'd be chosen, Weyrwoman Lessa," Breda said. "I've never been out of Crom, not even to a Gather."

"Did your family come?"

"No, Weyrwoman Lessa, my parents are dead. The Hall raised me."

In an uncharacteristic gesture, Lessa laid her hand on Breda's arm. "And you are to call me Lessa, my dear. We are both queen riders."

Breda's eyes widened.

"Who knows, my dear?" F'lar said, half joking. "You may be a Weyrwoman, too, one day soon."

Astonished, the girl stopped in her tracks. Amaranth pushed at her, urgently creeling her hunger.

Lessa tightened her hand on Breda's arm and led her briskly to meet the weyrfolk bearing huge bowls heaped with herdbeast flesh. "It is a possibility, you know. But first, we'll show you how to feed Amaranth. Don't let her bleating bother you. They always think they're starving after they've hatched."

Breda needed little instruction in feeding Amaranth, settling to the task with such ease that Lessa thought the girl had probably had to feed youngsters in the Hall that had raised her. Life in the Weyr was going to be quite different: Breda had just acquired a huge family.

Then Lessa turned to discharge the less enjoyable task of an Impression day: comforting the unsuccessful candidates. F'lar had already begun that process among the young men and boys. When Lessa looked about her for Nataly and Lord Groghe, she found them in a family knot at one of the tables. Manora was there before her, serving wine, klah, and fruit juices. Nataly was struggling to hide her disappointment and managing nobly, Lessa decided. Better than Silga and Tumara, who were in tears, with their families not really knowing what to say to console them. Cona was nowhere to be seen. Lessa wondered who had spirited her away, but decided that the girl's preferred kind of consolation might mend matters more effectively than any other available method.

She paused long enough to speak to Nataly and Lord Groghe and then moved on to help assuage the disappointment of Silga and Tumara.

The harpers had started to play, and although there were some long faces among the visitors, the music would soon brighten them. Weyrfolk were already busy pouring from wine sacks and serving enormous platters of the pit-roasted herdbeasts and wherries. Food was so often a sovereign remedy, Lessa reflected.

Finally, once the sated hatchlings were asleep on their pallets in the barracks, the Weyrlingmaster permitted the new dragonriders to join their families. With the honored guests present, the festivities went into full swing.

"A most positive young queen, hmmm?" Robinton said, sliding into an empty space beside Lessa. He raised his cup in a toast to F'lar, opposite her. "Made rather an entrance, didn't she?"

Lessa smiled and offered to fill Robinton's glass from the skin of Benden white that hung on her chair.

"Is Amaranth why F'lessan's been so interested in the vacant stakeholds in the South?" Robinton delivered his query in the guileless fashion that told Lessa and F'lar that he guessed a new Weyr was required.

F'lar gave a knowing snort. "He offered."

"He's more in Landing than he is here," Lessa added wryly. With three sons by as many weyrgirls, F'lessan had need to be absent from their entreaties. He had provided well for each of his children, but he was no more ready to settle down with one than any young, handsome, and popular bronze rider. Manora had even suggested that the absence of that young charmer for a while might result in one or more of the girls settling for an older rider in a more stable, lasting attachment.

Robinton cocked an eyebrow, suggesting to Lessa that he already knew about the demands on F'lessan. "He's an excellent choice of explorer. Is a Weyr situation the only thing he's to investigate?"

F'lar picked up on that. "Why? Is Toric restless again?"

Robinton took a judicious sip from his cup. "Not really. Now that Denol's tenure of the Big Island has been settled, Toric's making up for lost time with Aivas."

"And?" F'lar prompted.

"He hid his chagrin rather well when he discovered just how . . . mmm . . . less than vast the Southern Continent actually is. Fortunately he's decided that Southern must have Halls of both new Crafts. I believe that he and Hamian had rather a vociferous confrontation over the filler plant Hamian's been developing as an insulating material."

"The fibrous stuff that Bendarek's been going on about?" Lessa asked. "You know that he's genuinely concerned about the amount of trees that are needed to supply the demand for paper."

"Indeed." Robinton nodded vigorously. "I do see his point that a weed that grows rampant in Southern should be utilized instead of chopping down those magnificent forests of his."

"I thought that Sharra discovered the plant and recognized its usefulness," Lessa added.

"I believe that's Toric's contention," Robinton replied, his eyes sparkling with mischief. "That she found it on his holding while on a sweep for him."

"Will the man never be satisfied?" Lessa demanded with some heat.

"I doubt it," Robinton replied equably.

"Will we end up having to fight him for holdings in the South?" Lessa went on, shooting him a fierce glance for his casual manner.

"My dear Lessa, no one, absolutely no one, is going to challenge a man, or a woman, mounted a-dragon! And let us devoutly hope that there never is a point at which that is even remotely possible."

"Southern Weyr?" F'lar reminded the Harper severely.

"Well, yes, now, but that was not aggression—it was abduction." Robinton had good cause to remember the time Ramoth's egg had disappeared from the Hatching Ground and how very near Benden dragons had come to fighting the Oldtimer Southern dragons. Not wishing to remind the Weyrleaders that they had ostracized him at that point in time, Robinton held up his glass, looking plaintively at the wineskin hanging on Lessa's chair. She filled it for him. "Mind you, I think you're wise to send F'lessan to explore the tantalizing potential of Southern. When is he going?"

Lessa grinned, lifting her eyebrows expressively. "He should be there even as we speak."

The great plains rolled on below F'lessan and Golanth as the big bronze glided on a south-southwest path, aided by high thermals. A slight twinge of guilt marred F'lessan's happy contemplation of the scenery. He really should have been working up those equations for Aivas, who was under the impression that the young bronze rider's presence was required at the Benden Hatching. As F'lessan had no wish to have to explain to Nera, Faselly, and Brinna why he couldn't choose among them, he was glad enough to spend a free day obeying the injunction of F'lar and Lessa.

Golanth was so thoroughly enjoying himself that F'lessan decided it was unsuitable to belabor himself with unnecessary remorse. He had been unusually diligent in his studies—even enjoyed them. In truth, as F'lessan looked back over the past two Turns, he realized that he had devoted more time to Aivas than to the Weyr—save for Threadfall. He often flew as Wingsecond with T'gellan and the Eastern Weyr and with K'van in Southern. He liked fighting Thread, and he and Golanth were exceedingly deft at escaping injury.

One thing he hadn't dared to ask Lessa and F'lar: If he found a suitable site for another Weyr, was he in line to be Weyrleader? He dismissed that notion almost instantly. F'lessan had few illusions about himself. He was a good Wingleader, he understood draconic abilities, he knew which were the best riders in every Weyr and who were the most likely weyrlings in Benden, but he didn't think he was anyone's immediate choice for the next Weyrleader. And he was well aware of how such matters were decided: open mating flight for all unattached bronzes.

I'm big and strong, Golanth informed him with just a hint of boasting in his tone. *I'd've caught Lamanth that time, if Litorth had not done that clip-and-run dive maneuver. He'd been practicing with the greens!* he added petulantly.

F'lessan soothed his dragon with hand and voice. He had been a bit provoked about that himself. Of course, Celina was nearly as old as Lessa, but it was becoming a matter of honor for Golanth to fly a queen, and Celina was a nice sort. Anyone could get along with her.

A dust cloud caught F'lessan's attention, and he asked Golanth to veer toward it.

I'm not hungry just now, Golanth replied as they got near enough to distinguish the rumps of fleeing herdbeasts.

Get in a little closer, would you, Golanth? I've never seen any like these. Brown and white, and black and white. Big beasts. Nice and juicy, F'lessan added coaxingly.

If they are big now, they will be bigger when I am ready to eat.

F'lessan chuckled. There were times when Golanth couldn't be diverted. He glanced at the dial strapped to his arm, checking the time it registered against his reading of the sun. Accurate enough. Aivas called it a watch—and the first time F'lessan had worn it he had indeed watched, mesmerized, as the long second hand made its way around the dial. Jancis had presented it to him on his birthing day. She had designed and executed the device for him personally. F'lessan had felt both honored and elated to be the proud possessor of one of the few wristwatches on Pern. Jancis had only made six: Piemur, of course, wore one; so did Lord Larad and Lady Jissamy; Master Robinton and Master Fandarel were the other lucky recipients.

He and Golanth had been a-wing for the past five hours. If they didn't sight their objective soon, he was going to ask Golanth to land so that he could eat his lunch and stretch his legs. A six-hour stint during a Fall was one thing—then he was actively involved, too busy to become uncomfortable. Flying straight to a new location was a different matter altogether—always tedious. But it was necessary when one's destination was unfamiliar, unless one had been given a detailed description or could grab an image of the site from another dragon or rider's mind—which was not the case today. Golanth was making good time, catching the thermals and air currents to increase his speed, but it was a weary way to go.

Still and all, F'lessan enjoyed being first at something. He was not by nature an envious sort, but it did seem that Piemur and Jaxom had the larger portion of luck with their discoveries. He was very pleased that Lessa and F'lar had entrusted this search to him. They could have sent one of the older bronze riders, or F'nor. Nevertheless, it was F'lessan and Golanth who were winging over the great plains, toward the huge inland sea that the settlers had named Caspian, to a Hold called Xanadu.

Suddenly, off to his right, the sun dazzled him, reflecting off—water?

To our right, Golly, F'lessan said excitedly.

A very big water, Golanth added.

As he often had, F'lessan wondered if he would see clearer, better, farther if he had faceted dragon eyes.

I can see anything you wish for you, Golanth replied meekly.

F'lessan pummeled his neck affectionately. *I know, big fellow, and I'm always grateful for your help. I was just thinking what it might be like, that's all.*

Golanth began to stroke the air, beating upward. *Thermal,* he said cryptically, and F'lessan leaned down against the great bronze neck so as not to impede the ascent. He felt the alteration in the wind current and let out a triumphant yodel when Golanth flattened out and set his wings to glide on the hot air.

And that's something else you can do which I can't—tell where the air currents are. How ever do you know where the thermals are?

My eyes see the variation of air, I smell the difference, and my hide feels the altered pressure.

Really? F'lessan was impressed with the explanation. *Been listening in on my aerodynamics lessons with Aivas?*

Golanth thought that over. *Yes. You listen to him, so I thought I should. Ruth does, and Path certainly. Ramoth and Mnementh don't. They prefer to sleep in the sun while Lessa and F'lar are here. Bigath listens, and Sulath and Beerth. Clarinath occasionally, but Pranith always and Lioth whenever his rider's down. Sometimes the listening is very interesting. Sometimes it's not.*

Not only was that an unusually long speech for Golanth, but it gave F'lessan such food for thought that he was kept occupied with the ramifications until the edge of the vast inland sea became visible.

How are the air currents, Golanth? Shall we cross it, or fly around?

We cross it, was the immediate and confident answer.

We need a nor'norwest heading, Golanth, to reach the point where the ancients settled. Not that I think we'll find much.

As they crossed the water, passing through several squalls on the way, they noted all the little islands and the strange pinnacles of rock upthrusts, like bony fingers or clenched fists. On some, odd-shaped trees had managed to find soil enough in the rock crevices to support their roots. In two instances, naked roots twisted down the spires, seeking additional dirt and sustenance. The trees, with their closely packed heads, leaned precariously away from the prevailing winds. Or were those branches that were seeking the summits and sunlight? Sharra would want to know about these—she liked such oddities.

The western coastline was visible at last, a high palisade of cliff. The inland sea must have been formed in a vast subsidence, F'lessan decided, recognizing the geological formation from Aivas's survey lectures. That would also account for the spires and islands: the tops of sunken mountains. Now if those distant cliff faces also held caves, this would be a splendid place for a Weyr, he thought. All that water! One would never have a dry dragon in one's weyr.

He was to be disappointed, however, once they got close enough to see the solid granite composition of the high bluffs.

Dragons don't have cliff weyrs in Southern or Eastern and they don't complain, Golanth said helpfully.

I know, but I was asked to find a useful old crater or two.

The sun will find me in a clearing, and there are some very good-smelling trees on this continent.

F'lessan thumped Golanth, grinning at the bronze's effort to console him for the disappointment. *This isn't the only place I'm supposed to check out. There was a settler's hold, called Honshu, in the foothills of the southern barrier range. However, since we're here, let's look about for this Xanadu Stakehold.*

Golanth's sharp eyes spotted unnatural outlines on a slight prominence, not far from where a wide river had worn a deep gorge from the outer sea to the inner one. F'lessan wasn't sure about ruins, but he had to accept that wide steps had been cut in the palisade face. Someone had wanted an easy access to the lakeshore. Golanth landed neatly beside his alleged ruins. Looking around, F'lessan at first thought the dragon had been mistaken in seeing any shape whatsoever beneath the heavy vegetation.

This is not natural, Golanth insisted, tapping a vertical thicket of twisted vines and moss. Extending his wing, he hooked a wingfinger claw on a twisted branch and pulled away the obscuring greenery. As myriad creatures scuttled away from exposure to the sun, F'lessan found himself looking at a tall chimney of worked stone. So the rest of the ruin had to be the remains of the walls of a dwelling.

F'lessan shook his head for those foolish enough to build with so much vegetation all around them, making them twice as vulnerable to Thread. Taking a meatroll from his pouch, he ate as he walked around the hold walls, using his belt knife to scrape down to long-hidden dressed stone. It would have been a large dwelling. Golanth had shouldered his way into the thick forest and was calling his rider to inspect more ruins.

"Sizable place all right enough," F'lessan said, kicking at some rubble. "Xanadu, huh!" He turned back to the main building, snagging a ripe redfruit from a hanging limb as he walked. Chewing the juicy fruit, he contemplated the prospect of sea and distant shore that the original inhabitants must surely have enjoyed. Magnificent! If there hadn't been Thread to worry about, it would have been an endlessly beautiful vista. "We've another place to investigate, Golanth," he said abruptly, throwing off a sense of regret on behalf of those long-dead holders.

He asked Golanth to wheel over the site so that he could imprint the details in his mind for future visits. If—no, F'lessan corrected himself defiantly, *when* Pernese skies were Threadfree, this would be an admirable situation for an open-air weyr.

Golanth caught an updraft that put them quickly back into the westerly current. They had a long way still to go. Shielding his eyes, F'lessan glanced at the lowering sun and then, berating himself for his forgetfulness, looked at his wristwatch. Four more hours until dusk. Not that flying at night bothered Golanth, nor would it be the first night F'lessan had curled up in a bed made by his dragon's forepaws, but if they didn't hurry, F'lessan wouldn't see what he had flown all this way to lay his eyes on.

They flew onward, Golanth's wings tirelessly carrying them, until the great Southern barrier range developed from a pale lavender smudge to vast purplish blue massifs, dominating the horizon.

Bi-i-ig— F'lessan drawled the adjective—*mountains! Higher than anything we have in the North until you reach the Icy Wastes.*

The air would be very thin up there, Golanth observed. *Will we have to cross them?*

I don't think so. F'lessan rummaged in his jacket pocket for the map Aivas had printed out for him. It flapped so badly in the wind of their passage that he had trouble reading it. *No, this Honshu holding is in the foothills below the real range. We're just not close enough to distinguish them.*

The last of the brilliant sunset illuminated the general area of their destination. Only because sharp-eyed Golanth saw a line of herd-beasts ambling through a wide doorway in the foot of the cliff did they locate Honshu.

Are you sure you saw what you said you saw? F'lessan asked in surprise. *Surely they would have taken their beasts with them when they left.*

Maybe wild ones found the way into a place of safety, Golanth suggested. Speeding up his wing strokes, he reached the foot of the sheer cliff just as the last of sunset drained from western skies.

There was no mistaking the wide track worn smooth by usage that led to the cliff face and through a wide entrance angled into the cliff. Peering inside, F'lessan coughed at the stench of the place. High in the walls, window slits did not give him light enough to see much— and the smell alone was enough to discourage investigation. The herdbeasts bawled in surprise at his entrance and milled anxiously deeper into what he guessed was an immense cavern. Choking and with eyes streaming from the intense ammoniac smell, F'lessan backed out. Leaning against the cliff, he breathed deeply of the fresh evening air.

"Looks like you found me Honshu, Golanth," he said, running his hand up the beasthold entrance. "This was cut as neatly as a hot knife in cheese. Just like Fort Hold and the Weyr—when the ancients still had power for their stonecutters. So this has to be Honshu." His fingers also located a door, neatly retracted into the wall. "They left the door wide open, after all. Well, Golanth, let's find us a place to camp for the night. A fire would be right cheerful on a black night like this. I don't know if those big felines Sharra and Piemur talked about range this far south, but . . ."

No feline would challenge me!

"Not one who wishes to see tomorrow," F'lessan said with a laugh as he peered into the dark for someplace to settle down.

Follow me, Golanth said, and ambled to the left of the cliff face.

"You're better than a torch." F'lessan followed, taking care not to tread on his dragon's tail.

Dead wood was easy enough to find, and rocks to contain a fire, so very shortly F'lessan was comfortably settled against Golanth's shoulder, munching on his travel rations and sipping some Benden wine he had talked Manora into putting in his bottle. Then, because there was little else to do, F'lessan unrolled the fur that padded Golanth's neck ridge, nestled himself snugly between Golanth's forelimbs, and went to sleep.

He woke up just as the eastern skies were brightening. Enough embers remained from his fire to be coaxed back into sufficient warmth to allow him to heat his morning klah and break his fast with a warm meatroll. Golanth ambled down to the river and drank deeply.

This will be a good place to swim—once the sun is up, he said with the air of an expert. *And the cliff a good place to warm after a swim. The sun will catch the stone and radiate heat.*

F'lessan grinned as he sipped his hot klah. *You* have *been learning a thing or two from listening.*

Only the things that make sense to me.

Then F'lessan heard the low bleating and moaning of the animals sheltering in the hold.

Stay there, Golanth, or the animals won't come out, and I want to investigate this place.

I don't mind if I do, Golanth replied equably, *but they have nothing to fear for I am not hungry yet.*

Somehow I doubt they'd believe you, dear heart. F'lessan made a second cup of klah and then kicked dirt and gravel over his little fire lest the smell of burning wood alarm the beasts.

He did not have long to wait. Once the sunlight hit the entrance, the animals—which proved to be of more than one species of herdbeast—began to file out, ready for a day's browsing or grazing. Most of those had younglings at foot. Not stirring a muscle, F'lessan watched the exodus. Only when all had made their way down the track, spreading out on their separate ways, did the bronze rider approach the opening.

"Faugh!" The reek still discouraged F'lessan from entering—the dung had accumulated to the level of midthigh in some places. Holding his breath, he stuck his head in. The cavern was huge, as far as he could tell in the patches of early-morning light that filtered in through the high windows. It was then that he noticed a flight of steps to his right.

Golanth! I'm going in. There're steps here. Drawing his collar across his nose and mouth, F'lessan darted toward the steps and ran up to the first landing, where he stopped. There, to his right, was a large door that had once been secured by a lock, now a rusted shell that fell into dust at his touch. He pushed open the door and stood on another landing, from which steps led down to a large, high-ceilinged room. Window slits let in barely enough light to make out a bulky object, half a dragon length in size, which appeared to be covered.

I've found some sort of an ancient artifact! he told Golanth as he took the steps two at a time in his excitement.

The covering was of ancient manufacture, soapy and slick to the touch once he brushed aside the film of dust that had turned a bright green fabric to gray. Flipping a corner up, F'lessan peered at the unmistakable prow of a vehicle. Struggling to uncover more of the incredible object, F'lessan recognized it from some of the tapes Aivas has shown them as a sled, one of the larger sort.

Just wait till Master Fandarel and Benelek see this thing, Golanth! They'll go spare! F'lessan crowed with delight and anticipation at the stir this beauty would cause. He rolled more of the cover back, noticing how carefully the craft had been stored by its owners and wondering why they had left it behind. *No more fuel to fly it, probably.*

It's a cumbersome-looking thing, Golanth remarked.

Don't worry, love, I'd never trade you in for one of these. Cranky things from what the records tell us. Always needing to be serviced and have parts replaced. Don't have that worry with a dragon. F'lessan laughed heartily at the thought of the Smithcrafters swarming over the sled—for all the good it would do them. Still, it was quite a relic to find lovingly stored away. So few of the settlers' everyday implements had been discovered. Then he noticed the racks of dust-shrouded tools on the wall, a pile of empty plastic sacks such as the settlers had used to store all manner of items, and, under layers of fine dust, plastic containers in the settlers' favorite bright colors.

Well, when I tell Aivas what we've found, he won't be so upset, F'lessan added. *So I'd better survey the whole place for a complete report. Aivas respects complete reports.*

Then he bounded up the steps to the landing and proceeded on upward. He noticed that there were piles of dung on some of the steps and muddy hoof marks that, fortunately, ended at another closed door.

This one slid back into the wall—not without some grunting and shoving on F'lessan's part. Having achieved a wide-enough gap to squeeze through, he stepped onto yet another landing, with stairs leading down to a huge cavern—a workroom, to judge by the variety of tables and cabinets. Slightly amazed, he identified both a forge and a huge kiln, as well as workbenches. And there he saw his first signs of a hurried departure, for some cabinet drawers were half out of their slides and there were odd cartons, not quite lidded shut, on three work surfaces. He didn't go down to investigate further, for yet another flight of stairs led up to a higher level.

I'm moving up in the world, Golanth, with more marvels to report to Aivas. Oooowhee, but this place is a treasure trove. The people may have left, but for once they didn't take much with them. Robinton and Lytol are going to be fascinated!

Golanth's response was a deep grunt that echoed in F'lessan's ears; laughing at his dragon's lack of enthusiasm, the bronze rider galloped eagerly up the steps.

Nor was F'lessan disappointed. The door on this level opened onto what had to be the main entry to the hold. Through a graceful archway, he could see into what must have been the central living area. For the first time, he felt like an intruder as he stepped into the immense room, and he stopped in the doorway. He heard the slither of tunnel snakes, retreating from his presence. Peering into the room, he could distinguish little beyond shrouded forms in the darkness, but he could see the thin lines of light around window apertures.

Retracing his steps to the hall, he threw open the wide double leaves of the main door, blinking at the brilliance of the early-morning sun. The hold faced northeast, as a southern hold should, and an early breeze ruffled the thick cushion of dust on the floor. With that light to help him, he found the windows, which were set far above his head; he also found the long pole that opened them. He had opened five of the ten large windows before his eyes fell on the space above them.

Golanth! You should see this! It's amazing!

See what? Where are you now? Is there room for me?

"I—th—think so." F'lessan heard his own stammer echo back from the vaulted ceiling, a ceiling that had been decorated in brilliantly colored murals that had lost nothing of their brightness. And he now knew part of the story they depicted. "This ought to shut up the doubters—an independent verification of what Aivas told us!" he murmured, more to himself than to Golanth, as he gave the walls a fleeting glance before beginning a more studied perusal. So involved did he become with the mural scenes that it took him a moment to realize that the scrabbling noise he heard was Golanth's claws on stone.

This door is not wide enough for me, Golanth said, sounding distinctly annoyed. F'lessan glanced around and stifled a guffaw. Golanth had got head and neck through the opening, but not his massive shoulders.

"You're not stuck, are you?" the bronze rider asked solicitously.

They could have made the door a little bit higher and wider, since they made it as big as they did.

"I don't really think they had dragons of your size in mind when they built it, Golanth. But can you see the murals? There's even a scene about dragons—right overhead. Oh, you can't quite see it, but these murals are amazing. There are panels for every major event—" F'lessan pointed out the appropriate panels as he explained. "The actual landing in the shuttle craft; the ones in Ship Meadow; and yes, there are sleds just like the one down below; and the building of holds, and people working the land, and then Thread. They did that panel too graphically. Turns my stomach just to look at it. They've got lots of sleds, and smaller craft, and flamethrowers and—ah, high up in the ceiling, they've even got Rukbat and all its planets. If only we'd found this place a long time ago . . .'' F'lessan was silent a long moment, his eyes moving from one beautifully painted panel to the next. "They'll all want to see this place," he said at length with infinite satisfaction. "We did good, Golanth, dear heart. And we were first here!"

He looked around one last time, deciding not to investigate further so that others might have the pleasure of seeing the place as it had been left. Then he carefully closed the windows.

Golanth, crammed into the doorway, had been trying to see what he could. As F'lessan approached him, he carefully backed out onto the broad shelf that jutted out from that level. F'lessan closed the doors behind him, marveling at the workmanship that allowed the heavy metal to pivot so easily after so many centuries of disuse. He gazed up at the sweep of the hold: three more levels of windows were visible.

"Neither weyr nor hold but it would serve," F'lessan said, remembering the point of his search. "That is, once the artifacters and Craftmasters get their look-in."

Dragons would find this spot eminently suitable, F'lessan, Golanth assured him. *There is the river, which is deep, clear, and tasty to drink, and there are many ledges that face the sun all the day long.* The bronze dragon swung his head to left and right to bring those places to F'lessan's notice. *This would make a very good Weyr indeed.*

"And so we shall report."

12
▼▼▼▼▼▼▼

T he discovery of Honshu was partially eclipsed by S'len's discovery of eighteen usable space suits in the *Yokohama* EVA ready room. In Master Robinton's opinion, Aivas had received that news with a great deal more excitement than he had displayed when hearing about Honshu's state of preservation. Aivas said that the suits gave his schedule considerably more flexibility and dispensed with some rather awkward and possibly dangerous alternatives. However, some folk in the Smithcraft, and many in the Harper Hall, considered Honshu the more important, and certainly more immediately useful, discovery.

While Aivas was revising his plan, Jancis and Hamian were appointed by Master Fandarel to inventory the tools at Honshu and, if their use was not immediately apparent, to decide what function they had had. Aivas did take time to print out a manual for the sled, out of respect for the keen interest shown, but added the qualifier that any such investigations were esoteric since he could give no assistance in powering it. That provoked some resentment in those who felt that aerial transportation should not be restricted to dragonriders and "a chosen few."

Aivas's rebuttal to that accusation was to enumerate all the skills and technological improvements—which most of those same complainants objected to in theory—that would be necessary to produce powered aerial vehicles, including the development of an alternative and reliable power source.

"The settlers used power packs," Aivas reminded them. The subject had arisen before. "These units were rechargeable, but no recharging mechanism survived."

"But can't you tell us how to make the power packs?"

"There are two kinds of science," Aivas began in his oblique fashion. "Practical and theoretical. With practical, engineers use only what is known—and proved to work in the everyday world—to achieve certain predicted and predictable results. Theoretical science, on the other hand, pushes at the boundaries and laws that are *known* to work—and sometimes even steps outside of them. For the projects you have been working on, you already had enough background and know-how to learn the necessary science to follow my instructions. But for some things—such as the alien power packs—Pern simply has not the technology or the science to understand the theories well enough to apply them practically."

"In other words, we're stuck with this world and what's in it?" Jaxom asked.

"Precisely. And it is up to you to work this out for yourself, or to gain help from Lytol rather than from this facility."

And that was as much time as Aivas would spend on Honshu. With additional space suits available, he initiated new projects, which, it was made clear, were much closer to the major task at hand: the destruction of Thread.

Now that the life-support systems on the *Bahrain* and the *Buenos Aires* were fully operational, Mirrim and S'len were sent on their green dragons to make the necessary links between the bridge consoles on the two smaller ships and the *Yokohama* link with Aivas. The *Bahrain* and the *Buenos Aires* had, however, sustained more damage over the centuries than the *Yokohama*, losing antennae, exterior optics, and considerable areas of the outside skin from impacts that the shields had been unable to deflect. But that damage, Aivas was quick to state, would not interfere with the Plan.

Terry, Wansor, three of the Glass-smith's brightest journeymen, and Perschar, the artist, were ferried up by green dragons for long sessions on the *Yokohama*'s telescope, mapping the Red Star for any distinctive features. The vid-link down to Aivas was still imperfect; Aivas had been unable to discover the problem and so had to rely on human observations. They soon reported to Aivas that only one side of the planet was turned toward them. Perschar was to do large reproductions of whatever geographic features the surface of the eccentric planet presented. Wansor had to be peeled away from the console, so exhausted by his lengthy efforts that he actually fell asleep *between* on the return trip.

Teams made up of green and bronze riders—all transported by the smaller green dragons—explored the deserted levels of the *Yokohama* in case anything else had been left behind. But the ancients had stripped an amazing amount of material from the ship. The space suits—and the banks of coldsleep capsules—were all that had been deemed useless on the surface.

Then a team of Mastersmiths was sent to all three ships, starting with the *Yokohama*, so that all four could familiarize themselves with the cargo bays and engine rooms. The four—Fandarel, Belterac, Evan, and Jancis—were fascinated by the ship's construction, pausing to examine the way struts had been secured, how walls, ceilings and floors had been fitted into the skeleton of the ship. It was difficult for them to assimilate the fact that the *Yokohama* had been assembled in space at one of the old Earth's gigantic satellite shipyards, and that the heaviest portions had been pushed into position by single workers with computer-controlled machines.

Master Fandarel made full use of the *Yokohama* as a schoolroom, getting Aivas to explain the designs and the safety aspects of the compartmentalization. He was truly amazed at the rationale behind the odd design of the spacegoing ship and had many questions to put to Aivas about the apparent anomalies.

The main section of the *Yokohama* was a huge sphere of many levels, each of which could be closed off, as could sections of each level—to sustain life, Aivas told them, should the main hull be breached. Thus heat and oxygen could be maintained only where necessary, as was being done now, to conserve supplies. The bridge area, the environmental section and the lift accessing it, a small infirmary, and Airlock A were the most heavily shielded. According to Aivas, escape pods had once been attached to Airlock A, until the *Yokohama* had been recommissioned as a colony ship and those pod positions had been altered to access supply drones.

The huge matter-antimatter engines were housed on a long shaft, attached to the midsection of the main sphere but separated by the heaviest shielding on the *Yokohama*. Two great wheels on either end of the engine shaft had held the fuel and cargo pods that had been wrapped around the engines. Those had, of course, been emptied during the journey and launched to splash down in the seas off Monaco Bay. Retrieved, the basic metal had been smelted down and reworked. The ceramic fuel tanks had been put to different uses. Very little of the superstructure of the *Yokohama* and the other two colony ships remained. The narrower stern wheel on the end of the engine shaft still held its band of maneuvering jets which, powered by the solar panels and in conjunction with those around the main sphere, were what kept the *Yokohama*'s orbit stable. One of the first checks Aivas had commissioned was to ascertain how much fuel remained in the *Yokohama*'s main tank.

Fandarel, thinking about that fuel, wondered why the settlers had dared to leave the colony ships in an orbit that was ultimately destined to decay. Aivas replied curtly that that was not an immediate concern: So far, the orbits had not decayed, and the surface of Pern was not at risk—not, at least, from ship debris.

It was while Jancis was busy patching the main engineering board into Aivas while the others were examining the "readiness" run of the great propulsion units that one of the green riders activated the red alert from the bridge. Jancis's bronze fire-lizard, Trig, became so agitated that she had a hard time calming him down enough to make sense of his response. She could raise neither S'len nor L'zan on the com. And the red-alert signal continued to blink in the engineering facility.

"Thread attacking the *Yokohama*?" Jancis got that much from Trig's chaotic thoughts. "It can't, Trig. It can't. We're safe here! No, don't you dare breathe fire in here!"

Jancis then bellowed directions through the speaker to the bridge until S'len hit the right sequence of buttons to make voice contact.

"It's Thread, Jancis, I'm sure of it," S'len replied. "Not space debris. There's this flood of egglike things of varying sizes streaming toward us. Looks just like the stuff Aivas described to us in his lecture. Space debris wouldn't come in a steady flow, would it? This stuff goes back as far as we can see from the window. Only none of them ever hits the window, and the pilot's board is all lit up and the engineer's station is beeping at us." His words came tumbling out in his haste to describe the situation. Then his voice became agitated. "Bigath and Beerth are demanding that we go *outside*. They say it's Thread. I never should have even *thought* what I thought it is!" Then in an explosive aside: "No, Bigath, we *can't* fly this sort of a Fall. It's not Thread yet, if that's what it is! We haven't any firestone, and there's no air out there, and you wouldn't fly outside anyway—you'd float, just like in here. Shards! Jancis, I can't make her understand!"

S'len didn't panic easily, and Bigath was not as erratic as some greens. In the background, Jancis could also hear Aivas's loud reassurances. If Bigath was not obeying her rider, she certainly could not be disciplined by the Aivas. Her bugling challenge at Thread took on a frantic edge.

"Tell them Ruth says they're not to go! They obey him!" she said, latching on to an authority the greens respected. She didn't know a green dragon who wasn't partial to the white dragon.

"When is Ruth coming, Bigath wants to know!" S'len's tone had altered from dismay to desperation. Aivas's calm voice continued to exhort the green dragons to listen to reason, but he was using reason that the dragons were not in a state to hear.

Jancis was scribbling a note to Jaxom to come at once when S'len, with a cry of relief, said, "Ruth's here and everything's under control!"

Jancis looked at the note and then at her fire-lizard, who cocked his head at her quizzically. She considered the matter for a moment longer and then made a decision. There was absolutely no way in which Jaxom and Ruth would have known to come to the bridge. He was in Ruatha today, and Aivas had no way of communicating with him there. She checked the exact time on her watch and wrote it down on the note. She added a final phrase in big letters: "TIME IT!" Then she sent Trig off to Ruatha and Jaxom.

"But if Ruth and Jaxom are here, why send the note now?" Fandarel asked.

Jancis smiled at her grandfather. "Trig needs the practice, Granddad."

Trig was back almost immediately, looking inordinately pleased with himself.

"He needs more than practice," Fandarel said, dismayed at the apparent disobedience.

"I don't know about you," Jancis said as a diversion, striding over to the lift, "but I want to see this 'attack.' I've never been allowed out of Hall or Hold during a Fall, so now may be my only chance. Aren't any of you interested?"

The reaction to her challenge was immediate, and when Jancis found herself crammed into the lift with three big smiths she was sorry that she had issued it.

Then the lift door opened to a curious bedlam: two green dragons, wings plastered to the window, were so fiercely hissing and spraying saliva that the view was largely obscured, while Ruth, his wing fingers on those of the two greens, putting him at full stretch, overlapped their bodies. He was loudly emitting some sort of croon that was only just audible through their angry sputters.

Jancis managed to grab Trig before he took off to join the dragons in their futile posturing. She pinned him firmly under one arm while she hung on to the railing lest his violent attempts to free himself send her into a spin. Ruth turned his redshot eyes in their direction and barked peremptorily. The bronze fire-lizard immediately subsided.

The view—or the part of it that was not blocked by green and white dragon bodies—was awesome: the objects blanketed the entire panorama. Jancis had to exert a firm control over an urge to recoil as the shapes, zooming straight at *Yokohama*, were deflected at seemingly the last moment before impact by the ship's shields. But gradually, she and the smiths became accustomed to the spectacle and could appreciate it with detachment. Not that any of them found it as amusing as Jaxom did. He was clutching the pilot's chair in one hand to prevent himself from floating off, but he was nearly doubled up with laughter. S'len and L'zan, hovering circumspectly out of reach of furiously swishing dragon tails, looked on in chagrin and embarrassment.

Being the tallest man there, Fandarel had a reasonably unobstructed view. "An amazing spectacle. Aivas, is this one of those meteor showers you've told us about?"

"What you are seeing is not a meteor shower," Aivas replied. "Comparing the present onslaught with reports made by Pilot Kenjo Fusaiyuki during his reconnaissance flights and pending examination of a sample, it is reasonable to assume that Thread, in its space-traveling form, is flowing past the *Yokohama* on its way to your planet."

"But where will it fall?" Jaxom asked, unable to remember which Weyr was scheduled to fly Fall next.

"On Nerat, in precisely forty-six hours," Aivas replied.

Jaxom let out a long whistle.

"This swarm has a long way to go yet to reach the atmospheric envelope of the planet," Aivas continued.

"Hmmm," Fandarel said, moving closer to peer out the window. "Fascinating! To be amid Thread and unharmed by it. Truly astounding. It's a great pity we can't do something to stem the tide here, before it reaches the surface."

S'len groaned. "Please don't even think that," he said, flicking his hand at the willing creatures whom Ruth was visibly restraining at the window.

"Thread doesn't look so dangerous right now," Jancis said thoughtfully as she watched the ovoids sweep in and abruptly disappear.

"In its frozen state, it is unlikely to be life-threatening," Aivas said.

"But you don't know for sure?"

"Attempts were made by Nabhi Nabol and Bart Lemos to secure specimens, but their ship disintegrated before they were able to return with them."

"We could get some now," Jaxom suggested. "There're plenty out there."

There was a significant pause, and Jaxom winked at Jancis. It wasn't often that Aivas was caught speechless.

"You fail to recognize the hazards of such a venture," the Aivas replied at last.

"Why? We could stash the thing in Airlock A, for instance, and it would stay frozen. As you keep telling us, it takes the friction of the atmosphere for Thread to metamorphose into its dangerous state."

Jancis was mouthing words at Jaxom, shaking her head violently. Under her arm, Trig struggled with renewed vigor to free himself from restraint.

"The *Yokohama* is moving at approximately 38,765 nautical miles per hour or about twenty thousand miles per hour relative to the Thread ovoids. To attempt to capture one would be an impossible maneuver even for persons trained in extravehicular activities. It would also be essential to have nonheat-conducting tongs."

Trig squawked.

I would capture a Thread egg for you, Ruth said, turning his head at an impossible angle over his shoulder to his rider.

Jaxom looked in alarm at his white dragon and regretted his spontaneous suggestion. "Oh, no, you don't." At Ruth's crestfallen expression, he added, "No one else can keep those greens under control."

"Did Ruth just offer to go get a Thread?" Jancis asked, holding more tightly to the writhing Trig. "Let Trig go."

"You heard what Aivas said about the velocities and nonheat-conducting tongs."

"It doesn't look as if we're traveling anywhere near that speed," she replied. Then she sighed. "Even if I know we must be. Anyway, fire-lizard talons aren't exactly heat-conductive, are they? Trig seems to think he can."

"*What!*" Belterac demanded, his eyes bulging with horror. "Bring one of those—those things in here with us?"

"Not in here," Jancis told him. "Into the airlock, where we can examine it closely. In its frozen state, it poses no danger."

"Do you really think Trig would be able to manage?" Fandarel asked, his insatiable curiosity getting the better of an ingrained revulsion to Thread.

"If he thinks he can," Jancis said. She looked down at the struggling fire-lizard. "Letting him do something about Thread may calm him down." She looked out at the barrage.

"It has been noted," Aivas said, "that fire-lizards are particularly courageous in the presence of Thread. It has also been noted that, in both fire-lizards and dragons, the *thought* becomes the deed by some method which does not bear investigation. If Trig should *think* he can retrieve a specimen, despite the obvious difficulties, it would greatly facilitate a useful examination of the organism. Placing it in Airlock A would, of course, keep the specimen frozen, dormant, *and* impotent. Then it could be examined at leisure, a procedure your ancestors scheduled but did not implement. It would complete their biological investigations of this organism."

Jaxom looked warily at Jancis. All in all, he wasn't sure they should ask this of Trig. Didn't they know as much as they needed to know about Thread? And yet, to have a Thread impotent, at their disposal, locked in a primal form, would be subtly gratifying.

It wouldn't be at all hard to do, Ruth told Jaxom.

"Ruth!" Jaxom vetoed that with a sharp chop of his hands. "You stay out of this fire-lizard assignment. Show-off!"

To his surprise, Jancis laughed. "Does Ruth think he'd fit in Airlock A?" she asked, grinning at Ruth's reproachful expression. "First, let's see if Trig is certain he can manage. Now, dear . . ." She lifted Trig up level with her eyes, took his triangular head, and pointed it toward the window. "We want you to get one of those big eggs and put it in Airlock A. You remember where that is. It'd be like catching a wherry midair."

I'm telling him, too, in case he doesn't understand, Ruth said, turning a reproving eye on his rider. *I'd be perfectly safe. I'm much bigger than the Thread eggs. I wouldn't be thrown off balance as a little fire-lizard would be. And it's no more than a jump between.*

Trig gave a cheep, turned his head toward Ruth, and cheeped again, the whirling of his eyes speeding up with anticipation and resolve.

He understands. He says he can easily do that.

"Ruth has now briefed Trig thoroughly," Jaxom told Jancis.

"You're sure you can do this, Trig? You don't have to, you know," she said, but Trig's eyes were orange-red with challenge and confidence. With a sigh, she bounced him off her arm. He disappeared. A moment later they all saw him through the bridge window, catching an ovoid nearly as large as himself. Briefly, the force of the capture sent him spinning backward, but before he hit the window, he abruptly flipped out of sight again. Three heartbeats later, he reappeared on the bridge, chittering with satisfaction.

"His hide is so cold," Jancis said as she stroked him. "He's got stuff on his talons! Freezing! Ugh!" But, for all of that, she didn't dislodge him from her shoulder.

Everyone made much of him, including Ruth, with the notable exception of the two greens, who were sullenly rumbling their discontent at being kept inside the *Yokohama*.

"Apparently the extravehicular activity was successful?" Aivas asked.

Jaxom activated the optics in Airlock A and saw the ovoid floating gently above the lock floor.

Eyes widening in surprise, Jancis jiggled her finger at the screen showing the airlock. "Look!" she exclaimed. It took a moment for the others to realize that the ovoid was gliding across the lock. It hovered briefly by the wall and returned to approximately the same position in the center of the facility.

"Excellent demonstration of an incident of magnetic levitation," Aivas remarked.

"And congratulations from Master Robinton and D'ram. Warder Lytol is already mobilizing a team to examine the specimen."

"Is he indeed?" Jaxom asked flippantly, wondering who Lytol would tag with the unenviable task.

"The extent and density of this stream would be useful knowledge," Aivas went on. "Jancis, such readings can be taken from the navigator's console by activating the exterior optics, using the EXAM.EXE code."

"It occurs to me, Aivas," Jaxom began, winking at Jancis, "that this phenomenon was not on your agenda for today in space?" He was amused to see Fandarel regard him with astonishment for such an impudent question.

There was so profound a silence from Aivas that everyone on the bridge exchanged amused glances. Twice in one day they had confounded Aivas? Fandarel began to chuckle, a deep rolling sound, when an answer finally came.

"Regrettably, this facility did not compute that possibility, though calculations now indicate that the *Yokohama* and her sister ships have been in the line of Thread showers every fourth Fall."

"Well, imagine that!" Jaxom remarked, his eyes glinting with mischief. He had never thought to catch Aivas unprepared.

With what Jaxom decided was considerable aplomb, Aivas asked, "Is the shield destroying the ovoids, or is it deflecting them?"

"Deflecting," Jaxom replied. Then he absorbed the nub of that remark. "The shield has a destructive mode? We could destroy what's raining down on us? What an ingenious concept! There'd be just that much fewer to fall on Nerat. And that might persuade old Begamon that all this"—he gestured about the bridge—"is worth the effort."

"Jaxom, the destruct capability can be activated from either the captain's chair or the pilot's console. Call up the shield function program and alter DEFL to DEST."

"I hear and obey," Jaxom said eagerly, his breath quickening as he slid into the pilot's seat and activated the console. "Program altered." For a moment, he let his finger hover above the ENTER tab. "Engaged!"

In the next instant, the pellets streaking toward them dissolved in puffs, clearing a path so that the width and depth of the stream became all too visible.

"If you will activate the rearview screen, Jaxom," Aivas went on, "you will see how effective the destruct mode is."

Plainly a wide swath of Thread had been eliminated.

"That's beautiful! Just beautiful! Charring Thread in the air is one thing! *This* is much better. Much better!" Jaxom muttered. He turned the forward view back on and continued to watch the visible destruction of Thread with intense satisfaction. The green dragons had stopped spitting and were rumbling in delight.

"Is there any way to extend this destruction beyond the *Yokohama*?" Master Fandarel asked.

"No," Aivas replied. "The shield's main function is to deflect ordinary space debris. Considering the width, breadth, and depth of the stream, it would be analogous to trying to destroy a snow shower with a candle."

"Then how, Aivas, do you propose that we shall destroy this menace—as you promised we would?" Jaxom demanded.

"By removing the vector that brings Thread to Pern. That should have been obvious to you all by now," Aivas chided them. "The path of the eccentric planet must be altered sufficiently so that it does not come close enough to spin Thread into Pern's orbit."

"And how can we possibly do that?" Master Fandarel demanded.

"That will become apparent as you continue with the Plan. Everything you have learned, every seemingly simple exercise either here or on the ground is directed toward preparing you for that end."

No amount of wheedling or blustering could move Aivas to elaborate. "You cannot run before you walk," he repeated to almost every rephrasing of that question from Fandarel, Jaxom, Jancis, and Belterac.

Finally, Jaxom desisted and turned to the immediate situation. "Don't the *Buenos Aires* and *Bahrain* have similar shields?"

"They do," Aivas replied.

"Well, then." Jaxom rubbed his hands together in anticipation.

"Now wait a moment, Lord Jaxom," Jancis said. "You're not going to have all the fun today. I want my turn at destroying Thread."

"And I," her grandfather said, a rapturous grin replacing his usual composure.

"It would be a dangerous task for a young woman, a young mother," Belterac said, glancing anxiously at Fandarel to support him.

"I will not be done out of my opportunity on those grounds," Jancis said, her stance so belligerent that Belterac nearly recoiled in surprise. "Besides, I fit into a space suit. You're much too big, Belterac."

"I'm not," Evan said, speaking up for the first time.

"I thought that life-support systems had been reactivated on both the smaller ships," Fandarel said. "Am I not correct, Aivas?"

"You are, Master Fandarel."

"Well, then, space suits are not required."

"A knowledge of the sequence is, Granddad, and you always leave console work to someone else."

Fandarel drew himself up to his full height, swelling his massive chest importantly. "It did not seem too difficult. A few pecks and then the enter." He threw a quizzical glance at Jaxom.

"Cease!" Jaxom said, throwing up his hands and nearly propelling himself out of the pilot's chair by mistake. "As Lord Holder, I outrank everyone else, so I will make the decision. Master Fandarel deserves the chance for many reasons, and Jancis, too. However, Bigath and Beerth brought all you Smithcrafters up here, so they can just haul you across to the other ships, as well. You—" He pointed at Belterac. "—can be trusted with switching the screen from deflect to destroy. And you—" He indicated Fandarel. "—can then engage. Jancis, you reprogram the shield, and Evan, you can hit the ENTER key. So you'll all take part."

"It must be pointed out," Aivas said, "that the amount of Thread that would be destroyed, even utilizing the destruct mode of the shields on all three ships, is only point-oh-nine percent of an average Fall. Is this trip necessary?''

"That's point-oh-nine percent the dragonriders don't have to worry about, Aivas," Jaxom said jubilantly.

"Then let us make this efficient use of the available technology," Fandarel said eagerly.

"It is apparent that such participation would give immense psychological satisfaction, far outweighing either the risk or the actual destruction ratio," Aivas said.

"Immense satisfaction," Jaxom agreed.

"Raising morale to a new height," Jancis put in. "And to think I can have a part in it!"

"That is," Jaxom said, turning to the green riders, "if you and your dragons are amenable . . .''

S'len and L'zan were more than amenable. Jaxom drilled everyone on the steps necessary to alter the shield to destruct mode. Aivas did insist that everyone was to take along emergency oxygen equipment. The atmosphere on the two smaller ships was only minimal, and oxygen deprivation could not be risked.

When the greens, well laden with riders, departed, Jaxom found the bridge remarkably quiet.

"Jaxom," Aivas began, "how much weight can the green dragons carry? Their burdens today weigh more than their body weight."

"A dragon is capable of carrying as much as he thinks he can," Jaxom replied with a shrug.

"So if the dragon thinks he can carry any object, irrespective of its actual weight, he will?''

"I don't think anyone's actually tried to overload a dragon. Didn't you tell me that the earliest ones were used to transport loads out of Landing following the eruption?''

"That is true. But they were never, as you surmised, permitted to carry great weights. In fact, Sean O'Connell, the leader of those early riders, resented the fact that the dragons were used in such a capacity.''

"Why?''

"That was never explained.''

Jaxom smiled to himself. "Dragons can do a lot of inexplicable things.''

"For instance," and Aivas's voice altered subtly, "arriving in very timely fashions?''

Jaxom chuckled. "That's one.''

"How did you contrive such a serendipitous entrance?''

"Jancis was clever enough to put down the time. When I visualized the bridge for Ruth, I also visualized the bridge clock"—Jaxom pointed to the digital face—"at a minute before the one she gave. So, of course, we arrived—" He chuckled again. "—in time!"

Tell Aivas that I always know where in time I am, Ruth said, and Jaxom duly repeated the message to Aivas.

"A most interesting ability."

"Mind you, Aivas, that is for your ears only."

"This facility has no ears, Jaxom."

The discussion was interrupted by the jubilant return of the teams, the green dragons looking as gratified as their passengers.

"When Thread has passed by," Aivas said, "someone must return to the other ships and reset the shield to deflect. The solar panels do not supply unlimited power and will need to be fully recharged."

There was a unanimous agreement to that suggestion. By then, Aivas had accessed all the data he required, the Thread flow had diminished to a few stray globules, and the green dragons returned the teams to reset the shields.

"Aivas," Fandarel began when they were once again assembled on the *Yokohama*'s bridge, "has the matter of our excursions to the other ships been mentioned on the surface?"

"Master Robinton was on duty and approved," Aivas replied.

Fandarel cleared his throat. "No students listening to the exchange?"

"Only Master Robinton was in the chamber at that time. Why?"

"We can count on his discretion, then. This interesting facet of the *Yokohama* should be discussed before it is made public," Fandarel said. "I found it most exhilarating to initiate the destruction."

"Wouldn't it serve to convince the doubtful that these projects are useful?" Jancis asked.

"That is the question that must be discussed," Fandarel told her.

Jaxom and Ruth made their farewells and left the bridge. As Jancis and the other smiths returned to the engine room and their disrupted tasks, she fleetingly wondered if he had timed it back to Ruatha . . .

Jaxom did not return immediately to Ruatha. He felt obliged to inform the Benden Weyrleaders of the incident. Ruth was thoroughly in favor of a Benden destination, as he always enjoyed visiting his native Weyr.

Ramoth and Mnementh are happy to see me, he told his rider as they circled in to land at the queen's weyr. *Lessa and F'lar are within.* Then he turned his head up to Mnementh, and the two dragons touched noses. *Mnementh says that F'lar will be very pleased to hear what we did on the* Yokohama. *He and Ramoth are.*

As Jaxom entered the queen's weyr, Ramoth was watching for his appearance and rumbled a greeting.

She greets you as the bearer of very good tidings, Ruth told him.

"How about letting me deliver my own surprise?" Jaxom muttered with mock irritation.

"And what surprise is that?" Lessa asked, looking up from reinforcing a join on a long strap. F'lar had his harness stretched from a peg set high on the wall and was rubbing oil into the thick neck strap. These reminders of his near escape from cold-damaged leather sobered Jaxom. He had seen no further indication that the conspirators at Tillek were carrying out their threat against him. But then, he had been careful not to provide opportunities.

"Oh," he began casually, "just that the Fall over Nerat won't be as heavy as usual day after tomorrow."

"How's that?" F'lar swiveled about, giving Jaxom his complete attention. Lessa's stare suggested that the young Holder had better be quick with his explanation.

Grinning because it wasn't often that he could astound this pair, he related what had happened. When he had finished, and the two Weyrleaders had questioned him closely on details, Lessa looked less than pleased.

"I'd say we were very lucky not to have lost two green dragons. And don't tell me you didn't time it, Jaxom."

"Then I won't," Jaxom replied. "Bloody lucky Ruth's so clever at it."

Lessa opened her mouth to remonstrate with him, but F'lar held up a hand. "And there can be a reduction in the density of Fall, using the destruct mode of the shields?" the Weyrleader asked.

"It certainly looked that way to us out the back window . . . as it were." Then Jaxom halted in dismay. "You know, if I'd had the sense of a fire-lizard, I'd've reprogrammed the telescope and gotten a good look."

"It takes time to become accustomed to using all this new technology. Anyway, we'll confirm it at Nerat," F'lar said, smiling as he pushed back his errant forelock. "This'll be heartening news, Jaxom. Fall's right now at its densest, and unless Thread can re-form—which I doubt—during its descent through the upper strata, the wings will have a brief breather. And that'll cut down on our casualties."

"It may increase them," Lessa said with a scowl. "If we decide to take advantage of this capability. Riders'll become inattentive, expecting a lull."

"Oh, come now, love." F'lar gave Lessa's long, thick plait an affectionate tug. "You can be downright ungrateful for a favor."

She paused, reconsidered, then gave a grudging smile. "Sorry. I do tend to be gloomy just before a Fall."

"In that case, Lessa, you'd best come up to the *Yokohama* the next time this happens. I found it tremendously satisfying to be able to destroy so much Thread without endangering Ruth or myself!" Jaxom paused, then added, "We also have a specimen of Thread on the floor of Airlock A."

"*What?*"

Jaxom grinned at her startled, horrified expression. "Oh, it's safe enough. Airlock's got no oxygen, and it's the same temperature as outside. Aivas assured us that it's impotent in this form, can't alter. At that, we managed what the settlers never could—we captured Thread in its dormant stage."

Lessa shuddered in revulsion. "Get rid of it!" she said with a dramatic gesture of her hand. "Get rid of it!"

"Lytol's already assembling a team to dissect it."

"Why?" Lessa flinched again.

"Curiosity, I suppose. Though Aivas could merely be responding to another of those earlier imperatives of his he's so determined to implement."

F'lar gave Jaxom a long hard look. Then he held up the klah pitcher, gesturing for the younger man to join him at the table for refreshment. Jaxom nodded gratefully and took the chair F'lar indicated while the steaming klah was poured.

"I don't care what Aivas is implementing," Lessa said. "I don't like the idea of Thread on the *Yokohama*. Suppose—"

"Aivas would not expose us to danger," F'lar said, giving her a soothing smile. "I find Jaxom's comments on Aivas's mandates extremely perceptive." He settled in a chair and, cradling his klah cup, leaned across the table. "I'm curious, Jaxom, and you're more in Aivas's company these days than we are: This dissection business makes me wonder if Aivas's basic imperatives conflict with ours."

"Not where the annihilation of Thread is concerned. Though sometimes I don't understand at all why he has us doing some of those endless drills and exercises. Especially now that he has been revealed as fallible."

F'lar grinned. "Did Aivas ever say he was not?"

"He likes to give the impression that he's never wrong," Lessa said in a sharp tone, looking alarmed.

Jaxom grinned. "Good teacher image, and that's necessary when he has to pound all these radical ideas into our parochial heads."

"Is his fallibility a danger to us?" F'lar asked.

"I don't really think so. I'm just commenting on it since we are private today," Jaxom went on, "and because I was so surprised when Aivas did not know that Thread's descent passed so close to the *Yokohama*."

F'lar blinked, absorbing that information, and Lessa's frown deepened. "Surprised? Or worried?" she asked.

"Well, it's not his fault. The ancients didn't know it, either," Jaxom said with some satisfaction.

F'lar grinned back at him. "I see what you mean, Jaxom. Makes them more human."

"And Aivas not so inhumanly perfect."

"Well, it doesn't please me," Lessa snapped. "We've believed everything Aivas has told us!

"Don't fret, Lessa. So far Aivas has not lied to us," F'lar said.

"But if he doesn't know everything, how can we now be sure he's guiding us in the right direction with this great plan of his that's supposed to destroy Thread forever?" she demanded.

"I'm beginning to figure out what that's going to be," Jaxom said so confidently that Lessa gave him a long look. "Aivas is obviously teaching us at the rate at which he feels we'll be able to absorb the revolutionary ideas; these exercises are what we have to perfect before we can achieve his goals, which are ours, and were our ancestors'."

"And will you let us in on your conclusions?" Lessa's tone was as caustic as Jaxom had ever heard it.

"It has to do with having a Thread in the airlock and being able to analyze it unemotionally, the way Sharra, Oldive, and the others can identify bacteria and develop ways of combating infection. It has to do with becoming accustomed to moving in free-fall or in airless space, in using sophisticated equipment as if it were a third arm or an extra set of brains. That's all Aivas is, you know. An extra set of brains with a phenomenal, and infallible, memory." As Jaxom spoke, F'lar regarded him with growing respect. "And possessing a knowledge of the advanced technology we have lacked, so we couldn't do more than hold Thread at bay. But it's the dragons, and their riders, that Aivas needs to demolish Thread."

"That's obvious, considering the questions Aivas keeps asking us," Lessa put in sharply. "I'd feel happier if we knew what he wants our dragons to do." Ramoth gave a crisp bark of agreement. "I'd also like to know when he'll let the larger dragons up on the *Yokohama*." Both Ramoth and Mnementh bugled.

Jaxom grinned at Lessa. "Now, Lessa, don't be mean. It's not often that the greens get the jump on their bigger clutchmates. Allow them their moment of glory. At any rate, your chance comes soon. Sharra and Mirrim are monitoring the oxygen levels in the cargo bay, and as soon as the atmosphere's at the proper consistency, you'll be very welcome. Of course, you can always ask a green to fly you up there."

Emitting an angry rumble, Ramoth turned to fix Jaxom with eyes that whirled with occasional flickers of red.

"There! You know what Ramoth thinks of that idea," Lessa replied with a glint of amusement. "As if I'd consider for one moment being conveyed by a green," she added to soothe her weyrmate.

"A white?" Jaxom offered slyly.

Ramoth rumbled again, but not quite so angrily, and sneezed.

I'd be exceedingly careful carrying Lessa, Ramoth, Ruth said. *I fit on the bridge, which is warmer than the cargo bay, and Lessa would see much more on the bridge than in that dark cavern.*

"I heard," Lessa said when Jaxom opened his mouth to relay the message.

"I know that Aivas wants all the bronze and brown dragons to get used to free-fall conditions. The bay's the only large open area that they'll fit in. The algae farm is developing beautifully, so it shouldn't be long now."

Lessa cocked her head at Jaxom, her expression thoughtful. "Does Aivas plan for the dragons to move those ships?"

"Move the ships?" Jaxom asked, surprised.

"Why? How?" F'lar asked.

"Remember, F'lar, when Aivas insisted that the dragons should be able to move things telekinetically?"

"Dragons can only move themselves, their riders, and what they carry," F'lar said categorically. "They cannot move things they're not holding. And what good would come of moving the ships? If his plan is somehow to use the ships to blow up the Red Star, I don't see what good that would accomplish. Not as I understand his lessons in spatial mechanics."

"No more do I." Jaxom took the last gulp of his klah and rose. "Well, I've delivered my report of today's surprise."

"For which you have our gratitude," F'lar said.

"If that kind of predestruction turns out to be beneficial, we can set up a regular schedule to switch the shields," Jaxom said. "You can even have a chance at programming the mode yourselves."

"I'm sure it will be feasible, Jaxom. Anything that destroys Thread is helpful," F'lar said, rising to accompany the young Holder to the ledge.

"You won't worry about Aivas's fallibility, will you, F'lar?" Jaxom asked in a lowered voice when they were in the short corridor beyond the weyr.

"Me? No, certainly not," the Weyrleader assured him. "We've learned so much already from Aivas that, even if his vaunted Plan fails, we'll surely find our own ways of ridding Pern of Thread by the next Pass. But, somehow, Jaxom," F'lar said, gripping Jaxom's arm hard to show his implacable resolve, "I know we'll manage to do it in this Pass! Make no mistake about that! We'll do it in my lifetime!"

When the Smithcrafters returned to Landing, thoroughly elated by their time aboard the *Yokohama*, there was some contention over who should be allowed the opportunity to initiate the destruct mode. And of a more immediate nature, who would have the opportunity to dissect the Thread specimen.

"You'd have to choose carefully," Lytol said, "for too many folk believe that just being in the presence of Thread is followed by a terrible death. I've sent quite a few messages off to find qualified persons to perform the task, and so far, there's been no response."

"You might not get one," Piemur said. He had been waiting for Jancis's return, a sleeping Pierjan limp in his backpack. "I suppose the knowledge would be useful even if it'll become academic by the end of this Pass."

Master Robinton held up his hand. "I'll go, if no one else will."

He was so besieged with protests that he grinned. "So long as I can visit the *Yokohama* at some point in the very near future. And *don't*"—he glared about him—"tell me that my health won't permit it. I found data in the medical files on how heart patients were frequently sent to free-fall wards on satellites to recuperate. A visit to the *Yokohama* would, therefore, be *beneficial* for my health, and it could do my heart good to stab a sequence that destroyed Thread! Did one of your messages go to Oldive or Sharra, Lytol? Well, then, they're both busy folk, but they'll get back to you in time. And if one of them goes, why, I'd have my healer at hand."

Considerable consternation was roused when it became more widely known that a Thread ovoid had been procured. Aivas obliged with scenes of it reposing in Airlock A. It remained there unchanging for several days, proving that in its present state it posed no danger to anyone.

More importantly, Lessa and F'lar reported favorably on the reduction of Thread density during the largest Fall over Nerat. There had been three long columns entirely free of the deadly rain. So Lessa and F'lar came to landing to discuss adding that task to the on-board duties. Aivas had a tape of the incident so that Benden Weyrleaders could view it, which they did several times.

"Incredible to think Thread can be destroyed without dragon assistance," Lessa murmured in a low voice.

"Too bad there aren't a dozen more colony ships up there," Piemur said.

"Then dragons wouldn't have been needed, and *that* doesn't bear thinking of," Lessa snapped back at him.

"I spoke as a harper, Weyrwoman," Piemur said courteously, "as I, for one, am very glad dragons do exist."

"I think, F'lar, that we should go to the *Yokohama*," Lessa remarked. "There's enough oxygen for Ramoth and Mnementh in the cargo bay by now, isn't there, Aivas?"

"There is. It is essential that the larger dragons become accustomed to the conditions of space," Aivas replied. Lessa and F'lar exchanged meaningful glances. "The next stream should intersect with the *Yokohama*'s orbit in three days' time, at precisely 1522 hours ship time."

"That's late morning, isn't it, Benden time?" F'lar asked, turning to Lessa. "We'll go then, direct from Benden."

"Who's going to take me then?" Robinton asked, sitting straight up in his chair and looking aggrieved.

"I will," D'ram said. "Surely there's enough air for three big dragons, isn't there, Aivas?" The old Weyrleader's tone implied that there had better be.

"Certainly," was Aivas's prompt assurance.

"Well, then," Robinton said, brushing his hands together in complete satisfaction, "that takes care of that."

13
▼▼▼▼▼▼▼

Lessa was just a trifle put out when Ruth, with Jaxom, Sharra, and Oldive astride, joined the three big dragons the morning of their first ascent to the *Yokohama*.

"Sharra and Oldive volunteered to dissect the Thread egg," Jaxom said without apology, "and I'm to man the telescope and give Aivas fore and aft views of the Thread stream."

What Jaxom did not say was that Ruth might need to give the big dragons a few helpful hints on how to manage themselves in free-fall. So far, none of the green dragons had experienced any difficulty with the unusual sensation of weightlessness. The fire-lizards had been totally fearless and almost casual about coming up to see what the dragons, especially Ruth, were doing on the *Yokohama*. Mirrim was scheduled for algae-farming on the other two vessels that day, so that would give the party two dragons suitable for bridge-to-bridge transfer.

Going *between* from the brilliant sunlight and balmy air of Landing to the big, dimly lit cargo bay on the *Yokohama* brought exclamations from all the initiates.

"Jaxom, I thought you said there were lights," Lessa said.

"There are," he replied, agilely dismounting and expertly pushing himself toward the main switches on the wall by the lift. He was rather pleased that, with such an audience, he arrived effortlessly at the exact spot. Being well aware of the load soon to be taxing the solar panels, he activated only the ring lights, not the power-eating overhead globes.

"Amazing!" Master Robinton exclaimed, staring around the immense, empty facility.

Ramoth made an odd little noise in her throat as she viewed her surroundings, her eyes idly whirling. Mnementh lowered his head, sniffing at the scarred deck plates, peering into the corners, his eyes calm. D'ram's Tiroth stretched his neck until his head reached the ceiling. At that point, his feet lifted slowly from the floor, startling the big bronze into a bellow of protest.

You are in free-fall, Tiroth, Ruth said casually. *Every action has a reaction. Gently push yourself back to the floor with your snout. See? That was easy.*

Then Ramoth swung her head too rapidly about to see what was happening to Tiroth and started to drift.

Don't fight the motion, Ramoth, Ruth said, *just relax and let yourself go with the movement. Now, easily swing your head back. See, it's not hard at all. Look at me.*

"Ruth!" Jaxom said repressively, "don't you dare show off."

I'm not showing off, I'm showing! Ruth executed a slow backflip, careful to keep his wings tight against his spine where they would not interfere with his progress. *We weigh no more than a fire-lizard up here!* And then he twirled around on his tail end.

"Ruth!" Jaxom bellowed, his voice echoing off the walls of the bay.

"I think you've made your point, Lord Jaxom," F'lar said, a ripple of suppressed amusement in his voice. "Easy does it, right?" Moving carefully, F'lar swung out of his accustomed perch between Mnementh's neck ridges and found that he had propelled himself deckward. "An incredible feeling! Try it, Lessa. I know you don't weigh much under any circumstances, but I just drifted down! Amazing sensation! No strain for you, Robinton."

There were a few misjudgments as the passengers experimented. Sharra, discreetly assisting Masterhealer Oldive to the deck, made for the lift to start their day's project: a close examination of the egg in the airlock. Aivas has recommended that they take the Thread to the medical station on the top coldsleep deck. Laboratory facilities were still in place there, including a microscope more powerful than anything they had yet managed to build. The section had sufficient air but was not yet too warm, Aivas assured them. For an unemotional piece of machinery, Aivas was exhibiting an odd insistence for what Sharra would have thought a relatively unimportant element of the total project.

When the others had grown somewhat accustomed to the vagaries of free-fall, Jaxom escorted them to the bridge. Certainly he was as eager to show Lessa, F'lar, Robinton, and D'ram his familiarity with the *Yokohama*'s bridge as Ruth was to discreetly supervise the big dragons. Standing in the open lift, Jaxom's novices did not disappoint him: they were as genuinely awestruck by the view of Pern as he could wish. He gave them time to absorb the wondrous sight of the sunlit continent and the brilliantly blue sea, then gently shooed them into the room so that the lift door could close. They clung for a while to the guardrail, coming to terms with their experience.

Propelling himself smoothly to the captain's chair, Jaxom fed the telescope program, checked the ready room, where Sharra was helping Oldive into a space suit, and tuned one of the ceiling screens in to the laboratory.

F'lar dragged his gaze away from the riveting view of Pern to eye the specimen. "It's not as big as I thought it'd be," he said.

"No, it's not. That's why it'd be interesting to see how a big, long Thread fits into such a confined envelope," Jaxom replied.

Lessa shot one glance at it before turning back to the more compelling panorama. "Can we go to the window?" she asked.

"Just push yourself off gently—don't worry," he added when she started to float and tried to stop herself. "Just flow. Don't struggle." She went by him, rotating, and he reached up and halted the motion. Then, with a gentle shove, he aimed her at the window.

Robinton, having observed her mistakes, did not repeat them, and shortly he was beside her at the window, his feet dangling a handspan above the floor. D'ram gave a grunt and went hand-over-hand down to the nearest console, where he strapped himself into the chair.

"How long before the stream starts to intersect the *Yokohama*'s path?" he asked.

Jaxom set D'ram's screen at its highest magnification and called up the appropriate sector. As D'ram's screen refocused, the old bronze rider reared back in his chair, his expression blank with shock as the ragged beginnings of the wave appeared so immediately in front of him.

"It's not that close to us yet, D'ram. I just gave you an enhanced image. Here, I'll give you the actual perspective." Jaxom altered the magnitude so that the incoming stream was merely a sunlit smudge dropping toward them from the fourth quadrant.

"How near is it?" D'ram asked, his voice dry and cracking.

"Proximity monitor suggests we've a good ten minutes before contact," Jaxom said.

F'lar cautiously made his way to D'ram and hung on to the chair back, his legs almost horizontal to the floor. Then he levered himself into the other station and strapped in.

Are you all right down there? Jaxom asked Ruth as privately as he could so as not to be overheard by Ramoth.

She's far too busy enjoying free-fall, Ruth replied, his tone amused. *She's better at it then Mnementh and Tiroth, for all she's bigger. She's not using as much shove. I think they are doing much better without their riders watching. Watch your wings, Ramoth! Not much room in here!*

Jaxom grinned, then froze as he caught movement in the lab. Sharra and Oldive were entering the room, Sharra moving as gracefully as the magnetic boots allowed, one gloved hand guiding Oldive's jerkier progress. Jaxom watched, rapt, as they attempted to penetrate the hard shell of Thread. Then Mirrim, on green Path, arrived on the bridge.

"Who'm I taking to the *Bahrain*?" she asked, grinning at the sight of Lessa and Robinton stretched across the window.

"Whoever will go with you," Jaxom said. "Lessa? F'lar?"

Lessa made an injudiciously sharp movement of her head and flattened herself against the window. "I'll go with you, Mirrim." *No, Ramoth, it's perfectly all right. I assure you that you would not fit on the bridge here, much less on the* Bahrain's. *You learn to keep your balance down there in the bay where you have some space to maneuver.*

Jaxom asked Ruth to oblige F'lar, and the white dragon jumped *between* to the bridge.

"You know the drill?" Jaxom asked the Benden Weyrleaders.

Lessa gave him a hard stare as she floated across to Path, but F'lar chuckled and replied meekly, "I assure you, we've been practicing hard, Jaxom. My thanks, Ruth," he added as he glided up to the white dragon's back and settled himself.

"Bit easier to bestride than that great hulk of yours, isn't he?" Jaxom replied, grinning at the mild surprise on the bronze rider's face. "Have a good destructive time! You've got three minutes before contact."

"Where do I sit, Jaxom?" Robinton asked eagerly, pushing himself off from the window.

"Where F'lar was."

Much as Jaxom's fingers itched to insert the command, he found it equally gratifying to watch the expression on the Harper's face as he performed the task. As the smiths had on the previous occasion, Robinton and D'ram both recoiled as the ovoids hurtled toward the window. D'ram grunted as the first puffs signaled the destruction, then sat with arms folded across his chest, eyes narrowed, a look of deep satisfaction on his face.

"You know, D'ram, we really ought to get Lytol to come here one time," Robinton said. "It might ease his heart to destroy Thread. He never had the chance as a rider."

"Might do him some good at that," D'ram remarked thoughtfully.

"Aivas?" Jaxom opened the channel to Landing. "Are the pictures coming in clearly enough?"

"Yes, Jaxom, and the density is up by seven percent or more on the previous Fall."

"Then this predestruction will be welcome."

Jaxom turned his attention to the coldsleep laboratory, where the two healers were having trouble penetrating the shell of the Thread with the instruments they had brought with them.

"We've pounded, we've chipped, we've scraped—and we've not so much as scratched the surface," Sharra told Jaxom in disgust, waving a chisel in frustration.

"So much for those who fear it would leak out and devour us," Oldive said. He sounded more amused than frustrated. "Amazing envelope. Impervious to everything we thought would easily cut through it."

"Diamond cutters?" Jaxom suggested.

"You know, that might be just the thing," Oldive said, pleased. "Well, I certainly won't mind coming up here again. I've never felt so mobile." Although he generally paid no attention to his physical handicaps, his hunched back and crushed pelvis had given him uneven leg lengths and a crabbed gait. In weightlessness those problems were neutralized.

"This is an instance," Aivas said blandly, "when the teleportational abilities of the fire-lizards would come in exceedingly useful."

"Meer and Talla wouldn't know a diamond cutter if it bit them," Sharra said ruefully. Then Jaxom heard her ruffled breath of a sigh. "I doubt if even that sort of an edge will have any effect on this thing. Its casing is impervious."

"Not to heat," Jaxom reminded her.

"There is no way, Lord Jaxom of Ruatha," Sharra said, settling her hands on her hips in a characteristic posture, "that you will get us to heat that thing up to simulate the friction of an ovoid's passage through atmospheric levels! Not that one could use a flamethrower in such a confined space as this lab."

"You do not have the technology necessary to produce a narrow heat beam such as a laser that would be effective on such a casing," Aivas added. "Another area in which you will have to make great progress over the next Turn."

"Oh? Why?" Jaxom asked, noting the quick interest of both Robinton and D'ram.

"There is no point, at this juncture, to elaborate on device or need," Aivas replied. "It is a matter that has been placed in the Mastersmith's hands but does not have priority over other, more essential, projects."

"Haven't you any helpful suggestions for us?" Sharra asked Aivas caustically.

"The diamond-cutter edge will be effective."

"Then why on earth didn't you suggest that we bring one along on this trip?" she demanded.

"The question was not put to this facility."

"The trouble with you, Aivas," Sharra continued with some asperity, "is that you only tell us what you think we should know: not necessarily all we *need* to know or what we *want* to know."

A long silence ensued, during which she and Oldive left the laboratory, sealing the door behind them.

"Sharra's right, you know," D'ram remarked at last.

"Indeed," Robinton said.

"But would we have thought that a diamond cutter would be necessary, considering the selection of edged tools Sharra and Oldive *did* bring with them?" Jaxom asked, though he agreed completely with his mate and was rather proud of her for speaking so bluntly. It was significant, too, that Aivas had not refuted the accusation.

Robinton shrugged in answer to Jaxom's question. D'ram, however, pulled at his lower lip.

"Diamond cutters are used for gemstones and glass etching. Why would we think to use them to cut open a Thread capsule?" the old Weyrleader asked. He lifted his hands, expressing inadequacy.

"Master Fandarel would have," Robinton remarked. Then he

sighed. "We have so much still to understand, to learn, to appreciate. Is there ever an end, Aivas?"

"To what?"

Master Robinton turned a wry smile to Jaxom. "The question was rhetorical, Aivas."

From Aivas, there was silence.

Later, when the group returned to Cove Hold, the consensus was that the sojourn on the *Yokohama* had been eminently successful. The dragons had become comfortable in free-fall; the humans had had the gratifying experience of cutting ship-shaped tunnels through incoming Thread at no risk to themselves or their dragons. Once their riders had dismounted, the dragons headed for the warm water of the Cove lagoon; and the humans, themselves, were by no means averse to a relaxing swim. Fortunately, Lytol had anticipated these needs and arranged for the meal he had ordered to be delayed until everyone had been refreshed.

Ramoth had become so accustomed to fire-lizards by now that she did not object when wild ones came to assist the riders in scrubbing their dragons. In fact, she insisted that because she was the largest, she needed more to help Lessa scrub her, Lessa being not as big as the other riders. *And Ruth has Jaxom and Sharra to bathe him,* she added imperiously.

When a laughing Lessa repeated Ramoth's remark, Robinton announced that he was more than willing to scrub a queen. Then D'ram said that there were far too many fire-lizards helping Lessa, whereas Robinton had been flown to the *Yokohama* by Tiroth and so the Harper ought, out of courtesy, to wash the bronze. In the end, all the apprentices and journeyfolk working at Cove Hold, save Lytol, waded into the waters and helped bathe the five dragons.

After a very pleasant evening meal spent in most congenial company, Jaxom, Sharra, and Oldive reluctantly departed for Ruatha. Jaxom was growing as accustomed to these long days as Sharra. Making use of the extra hours allowed him to acquit his Hold responsibilities while continuing to indulge himself in the Aivas schedule. While Sharra and Oldive dealt with the patients in the Hold infirmary, he located Brand and oversaw the enlargement of the beasthold at Riverside, and checked over the improvements to two more minor hold properties.

Having put in a twenty-hour day, he was not best pleased then to be awakened in the black of the night by an urgent message from F'lessan, relayed to him by Ruth.

Golanth says that the roof of Honshu caved in and something very curious, and quite possibly very important, has been discovered in a secret room, Ruth said, faithfully repeating what he had been told. *Golanth has informed Lessa, F'lar, K'van, and T'gellan. Messages have also been sent to Master Fandarel, and for Master Robinton, to relay to Aivas.*

Jaxom did not move for a long moment, though his mind actively considered the information. He resented being roused from much-needed rest and yearned to go back to sleep.

Golanth does not ever bother us unnecessarily, Ruth added almost contritely.

I know that! Jaxom replied wearily. *Any indication of Aivas's response to this message?*

If you are not in Aivas's presence, I can't hear what he says. Ruth was silent for a long moment while Jaxom argued with himself about leaving the warm bed and his sleeping wife and making an adequate response to this new summons.

Tiroth is bringing all three from Cove Hold with him, the white dragon went on at last. *He says that Lytol believes this could be very important. Aivas was insistent that these sacks be investigated as soon as possible. Ramoth and Mnementh will come. Everyone who was asked is coming.*

Stifling a groan, Jaxom eased himself out of bed, careful not to disturb Sharra. She needed the sleep as much as he did. Maybe this wouldn't take long and he could get back before she discovered him gone again. She and Oldive were keen to return to the *Yokohama* with a diamond cutter. He would hate to disappoint them because he had been called elsewhere.

He dressed, putting on light clothing under his riding gear in anticipation of the warmer weather in Honshu. He was pleased that, sleepy as he was, he could remember such details. But he did not, as he frequently did, check the riding harness that he always left openly on the peg in Ruth's weyr. With the deftness of long practice, he rigged his covert gear on Ruth and, throwing open the wide doors to the weyr, followed the white dragon out to the courtyard to mount. The watchdragon, the watch-wher, and some of the Hold's resident fire-lizards silently observed their departure, bright eyes gleaming blue or green spheres in the night.

What a time to send for folk, Jaxom thought as Ruth leaped skyward.

What time is it in Honshu? Ruth asked.

''Sunup, probably!'' Jaxom replied testily, envisioning the facade of Honshu Hold that F'lessan had vividly described to him.

Between, Jaxom shivered despite his fur-lined riding jacket. Two breaths later they were hoving above a sea of mist, with dawn just breaking. Around them were other dragons, clinging to pinnacles that rose above the obscuring vapor. Ruth descended to the nearest vacant spire and nodded greetings to the other dragons.

''And where is Honshu?'' Jaxom asked.

Ramoth says it's obscured in the river fog to our right. I knew where I was going. It just isn't visible yet, Ruth replied. *Today begins beautifully, doesn't it?* he added unexpectedly, gazing eastward, where the sky was a lighter blue.

Grudgingly, Jaxom agreed as he contemplated the view. To his left, both moons were visible, half full, hanging in a sky of an unusual clear and cloudless blue as night retreated westward—where he should still be in his bed, he thought ruefully. He suppressed the urge to lean forward in his saddle, rest his head on Ruth's neck, and go back to sleep until the mist cleared. But the longer he looked on a day so beautifully beginning—he hadn't known that Ruth could be so lyrical—he found it increasingly difficult to look away.

More dragons arrived, hovering in surprise to discover their landing site so totally obscured and eventually settling wherever they could.

Golanth apologizes, Ruth informed Jaxom. *The mist rolled up from the river just as day broke. He says that once the sun is up, this will clear away. He says he will go stand near the place where the roof collapsed.* The white dragon turned his head in the appropriate direction, and Jaxom spotted Golanth's bronze shape rising out of the mist to settle on a still invisible surface. *Golanth says that there is hot klah and porridge waiting and so few of us have seen Honshu that we have a nice surprise coming. He says there is very good hunting in the valley—when it's visible.*

Ruth's qualifier touched Jaxom's sense of humor, and he chuckled himself out of irritability just as the sun rose, shooting bright, hot rays across the mist. Then a breeze picked up energy and very shortly the mist cleared away, revealing at last Honshu's cliff face and Golanth, perched on the heights.

Golanth says for us to land you on the upper level by the hold's main door. There should be enough room for all. More of the roof might collapse, and on the lower level, the beasthold hasn't been completely cleaned out yet. F'lessan doesn't want anyone entering that way.

Almost as one, the waiting dragons lofted themselves. Perhaps it was the downdraft of great wings wafting away the last tendrils of mist, but by the time the dragons were ready to land, the vapor had cleared right up to the second tier of window slits.

F'lessan and the other weyrfolk who were making Honshu livable were waiting in the wide doorway, cheering the arrivals.

"Thanks for coming so promptly," F'lessan said, grinning broadly. "I don't think you'll be disappointed. Sorry to get you out of your bed, Jaxom, because I know you had a long day, but you'd hate me to leave you out of this." The young bronze rider threw a companionable arm about Jaxom's shoulders, his expression so uncharacteristically anxious that Jaxom felt obliged to reassure him.

"It's thoughtful of you to have food and klah laid on, F'lessan," Lessa said as she crossed the entrance hall, "but I'd rather see your discovery first."

F'lessan pointed to plastic sacks on the long table in the main room. "You can see the secret room, too, if you don't mind a long climb up winding stairs."

Everyone but Jaxom hurried to the table. He stood on the threshold, staring up at the amazing murals, their colors as brilliant as the day they had been first applied. Vaguely he recalled Lytol and Robinton talking about the decorations at Honshu, but he had not expected anything nearly so magnificent.

"Rather spectacular, isn't it?" F'lessan asked, turning back to his old friend. He spent a long moment admiring it, too. "The place is not really big enough for a Weyr, though Golanth says that there're plenty of good ledges to lie on. And good eating."

"Southern Weyr had less than this originally," Jaxom reminded him.

"True. But it's arranged as a hold. I just don't want anyone lording it in here," F'lessan said with unexpected fervor. "People know they can come and go freely in a Weyr. C'mon, you'll want to see the stuff I found. And now that I've got you here at last, you're going to see the whole place. It is remarkably well preserved and full of the most fascinating tools and equipment. All the smiths are drooling over them."

"I've had the complete inventory from Jancis," Jaxom said with a wry grin.

F'lessan's find was most unusual: liquid carefully stored in plastic bags. Each had been tied shut around the neck by rigid strips that ended in wide tabs, which were inscribed with strokes in odd patterns, the like of which neither Robinton nor Lytol had seen in all of Aivas's records.

"I opened one," F'lessan said, pointing to the sack sitting in the bowl, its mouth carefully peeled back so that its contents were accessible. "I thought at first it had to be water, but it's not. It's got an odd sheen to it, and anyway, water would long since have evaporated, I think. It smells funny. I didn't taste it."

Lytol and Fandarel nearly bumped heads as both leaned over to sniff the liquid. Fandarel dipped in a finger and smelled it, grimacing.

"Definitely not drinkable."

"We should take this sack to Aivas for examination," Lytol said. "Is this all there were?"

"No," F'lessan replied blithely. "Thirty-four more, plus the six here. They don't all contain the same amount of whatever it is. There were a few empty sacks in the attic so some leakage occurred. Or maybe tunnel snakes chewed their way through. They'll eat anything."

"You said something about a stairway?" Lessa asked.

"Well, the steps weren't completely cut. Just a toehold up the final curve. We didn't bother to explore that level—until Benmeth crashed through."

"You didn't say whether she hurt herself or not," Lessa said almost accusingly.

F'lessan grinned, rarely affected by his mother's moods. "Scraped her right hind leg, but J'lono's slathered numbweed all over her. She's down in the workroom."

"Show me where the stairs are, F'lessan," F'lar said, and when the young bronze rider had indicated the doorway, the Benden Weyrleader led the way, followed closely by Fandarel, Lytol, K'van, and T'gellan.

"Oh, no, you don't," Lessa said, grabbing Robinton by the arm. "Free-fall's all right but stairs are not, Robinton. And you won't have eaten yet if I know you."

Not fancying a long hike, Jaxom added his persuasions to Lessa's, and F'lessan insisted that Robinton would insult the weyrfolk if he didn't sit down right that moment and enjoy Honshu's hospitality.

"It is fuel," Aivas said, and Robinton could have sworn he heard jubilation in his voice. "Fuel!"

"Yes, but is it any good after so many centuries?" Fandarel asked.

Jaxom had a brilliant vision of the three shuttles lifting off the ship meadow, but canceled it almost immediately as a total impossibility. Those ships would never fly again. Pern hadn't the technology necessary to repair them properly.

"The fuel does not deteriorate with age, nor does the sample you brought appear to have suffered any contamination. Since this discovery is in Honshu, Kenjo Fusaiyuki's Stakehold, it is logical to assume that this is part of the fuel he had diverted for his personal use. Mention was made of this cache in Captain Keroon's records; a search for the fuel cache was conducted at Honshu, but it was never found."

"But the sled was so well preserved, couldn't we—" Fandarel began excitedly.

"The sled used power packs, not fuel. The forty sacks that have been recovered will be put to excellent use," Aivas said.

"Where? Why? In what?" Jaxom demanded. "I thought you said the *Yokohama* used matter/antimatter engines."

"For interstellar travel only," Aivas explained. "This fuel was used for propulsion in-system."

"The shuttles in the field?" Piemur asked, his face flushed with anticipation. And Jaxom realized that he was not the only one who had had dazzling visions.

"Even were you technologically more advanced, they have deteriorated past repair," Aivas said. "This unexpected dividend will be put to very good use when the alternatives have been thoroughly reviewed."

Jaxom and Piemur exchanged expressions of disgust.

"Let me guess, Aivas," Jaxom said. "We could put all the fuel in the *Yokohama*'s tanks, or split it up between all three ships. There'd be enough to give us half-grav, some maneuverability—that is, if we wanted to go anywhere in those ships . . ." He finished on a querying note.

"There is insufficient fuel to reach the Oort Cloud," Aivas said. "Or to follow the direction of the Thread stream and use the destruct capability of the shields to reduce the density of the ovoids."

Trying not to let his frustration show, Jaxom made himself grin at Piemur. "Well, he thought of one course that I didn't."

"Who are we to outguess Aivas?" Piemur asked, but Jaxom noted the suppressed anger in the harper's eyes.

"One of these days . . ." Jaxom said just loud enough for Piemur to hear, and Piemur nodded.

"But, Aivas, since there is this sample," Fandarel said urgently, "can you not analyze its composition so that we can duplicate it? Surely we can make enough fuel to take at least one ship to the Oort Cloud."

"For what reason?"

"Why, to blow up the Oort Cloud! Destroy the Thread organism that is generated there!"

Another of Aivas's curious silences ensued, and then suddenly the Rukbat system came up on the screen, the sun dwarfing its satellites. Abruptly the picture altered, the brilliant sun diminishing to a pinpoint of light, the planets reducing out of visibility on the new scale, and the swirling nebulosity of the Oort Cloud appearing to flow across the screen, blotting out even the distant Rukbat. As in so many previous demonstrations, a red line began to describe the orbit of the Red Star, moving through the Oort Cloud and back into the system, swinging around the primary, inside Pern's conventional path.

"Aivas certainly knows how to cut us down to size," Piemur murmured.

"Oh!" Fandarel said, resigned. "It is indeed difficult to appreciate the massive scale of the Cloud and the insignificance of our tiny world."

"So what *do* we destroy to be rid of Thread?" F'lar asked.

"The best way to reduce the threat of Thread is to alter the orbit of the eccentric planet that brings it into Pern's system."

"And when will you tell us how we accomplish that?"

"The research and technology required will shortly be completed."

"Then finding the fuel makes no difference?" F'lessan slumped in disappointment, his usually merry expression glum.

"It may make a difference in another area, F'lessan. It is always good to have alternatives. You have all done exceedingly well." That, from Aivas, was praise indeed. "Do not succumb to apathy."

"What should I do with all these fuel sacks then?" F'lessan asked dispiritedly.

"They should be transferred to a safe storage facility in Landing."

"I shouldn't put them into anything else? Those sacks are old."

"If they have lasted 2,528 years, they will suffice for another." A chart appeared on the screen. "Now, here is the schedule for bronze and brown dragons to jump to the cargo bays of all three ships. The latest readings indicate sufficient oxygen levels to allow every dragon and rider some experience in free-fall."

"Why?" F'lar asked.

"It is essential for the success of the Plan that all the dragons of Pern learn to handle weightlessness."

The schedules were forwarded to the Weyrleaders of all eight Weyrs, and there was a good deal of jubilation from all but a few— and those were mainly riders of elderly dragons for whom even hunting was becoming difficult. The weyrlings were ecstatic, and Weyrlingmasters hard put to maintain discipline.

Each group was sent up with someone experienced in free-fall; even Jancis, Piemur, and Sharra were sent as monitors. There were often full fairs of fire-lizards tagging along, and though that occasioned complaints, Aivas approved of their interest. A new enthusiasm swept through all the Weyrs, overcoming the mid-Pass apathy.

Three days later, fires were set among the fuel sacks, but fire-lizards gave the alarm so no harm was done. On hearing of the near disaster, Aivas was unperturbed and, in an offhanded tone, informed the agitated Lytol and D'ram that the fuel was nonflammable. The relief was palpable, but when Fandarel heard, he immediately wanted to know exactly how such fuel provided the desired effect. Aivas responded with a lecture on the intricacies of seven kinds of jet engines, from the simple reaction engines they had learned about, which made little sense even to Master Fandarel, to more complex multistage affairs.

That evening Master Morilton dispatched his fire-lizard with an urgent and horrified message that someone had destroyed all the lenses his Hall had ready to be installed in microscopes and telescopes, ruining months of hard and patient work. Later the next morning Master Fandarel found that the metal barrels he had been producing to house the lenses had been thrown into the forge fire and distempered overnight.

It was as well that the orientation program for dragons was going so well, or morale would have hit a new low. Then Oldive and Sharra at last were successful in penetrating the shell of the Thread egg with a black diamond cutter.

"I'm not much wiser," Sharra told Jaxom when she returned home that evening. "It's a complex organism, and it's going to take us time to analyze it. We have to work so slowly. I think that may be why Aivas taught us how to culture bacteria. Good training for this investigation."

"What did it look like—inside, I mean?"

"The most astonishing mess," she said, frowning in perplexity. Then she gave a disparaging chuckle. "I don't know what I thought it'd look like. In fact, I never thought about it at all. But the ovoid is coated in layers of dirty, rock-hard ice, with all kinds of pebbles and grains and—and junk mixed up. It's sort of whitish, yellow, black, gray . . . Is the yellow helium? Were you there for those lectures on liquefying gas? No, that was Piemur and Jancis.

"At any rate, there are rings that wrap round and round. You can separate the rings from the other material. There are tubes, and patches of bubbling stuff. Aivas said it was a very disorganized life-form."

Jaxom laughed in surprise. "It certainly disorganizes us!"

"Silly! He doesn't mean it that way. But we couldn't do much today because we don't have the proper tools to work in three-degree absolute temperatures." She grinned in reminiscence. "The tools we brought sort of went brittle and disintegrated in the cold."

"Metal? Turned brittle?"

"Good Smithcraft steel, too. Aivas says we have to use special glass."

"Glass, huh." Jaxom thought of all the time Aivas had spent with Master Morilton and grinned. "So that was why. But how could Aivas have known then that we'd capture Thread when he didn't even know we could?"

"I'm not sure I followed all of that, Jaxom."

"I'm not sure I did, too, lovey. I wonder who's getting the bigger surprises? Aivas, or us?"

The next morning, Sharra asked Jaxom if he would mind letting Ruth convey her to Master Oldive to confer on who else they would need to assist them in their study. Ruth was always glad to oblige Sharra, so Jaxom was free to remain behind in Ruatha to preside with Brand over a long-delayed Hold disciplinary meeting.

He was just taking his seat in the Great Hall when he caught a glimpse of Ruth departing with Sharra on his back. He bounced back to his feet in alarm.

The harness, Ruth! Which harness did Sharra use?

At the same moment that Ruth replied, *She's safe,* her two fire-lizards screamed so loudly that Lamoth, the elderly bronze on Ruatha's heights, bugled a warning. As Jaxom watched paralyzed by shock, he saw Ruth slowly descending, Sharra clutching him tightly about the neck; Meer and Talla hooked their talons in the shoulders of her riding jacket. The main riding strap dangled loosely between Ruth's legs.

Trembling in fear for what might have been, Jaxom forgot dignity and duty as he tore out of the Great Hall. In his wish not to worry her with an incident he had almost forgotten, he had nearly cost her her life. As Ruth delicately landed in front of him, his hands were still shaking as he helped Sharra down from her precarious perch and embraced her tightly.

I should have asked which harness she had with her, Ruth said, his tone remorseful, his hide tingled gray with anxiety. *I could have told her where you hide the harness you're using now.*

"It's no fault of yours, Ruth. You're all right, Sharra? You didn't hurt yourself? When I saw you hanging—" His voice broke and he buried his face in her neck, aware that she was trembling nearly as much as he.

Sharra was quite willing to be comforted, but soon enough she became aware of the audience and, with a weak, embarrassed laugh, struggled to be free. He eased his hold but did not let her go. If she had not been such a skilled rider . . . if Ruth hadn't been such a clever dragon . . .

"I thought you'd mended that harness," she said, anxiously looking into his eyes.

"I had!" He couldn't tell her the truth, not with so many within earshot, and despite the bond between them, she did not apparently realize he was not being entirely candid.

"I've got to go, Jaxom," she said, duty warring with fright. "Would Ruth be totally offended if I went with G'lanar on Lamoth?"

"You'll go on?" Jaxom was both amazed by and proud of his wife's courage and resilience.

"It's the best thing I can do, Jax, to get over this shock." She leaned across him to stroke Ruth's nose. "I know it wasn't your fault, dearest Ruth. Please relax! That shade of gray is not becoming!"

I felt the strap go as I leaped, Ruth told Jaxom. *I should have asked her which straps she used. I should have.*

"It's all right. You saved Sharra," Jaxom repeated, never more grateful to his dragon than at this moment. "She still has to get to the Healer Hall. On Lamoth with G'lanar."

Ruth eyed his rider, the orange of panic beginning to recede. *He's all right for an Oldtimer*, Ruth allowed grudgingly. *I wish that Dunluth and S'gar were back.*

"You know that pair can't fly Thread now. G'lanor's failing and Lamoth can barely chew his food anymore, much less firestone." Jaxom didn't think more of Ruth's comment then but tactfully called to the elderly dragon and rider to convey Sharra to the Healer Hall. He stripped off the dangling harness and rolled it up until he could examine it.

He watched the three until Lamoth went *between*, Meer and Talla following without fuss. Then he retraced his steps to the Great Hall, while Brand and the understewards gestured for those attending the court to settle themselves.

"You never told her?" Brand murmured in Jaxom's ear as they sat down.

"I will now. That was too close." Jaxom saw that his fingers were trembling as he sorted the papers he had scattered in panic.

"Indeed and it was. Does this . . . obvious attempt on your life have anything to do with all the recent incidents?"

"I wish I knew."

"You will speak to Benden now, won't you?" Brand's look was severe and implacable.

"I will," Jaxom agreed with a faint smile, "because I know that you intend to."

"So long as that's understood." Then in a louder voice, Brand went on. "The first case concerns the alleged misuse of Hold supplies . . ."

That evening Jaxom told Sharra every detail of the incident at Tillek Hold and the investigations that Brand had set in motion—investigations that had produced no results at all, for Pell professed himself to be quite content working in his father's craft. No one had asked him about his Ruathan Bloodlines, he assured them. And he was only a second cousin at best.

After Sharra had torn strips out of him for "sparing" her anxiety, they went over the entries in the Hold visitors' book and could find no one in the least bit suspicious. Ruth could not even be encouraging, for he was not always in his weyr when Jaxom was at home. He usually joined whichever dragon was on duty on the heights.

Even old Lamoth, he added. *I scratch his itches; he scratches mine.*

Both Sharra and Jaxom were due at Landing the next day for a meeting concerning the vandalism.

"If you don't come clean about this incident, Jaxom, I will," Sharra said, her expression fierce.

"That was about succession, Sharrie," he objected. "The destruction is a different matter entirely."

"How do you know that?" she demanded, clenching her fists on the armrest and shooting him an angry and reproachful glare. "Especially when you're the leader for all of Aivas's plans."

"Me? The leader?" Jaxom stared at her in complete surprise.

"Well, you are, even if you don't realize it." Then her severe expression softened. "You wouldn't." She gave him a sweetly condescending smile. "You are, though. Take my word for it, and everyone on the planet knows it."

"But I—I—"

"Oh, don't get fussed, Jax. It's one of your most endearing traits that you don't get puffed up with importance and irritate people with an inflated self-consequence."

"Who does that?" Jaxom rapidly thought of all those working so diligently with him.

"No one, but you'd have the right to." She came to sit on his lap, coiling one arm about his neck and stroking his frown smooth. "That's why you might well be a target for the dissidents. You certainly can't hide from the fact that dissatisfaction about Aivas's far too long-term project is increasing."

Jaxom sighed, for it was but one more thing he had tried to play down. "I'm all too aware. In fact, it's almost a relief to know they've come out in the open."

Sharra stiffened in his arms. "You know who they are?"

He shook his head. "Sebell knows who's likely to be involved, but none of his harpers have been able to produce any evidence. And you can't really accuse a Lord Holder without pretty substantial proof."

She murmured agreement and laid her head down on his shoulder. "You are being careful, aren't you, Jax?" she asked in a low and anxious voice.

He hugged her to him. "More than you are. How many times have I told you to check the riding harness before you use it?" he asked. He met her outraged reaction with a grin.

W hen the meeting convened the next day in Landing, Aivas took charge, first ordering the building cleared of all but those immediately involved.

"While these incidents are clearly directed at the new technology you are developing," Aivas said, "none, so far, threatens the success of the main drive of your efforts."

"Not yet," Robinton said darkly.

"I disagree," Sharra said, and fixed Jaxom with a steady glance. When he hesitated, she added, "Someone's trying to kill Jaxom."

When the commotion subsided, Jaxom gave a full and concise report.

"That is disturbing," Aivas said, raising his voice over the babel of questions. "Is not the white dragon protection against such attempts? Can he not prevent them?"

"Don't get so upset," Jaxom said, annoyed at the fuss, though he wanted to set his mind at rest over any further threat to Sharra. "Ruth knew the moment the leather went, and he saved Sharra's life. I left those riding straps right out in the open, and hid the set I use. It was only—"

"He was trying to keep me from worrying," Sharra said in an acid tone. "Brand is trying to find out who could have sliced the leathers. It was done very cleverly by someone who knew exactly what stress would be put on riding straps."

"A dragonrider?" Lessa's voice rose to a near shriek, and outside half the dragons on the heights bugled in alarm. "There isn't a dragonrider on Pern who'd endanger Jaxom or Ruth!" And she glared at the young Lord Holder as if he were at fault. He glared right back.

"Nor any way a dragonrider could do so without his dragon's awareness," F'lar said emphatically.

"Nothing would be gained by—" Lessa faltered. "By disposing of Jaxom."

"Could it have been as protest to my involvement with Thread?" Sharra asked.

Jaxom shook his head violently. "How could it? Who would know that you'd want to have Ruth fly you to the Healer Hall?"

"Since it is usually Jaxom who flies Ruth," Aivas's calm voice said, "it is logical to assume that he was the target. No further attempts on his life must be permitted."

"Meer and Talla have their orders," Sharra said resolutely.

"What about Ruth?" Lessa demanded, and was silenced by a cacophony of bugling from the massed dragons at Landing. She blinked in surprise at their belligerence. "And, it would appear, every other dragon on Pern!" Then she leaned across to lay her hand on Sharra's arm. "We're alert to the danger now." She swung her glance to

Jaxom and radiated rebuke. "We should have known much earlier, young man!"

"I have not been in danger," Jaxom protested. "I have been very careful."

"You would be wise to increase personal vigilance, Jaxom. Also, proper security measures must be promptly inaugurated to prevent further vandalism in every Crafthall that has undertaken to do specialized work," Aivas said sternly. "The recent destruction certainly delays the completion of useful equipment, but the vandals were, fortunately, not aware of the true significance of other crucial projects: the space helmets, the oxygen tanks, and the additional space suits which are vital to the success of our endeavour."

"All that work is divided among several Halls and different locations," Fandarel said with an air of relief. Then he shook his head, his expression doleful. "I find it very hard to believe that some member of my Crafthall could so wantonly destroy the hard work of his colleagues."

"Your society is a trusting one," Aivas said, "and it is sad to see that trust betrayed."

"It is indeed," Fandarel agreed, his voice heavy with sadness. Then he straightened his shoulders. "We will be vigilant. F'lar, would there be any riders available for extra guard duty?"

"Watch-whers would be more effective," Lytol said, entering the discussion for the first time. He had turned very pale, despite his southern tan, during the disclosure of Jaxom's peril. "They would be most effective, and I am of the opinion that the Weyrs are stretched as far as they should be right now."

"Watch-whers *and* fire-lizards," Fandarel said. "Many of the Craftmasters involved have fire-lizards, and once they know that they are to be vigilant, they will be."

"My brother Toric had had good luck using some feline cubs," Sharra put in. "Of course, they have to be caged in the daytime, for they are ferocious beasts."

"Recruit whatever guardians are necessary, but do not permit the essential manufacturing to be damaged," Aivas ordered. "Tomorrow the dragons assigned to exercises in the *Yokohama* are to transport the fuel sacks. Master Fandarel, you will see that the sacks are emptied into the main tank. That will eliminate one security problem."

"Would that we could remove all the vulnerable materials to the *Yokohama*!" F'lar said. "Could we?" he asked Aivas.

"Unfortunately that is impossible, for a variety of reasons. However, as soon as certain items have been completed, they should indeed be transported to the safety of the *Yokohama*."

"Is there any guarantee that they'd be safe there?" Lytol wanted to know. He ignored those who regarded him with anger, dismay, disbelief, or anxiety as he waited for Aivas's reassurance.

"This facility can efficiently and easily monitor the *Yokohama* as you cannot your individual Holds, Halls, and Weyrs," Aivas replied.

"And the guardian guards himself!" Lytol added in a low voice.

"Q.E.D.," Aivas said.

"Cue ee dee?" Piemur asked.

"That has been demonstrated."

14

On the bridge of the *Yokohama* the next afternoon, Jaxom and Piemur leaned over the engineering console.

"I know we emptied all those sacks in," Piemur said in an aggrieved tone, "but you wouldn't know it from the gauge."

"Big tank," Jaxom said, giving the dial a tap. "Drop in the bloody bucket."

"All that work for nothing," Piemur added, disgusted. They had had to suit up, because the fuel auxiliary intake pipe had been in a low-pressure section. The harper did not like the restrictions of a suit and the smell of tanked air. Despite weightlessness, the sacks had been awkward to manage: they could only take two at a time to the engineering level from the cargo bay where the dragons had transported them. And they were even more awkward to empty into the intake, following Aivas's instructions on the procedure for handling fluids in free-fall.

"Not for nothing," Aivas replied. "It is now safe from any tampering."

"Then it was dangerous?" Piemur asked, shooting Jaxom an I-told-you-so look.

"The fuel was not flammable, but if it were spilled, there would be toxic effects. Also, soil impregnated with the fuel becomes sterile. It is wise to avoid any unnecessary problems."

Jaxom rotated his shoulders, easing tense muscles. Sometimes working in these free-fall conditions was harder than performing a similar task on Pern.

"We have quite enough trouble as it is," Piemur said, and then turned to Jaxom. "Klah?" He lifted the hot bottle, one of Hamian's new contraptions: a large, thick, glass bottle, insulated by teased fibers of the same plant Bendarek was using to make paper and set inside a casing of Hamian's new hard plastic. It kept liquid warm or cold, though some people could not understand how the bottle knew the difference. "Meatroll?" He held out several wrapped rounds.

Jaxom grinned as he sipped from the bottle, taking care not to let any droplets escape into the air. "How is it that you always seem to have the very latest thingummies?"

Piemur rolled his eyes expressively. "Aivas said it was a thermos, and harpers traditionally try new things out! And besides, I'm resident at Landing, where Hamian has his manufactory, and you're just a runner-in, always missing the fun."

Jaxom refused to rise to the jibe. "Thanks for the food, Piemur. I'd worked up quite an appetite."

They had taken off their helmets and gloves upon entering the bridge and now made themselves comfortable in the console chairs. After the first edge of their hunger was allayed, Piemur gestured to Ruth, Farli, and Meer, who were plastered across the window, staring out.

"Do they see something we don't?" he asked.

"I asked Ruth," Jaxom said. "He says he just likes to look at Pern, all pretty laid out like that. With the clouds and the differences in light, it never looks the same twice."

"While you are eating," Aivas said, "this is an opportunity to explain another very important step in the training process."

"Is that why we got the sack duty?" Piemur asked with a wink and a grin at Jaxom.

"You are as perceptive as ever, Piemur. We have a secure channel here."

"We're all ears," Piemur said, then added hastily, "figuratively speaking, naturally."

"Accurate. It is essential to learn how much time dragons can spend in space unprotected by such suits as you are now wearing."

"I thought you'd figured that out, Aivas," Jaxom said. "Ruth and Farli suffered no harm at all during the time they were on this bridge. They didn't seem to notice the cold and certainly weren't in oxygen debt."

"They were on the bridge for precisely three and a half minutes. It is required that dragons function normally for a minimum of twelve minutes. Fifteen would be the upper time required."

"For what?" Jaxom asked, leaning forward, elbows on his knees. Piemur's eyes were bright with excitement.

"The exercise is to accustom them to being in space—"

"Having already become accustomed to weightlessness?" Jaxom asked.

"Exactly."

"So we're at the walking stage?" Piemur asked.

"So to speak. The level of adaptability of your dragons is commendable. There have been no unfavorable reactions to the experience of free-fall."

"Why would there be?" Jaxom asked. "It's on a level with hovering, or being *between*, and dragons have no problem with that. So now, they're to go extravehicular."

"Wouldn't they float away?" Piemur asked, casting an anxious look at Jaxom. "I mean, like the Thread eggs do?"

"Unless a violent movement was made, they would remain stationary," Aivas said. "As they will exit from the *Yokohama*, they are moving at the same speed, not at a different velocity as the incoming Thread spheres are. However, to prevent any panic—"

"Dragons don't panic," Jaxom said in flat contradiction, speaking before Piemur could utter a similar rebuke.

"Their riders might," Aivas replied.

"I doubt it," Jaxom said.

"Perhaps dragonriders are a breed apart, Lord Jaxom," Aivas said at his most formal, "but records of many generations indicate that some humans, despite training and reassurance, can find themselves overwhelmed by agoraphobia. Therefore, to prevent panic, the dragon should anchor itself—"

"Himself," Jaxom automatically corrected.

"Or herself," Piemur added, waggling a finger at the white rider.

"For the dragon to be anchored securely to the *Yokohama*," Aivas finished.

"Lines? We can get rope or some of that strong fine cable Fandarel's been extruding," Piemur suggested.

"That will not be necessary, as something suitable is already available."

"What?" Jaxom asked contritely, realizing that their banter was delaying details that they had wanted to hear for Turns.

The screen in front of them lit up, showing a graphic of the *Yoko-hama* profile. The display altered to a close-up of the long shaft on which the engines were fitted—and the framework of spars that had once held the extra fuel tanks in place.

"Dragons can hang on the frames!" Jaxom cried. "That would definitely offer a secure grip. And, unless I've misread the dimensions, those rails are as long as a Weyr Rim. Imagine, all the Weyrs of Pern, Piemur, out in space, along those girders! What a sight!"

"The only drawback to that," Piemur said pragmatically, "is that there aren't enough space suits for all the riders of Pern."

"There will be sufficient space suits available when required," Aivas informed them calmly, "though not quite all the dragons in the Weyrs of Pern will be needed. Since you are still suited, Lord Jaxom, and have taken nourishment, perhaps you and Ruth would attempt an extravehicular activity today?"

Piemur's eyes grew wide and round as he assimilated Aivas's astounding suggestion. "By the first Egg, it's not the humans you've got to be wary of, Jaxom. It's Aivas who's trying to kill you!"

"Nonsense!" Jaxom replied hotly. But he had felt his stomach leap almost in time to the accelerated beat of his heart at the notion of an EVA. "Ruth?"

I'll see a lot more from there than I can from the window was the white dragon's thoughtful response.

With a laugh that was only a trifle shaky, Jaxom told Piemur what Ruth had said.

The harper gave him a long incredulous look and sighed. "I don't know which of you two is more outrageous. You'd dare anything, the pair of you would." Then in a wry tone, he added, "And I'm supposed to be the reckless one."

"But you aren't a dragonrider," Jaxom said gently.

"The dragon makes the man?" Piemur shot back.

Jaxom smiled, sending a loving look at Ruth, who was watching the two humans. "With a dragon to guide and guard you, you tend to feel secure."

"So long as your riding straps hold" was Piemur's quick retort. Then he shook his head. "Come to think on it, with Aivas as your mentor, you don't need to worry about what mere men could do to you."

"Lord Jaxom will not be in any jeopardy, Harper Piemur," Aivas said with customary composure.

"So you say!" Then Piemur fixed Jaxom with a fierce stare. "So you're going to do it? Without checking with anyone?"

Jaxom glared right back, anger rising. "I don't need to check with anyone, Piemur. I've been making my own decisions for a long time. This time I get to make it without anyone else's interference. Not yours, or F'lar's, or Lessa's, or Robinton's."

"Sharra's?" Piemur cocked his head, his eye contact unswerving.

It doesn't seem to be a hard thing Aivas asks us to do, Jaxom, Ruth said. *It is no more dangerous than going* between, *where we have nothing to hold on to. My talons are strong. My grip will be secure for both of us.*

"Ruth sees no problems. If he did, I would certainly listen to him," Jaxom said, very much aware that Sharra would undoubtedly share Piemur's reservations. "I don't know why you're upset about an EVA. I thought you'd want to be first."

Piemur managed a flicker of a smile. "One, I don't have a dragon to reassure me. Two, I dislike being trussed up in this thing." He flicked his hand at the space suit. Then his expression changed to a cocky grin. "And three, it's just likely I'm one of those humans who'd panic out there with solid earth a million dragon-lengths away from my feet. So," he finished, rising to his feet and reaching for Jaxom's helmet, "since I can't talk you out of it, go and do it. Now! Before I get myself in a knot!"

Jaxom gripped his shoulder. "Don't forget that Aivas cannot endanger human life. And we've seen tapes of spacemen doing EVA drills."

So let us go. Ruth pushed himself away from the window with just enough force to arrive by Jaxom. He peered down at Piemur's scowling face. *Tell Piemur that I won't let anything happen to you.*

"Ruth says he won't let anything happen to me," Jaxom said.

With a roughness born of anxiety, Piemur adjusted Jaxom's helmet, securing the fastenings, checking the oxytank unit, and gesturing for him to turn on the helmet's audio.

"Keep up a running commentary, will you, Jaxom?" he asked.

"Nod if you can hear me all right." The sound of his own voice echoing in the confines of the helmet still sounded unnatural to Jaxom.

Piemur nodded, his expression carefully blank.

"Aivas, show us where we're going so Piemur can watch." Jaxom gave his friend one more buffet and then, pulling first one foot and then the other free of the deck, he floated up to Ruth. Hauling himself into position, he attached his riding straps to the toggles that had been designed to hold snap-on equipment for EVA.

"You wearing the right riding harness?" Piemur asked acidly.

"That's the second time you've asked me that today."

"Bears repeating. Can you see the screen perched up there?" Piemur's tone was even more acerbic. Jaxom wished the harper wouldn't worry so much. But that was yet one more difference that only another rider would understand: the supreme confidence one could have in one's dragon's abilities. And Ruth had more than most.

"I can see it," he said, his voice high and tinny to his ears. *D'you know where we're going, Ruth?*

Certainly. Shall we go?

Jaxom was accustomed to very short passages *between*, but this must have been the shortest they had ever taken. One moment they were on the bridge; the next, they were surrounded by a different sort of darkness. For one heartbeat, Jaxom tasted as deep a fear as he had ever known. But Ruth's head, erect and swinging around as he surveyed the scene, was all the token of reassurance Jaxom needed. Then he became aware—unlike the total lack of sensation in *between*—of his legs pressing against Ruth's neck and even the tug of the straps against his belt.

I won't let go, Ruth said as calmly as ever. *I could hang by my claws. The metal is so cold it feels hot.*

Jaxom peered down over the lower edge of his helmet and saw that Ruth had, indeed, curled his talons about the spars—two different spars. Carefully the white dragon had extended his forepaw talons to grip the upper bar and had arranged his hind feet on tiptoe, one in front of the other, for a purchase on the lower one, stretching comfortably between the two levels.

I'm holding my breath, but I am in no discomfort, Ruth continued as he gazed alertly around. His left eye was whirling ever so gently in the blue of interest. Above, Jaxom could see more horizontal spars, a longitudinal framework that circled the engines. Their mass was behind the grid, an immense rectangular boxlike structure in which the matter/antimatter drive provided propulsion for interstellar travel.

"Are you all right, Jaxom?" Aivas asked.

"Perfectly," Jaxom replied. He would have been unwilling to give any other response, but in truth, he felt his muscles relax just a trifle even as he spoke. After all, nothing had happened.

"Ruth suffers no discomfort?"

"He says not. He's holding his breath."

I wish to climb higher, for a better view. There is nothing to be seen here but the engines. They are uninteresting. Before Jaxom could forbid him, Ruth had reached for the spar above his head.

Whatever you do, Ruth, don't let go entirely, Jaxom said urgently.

I'd only float.

Jaxom wondered at his dragon's nonchalance in this new and dangerous environment. But then, didn't dragons meet danger head on everytime they flew Thread? At least there was none of that here to score the white hide or pierce a fragile wing—or his space suit.

See? And Ruth did begin to float, rather than climb, upward. Jaxom was so surprised by his dragon's initiative that he could think of nothing to say. *And it doesn't matter if I float*, Ruth went on, *because all I have to do is jump* between *wherever I need to go. Is it not beautiful up here?*

Jaxom had to agree. Ruth had them perched on the topmost rail, and before them, the globe of Pern glowed in brilliant greens and blues: He thought he recognized the Paradise River Hold estuary and, just at the curve of the horizon, the purple hills of Rubicon and Xanadu. Above were the stairs; behind him, shining far too brightly, was Rukbat's blaze. He thought he caught sunlight glinting off one of the other ships—the *Bahrain*, no doubt. And far, far above him, at an impossible distance, was the Red Star and the Oort Cloud that the erratic planet would penetrate yet again in another hundred or so Turns.

Abruptly Meer and Farli appeared floating beside Ruth, blinking out a moment later only to reappear, hanging on to the spar with their claws, daintily keeping their flesh from contact with the absolute chill of the metal. Their eyes began to whirl into excited reds.

We're not staying much longer. You'd better go in. You can't hold your breaths as long as I can, Ruth told the two fire-lizards. *They say space is much too big*, he said to Jaxom. *It is also colder than* between. *I think we will go in now. I feel the need to breathe.*

Once again, before Jaxom could direct the proceeding, Ruth had executed his intention. Almost without any sensation of transfer, they were back on the bridge of the *Yokohama*.

That was splendid! Ruth exclaimed, chirping happily.

Piemur's complexion, Jaxom noted, was noticeably pale under his southern tan, and his expression was unusually grim for a man who traversed the Southern coasts for months with only a gold fire-lizard and a runt runnerbeast for company and never lost his sense of humor.

"Did you have to make Farli and Meer come?"

"They came of their own accord. Ruth says they think space is too big." Jaxom laughed at their understatement. "Ruth thoroughly enjoyed it," he went on, realizing even as he said it how inadequate the comment was. "And so did I," he added staunchly, picturing again that vision of grandeur and immensity, "once I got used to it." He undid his helmet and grinned down at Piemur. "No difference really, from *between*, and not really as dangerous. As Ruth pointed out, all he has to do is go *between* wherever he wants, so we'd never really be in any danger in space."

"You sound to me a bit like a man convincing himself against the evidence of his own senses," Piemur said, regarding his friend through narrowed eyes.

"Well, it does take getting used to," Jaxom repeated, running his fingers through sweat-damp hair and grinning in what he hoped was a more convincing fashion. He wouldn't admit to Piemur that he had been apprehensive, though he could now appreciate the sour smell of sweat rising from his suit.

"I wonder," Piemur went on, "just how Sharra, and Lytol, and Lessa, and F'lar, and Robinton will view your latest escapade."

"Once they've tried it, they'll see that it's not really dangerous. It's just . . . a different aspect of travel on a dragon!"

Piemur let out an exaggerated sigh. "And if you and Ruth can do it, every other dragon and rider on Pern will feel required to follow your example. Is that what you wanted, Aivas?"

"The result is inevitable, given the friendly competitiveness of dragonriders."

Piemur raised both hands in a gesture of resignation. "As I said, with a friend like Aivas, you don't need enemies!"

J axom had let himself in for a series of harangues once they got back to Landing.

"True harper instincts!" he remarked acidly to Piemur, when the journeyman bellowed the news to Lytol on the duty desk. His old guardian turned pale and stern, and Jaxom had the satisfaction of seeing Piemur blanch. "Just let's keep this all in perspective, shall we?" he added, striding to Lytol. "I'm all right, really I am. Ruth wouldn't put me in danger any more than Aivas would. Someone!" He raised his voice. "I need some help here!"

Jancis came running down the hall, halted as she took in the scene, and darted into a side room. She was back in a moment with a hot bottle and poured Lytol a cup of klah.

"Just don't stand there, Piemur, get some wine. Some of that fortified wine would be best," she called after him as he scurried for the kitchen. "And just what have you been up to?" she demanded of Jaxom.

"Nothing as dangerous as springing news on—" Jaxom caught himself before saying "old man." "—someone with no advance warning or preparation. I gather Aivas did not mention what he had planned for us today."

"How could emptying fuel sacks be dangerous?" Jancis asked, her pretty eyes wide with astonishment.

"I'm perfectly all right," Lytol insisted. After he had obediently taken several sips of the hot klah, his color had improved.

Piemur burst back into the hall, a wineskin in one hand and several glasses in the fingers of the other. He set these down on the table with more force than needed, but he could see that Lytol was recovering. "I need a drink as much as anyone else," the harper said, splashing wine into the first glass so sloppily that Jancis, uttering a protest, took the skin from his hand. "Thanks. I needed that!" And Piemur downed the glass he had filled and held it out for a refill.

"You wait your turn," she scolded.

Jaxom gestured for her to pour wine into Lytol's cup and for the older man to drink again.

"Now, whatever made you attempt such a dangerous maneuver?" Lytol demanded.

Jaxom sighed. "It wasn't dangerous. Aivas asked Ruth and me to do an EVA, and we did. Ruth and I were quite safe. He had his claws hooked on that framework around the engine section and I—I was hanging on to him." Jaxom grinned at the consternation on Jancis's face.

"Dragonriders!" In that tone, Jancis's single word was a profound condemnation.

"Wouldn't you agree, Lytol, that a dragon won't endanger his rider? That a dragon can take himself and his rider anywhere *between* to safety?" Suddenly Jaxom realized that this was the first time in many Turns that he had asked Lytol to verify draconic abilities. He could see the muscles along his guardian's jaw clench, and wondered if he had overstepped the bounds of tact.

Lytol exhaled. "On occasion I have thought that Ruth acted too much on impulse, but you, Jaxom, have always been cautious; thus the two of you balanced each other. He would no more endanger you than you would put his life in jeopardy. But your extravehicular activity should have been discussed beforehand."

Piemur shot Jaxom a righteous glare, and Jaxom shrugged.

"We did it, and we have proved that it can be done with no harm."

I am going to sleep in the sun, Ruth told him. *You're going to be talking for hours. I'm glad we didn't talk about doing it first. It could have taken days to arrive at permission. We might never have gotten to do it.*

Jaxom did not repeat Ruth's less than diplomatic remarks or his appraisal of talk to come—talk that grew into harangue as Lessa, F'lar, Robinton, and D'ram were informed of the EVA.

"One more incidence of Aivas's obsession," Lessa said, not at all pleased to be summoned to the hastily convened meeting.

"I wish you would all address the meat of the exercise," Jaxom said with more irritation than he had ever before betrayed in the Benden Weyrleaders' presence. "The important fact is that it can be done, has been done, and that Aivas says that EVA by dragons and riders is crucial to his plan."

They were not in the Aivas chamber, but in the conference room.

"Why on earth would he want dragons clinging to that bloody framework, thousands of miles above Pern?" F'lar demanded.

"To accustom dragons to being in space," Jaxom replied.

"That's not all," Robinton said in a slow, thoughtful tone.

"No." D'ram sat erect and alert. "The dragons must move the *Yokohama.*"

"Why?" Lessa asked. "What good would that do?"

"To ram it at the Red Star," D'ram said.

Jaxom, Piemur, and F'lar shook their heads.

"Why not?" Lessa demanded. "That must be why he wanted the fuel in the tanks."

Jaxom smiled wryly at her ignorance. "That drop of fuel would not explode on impact, and ramming the Red Star with the *Yokohama,* ponderous as it is, would not alter its orbit one bit. But I grant you, he needs the dragons to move something."

"Let's ask him!" Robinton suggested, standing and starting for the door. When the others did not move, he turned back at them. "Well, don't we *want* to know?"

"I'm not so sure I do," Lessa murmured, but she rose and followed the others as they trooped down the hallway to Aivas's room.

Jaxom, Jancis, and Piemur closed the doors into the various rooms occupied by students and, when all were inside Aivas's chamber, that door was closed. Piemur leaned back against it.

"What do the dragons have to move and where?" F'lar asked with no preamble.

"So you have perceived part of the plan, Weyrleader."

"You mean to use the *Yokohama* to ram the planet?" Lessa asked, still sure that she had the answer.

"That would be totally ineffectual, and the *Yokohama* is needed as a vantage point."

"Then what?" F'lar insisted.

A picture came up of the Red Star, with details gleaned from Wansor's patient study of the face the planet presented its viewers. A deep chasm could be seen running diagonally across one hemisphere—an unusual feature caused, Aivas had said, by an earthquake of incredible force.

"You all see this fracture. It is entirely possible that the chasm goes deep into the planet. It is probable that an explosion of sufficient magnitude at this point would have the desired effect of altering the planet's orbit. Especially when the planet is already perturbed by its proximity to the fifth satellite of this system." The visual altered to the familiar diagram of the Rukbat system. "Ordinarily an explosion of this magnitude would be impossible to effect. Not only because of the difficulty of amassing the elements required to make such a blast, but because it is nearly impossible to prevent chaotic elements from entering the equations of motion of the Red Star and even of the other planets.

"It is apparent from Master Wansor's investigations that the fifth planet is devoid of atmosphere and life. It is also at its farthest distance from Pern. There will be some perturbations throughout the system, but these have been calculated as negligible in the face of the desired result, the relief from any further incursions of Thread on this planet."

For a very long moment, no one spoke.

"We have no such exploding capability," Jaxom said.

"You do not. The *Yokohama*, the *Bahrain*, and the *Buenos Aires* do."

"What?" F'lar demanded angrily.

"The engines," Jaxom said. "The bloody engines. Oh, you are devious, Aivas!"

"But the engines are dead!" "There's not enough fuel!" "How would we get them there?" Everyone tried to be heard.

"The engines are dormant," Aivas said over the uproar. "But it is the material in the engines that will provide the explosive power. If antimatter is allowed to contact matter without controls, the result will suit your needs."

"Now wait a moment—" Jaxom called for order over the babel of questions. "You specifically stated in those engineering lectures to Fandarel that the antimatter is held out of contact with matter in the densest metals Mankind has ever forged. We don't have the equipment to penetrate those casings. Or is Fandarel working on something we don't know about?"

There was a little pause, and Jaxom found himself agreeing with Master Robinton that Aivas seemed to laugh to himself sometimes.

"It is true that the safety factors built into the great interstellar engines were immensely sophisticated, and that schematics for their design are not available in the engineering data," Aivas said at last. "But it has long been the case that complex things can be attacked best by simple methods. This facility must also obey the stipulation that you are not to be instructed in levels of technology beyond that of your ancestors. Fortunately you already have an agent that will provide the penetration. You have used it in every Fall for many centuries."

"HNO$_3$!" Piemur said in a gasp.

"Correct. The metal casings of the matter/antimatter drives are not impervious to its erosive effect." The visual of the *Yokohama*'s engine shaft reappeared, but now there were large extraneous tanks placed on the drive cube. "It will take time, which is why there is a wide window of two weeks for this part of the activity, but the acid will penetrate the casings, and once the magnetic chamber is broached, matter and antimatter will self-destruct, causing the cataclysmic explosion necessary to shift the Red Star's orbit. Any further questions?"

Jaxom broke the silence that time. "So all the Weyrs of Pern will be needed to take the engines, not the ships, *between* to the Red Star. To drop them into the chasm?"

"To drop them might displace the HNO$_3$ tanks."

"How heavy are those engines?" F'lar asked.

"Their mass is the one weak point of the plan. However, you have constantly stated that the dragons can carry that which they think they can carry."

"Correct, but no one has ever asked them to carry engines!" F'lar replied, awed by the scale of the loads.

Jaxom began to chuckle and received offended stares. "That's why the bronzes have been exercising in free-fall—to get them used to things being so much lighter in space. Right, Aivas?"

"That is correct."

"So if we don't tell them how much those bloody things weigh . . ."

"Now, really, Jaxom," F'lar began.

"No, really, F'lar," Jaxom replied. "Aivas is applying a valid psychological tactic. I think it'll work. Especially if *we* think it can work. Right?" He gave F'lar a challenging look.

"Jaxom makes a good point," Lytol said. Beside him, D'ram nodded accord. "With many dragons, all working together . . . it could be done. No one dragon bearing more than his fair share of the burden, everyone believing that he can succeed. That framework is convenient. Each dragon will be able to grip the load."

"With padding on their feet to reduce the effects of space-cold metal," Aivas added.

"And take that much weight *between*?" Lessa asked, still skeptical.

"You know," F'lar said, rubbing his jaw speculatively. "I think they could do it—if we think they can. Tell me how Ruth reacted to being in space, Jaxom."

"Wait a minute," Lessa said, holding up her hand, her brow wrinkled in concentration. "How long would such a maneuver take? We could get an engine *between*, but to go that distance *between* . . ."

"You and your queen Ramoth traveled backward in time . . ."

"And nearly died," F'lar said, his tone as bitter as the look he gave his weyrmate for the anguish he had suffered then.

"The riders will all have oxygen—which is doubtless what you lacked, Weyrwoman—to breathe, and protective suits."

"There aren't that many!" D'ram protested.

"Not yet," Piemur said, his eyes glinting, "but Hamian's turning out the plastic-coated fabric faster than Master Nicat's men can glue the pieces together."

"From what has been said by every rider interviewed, only eight seconds elapse to reach most destinations here on Pern," Aivas went on. "Of those eight seconds, the dragons seem to use a basic five or so to assimilate their coordinates, and the rest of the time for the actual transfer. Using this premise and adapting it to a logarithmic computation, assume that travel takes 1 second for 1,600 kilometers, 2 seconds for 10,000, 3.6 seconds for 100,000, and 4.8 for 1 million and 7 to 10 seconds for 10 million. While this method of transference is still incomprehensible to this facility, it does appear to work. Therefore, knowing the approximate distance from Pern to the Red Star, it is easy to compute an interplanetary jump. It has also been established that dragons are able to function for fifteen minutes before their systems are in oxygen debt—more than enough time to make the journey, position the engines in the chasm, and return. The dragons are accurate fliers.''

''I'd want to try that journey,'' F'lar said. Lessa turned on him, but before she could speak, he went on. ''Love, if we believe in our dragons, we can believe in our own abilities, as well. Before I ask the Weyrs to undertake such a trip, I must be sure it is feasible, and I won't risk anyone. Not this time!'' Everyone knew he was alluding to F'nor's nearly fatal attempt to reach the Red Star so many Turns before. ''Is there any air to breathe on the Red Star?''

''No,'' Aivas replied. ''Certainly not breathable atmosphere, but there is some, mostly noble gases and nitrogen. Whatever denser atmosphere it once had would have been lost when it escaped from its original system. There is no water, as repeated circuits past Rukbat have boiled off much of its volatiles, too. F'nor has seen this in process. Gravity on the surface would be not much more than one-tenth of Pern's, so the atmosphere is much less dense than what you are accustomed to.''

''You will not take such a perilous expedition by yourself, F'lar,'' D'ram said, rising to his feet, his expression resolute.

''D'ram . . .'' Robinton reached for the old dragonrider's arm, while Lytol's expression was both pitying and approving.

''D'ram, this is a young man's duty,'' the ex-warder said, shaking his head sadly. ''You have long since done yours.''

''F'lar?'' Lessa's face was screwed up in an anxious grimace, as if she couldn't deny him but wanted desperately to do so. She shook her head, her gray eyes wide with fright, as she realized that nothing she could say would dissuade him.

''I will go,'' the Weyrleader repeated.

''Not by yourself,'' Jaxom said, shaking his head. ''I'll go with you.'' He held his hands up to silence the others, but had little effect. He raised his voice over the uproar. ''Ruth always knows where he is and when he is. No other dragon has that ability, and you all know it. I'll go without permission if you keep on at me like this!'' He allowed his anger to be seen as he glared at Lytol, Robinton, and D'ram. Lessa glared back, but she didn't join in the arguments.

''Jaxom, you may not come with me,'' F'lar stated. ''You've responsibilities—''

ANNE McCAFFREY

"I'm going, and that's that. I trust Ruth as you trust Mnementh.
Let's keep this expedition down to as few as possible. Right?"

"What happens, though," Robinton said, his composure recovered, "if the one man"—and he gestured to F'lar—"who can keep
this planet united and the young Lord Holder who has earned the
respect of Hall, Hold, and Weyr should be lost to Pern at this very
critical stage?"

F'lar gave a rueful laugh. "I don't intend to be lost, and if I will
not go where I expect the Weyrs to follow, how can I ask them to
go?" He took Lessa by the arms, appealing to her. "I must go, Lessa.
Surely you see that."

"I do," she snapped. "But I don't have to like it. Furthermore, I'll
go with you two fools!" She laughed at the startled reactions. "Why
not? There're plenty of queens now to continue dragonkind. Ramoth's still the largest dragon on the planet and the bravest, going
where no one dared go before. I think we three deserve the right!"
She lifted her chin, haughtily oblivious to persuasions. "When do we
go?"

Piemur let go a bark of laughter. "Just like that?"

"Why not? We don't have Threadfall for another two days. Jaxom?"

Three dragons bugled from the mounds beyond the building.
Lessa, F'lar, and Jaxom smiled.

"I won't tell Sharra." He paused while Jancis savagely muttered
something to the effect that Sharra wouldn't let him go. "I wouldn't
be so sure of that, Jancis," he said, giving her a quelling look. "But
there are a few things I must put in order. And to be perfectly candid,
I'd like a good night's sleep. It's been a busy day!"

"Tomorrow then?" Lessa said, pinning him with a fierce stare.

"Certainly! I'll send Meer to Ruatha with a message that I'm staying over at Cove Hold."

"A good idea," F'lar said, quirking one eyebrow in amusement.
"Mnementh is pretty excited . . ."

"Ramoth, too," Lessa said, and frowned. "We can't risk some
other dragon sensing what we plan. There are fortunately no other
dragons at Landing right now."

The three riders discussed with Aivas and the others every aspect
of their unprecedented leap *between*. As the riders became more and
more confident of success, the others began to cease their opposition,
lapsing into nearly morose silence.

"If we do not leave soon," Robinton said into a pause as the three
dragonriders were studying their landing site at the highest magni-

fication Aivas could produce, "some of our more perceptive students will start speculating about the length of this meeting."

"A good point," F'lar said cheerfully. "Aivas, can you print out a copy of what's on the screen right now? We can study it further at Cove Hold."

"I'd've thought it was burned in your brains already," Lytol remarked caustically.

"Nearly," Jaxom replied gaily. He was buoyed by the confidence that F'lar and Lessa exuded, not realizing that each was infecting the other. Jaxom had not missed Lytol's frequent brooding looks, but after those first protests, his old guardian had only been silently reproachful.

Aivas printed three copies.

"This facility would not recommend such an exploration if any foreseeable danger was involved," Aivas said to reassure the skeptics.

"Foreseeable is the important word," Lytol said, and walked out.

15
▼▼▼▼▼▼▼

"I've never seen so many fire-lizards!" Jancis exclaimed as she helped Piemur and Jaxom wash Ruth in Cove Hold's lagoon.

Lessa, F'lar, and D'ram were similarly occupied, assisted by other members of the Cove Hold research staff. Lytol and Robinton had gone to oversee the preparation of the evening meal. The atmosphere was tense with anticipation, and Jaxom hoped that the stress would not be communicated to the Hold people; fortunately it was not unusual for the Benden Weyrleaders and the Ruathan Holder to enjoy Cove's hospitality.

Ruth, have the fire-lizards twigged tomorrow's journey? Jaxom asked. He refused to think of it as an "attempt," which implied the possibility of failure.

They're excited because I am. Ramoth and Mnementh are, too. Look at their eyes! But the little ones don't know why they're excited.

Jaxom put some extra effort into scrubbing Ruth's left wing. There were hundreds of questions rattling about in his brain, but to settle on any one of them and find an answer was beyond him. This was not at all like the day that he and Ruth had gone hunting for Ramoth's queen egg. He had been a boy then, struggling to achieve manhood, to be both Lord Holder and dragonrider and to advert a major confrontation between the Southern Oldtimers and Benden Weyr. This also wasn't as spontaneous an acceptance of challenge as that morning's EVA had been. This was a planned expedition to be made in the company of two of the most important people on Pern.

And the three best dragons, Ruth added.

Aware that his roiling thoughts might also leak to the fire-lizards, Jaxom earnestly pulled soothing images to the fore in his mind. Just then a fire-lizard arrived from *between* with the faint pop of reentry. It was Meer—in all the excitement, Jaxom hadn't even noticed that he had disappeared.

So it did not exactly surprise him when Sharra strode into the Hold while they were finishing their dinner. Still, he had no idea what Meer might have conveyed to her, so he decided he would be best off playing innocent.

"Darling, what an unexpected surprise," he said, rising to greet her with an embrace. "There's nothing the matter at Ruatha, is there?" he added with a fair pretense of alarm. He ignored Piemur, who was rolling his eyes.

"No, nothing's wrong at Ruatha," Sharra said in the tone that always made him wary. But she smiled with genuine warmth at the others. "It's just that the biology team is starting the dissection tomorrow. Mirrim said she'd convey me up. G'lanar point-blank refused. I hope I'm not interrupting . . ."

She was disabused of that notion by offers of klah from Lessa, wine from Robinton, and sweet breads from Jancis, while Piemur hastily drew another chair up to the table.

"G'lanar bring you?" D'ram asked.

As she nodded, Jaxom left Piemur to settle his wife and strode out to the porch to offer hospitality to the Oldtimer. But Lamoth and his rider were already airborne, circling to the east above the lagoon, disappearing into the night sky.

"I didn't catch him," Jaxom said. "He ought to have at least joined us for a cup."

D'ram brushed away Jaxom's discontent. "G'lanar was always a surly one. How does he happen to be at Ruatha these days?"

Jaxom grinned. "The weyrling we had was judged old enough to fight and was sent to join K'van's wings. He asked us to accommodate G'lanar and Lamoth in their stead. The old bronze sleeps almost as much as G'lanar does."

"It does them both good to feel needed," Sharra said, her eyes glittering at Jaxom although her tone was social.

Jaxom wondered what on earth Meer had conveyed to her that had brought her to Cove Hold. His own message had been innocuous enough: the Egg knew staying over at Cove Hold was nothing out of the ordinary. But he was glad to see her.

It was also very like Sharra to say nothing to the point in company. But he began to worry about how to dissemble when they were alone in their sleeping quarters. As the dragonriders whiled away the after-dinner hours, no hint of their morning's plans was raised—partly because the young men and women of the Archive were present, but especially because Sharra was there.

"I've a new song from Menolly," Master Robinton said, gesturing for Piemur to bring him his gitar and to get his own. He unrolled the score, passing a copy to Jancis to put on the rack for Piemur. "An odd tune, unusual for our Masterharper Menolly. She says the words were written by young Harper Elimona," he went on, plucking a string to tune the instrument. Piemur corrected the pitch of his and, reading the music, soundlessly fingered through the chords. "But a lovely haunting melody and words to lift hearts at this point in a Pass."

Then he nodded to Piemur and they began. Having sung and played so often together, they interwove and harmonized as if they had rehearsed the brand-new song a hundred times already.

> A heart that's true in harper blue
> makes song from heart's own fire,
> and though betrayed, is not afraid:
> in danger, leaps up higher.

Jaxom suppressed the start of surprise the words gave him, and dared not look at either Lessa or F'lar.

> No world is free of minstrelsy,
> nor noise, nor rage, nor sorrow.
> A harper must discharge his trust
> before he asks to borrow.
>
> My Harper Hall is free to all
> who serve with song and playing.
> But you who'd hide your song inside
> are very sadly straying.

At those words, Jaxom wondered what cryptic message Menolly and Elimona were giving, and to whom. The next verse was even

more germane to the problem of those who considered Aivas to be
"the Abomination."

> *Will you withdraw beyond the law,*
> *lie safely in your slumber,*
> *while dangers shake your world awake*
> *and Death makes up his number?*
>
> *Did harper here betray those dear*
> *he'd feel more than my tongue.*
> *If place you'd earn, you'd better learn*
> *more music than you've sung.*
>
> *For if you die, while safe you lie*
> *halled in your selfish bone,*
> *no chant will come, no harper drum,*
> *and you'll lie long alone.*

Jaxom, watching Robinton's face as he sang, wondered if the words
could possibly have been prompted by Robinton or Sebell, who so
often suggested themes to their harpers. But then, Menolly had such
an uncanny knack of catching exactly the mood of the moment that
this could have been merely serendipitous. The two harpers played
a bridging passage; then their voices, which had been light and almost taunting, deepened for the final verse.

> *Get up, take heart—go, make a start,*
> *sing out the truth you came for.*
> *Then when you die, your heart may fly*
> *to halls we have no name for.*

As the last chord died away there was a respectful silence before
the audience burst into loud applause. Robinton and Piemur dis-
claimed humbly, Robinton saying that with such music any harper
would find himself doing his very best.

"Who's next?" Piemur asked, strumming his gitar into a complicated alteration, minor to major.

The next hour was spent happily enough so that Jaxom relaxed,
holding Sharra's hand and playing with her long fingers—and trying
to ignore the distance she had put between them. Talla was coiled
up on her shoulder, but he saw nothing of Meer.

Ruth, did Meer tattle on us? he asked when Sharra was occupied in singing descant for one of her favorite songs.

He has curled up on the beach and pretends to be asleep. What could he tell her that would make sense?

Sharra's perceptive, Ruth. She could guess.

She knows you are always safe with me.

But she also doesn't want me risking my neck . . . more than I already do.

She will not refuse you, Ruth added encouragingly, though his tone held a nuance of doubt.

At last Lessa called an end to the evening's entertainment, murmuring something about never quite becoming accustomed to double-ended days. Robinton acted the perfect host, making certain, with Jancis's help, that all the guests were comfortably installed; his behavior was so calm and ordinary that when Sharra and Jaxom were alone in their usual corner room, she frowned in puzzlement.

"Why was Meer so agitated, Jaxom?"

"He was? Not much happened today." He began to pull his shirt off, which served to muffle his voice and hide his face lest his expression give him away. Sharra had become adept at reading him, a skill that usually smoothed matters between them, but this time he really didn't want to risk upsetting her unnecessarily. He had written notes for Brand and for her and given them to Piemur—not that he expected that Piemur would have to deliver them, but he had to plan for contingencies. "Anyone at Ruatha got a randy green or gold?" he continued as nonchalantly as possible.

He could see her considering that possibility. "I don't think so," she said finally. "Are you all going up to the *Yokohama* tomorrow?"

"Yes." Jaxom gave her his best grin, which he expanded into a yawn as he gestured for her to climb in first. When she was settled, he lay down and put his arm around her, cushioning her head on his shoulder as he so often did—only now he did it consciously, not merely in response to the habits of five Turns.

"What's the schedule?" she asked.

"More of the same. Getting accustomed to free-fall."

"Why?"

"Well, Aivas let us in on that today," Jaxom said, choosing his words carefully. "Seems like all the Weyrs of Pern are going to be needed to hoist the engine part of the ships to that big rift on the Red Star."

"What?"

He pushed her back down in the bed, grinning at her astonished expression, clearly visible in the moonlight flooding the room. "That's what I said. He's going to call our bluff that dragons can lift anything they *think* they can."

"But—but—why?"

"Those engines will be made to blow up, and the force of the explosion will nudge the Red Star into a new orbit."

"Oh, my!"

Jaxom grinned. It took something as fantastic as that to reduce his beloved to an incredulous whisper. He pulled her close enough to lay a kiss on her forehead, meaning only to reassure her. But as his lips touched her soft skin and his nostrils inhaled the spicy fragrance she used, he felt desire well up inside of him. And, though at first her response was reflexive while she was still mulling over his news, he had no trouble in getting her complete attention.

Later, he was awakened by the scratch of a fire-lizard claw on his cheek. It was Meer, his sense of smell told him—and a Meer who was worried and puzzled.

Jaxom! Ruth's anxious tone reinforced Meer's warning. *There is someone in the hall by your door. Meer senses danger. I'm coming!*

For the love of the egg that hatched you, keep him quiet right now, Jaxom told Ruth. *And be as quiet as you can.*

You know how quietly I can move, Ruth replied, slightly aggrieved.

I want this one alive—and identifiable!

Carefully, so as not to disturb Sharra or alert the intruder, Jaxom rolled out of the bed and went for his belt and the knife sheathed there. In the darkness, Meer blinked orange-red eyes that were whirling in a gradually increasing speed, but the little bronze made no move.

An alteration in the shadows of the room told Jaxom that the door was being stealthily opened. He stayed where he was crouched, muscles relaxed but every fiber of him ready to move.

The door shadows separated into a crouching figure, knife-holding hand raised in a strike position as the intruder crept toward the bed—then paused. Realizing that the man had discerned that only Sharra lay in the bed, Jaxom sprang, encircling the figure with his arms.

"Oh no you don't!" he cried in a hoarse whisper, still not wanting to wake Sharra. But there was no hope of that.

Meer, swooping at the man's face while Jaxom struggled to hold him, bugled with no regard for sleeping folk. Outside, Ruth bellowed, and half the fire-lizard population of the Cove tried to fly in through the open window.

Though the man struggled, breathing hoarsely in his desperation, Jaxom was the victor of far too many wrestling matches to have his hold broken easily. But he didn't quite avoid the slashing blade, which scored his bare shoulder. Cursing, Jaxom grabbed the dagger hand and, twisting it in a move F'lessan had taught him, broke the man's wrist. The attacker crumpled, crying aloud in pain just as F'lar, Piemur, Lytol, and D'ram came bursting into the room. Someone behind them was carrying an open glowbasket, and light spilled past the reinforcements to fall on the face of the man Jaxom had downed.

"G'lanar!" Jaxom fell back in surprise and shock.

The old bronze rider snarled up at him, batting at the shrieking fire-lizards who were still swooping at him, claws extended.

"G'lanar?" D'ram grabbed the man by the arm and, with F'lar's help, hauled him to his feet.

Jaxom told Ruth to call the fire-lizards off and, still screaming their challenge, the fair swooped back out the window.

Sharra stared from the bed as Jancis and Lessa crowded into the room, each holding a bright basket.

"What did you intend, G'lanar?" F'lar demanded, his voice coldly implacable.

"He's to blame . . ." G'lanar cried, spitting in his fury, cradling his broken wrist to his chest.

Jaxom stared down at the old rider. "Blame?"

"You! I know who it was now! It was you—and that white runt that ought to have died the moment it was born!" Outside, Ruth roared exception to the insult, then thrust his head through the window. "If it hadn't been for you, we'd've had our own fertile queen! We'd've had a chance!"

Jaxom shook his head slightly, trying to understand the accusation. So few knew that he and Ruth had recovered the abducted queen egg from Benden Weyr. How had G'lanar learned?

"So it was you who cut the riding straps?" Jaxom demanded.

"Yes, yes, I did, and I'd've got you. I'd've kept trying till I did. Nor wept if your woman'd died that morning. Save Pern from more like you and that abortion!"

"And you, a dragonrider, would seek the death of another?" D'ram's scorn and horror made G'lanar flinch—but only briefly.

"Yes, yes, yes!" His voice climbed in fury and frustration. "Yes!

Unnatural man, unnatural dragon! Abominations as vile as that Aivas thing you worship.'' G'lanar's eyes glittered; his features were contorted.

"That's enough of that,'' F'lar said, stepping forward purposefully.

"It is! Enough!'' Before either Jaxom, who had stepped back from the man, or F'lar, who was moving toward him, could act, G'lanar plunged his dagger into his own breast.

His action shocked everyone to immobility.

"Oh, no!'' Jaxom breathed, dropping to the man's side and feeling for the throat pulse. With the rider dead, the dragon would suicide. Had G'lanar's thrust been true? His heart quailed, waiting for the keen all dragonriders dreaded to hear.

Ruth had pulled his head from the window, and Jaxom could see him, rearing back on his haunches and stretching to his full height, wings spread to balance him. The sound he uttered was muted, an oddly strangled noise. There were other sounds in the night, and then Ramoth and Mnementh landed outside the room, deepening the shadows.

Lamoth dies. In shame. Ruth sank back to the ground, wings limp against his back, his head low. *They were mistaken to steal Ramoth's egg. We only set matters right. I am not an abomination or unnatural. And you are a very natural man, Jaxom. How can Aivas be wrong when he does everything to help us?*

Lessa moved to Jaxom and lifted him up from the dead man; her eyes watered with tears and her expression was dreadful, but her hands were gentle. Sharra, wrapping the sheet around herself, ran to him and put her arms around him, draping a corner of the sheet over his nudity.

"I don't understand this,'' D'ram said, running trembling fingers through his thick, gray hair. "How could he so corrupt the truth? How could he seek the life of another dragonrider?''

"There have been moments,'' Lessa said in a broken voice, "when I wonder what good I did bringing the five Weyrs forward.''

"No, Lessa.'' D'ram recovered from regret to touch her shoulder supportively. "You did what was necessary. So did Jaxom, though I never realized it was he who saved that situation.'' He shot an approving look at the young Lord Holder.

"Why did no one realize that G'lanar harbored such a grievance?'' F'lar demanded.

"I'm going to get to the bottom of this,'' Lessa said resolutely.

"I'd thought the Weyrs were united in this project! Surely even Old-timers are! They've fought two lives' worth of Thread . . ."

D'ram was scrubbing at his face, shaking his head, his shoulders hunched against the night's treachery. "Every Oldtimer I've spoken to—and there are few enough of us old ones now—and all the younger riders are definitely in accord with Benden. Everyone sees the help, the training, the promise Aivas holds out as the culmination of the Weyr objective since the first egg hatched. The project has given us all hope at this critical point in a Pass."

"Ramoth has started speaking to the other queens," Lessa said, her voice strained. "We'll know by morning if there are any other disaffected riders in any Weyr."

"I'll take care of this," F'lar said, gesturing to Piemur and Jaxom to help him with G'lanar's body.

"No, I will," D'ram said, stepping over the corpse to heave it over his shoulders. His face was devoid of expression, but his cheeks were tearstained. "He was a good rider before he went South with Mardra and T'ton."

The others stepped back so he could pass with his sad burden. Sharra handed Jaxom his long-tailed riding shirt, and as he slipped into it gratefully, she hurriedly pulled on a tunic. The night breeze was chilly. She went past Jaxom to the door.

"A cup of hot wine is indicated," she said, and Jancis followed her to the kitchen.

Sharra had added something to the wine, Jaxom decided when he woke and found morning well started. She was still asleep beside him, so he assumed that she had taken her own medicine. A boon for him, since he had no intention of delaying that day's plan. He eased out of the bed, scooped up his clothing, and went to dress in the head. When he entered the main room, he found Lessa cradling a cup of klah in her hands while F'lar, a set expression on his face, was spooning cereal into his mouth. Without a word, the Weyr-woman rose and filled a cup and a bowl for Jaxom.

"Is everyone else still asleep?"

Lessa shook her head. "Piemur and Jancis have gone to Landing with D'ram and Lytol. Robinton's to sleep himself out." She took another sip of klah. "Ramoth says the queens report no other traitors in our midst." Her tone was as bleak as her eyes. "She says that

Southern's queen is inexperienced and Adrea too young to understand G'lanar's grievances. However, apparently old G'lanar had begun to get quite testy, going off a lot on his own after Tillek. When S'rond was due to join the fighting wings at Southern Weyr, G'lanar begged for the duty at Ruatha. That would have made me suspicious!''

"Why?" F'lar asked. "Ruatha's the duty everyone wants." He gave Jaxom an encouraging smile and spooned more sweetener over the remains of his porridge.

Noticing that, Lessa opened her mouth to scold and then shut it, looking away in her disgruntlement. F'lar winked at Jaxom, pretending relief.

"No, the Oldtimers who chose to go south with Mardra and T'ton were already antagonistic to Benden's aims," the Weyrleader said, "as much because Benden suggested them. G'lanar would've brooded long enough, ripe for any scheme to support his grievances. And we already know there's a fair number who see Aivas as an Abomination."

"There may be more after today," Lessa muttered.

F'lar dropped his spoon with a clatter. "No one's going to know about today . . .''

She shook her head, surprised at his remark. "I didn't mean what we plan to do," she said with some exasperation. "I meant, G'lanar's death. Well, the Weyrs know the old fellow died but certainly not why. We can at least keep the attack quiet."

F'lar shot an anxious look at Jaxom, who shrugged acquiescence. He certainly didn't wish to have the story bruited about.

"That's what D'ram's going to insure: that everyone thinks old G'lanar suffered a brainstorm."

"That's lame. The dragons'll know . . .''

"Ramoth says not. Lamoth had gone to sleep in the clearing, totally unaware of what G'lanar was doing here. Of course, he knew when G'lanar died, and he floundered *between* somehow. To be doubly cautious, D'ram means to speak to each of the remaining Oldtimers. Tiroth may not be a queen, but no dragon could hide his heart from that bronze."

"*How*," Jaxom asked, "did G'lanar realize that Ruth and I rescued Ramoth's egg?"

"Have you been timing it much lately?" Lessa asked bluntly.

Jaxom tried to shrug the question away. "Not often."

Lessa raised her eyebrows in resignation. "I keep telling you that timing it is dangerous. It was bloody sure dangerous for you. Lamoth would have known. He would have told G'lanar. G'lanar was misguided but not stupid. I know that all the Oldtimers at Southern have puzzled over who rescued the egg. In spite of our precautions, they all know Ruth's abilities and might have suspicions.''

''G'lanar's the only bronze rider left from that group,'' Jaxom said, after a quick mental review.

''We have a more important task to perform today than to fret over this incident,'' F'lar said, rising to clear the table of his bowl and cup. ''That is, if you feel up to it, Jaxom . . .''

Jaxom regarded F'lar scornfully. ''I've been waiting on you. Let's do it.''

''From here, or the *Yokohama*?'' Lessa asked.

''The *Yokohama*,'' Jaxom said, grabbing his riding gear from the beach beside him. ''We don't have the space suits down here.''

''You're sure there's one to fit me?'' Lessa asked, shrugging into her leather jacket.

Jaxom grinned. ''There're two small ones. One ought to fit, even if we have to truss you up some.'' As he came out onto the porch, Meer chirped at him. ''Lessa, to preserve my image in my wife's eyes, would you ask Ramoth to keep Meer from following me today? Ask her to tell him I'm safe with you two.''

Lessa quirked her eyebrow, grinning up at him. ''You're sure of that?''

Tucks had to be taken in the arms and legs and waist of the smallest of the suits, which caused some amusement to F'lar and Jaxom but none to Lessa. They contacted Aivas when they were ready to proceed. He brought up their objective, the immense long scar on the Red Star, on the screen in the cargo bay.

F'lar frowned at it again, not so much in order to imprint the scene firmly into his mind as to rationalize what he was seeing.

''When F'nor made his flight to the Red Star, he said there were roiling clouds . . .''

''There probably were,'' Aivas replied easily. ''In orbiting so close to Rukbat, the planet's surface would have become heated, hot enough to melt rock and certainly causing steam from the ice that coats Thread ovoids. It can be posited that the planet itself is coated with the debris of the Oort Cloud. Steam or dust clouds of considerable density are entirely possible. That is undoubtedly what F'nor saw, not the actual surface. His memories of the event, even the abrasive injuries he and Canth sustained, bear out the supposition. At this point in its orbit, the surface has cooled, that phenomenon has subsided, and you see a sterile planet, its surface slowly freezing again.''

"Well, let's do it!'' F'lar vaulted to Mnementh's shoulder, grabbing the riding straps to swing himself to his customary position between neck ridges.

Despite free-fall, Lessa moved more clumsily.

"How anyone can be expected to move anywhere in this sort of gear . . .'' she muttered, finally settling herself in place. She had a bit of trouble snapping the riding straps onto rings lost in the folds about her middle. "Can't see what I'm doing, trussed up like a wherry for the spit, and this helmet obscuring my sight . . .''

Jaxom grinned at her and looked toward F'lar. "Are you leading this expedition?''

Something like a growl came over Jaxom's helmet com and he chuckled.

"Do our dragons know where we're going?'' Lessa asked. She held her suited arm up high above her head, looking first to the left at F'lar and then to the right at Jaxom; all three were concentrating on the image of that tremendous fault. "Very well, then, let's go!'' And she dropped her arm.

Jaxom counted as Ruth shifted them *between*. He remembered to continue breathing, an exercise he frequently suspended on such trips. He didn't think of the blackness or the frightening cold of the familiar oblivion: he thought only of where they were going . . .

I know where we're going, Ruth assured him patiently.

. . . and how long it was taking them. Jaxom had counted twenty-seven slow seconds, seconds that seemed an eternity. He wondered if Lessa had counted when she had gone back four hundred Turns to—

And then the three dragons emerged simultaneously over a chasm that made Ruth extend his wings uselessly in an attempt to slow his entry in the light gravity and thin atmosphere.

"Aivas?'' Jaxom cried, though in the next second he knew that they were too far from Aivas for any contact.

"Shards! Jaxom, we can handle this without his supervision!'' F'lar roared. He moderated his tone as he went on. "There are times when

I think we've gotten too dependent on Aivas. Slow your descent, Jaxom! We want to land on the edge, not in that bloody rift.''

Just beyond Ruth, the rift widened into a crater more immense than the Ice Lake. Jaxom's body gave a massive shudder, and he had the most incredible feeling that he had expected to see that crater all along, though the detail had not been on the visuals. To center his wandering attention, he concentrated on the rim below him, and in the next breath, Ruth obediently glided to the hard-packed surface of the planet, his wings fully extended. Mnementh and Ramoth, necks stretched out and eyes whirling in a brilliant rainbow expressing their consternation, landed gracefully beside him.

"Quickly, now, mark those boulders . . .'' F'lar pointed to the huge stone shafts that made a rim, like so many immense jagged teeth, across the mouth of the huge aperture.

"That crater's a fine landmark,'' Jaxom commented.

This place is strangely familiar, Ruth said, walking forward to peer over the edge.

Watch it! Jaxom warned his dragon as Ruth's feet sank into what appeared to be a mass of oval shapes. "Look, F'lar! Thread ovoids.''

F'lar peered over Mnementh's shoulder while the big bronze dropped his head to examine the surface under his feet. He didn't appear particularly concerned.

"I don't like this place,'' Lessa commented. Ramoth seemed to share her distaste, placing her feet with extreme care as if she were walking through putrid mud.

"And watch that edge, too, Jaxom,'' F'lar added.

Ramoth was looking straight ahead, trying to see to the other side of the gorge. Jaxom could not see the far side in the dim light available. When he looked over his shoulder toward Rukbat, he had no trouble looking directly at the dim sun, but it did give sufficient light for him to pick out details of the terrain beyond the canyon. Not that there was much to see. The surface of the Red Star was pocked and slagged, minor fissures and fractures speading out from the immense fault across what looked more like bare rock than sand. The black chasm stretched in both directions into the tenebrous distance. Jaxom looked behind him. There were some jagged projections, from small terraces to great sheets that would have taken up most of Benden's Bowl. An appallingly sterile landscape. Jaxom could almost feel sorry for the battered planet.

It's a long way across, isn't it? Ruth remarked.

You can see across it? Jaxom asked, squinting in the dismal gloom at the shadowy far edge.

There isn't much to see but more of the same.

"See how those levels are situated?" F'lar said, peering down. "We could settle the engines along them."

"Are they stable enough to hold that sort of weight?" Lessa asked.

F'lar shrugged. "I don't know why not. Don't you feel how much lighter we are here? The engines should weigh less, too. And look at the size of the slabs! Gigantic."

"Like teeth. You know, this looks as if some force broke the planet's surface as you or I would open a redfruit," Lessa said, her voice awed.

Ruth, can you drop down to that first level of rock? Take it easy now. We want to see how stable the protrusion actually is.

"Easy now, Jaxom!" F'lar cautioned, raising one hand as if to cancel the experiment.

There was plenty of wing space, and Ruth delicately lowered himself in the thin atmosphere past the lip of the canyon and down onto the first stone sheet. He dislodged a small boulder, which continued to fall. Jaxom listened for a long moment.

Have you got all your weight on this, Ruth? Jaxom asked.

Jaxom could feel Ruth grunting as he bent his knees and pressed downward.

It's not going anywhere. And I don't weigh so much here.

True. "We should have brought some lights," Jaxom told the others, peering along the stone protrusion. "But this shelf looks plenty long enough to hold even the *Yokohama*'s engine. D'you want me and Ruth to see how far down we can go before the canyon closes up?"

"Shards! No!" F'lar said. "What you're doing is dangerous enough."

"How much time has elapsed?" Lessa asked. "The dragons have only so much air in their bodies."

"We're only seven minutes here," Jaxom said after glancing at the built-in suit chronometer. As a leader, he was wearing one of the original space suits, not one of those Hamian had so cleverly contrived.

"C'mon up out of there, Jaxom," F'lar said. "If the jaws of that canyon should snap shut . . ."

Jaxom, who had been thinking the same thing, was quite willing to comply. Beating his wings much faster than he'd need to on Pern, Ruth rose from the black chasm, facing the other two dragons.

ANNE MCCAFFREY

"This would be one likely site then," F'lar said. "I'll go up, you go down. Lessa, see what the other rim is like. How much time, Jaxom?"

"Five minutes! No more!"

Jaxom found it somewhat unnerving to fly over this aperture, knowing that it likely extended to the depths of the planet. He kept his eye open for unusual extrusions to use as landmarks, but the sides had sheared clean for almost four minutes of flight. Then, a dragon-length below the lip, he saw another long, thick sheet of pale mottled rock. He asked Ruth to mark it in his mind.

Ramoth says we must return. They have found a third place, Ruth told Jaxom.

Then our mission is accomplished. Let's join 'em and go back.

Ramoth says to jump back from where we are.

Are you all right? Jaxom asked. *Are they all right?*

I'm all right. They're all right. But it would be good to get back to the Yokohama *and breathe.*

Let's go, then. And Jaxom thought with longing of his own for the safety of the cargo bay.

A fraction of a breath after Ruth and Jaxom arrived, the two big Benden dragons appeared. Even in the dim light of the cargo bay, Jaxom could see that their colors were grayed. Apprehensively, he looked down at Ruth, but no fading was visible. Then he saw that their journey had had an elapsed time of 12:30:20 minutes.

Are you all right? he asked, leaning forward on Ruth's neck, aware that the white dragon's mouth was wide open as he inhaled and exhaled, great deep breaths. Jaxom could feel him trembling.

"Jaxom? Lessa? F'lar?" Aivas's voice sounded very loud in the helmet.

"We're here," Jaxom replied. "We're all right. We've found three points for the engines. Well down in the chasm, wide ledges. Perfect." He looked at the chronometer. "Twelve minutes, Aivas. Twelve. Strange place," he added, recalling what he had seen of the lifeless surface and the jumbled, tortured terrain, with the vast canyon like a gaping wound that had killed the planet. Had anyone ever lived on it?

I am thirsty and I need a bath, Ruth said so plaintively that Jaxom laughed. *Ramoth and Mnementh agree.*

"I think we'll just let you get your full breath back, Ramoth dear," Lessa said, unsnapping the riding straps. "There wouldn't be any klah up here anywhere, would there, Jaxom?" she asked, almost as

- 311 -

plaintively as Ruth had. "I'm thirsty, cold, and I feel as if I've been gone from Pern for a century."

"Water's all we've got up here," he told her. "But we're not that far from hot klah." He wouldn't mind a pitcherful or two himself. His guts felt cold from his navel to his backbone.

But the water cask proved to be empty, and Jaxom cursed under his breath. He would have a hard word or two for whatever dimwit hadn't had the consideration to refill the on-board cask.

Lessa was furious, too, but that made them quick to shed their suits and rack them carefully away. By then, all three dragons insisted that they were restored and wanted nothing more than a long drink and a longer swim.

"One thing," Lessa said as she remounted Ramoth. "This trip was much farther away, but it didn't take as long as I thought it would. I wonder . . ."

"We've enough to wonder about, Lessa," F'lar said firmly, "and I want to get the details down as soon as possible before they fade."

"My impressions of that sterile place won't fade," Lessa replied emphatically. "I could almost feel sorry for it."

"It has been a dead planet for longer than Pern has been viable," Aivas said.

"That doesn't make me feel any better," Lessa replied.

Meer was waiting at Cove Hold, and he gave both Jaxom and Ruth such a scolding of agitated dives and fierce shrieking that Lessa and F'lar doubled up with laughter.

Ruth calmly reassured the little bronze and, ambling down toward the beach, invited him to help with the dragons' bath. *You are not coming?* he added plaintively when he saw Jaxom heading in the direction of the Hold.

"Can't, dear heart. Got to put down the details while they're fresh in my mind! Be with you soon enough," Jaxom called as he jogged up to the beach with Lessa and F'lar. Fairs of fire-lizards erupted into the air, diving for the dragons. "Not that you need us!"

The spacious living area of the Hold was empty, and calls for Robinton and Sharra went unanswered.

"I wonder where Sharra's gone," Jaxom said, remembering all too clearly how he had left her asleep and diverted Meer. She would be worried. Or angry! And with genuine cause, he thought, wincing.

Lessa grinned at him, understandingly. "You were with us."

"That'll be no excuse," Jaxom said glumly, wondering how he was going to restore himself in Sharra's eyes. Then he gave himself a mental shake and turned to immediate tasks.

As the Benden Weyrleaders collected drawing materials, Jaxom found a pitcher of cold fruit juice in the cooler; they all emptied the large jug while they recorded their visit. When they compared the images, there were few deviations.

"That's done!" Lessa said, with a sigh of relief.

"You know," Jaxom said, propping his head on one hand and grinning at the other two, "I still don't believe we've been there and back!"

F'lar grinned wryly. "I don't know what I expected—especially after F'nor's try—but it's incredible that something as dead as that has threatened us for so long."

"Well, it has!" Lessa said, planting both hands on the table and pushing herself to her feet. She picked up the sketches and thrust them at Jaxom. "Put them somewhere safe until you can show Aivas. Now, I'm going to swim!"

Though he wanted a swim as badly as the others did, Jaxom detoured through the room he had shared with Sharra, hoping that she had left him a message. There was none, and he felt more dejected than ever. He shucked off his clothes, thankful that he always kept a spare change at Cove Hold, and made his way down to the lagoon.

Meer and Talla separated themselves from those scrubbing Ruth and circled his head, chittering happily. Not entirely encouraged by their response, he waded out to Ruth.

Sharra's above. She wouldn't let Meer or Talla go with her. They'd get in the way, Ruth told him.

Jaxom slapped his forehead in dismay: she had told him, too, and he had forgotten about it, once again so immersed in his own business that her doings hadn't quite registered in his brain. He laughed in self-deprecation. At times he *knew* he didn't deserve a woman like Sharra, and this was one of them. How conceited he was! He missed her. Even if he couldn't have told her about the marvelous journey he had just taken, he missed her.

I'm here, Ruth said in subtle reproach.

Indeed you are, my dearest friend, as you always are! And Jaxom waded out in the warm water to help the fire-lizards give his lifemate a good scrubbing.

16

When Mirrim had come to collect Sharra for the trip up to the *Yokohama* to begin their own project, she had found Sharra still asleep.

"Sharra? We're to start this dissection business? Remember?" Mirrim said as Sharra groggily roused, plainly disoriented.

"You know about Lamoth and G'lanar?"

Mirrim wrinkled her nose. "I feel sorry for the dragon. Didn't know one would die of shame. You get dressed. I'll get you some klah."

As Sharra quickly dressed, she hoped that Mirrim's feelings would be shared by others. She found some reassurance in the knowledge that Mirrim would not necessarily side with Jaxom if she felt he was wrong.

"You'd better eat, too," the green rider said, returning with the klah. "And let's bring some food, fruit, and juice. I thought I'd faint with hunger during that last session Aivas put us through. Maybe he's sophisticated, but my stomach's not. It's real primitive. It likes to be filled at regular intervals."

Sharra smiled over the rim of her cup. That was Mirrim, talking up a storm to hide her real emotions. The death of any dragon for any reason upset all riders. Sharra just let her friend talk on. Then, with the klah stimulating her, she lent Mirrim a hand to pack provisions.

ANNE MCCAFFREY

"No meatrolls!" Mirrim said with a dramatic shudder as Sharra reached into the cupboard for some. "I'll puke if I have to eat any more. Thank goodness Master Robinton likes proper bread and sliced meats and raw vegetables." They placed fresh fruit in the special quilted sacks that were a spin-off product from Hamian's search for space-suit paddings, and filled thermoses with cool drinks. "All right, then, let's lift."

"Isn't Brekke coming with us?" Sharra asked.

"No, F'nor's to do something aboard the *Yokohama* today." Mirrim grinned. "Probably the same thing Jaxom and T'gellan are doing, only I'm not to ask."

"Is it dangerous?" Sharra spoke casually, but she knew Jaxom well enough to know that he had *not* been telling her something the previous night—a something that had fretted Meer badly enough to send the little bronze skittering back to Ruatha in fright.

"I doubt it! Riders take good care of their dragons, and the reverse is true. The dragons are all very happy with themselves. I wouldn't let *today* worry me, Sharra," Mirrim said sympathetically.

More bolstered by Mirrim's breezy tone than by her words, Sharra followed her friend out to where Path awaited them, her green hide gleaming with undertones of deep blue, her eyes dazzling in a green that exactly matched her hide.

"Does she do that often?" Sharra asked, pointing to eye and hide.

Mirrim flushed and ran a hand over the short front locks escaping the tieback. "Sometimes." Though she had a slight grin on her face, she wouldn't meet Sharra's eye. T'gellan was very good for Mirrim, Sharra thought.

When the two women arrived at the *Yokohama*, Mirrim left Path to amuse herself at the big window of the bridge, an occupation that would engross the green dragon for hours on end. Hefting their provisions, they made their way to the first level of the coldsleep storage facility where they, and the others Master Oldive had inducted to assist in the project, would attempt to understand the complexities of Thread. It was a project that would take far longer than any of them had estimated; it would occasionally cause them to wonder, over the next few weeks, why they had started such an investigation in the first place.

Whenever she could, Sharra cadged a ride back to Ruatha, to spend a few hours with her sons, whom she missed terribly—when she had time to miss anything. She was relieved that Jaxom seemed so in-

· 315 ·

volved in his own project that he apparently didn't notice, or mind, her preoccupation. Sometimes, when she and the others found themselves working long hours, they stayed up on the *Yokohama*. Mirrim, of course, had to fly Threadfall, but the others had been released from any other duties for this important investigation.

Other times, when the team had to perform endless boring tasks, they grumbled about Aivas's obsession with the biology of the Thread organism, especially as once the primary task of shifting the Red Star's orbit was accomplished, Thread would be relegated to a myth with which to threaten disobedient children. But Aivas repeatedly insisted on the necessity of this research: how vital it was to *understand* the organism. They were all, including Oldive, so accustomed to obeying an Aivas directive that they complied.

Caselon, who now sported journeyman's knots as well as a unique pattern of tiny white scars on his tanned face, did comment about the irony of their grabbing a few hours' sleep in the very capsules that had brought their ancestors to Pern.

Skillfully guided by Aivas, they had sufficient successes to keep a high level of enthusiasm and interest, and to ignore discomforts. As Aivas often reminded them, the routines they were learning in dissecting the very complex organism that had menaced their world for centuries could be applied to other organisms. So the discipline was an end in itself.

Aivas did insist that they bring one ovoid up to "normal" temperatures in an airlock on the far side of the *Yokohama*, away from the sections that were normally being used. With no friction to destroy the tough outer layer, the ovoid remained inert.

"The friction, then," Aivas observed, "is essential to free the organism."

"Let's not free it," Caselon suggested drolly.

"It is as well," Master Oldive remarked thoughtfully, "to know that it is helpless."

"At our mercy," Sharra added, grinning.

"The observation will be continued," Aivas said.

"Do let us know if its condition changes," Sharra said.

Besides Caselon, Sharra, Mirrim, and Oldive, Brekke had volunteered and brought Tumara, the unsuccessful queen candidate, for the girl did not seem to mind monotonous tasks as much as others did. Two more healers, Sefal and Durack, and Manotti, a Smithcraft journeyman, completed their staff. There were times when they could have used twice the number, but all had been trained by Aivas and soon worked well together, smoothly and efficiently and in good spirits.

Initially they had the barest essentials for the task at hand. In the laboratory there were two cubicles. On the top of the work benches were disks that lit up with various kinds of light; Sefal, a dour but diligent sort, was fascinated by the effects obtainable during initial demonstrations. Most important for their purpose was the binocular stereo microscope that they all had to learn to use. The x and y dimensions caused no problem, but to learn to use the z proved to be far more difficult. To demonstrate, Aivas had Sharra take a hair from her head and tie knots in it under the microscope—not as easy as it sounded, as each of them learned when they tried it.

To one side of the microscope was a flush drawer with a sliding cover, in which some oddly truncated glass instruments were found. These, Aivas told them, they had to learn to duplicate in order to do the dissection work required.

Two more workbenches and stools were found and dragged into the two cubicles, although that limited what free space there was.

While Sharra was tying knots in her hair using the binocular microscope, Aivas had Sefal and Manotti take apart one of the two refrigerators to obtain the parts necessary to bring the third one down to −150 degrees, the temperature they would need to work on the Thread organism. They might have to reduce its temperature to that of the Oort Cloud from whence it came, −270c or 3° absolute—but for the present, they could be content with maintaining the Thread's temperature in Pern orbit.

"I don't know what I'm doing," Manotti complained at one point as he gutted the dispensable refrigerator unit.

"That is not at issue," Aivas reassured him. "You need only follow instructions, for there isn't time to teach you cryogenics or refrigeration engineering. Do as you are told."

"I will, I will." Manotti said, grimacing as he very carefully removed a coil of tubing from the back of the first refrigerator. "Now where does this go?"

Aivas explained. When the transfer was completed and the machinery purred into activity, Manotti gave a whoop of triumph. Next, several of the cold capsules were altered to provide additional three-degree-absolute temperature storage for their specimens. For they needed many more than the original Thread ovoid that Farli had caught. The ovoids, as they shortly learned, came in a variety of sizes and in many conditions and, surprisingly, temperatures.

"You'd think one would be enough," Mirrim muttered to Sharra.

"Humans are not duplicates of each other," Aivas replied, though she had not intended to be overheard. She rolled her eyes at Sharra. "Patently the Thread organisms will also exhibit anomalies—ordinary deviations and quite likely mutations. They are as much a life-form as humans are, and they are in a very stressful environment so near Rukbat."

"That puts us neatly in our place," Oldive said with a grin.

Over the next few days, each team member had to learn to cope with the binocular microscope. Tying knots in a strand of hair gave way to carving flowers from splinters of wood and making paper flowers one millimeter across. Sharra proved the deftest of all, with Brekke and Mirrim not far behind her.

Caselon and Manotti, aided by Sefal and Durack, assembled a microforge with a flame two millimeters long, in which they heated the special glass Aivas had had Master Morilton mix, a glass with such a high lead content that even the amenable Morilton had protested. After Aivas told him that he could make knives with the high-lead mix sharp enough to cut bread, Morilton was at least curious enough to wish to experiment. So Aivas and Caselon got the unusual material.

Working carefully, Caselon pulled glass in the tiny flame, then took the resultant tube down to the 3° absolute in which the finished product would be used. When the first rod shattered, he reflexively jumped back despite the fact that he wore protective face and body shields. He glanced around sheepishly.

"A good habit to acquire, Caselon," Aivas remarked approvingly. "Try again."

When the fourth rod had shattered, Caselon was disgusted.

"The glass may not have been blended well enough, Caselon. Master Morilton supplied you with several different mixes. Use the one with the highest lead content. The instruments must be flexible, bending rather than shattering," Aivas said, projecting such a reassurance of eventual success that Caselon took heart.

The fifth attempt bent slightly in the extreme cold but it did not shatter or crack.

"Now, using that mix, make more rods, which you will then fashion into knobs, spikes, and blades. Each of you will work your own tools, with Caselon as your instructor. To further dissect Thread, you will need what are ordinary tools, hacksaw, chisel, mallet, scalpel, but in miniature. Carborundum stone will sharpen edges."

Caselon's set was much admired by the others, though Mirrim thought them stubby inelegant implements. Consequently, when she, on her competitive mettle, made her set longer, she discovered that the flexibility of the length proved a disadvantage when the instruments were used.

"There is so much to do before we *do* anything," she complained. "We've wasted weeks on all this!"

"And you will spend weeks on the next procedures, Mirrim," Aivas said in a tone that chided her for impatience. "You have worked with great diligence and achieved feats of expertise that two Turns ago you would not have been capable of performing. Do not despair. You are about to embark on the truly interesting phase."

"What?" Mirrim asked bluntly.

"Dissecting Thread."

"But haven't we?" Sharra exclaimed, pointing to the cold capsule where the sectioned Threads were housed.

"You have cut the ovoids apart, but you have not truly examined them as minutely as you shortly will. Now, let us see if the waldoes still operate."

Caselon had been fascinated by these devices, which would allow them to work in a chamber maintained at the very low temperatures at which the Thread specimens were kept. He volunteered to be first, but Aivas chose Sharra, as she had already done more microscopic work than the journeyman. The apparatus was powered up, the specimen and the glass tools placed inside the waldo chamber, and the binocular microscope swung into position.

Resolutely, Sharra put her hands into the gloves and gave a little shudder.

"Cold!" she said, and attempted to move her fingers. "I thought you said these waldoes would follow my movements."

"Meters show that current is being taken into the mechanism," Caselon said, looking at the dials. "Here, let me."

Sharra withdrew her hands, but Caselon had no more luck than she.

"All right, Aivas," she said. "What do we do now?"

There was one of the brief but noticeable pauses they had all come to expect whenever Aivas conducted an internal search.

"The mechanism has been unused for twenty-five hundred years. It is not unreasonable to assume that maintenance might be required. A lubrication of the finger joints with silicone fluid may restore mobility."

"Silicone fluid?" Caselon asked.

Manotti raised his hand. "I know what he means. Aivas, is there a smith journeyman or master available?"

"I can send Tolly down for it," Mirrim suggested.

Manotti gave her a sardonic look. "He'll have a day's wait."

She groaned. "Then I'm going down," she said. "I feel the need of a swim and fresh food and some time with my mate."

"If we really are out of action until the silicone fluid is prepared, I ought to take the day off, too," Sharra said, thinking it had been an age since she'd had any time with her sons, or Jaxom.

Caselon grinned. "I'll stay here and manufacture some more tools. If I go down, someone's surely going to find work for me."

Aivas gracefully gave permission for the departures, but to those who remained, he immediately assigned other tasks.

J axom was as absorbed in his current tasks as Sharra was in hers, but these days he managed to spend more time at Ruatha, with the two boys, than she was able to. When she was home, he would listen to her descriptions of her projects—the failures and small successes— and encourage her.

"Aivas knows what he's doing, even if he doesn't devote much time to explanations," he told Sharra on more than one occasion. "He's done so much for us already, we simply have to take the enigmatic on faith and follow his instructions." Jaxom reminded himself to take his own advice.

To the chagrin of Lessa and F'lar, Aivas had insisted that Jaxom and Ruth be involved in every aspect of training the dragons and riders in extravehicular activity. According to Aivas, Jaxom and Ruth would also be the ones to guide all future excursions to the surface of the Red Star.

"Ruth is the younger dragon," Aivas said at its most diplomatic, "and has not suffered the strains and stresses of Threadfall—"

"I ride Fall with Fort Weyr all the time," Jaxom protested, as much to soothe Lessa as to make clear that he and Ruth did not fail of their primary obligation.

"No offense intended," Aivas said deferentially. "Be all as it is, it is not recommended that such a long journey be made without good reason."

"It's certainly no gather site," Lessa said.

"I do propose one more investigative trip," F'lar said, "taking along an observer to record the abyss in a permanent form. Every dragon and rider who is to help bring those engines there must have a vivid picture in his mind of where he's going."

"Apart from that necessary contingency," Aivas went on smoothly, "this undertaking should be recorded. There is nothing to match this endeavor of yours in the annals of any other world."

"Not that any other world is interested in our feats," Master Robinton said in a droll murmur.

"Mankind needs heroes," Aivas replied. "This project is of heroic stature."

F'lar gestured in disclaimer. "What has to be done can scarcely be termed heroic!"

Master Robinton shot the Weyrleader a long, thoughtful look.

"We have three engines to place," F'lar went on, ignoring the Harper's stare, "so the leaders of each group need to visit the place. I lead one . . ."

"Jaxom leads another," Aivas said crisply.

"All right," F'lar allowed.

"And I lead the third," Lessa said.

F'lar immediately objected. "You've risked yourself and Ramoth enough already."

Lessa's expression hardened. "If you go, I go. Ramoth's scarcely the only queen on Pern these days."

Suddenly F'lar's resistance dissolved, which surprised Jaxom but not Ruth.

Why not? Jaxom asked his dragon very privately.

Lessa would not risk Ramoth if she is in clutch, would she?

Jaxom hurriedly covered his mouth with his hand and turned a guffaw into a cough. No wonder F'lar hadn't pressed the point of Lessa's involvement in the event—and Mnementh would cooperate by getting Ramoth in clutch. F'lar had learned subtlety in handling his weyrmate!

"On this one admissible expedition," Jaxom said, "I think F'nor ought to be included."

F'lar gave Jaxom a friendly clout, grinning broadly. "I was about to insist that F'nor and Canth deserve to see the place."

"It's only fair," Robinton said, nodding wisely. "And Canth won't object to taking Perschar, who's got the best eye for detail. D'ram must be allowed this opportunity. And Tiroth can easily convey me," he added, daring protest.

"You can't be put at risk," Lessa said, rising to the bait.

"There'd be no risk involved, would there, Aivas?" Robinton said, shamelessly appealing to the one authority that Lessa would respect.

"The Harper would not be at risk."

"Tiroth's too old!" Lessa declared, glowering at Robinton.

"Tiroth is sturdier than most beasts his age, and the insight of both his rider and Master Robinton might prove invaluable," Aivas said.

It took a few moments for Lessa's irritation to subside, but the matter was soon settled. One more exploratory jump would be made to the Red Star's surface. The group would include D'ram, F'nor, N'ton, and Jaxom, with the dragons carrying Master Robinton, Fandarel, Perschar, and Sebell as observers. The discretion of these few was unassailable, so there would be no chance of careless talk generating more rumor and misconception than already abounded.

Lord Larad of Telgar and Lord Asgenar of Lemos asked Masterharper Sebell to meet them at Telgar Hold at his convenience.

Since Sebell appreciated the diplomatic tone, he dispatched his fire-lizard, Kimi, with a message that he would attend them an hour after the evening meal at Telgar.

"What do you suppose is bothering them?" Menolly asked when Sebell told her of the meeting.

"Rumors have abounded lately, pet," Sebell said with a sigh.

Menolly leaned back from the lectern on which she composed much of her music and, grinning slyly, cocked her head at her husband. "You mean the ones about Sharra and Jaxom, the ones about G'lanar and Lamoth, the latest Abomination mischief, or why the bronze dragons are looking so inordinately pleased with themselves?"

"I'd rather not have so much choice." He carefully tucked a vagrant strand of her long hair back into its clasp before bending to kiss her neck. "I hadn't heard of either Telgar or Lemos having any problems with vandalism, so it can't be that."

"Those who approve do so wholeheartedly, while those who are fearful, apprehensive, or downright skeptical scuttle around the edges and ruin what they haven't the wit to understand."

"It's our task to see that they do understand," Sebell said, gently remonstrating.

"But some don't *want* to," she replied in a rebellious tone, stretching both arms well above her head to ease her back. "I know the breed. Oh, how I know the breed! It's just too bad we can't leave them alone with their closed minds, but they're standing in our way forward."

"We are altering the fabric of their lives. That frightens people. It always has; it always will. Lytol's sent me some fascinating excerpts from Aivas's historical data. Fascinating. People don't change, love. React first, think later, regret at leisure."

He bent to kiss her cheek. "I've time to tell Robse and Olos a story before I go."

Menolly snaked an arm around his neck before he could straighten. "You are such a loving man," she said, and then kissed him again deeply before releasing her hold.

When he paused at the threshold to look back at her fondly, she was already bent to her composition. He smiled at the concentrated pose of her back, one shoulder angled up. She did love him, but he accepted the fact that he would have always two rivals—music and the Master. He had the same loves. With that thought, he went down the corridor to sing to his sons and to admire his daughter, Lemsia, who was too young for more than adoration.

Laradian, Larad's oldest son, was waiting for Sebell in the well-lit court when the obliging Fort Hold dragon deposited the harper at Telgar.

"My father and Lord Asgenar are in the small study, Masterharper," Laradian said formally, and then, relaxing, grinned a welcome at Sebell.

A fine fire was burning on the hearth angled in the corner of the pleasant room, the walls of which were hung with rich tapestries and framed sketches—probably by Perschar, if Sebell didn't mistake the skill—of the current Holder's offspring. Several heavy old wherryhide chairs, sagging from the comfort they had given several generations of weary bodies, and the huge desk and table where the Lord Holders of Telgar had done their accounts for centuries, furnished the room adequately. Sebell immediately noticed the latest addition: a very good rendering, though considerably reduced in scale, of the Honshu mural.

"Hmmm, yes," Larad said, noticing his glance. "My daughter,

Bonna, went along with Perschar's group and brought that back. Of course, she was under Master Perschar's eye all the time, but it's judged to be a fair representation."

"You'd be welcome to see the original," Sebell said, nodding to Asgenar, who was ensconced in one of the armchairs.

"What?" Larad asked, his pleasant face affecting a horrified expression. "And let rumor have it that I wanted the place for one of my sons?" He gestured for Sebell to take a chair and held up a wine bottle. "It's Benden." His grin was for the allusion to a harper preference for that wine; but his reference to rumor told Sebell that he was seriously concerned.

"I follow many of Master Robinton's traditions," Sebell said, accepting the generous goblet. He sipped judiciously and raised his brows in appreciation. "A 'sixteen?"

"Indeed, and it was Master Robinton who urged me to acquire as many skins as I could wheedle."

"So?" Sebell turned politely to the two Lord Holders. "Rumor bites?"

"I wish it were only rumor, Sebell," Larad said. He took a small message roll from his sleeve cuff and handed it to the harper. "This is far more serious and demands your urgent consideration. I know the sender well enough to heed his words."

After a glance at the message, Sebell shot out of the comfortable chair, seething with anger and swearing blackly. " 'I have good reason to believe that Masterharper Robinton may be abducted to force those at Landing to destroy what they call the Abomination.' " Sebell was consumed with outrage. "Hazard the Masterharper! Ransom him for the destruction of Aivas!" Outrage gave way to panic. "Who is this Brestolli who signs the note?"

"He's a wagonmaster. We both know him." Larad gestured toward Asgenar, who nodded earnestly. "He wouldn't send a false alarm. Actually, it was delivered by his fire-lizard to his employer, Trader Nurevin, who's here now. Nurevin brought it straight to me, leaving his train a day's trip out. He said that he'd had to leave Brestolli at Bitra with a broken leg and cracked ribs from a wagon accident."

"Nurevin's just outside. I'll ask him in," Asgenar said, and slipped out of the room.

Larad gave a wry smile. "Nurevin felt you would heed this message more if we presented it to you."

"He'd need no one vouching for him to me," Sebell said, rereading the message. "This has the ring of truth. Nothing Bitra initiates surprises me."

"Then you also know that your harpers at Bitra Hold have been put in quarantine for a virulent disease?"

"The Bitran euphemism for 'reporting truth'?" Sebell asked. He ran his fingers through his hair, a gesture of exasperation. "We haven't heard from them recently by the usual route. I should have sent at least one who had a fire-lizard."

"Our Master Celewis can mount a rescue mission, if you'd like," Larad suggested.

"If that can be done without jeopardizing Brestolli," Sebell replied.

Larad raised his eyebrows and grinned slyly. "Surely you know Celewis's abilities . . ."

"Indeed I do," Sebell said with an answering grin.

"Then you may be certain that he'll be adroit in the matter."

Nurevin came in just then, preceding Asgenar.

"I've not had occasion to pass time with you, Trader Nurevin," Sebell said, smiling as he extended his hand and returned the strong pressure given. "But I can tell you that the Harper Hall is more than grateful to you for passing this message."

"Brestolli's not the sort makes things up for mischief, Master-harper," Nurevin said, cocking his head to emphasize his opinion. He was a swarthy man of medium height, with grizzled hair worn in a long plait that had recently been neatly redone. His clothing was of excellent quality but road-worn. "So I knew I'd best get it to someone who could see it was handled proper. I hated to leave him in Bitra Hold, but he'd broke his leg in three places, mangled his arm, and cracked some ribs when a cart overturned. Caught a wheel on uneven flags in Bitra Court. Healer said he couldn't be moved, so I paid the brewer both good marks and trade goods to tend him. Brestolli's one to keep his eyes and ears open, despite he talks such a streak you wouldn't think he'd hear for the constant sound of his own voice. But if he's heard what that message says he heard, then he's heard it. Make no mistake about that. I wouldn't want it said we didn't give warning when there're them what'd harm good Master Robinton. No, I wouldn't."

Larad offered him a goblet of Benden wine, and Nurevin's eyes lit up with appreciation after his first sip.

"You honor me, Lord Larad."

"Telgar is in your debt, Trader Nurevin."

"Not just Telgar, Trader Nurevin," Sebell added solemnly as he tilted his glass to him and drank ceremoniously. Nurevin flushed at such courtesy.

Sebell called to Kimi, who had been visiting outside with Telgar Hold's fair. Silently, Larad proferred writing materials and a message tube.

"I'm sending this to Lytol, who will take appropriate measures," Sebell said after penning some quick lines. Kimi extended her leg for him to attach the capsule, knowing exactly what was required of her. "Kimi, take this to Lytol, in Cove Hold, where our Master lives! Where Zair lives. Yes?"

Kimi had listened intently, cocking her head this way and that, her eyes whirling with noticeable increase in speed. She gave one chirp and disappeared.

"Forewarned is forearmed, Trader Nurevin. Has Brestolli's fire-lizard returned to him?"

"Yes. It's only a blue, but he's got it well trained. I can send my queen if you need more information. I've been keeping in touch with Brestolli to be sure he's well tended." Nurevin winked and grinned. "Bitrans need me more'n I need them, since they're so hard to deal with. I'm the only trader who does their route in these parlous times. So I've an edge on 'em, so to speak." He paused, his expression grim. "Did Lord Larad tell you about your harpers?" When Sebell nodded he went on. "That was done a-purpose, or I'll be scored next Fall!"

"When a harper is silenced, all men should listen harder," Sebell said.

Nurevin nodded solemnly. "I heard some other stuff whilst I was at Bitra . . ." He hesitated.

"Be easy, man," Larad encouraged him. "There's not much a harper doesn't hear sooner or later. And, if it's along the lines of Brestolli's message, perhaps Master Sebell'd better hear it from you."

"Well, it's them rumors." Nurevin paused again, obviously not happy to utter them, but by gesture and expression, all three men encouraged him to speak. "It's said that Lord Jaxom and that white dragon of his killed G'lanar and Lamoth—deliberate."

"Shards! How could anyone repeat such a foul slander?" Asgenar asked, incensed.

"Oh, there've been worse," Sebell said, but he turned to Nurevin. "Master Robinton was there himself and told me that Jaxom was victim, not assailant, and Lamoth died of shame that his rider would turn on another rider. Any more?"

"Well, and this's stupider," Nurevin went on, both reassured and encouraged by his audience. "That dragonriders will take the three colony ships and disappear from Pern, leaving us with only flame-throwers to kill Thread!"

"Did you hear the one that suggests that the dragons will take the old shuttles and throw them at the Red Star and destroy it?" When Nurevin shook his head, Sebell continued, his expression serious. "There's one that the Masterhealer has been given medicine by Aivas that will paralyze folk so that pieces can be carved out of their bodies to repair others who have sickened."

Nurevin snorted. "I heard that one at Bitra. I didn't believe it then and I don't believe it now. That Aivas thing is scary, but I've not seen anything produced yet that didn't help us in some way or t'other. Best axle grease I ever had was something that Aivas gave the Smithcrafthall. And that new metal for cotter pins that don't bend or snap when the wheels are stressed."

Kimi reentered, chittering about the success of her trip and strok-ing her golden head on Sebell's cheek before she held out her message-laden leg. Excusing himself, Sebell read the message.

"Late as it is there, I'm bid to Cove Hold. If you'll excuse me . . ."

He was ushered out by the two Lord Holders.

"You wonder sometimes, don't you, Asgenar," Larad said sadly as they turned to reenter the warm, comfortable room, "why people can be so ornery."

"I think it has to do with a resistance to being done good to."

"Not if they're putting Master Robinton at risk," Larad said, still horrified by that possibility. "He's never harmed anyone in his life. This world would rise up to the least child to protest such infamy."

"Which, unfortunately, makes him the most useful hostage," As-genar said with a sigh of regret.

B y the time Sebell reached Cove Hold, it was early morning there. He and the brown dragon who was conveying him were immediately greeted by swarms of chittering fire-lizards as dense in the sky as Thread. Tiroth, ensconced on the grassy sward before the hold, blinked orange-laced eyes until he and brown Folrath identified each other. Sebell was pleased to see so many guardians already in place. Not that the whilom abductors could as yet have gotten so far as Cove Hold, given the journey they would have to make from Bitra, or even from the nearest seaport.

Every glowbasket in the main room was wide open, shedding light on Robinton, D'ram, Lytol, and T'gellan, who were sitting at the big round table. A collapsed wineskin indicated that much discussion had already taken place. Sebell was glad to see the Eastern Weyrleader present.

"Ah, Sebell," Robinton cried, raising his arm in welcome, his expression so merry that Sebell thought the Harper was perversely enjoying his jeopardy. "Any more news of this scurrilous scheme?"

Sebell shook his head, grinning at his reception but noting immediately that the Harper's ebullience was not echoed by others at the table.

"You know as much as anyone, though Nurevin has assured me he'll keep in touch with Brestolli, by fire-lizard, in case the man hears more to the point."

"I've sent Zair with a message to Master Idarolan," Robinton said, "in the hope that he can intercept the conspirators."

"We've had quite enough of petty vandalism and wanton destruction of property," Lytol said, a deep angry scowl on his face. "This time we must catch the scofflaws and discover everyone who has aided and abetted them. For anyone to even contemplate harming Master Robinton, a man to whom all Pern owes a very great debt . . ."

"Now, now, Lytol," Robinton said, circling Lytol's stiff shoulders with a soothing arm, "don't carry on so. You're embarrassing me. And this whole scheme only shows how basically stupid our detractors are. As if they had a chance of penetrating my loyal minions." The Harper gestured to the storm of fire-lizard fairs outside the window.

"I know they can't reach you, Robinton," Lytol said, banging his fist on the table and making the goblets jump, "but the fact that they would *dare* . . ."

Robinton grinned maliciously. "Maybe I should let myself be captured? Hauled off unceremoniously," he began as Lytol stared at him, aghast, "taken to wherever they plan to incarcerate me, and then—" He lifted his free hand and clenched it suddenly into a fist. "—let the avenging wings swoop down on the despicable rabble and carry them off forthwith to be dropped in the deepest of Larad's mines, condemned to toil off their misspent energies in useful work."

Lytol's expression turned to resignation and disgust. "You should take this seriously, my friend."

"I do. I really do!" Robinton altered his mobile face. "I'm deeply saddened that I, or anyone, on Pern could be victimized in this horrendous fashion. But," he added, holding up one finger, "it's more ingenious than trying to burn space-engine fuel or sabotage Aivas. We really ought to ask his advice, you know."

"If it weren't for Aivas—" Lytol began heatedly, then broke off when he realized what he had said. T'gellan and Sebell tried to smother their spontaneous guffaw. Lytol abruptly got to his feet and strode out of the room.

When Sebell made to go after the old Warder, Robinton held up his hand, and the younger harper settled back into his chair.

"He has every right to be upset," D'ram said in a slow, sad voice. "It is terrible to think that there are people who oppose all the good that Aivas has done for us and would go to such great lengths to destroy him and those of us who have the vision to appreciate the potential."

"Look, I see no real chance of anyone reaching Master Robinton," T'gellan said, leaning forward on his elbows across the table. "They cannot have thought this through very carefully. They can know nothing of Cove Hold or how many people are in and out on a daily and—" He gave Sebell a wry grin. "—early-morning basis."

"Have you forgotten the raid on Landing?" Sebell asked. "Horses, gear, experienced mercenaries. If Aivas hadn't his own defenses, that could have succeeded. We can't allow ourselves to be complacent."

"Well said, Sebell," D'ram replied. "However, what Robinton suggested so glibly has merit. If we wish to find the ones behind these attempts, it would be smart of us to set no apparent"—and he held up his hand to emphasize that adjective—"reinforcements, make no obvious alterations of our daily routines."

"Agreed . . ."

"All the while making certain that Robinton is never left alone."

"As if I ever am," Robinton said, feigning an outraged glower.

"I apologize in advance," Sebell said in a contrite tone, "for suggesting this. But if G'lanar was disaffected . . ."

D'ram raised his hand in understanding, but it was T'gellan who answered, his expression bleak.

"Ramoth herself spoke to the remaining Oldtimer dragons— they're the only ones who might still be contentious enough to cause

problems. But every one of them was appalled by G'lanar's action,''
the bronze rider said, "and none can dissemble before Ramoth!"

Sebell looked immensely relieved. "Then we can rule out that possibility."

"Somehow that doesn't greatly reassure me," D'ram said in a
lugubrious voice. "We're not dealing with fools."

"No, we're dealing with fearful men, and they're more dangerous."

T he silicone fluid, worked well into the joints of the waldo gloves,
restored mobility—except in the third finger of the left hand, a limi-
tation that posed no great problem.

"What would we have done if the silicone fluid didn't work?"
Manotti asked, winking at his colleagues to indicate that he was teasing their mentor.

"There is always an alternative course of action, though it may be
less efficient and productive," Aivas replied. "Now, Sharra, be good
enough to place a Thread section in the chamber and, using a blade,
slice the specimen at a slant, thus exposing all layers. Now, what do
you see?"

"Rings, springs, and the shapes you called toruses," Sharra said.
"An odd goo, a yellow liquid, some strange pastes in peculiar shades
of yellow, gray, and white, and some other substances that seem to
change color."

Tumara made a revolted noise deep in her throat and turned away.

"You must all realize," Aivas began in a stern tone, "that the most
important piece of apparatus in the laboratory is your brain. Just as
you made the microtools to effect this dissection, you must make
your brains the right instrument for this task. The most useful thing
is the moment-by-moment interaction of your brain seeing these
things for the first time. Even your reaction, Tumara, has a certain
validity. Now, set that reaction aside, and observe. What else do you
see, Sharra?"

She tapped her microblade on a ring. "This feels like metal."

"Then excise it and any more like it that you see, and have the
items sent to Master Fandarel for analysis. What else?"

"There're a lot of particles lodged in the pasty parts, and—and it's
hollow in the center. Could that yellow be liquid helium?" Sharra

went on. "It's just like the stuff you showed us in the liquid gas experiments, and it boils as soon as it's exposed to the −150° atmosphere. We haven't yet tried it at 3°."

"There is no reason why it cannot be helium. Helium is liquid at the temperatures that Thread inhabits. Isolate a sample, and a positive identification can be made."

"This whole thing resembles those micrographs you displayed, Aivas," Mirrim said.

"You are quite right, Mirrim. This is the real thing, though, not a slide. Continue, Sharra."

"How?"

"Dissect another ring. Slice it so that you go through more than half the torus. That will show more of its composition."

"That's odd," Brekke said. "Compare that ring with the other one. The first has all kinds of springy-like things sort of layered, while in the other they're all twisted up—oooh, shells!"

Sharra had prodded one of the rings, and suddenly it flipped away from the tool, sticking to the wall of the examination enclosure.

"This could be their method of reproduction," Aivas said. "Or it could be a parasite, escaping from the dying organism. But this is quite interesting. Try another ring to see if the reaction is the same."

Though Sharra's second prod was more tentative, there was another eruption.

"Now, apply your blade to the springs in the first torus," Aivas instructed. "Nothing happens. Now you have seen two entirely different facets of this organism. You are investigating a wholly new creature, and we must see everything that it is."

"Why?" Mirrim asked.

"Because you must know how to destroy this organism, so that it cannot reproduce, so that it cannot multiply anywhere in your system."

"If it doesn't fall on Pern, that's enough, isn't it?" Brekke asked.

"For you, perhaps, but the sensible thing would be to destroy it at source."

Caselon recovered first. "But if the Red Star is moved . . . ."

"That doesn't destroy Thread. It only removes its vector. Your task is to discover how you can destroy the Thread organism itself!"

"Isn't that a bit ambitious for us?" Sharra asked.

"The means are available. Even in your very brief investigations today, you have discovered much about the organism. Each day you will discover more. It is possible that some of those bits are parasites, smaller entities built on the same plan. Parasites or progeny. Or predators.''

"Like those limpets on the tunnel snakes?" Oldive asked. "The ones that attach themselves to the snakes and eat their muscle tissue and then leave when they're sated?''

"A good example. Were they predators, or were they parasites?''

"I don't think we ever decided,'' Oldive remarked. "According to your definition, a parasite does not always cause its host lasting harm, and tends to be unable to survive apart from this host; while a predator usually kills its victim and moves on. As the snake limpet leaves its host/victim alive and able to heal, it is more of a parasite, not quite a predator.''

"What must be found are parasites that can be made into predators, guaranteed to kill their hosts—just as you isolated bacteria and altered it to create bacteriophages to reduce wound infection.''

"I still don't see the purpose,'' Mirrim muttered.

"There is one,'' Aivas said so emphatically that Mirrim grimaced in dismay and pretended to be frightened.

"Sharra, have you isolated those parts that must be subjected to other tests?''

"I've got a lot of messy bits, and springs and metals, and lumps and bumps, if that's what you mean.''

"Good. Place them on the petri dishes and we can proceed with the investigation. You are to examine them under high pressure, with inert gas—xenon, which we have in that cylinder—to discover if those tubes are full of helium. Now that you have opened the containing tubular vessels, you are losing all the helium, if that's what it is, very rapidly.''

When Lessa and F'lar learned of the threat against Master Robinton, they were all for sending him up to the *Yokohama*, or to Honshu, or back to the Harper Hall.

"I'm not a child,'' he said, considerably incensed by such protectiveness. "I'm a grown man and have faced down every danger that has come my way. Do not deny me that right. Besides, if these conspirators should learn that their victim has been put beyond them, they'll merely think of something else we might not learn about in time to counter. No, I'll stay here, with half the fire-lizards of Pern

as my escort and whatever other"—he held up a warning hand—
"discreet guardians you choose to appoint. Beat a cowardly retreat I
will not!" With his head up, his eyes flashing, his breath rapid, he
forestalled all further protests.

If he noticed those set to guard him in the following weeks, he did
not register the surveillants with so much as a flicker of his eye. Master Idarolan, as irate as everyone else, sent messages to all harbor-
masters, consulted at great length with his most trusted captains, and
dispatched his fastest courier ship to Monaco Bay. Menolly sent
Rocky, Diver, and Mimic to assist Robinton's Zair, and Swacky and
two other big mercenaries were established at Cove Hold. Master
Robinton continued his duties at Landing and on the *Yokohama*, pretended to be highly intrigued by the biological team's exacting work.

How Aivas learned of the threat no one knew, or admitted, but it
gave Fandarel the schematics for a small device that Master Robinton
was to wear at all times. "A locator," Aivas termed it. "Wearing that,
you can be traced anywhere on this planet and as far as the spaceships."

That afforded all his friends far more relief than any would admit.
With Aivas as protector, Master Robinton was surely safe.

17

▼▼▼▼▼▼▼

By the end of the summer, there was still no sign of would-be abductors. Nurevin collected Brestolli from the brewer's cot in Bitra, limping but still adamant about what he had overheard; a visit to Lord Sigomal by Benden Weyrleaders secured the release of the "contagious" harpers, and Master Sebell told the Bitran Lord Holder that, regretfully, he had no replacements suitable for a Hold of such stature. Several other Crafts withdrew their masters, leaving the Bitran Halls staffed by minor journeymen and apprentices of local origin.

A similar withdrawal occurred at Nerat but not at Keroon, for despite his increasingly vocal distrust of all improvements originating from the "Abomination," Lord Corman did not interfere with any of his Crafthalls or with the performance of their traditional duties to his Hold. He also made plain that he was distancing himself from Sigomal and Begamon.

Every Weyrwoman kept her queen on her mark, and every harper tracked down the faintest whisper of clandestine activities. Major Crafthalls discreetly doubled security measures. And dragonriders continued to drill outside the *Yokohama*, the *Bahrain*, and the *Buenos Aires*. Hamian and his crews worked overtime producing protective covering for riders, as well as a garment that would fit like a glove on dragon hind paws to shield flesh from the burn of ice-cold metal. Oldive, Sharra, Mirrim, Brekke, and the others labored under Aivas's close guidance to analyze and describe the peculiar organism that was Thread—or, rather, that *became* Thread as it met its fiery frenzied doom in the skies of Pern.

Sharra tried to explain to Jaxom the task Aivas had set his investigators, as much to hear herself explain what she was doing as to make it clear to her mate.

"We had one marvelous day when Mirrim discovered the beads under the microscope. Aivas was excited, too, for he feels certain that the beads are the genetic information of the Thread organism." She grinned as she remembered that moment of triumph. "The microscope was at sub-high for maximum magnification, so we could all see these tiny, tiny beads strung along one of those long wires I told you Thread has. Not the springs, but the wires, which are coiled ever so tightly in a volume no bigger than the tip of my finger. Aivas says these ring beads use the material of the Thread ovoid to reproduce themselves." She made a face, indicating her ignorance of how that was done. "What he wants us to find now is a bacteriophage to infect the beads and then discover just the right one that will replicate itself fast before it uses up all the Thread material. We've done something of a similar nature, you know, when we located bacteria from wounds and learned how to disimprove their symbiotic bacteriophages so that they would kill their hosts. Our ancestors could certainly do marvelous things biologically to heal people. I hope we can begin to do as well as they did. *This* exercise could heal our planet."

"Then why didn't *they* do it?" Jaxom asked. "Why are we left with the job?"

Sharra grinned smugly. "Because we have dragons to replace fuelless shuttles, fire-lizards who can nick Thread ovoids out of space, and Aivas to tell us exactly what to do. Even if I don't always understand what we're doing or why we're doing it."

"I thought you said it was to disimprove the Thread's symbionts. Though why that's necessary with what the dragonriders are to do, I don't know."

Sharra was silent a moment, considering that. "Aivas hates Thread, inasmuch as an inanimate machine is capable of hatred. He hates what it did to his captains and Admiral Benden. He hates what it's done to us. He wants to be sure it can never menace us again. He wants to kill it in the Oort Cloud. He calls the project 'Overkill.' "

Jaxom regarded her in puzzled astonishment. "He's more vindictive than F'lar!"

Sharra sighed dejectedly. "I'm not sure that we can *do* what he wants. It's all so very complicated. And we're so limited in our understanding. He may be the machine, but I feel like one, doing this and that without knowing why."

She was more buoyant three days later when she told Jaxom that Aivas had fond the appropriate parasitic vector.

"He says that similar life-forms were found in microgravity conditions in the asteroid belts. It's very like the one found in the ecology of the Pluto/Charon pair in the original Earth Solar system." Sharra frowned in perplexity. "Well, that's what he says. He has named the springs 'zebedees.' And zebedees are what we will now use to make our tailored parasite, like a virus, jump from one Thread ovoid to the next . . . once the parasite has disimproved itself as a symbiont and became really destructive! We've got to culture it now, though."

Jaxom managed a suitably appreciative grin for her enthusiasm. "Who are we to protest an Aivas pronouncement? What next?"

"Well, he's got all the fire-lizards searching the ovoid streams for the springs. Sometimes they're embedded right on the surface of an ovoid. We've had to start up nine more cold capsules to contain the things and infect them with the zebedee-makers."

"Zebedees, the Thread fleas!" Jaxom said, teasingly.

"Well, fleas *are* parasites, and I could wish we were able to disimprove some of them quickly! As it is, the time we have is nowhere near long enough for the work we have to do."

She had been disgusted to discover canine fleas on Jarrol, who was incurably attached to one of the kitchen-spit animals. "Fleas!" She shook her head. "That will be my priority project, as soon as we're finished with Aivas's: to disimprove fleas."

"Whenever that'll be," Jaxom added. There were so many Aivas endeavors, at various stages of completion, that he wondered if any of them would get finished on time now that the deadline drew nearer.

"Would you and Ruth have time to get me back to the *Yokohama* tomorrow before you fly Fall?" Sharra asked.

Jaxom groaned. "I thought you'd be here a few days."

Sharra looked properly repentant. "I've been over everything for the Gather with Brand and the other Stewards, and all's ready for our guests. But this is an especially critical time, Jaxom . . ." Her eyes pleaded for his understanding.

"You'll be exhausted. You won't enjoy the Gather . . ." he heard himself saying, and then he pulled her into his arms, savoring the feel of her body against his, and the spicy fragrance of her hair. Gathers were always special times for them.

"Please, Jaxom?" Her lips brushed his neck.

"I'm just griping, love. I could never keep you where you didn't wish to be."

"Won't it be wonderful, when this is all over, to be just us again?" she asked. "I want a daughter, too, you know."

That earnest wish elicited a response he was glad to make.

Threadfall was uneventful, though it was not one in which the spaceships' shields had carved tunnels of Threadfree air. Then Hamian sent a message that he had a new glove for Ruth to test on an EVA. So, after Ruth had tested it and found it comfortable as well as a good shield with an easy buckle attachment to hold it in place, Jaxom reported the success to Aivas to pass on to Hamian. For a change, Jaxom and Ruth were alone on the bridge: Ruth was spread across the big window as usual, devouring his favorite view.

"Aivas, just why are you so obsessed with this zebedee project?" Jaxom asked when he had delivered his message to Hamian. "Sharra says you call it Overkill. Why isn't blowing the Red Star out of orbit sufficient?"

"You are alone?" Aivas asked.

That was an unusual question, as Aivas usually unerringly sensed additional presences.

"Yes, I'm alone. Are you going to come clean?" Jaxom asked, half joking.

"This is as good a time as any," Aivas replied, startling the young Holder.

"That doesn't sound good."

"On the contrary, it is all to the good to know what has been expected of you since this facility learned of Ruth's unusual abilities."

"His knowing when and where he is?" Jaxom asked slyly.

"Precisely. An explanation is needed."

"They usually are, with you!"

"Flippancy has always covered apprehension. Candor is required. There are three engines that must be exploded to push the Red Star out of an orbit hazardous to Pern. Two of those explosions have already taken place."

"*What?*" Jaxom sat upright in the comfortable chair and stared at the screen in front of him.

"As you are aware, records from every Weyr, Hall, and Hold were presented and analyzed. Two small entries illuminate an anomaly.

"Based on the position of the Red Star when Mankind first landed on Pern, that planet is not now in the orbit it should be tracking at this point in time. Repeated calculations were made during the First Fall by captains Keroon and Tillek. Eccentric it might be, but its current position differs from an extrapolation of those original calculations. Its path shows that it has suffered a perturbation of nine-point-three degrees off its original elliptical orbit. That is not consistent with the extrapolated position. Therefore, something has already altered its path. Substantiation occurs in two minor references found in Istan and Keroonian records in the Fourth and Eighth Passes, which were each prior to a long Interval. During each Pass, bright flashes were observed when the Red Star was at apogee in reference to Pern. Bright enough to be remembered and noted."

Stunned, Jaxom blinked, as if closing and opening his eyes would help him focus his thoughts on what Aivas was saying. "Those two craters?"

"Your perception is acute."

"My fear is also, Aivas!"

"Man is wise to fear: it sharpens the sense of self-preservation."

"But what I felt when I saw the first crater was not fear. It was—it had to be—it was as if I knew it had to be there! I discounted such a ridiculous notion at the time. And you, Aivas, would not have me believe that I have been there before?"

"The time paradox has bewildered many. Your presentiment of involvement with the crater is unusual, but similar incidents are reported in the annals of psychic phenomena."

"Are they?" Jaxom asked facetiously. "I'm not at all sure I appreciate the position you've put me in—that is, if I understand you correctly."

"How do you understand what has been said?"

"That somehow I, on Ruth, with enough dragonriders to perform the task, took an engine back in time and deposited it in that Rift? Where it blew up to form the crater I find on my initial trip to the Red Star some eighteen hundred Turns in the later?"

"You have done it twice. The second time was six hundred Turns ago. It is the only explanation. Furthermore, *you* know that you've done it."

"I don't want to do it," Jaxom protested, thinking how far back he would have to ask Ruth to take him and the others. Yet Aivas had been accurate in so many other unlikely things. "What if something went wrong?"

"True to the time paradox, if something had, you wouldn't be here, and there would be some thirty or forty dragons missing from this time."

"No, that's wrong," Jaxom said, struggling to understand. "We wouldn't have gone yet. So we'd still be here. We won't be here if we fail when we try it. No, no!" He waved one hand irritably at his confusion.

"You have gone. You have been successful, and each of those previous explosions has caused Long Intervals—which are inexplicable by any other rationale—thus setting up the planet for the final orbital dislocation."

"Now wait a minute," Jaxom said, waggling his finger at the screen in an aggravated fashion. "We've done a lot of queer things to propitiate you, Aivas, and we've done them because you've proved to be right . . ."

"This facility is correct in its findings and conclusions in this matter, as well, Lord Jaxom."

"Don't try that tact on me, friend. It doesn't work! The dragonriders are not going to go along with this. Timing it has always been extremely tricky. You know that Lessa nearly died going back four hundred Turns. You want us to go back eighteen hundred?"

"You will be carrying your own oxygen supplies, so you will not suffer from asphyxia as she did. You are aware of the sensory-deprivation syndrome and will not be disturbed by the disorientation . . ."

Jaxom kept shaking his head. "You can't ask bronzes to do that, even if they are able to. I don't think F'lar times it. In fact, the only one I do know who has is Lessa."

"And your Ruth. Furthermore, you have been proud of the fact that the white dragon always knows where and when he is going."

"You have said that Ruth always knows where and when he is going."

"I have, but—"

"If Ruth knows where and when he is going—and specific guides are available—he can supply the necessary visual coordinates."

"But I know that the other riders won't stand for this . . ."

"They will not know!"

Jaxom stared straight at the screen for another long moment.

"How," he asked at last in a very patient, saccharine tone, "will they *not* know?"

"Because you will not tell them. And since you now have been to the Red Star on several occasions, and since the distance in terms of travel *between* will not be appreciably longer than what they would expect, they will not know that they have been transported back in time and to the Red Star in the position required by the equations that cover the two disparate explosions.''

Jaxom mulled that over and, inhaling deeply, realized that in his state of shock he had not been breathing regularly.

I think we can do it, Ruth remarked with more confidence than Jaxom was feeling at that moment.

Jaxom turned toward his beloved friend. ''You may think we can, but I'm going to be bloody sure we can. Now, Aivas, let's go through this again . . . The other riders are not to know the time of our destination. But there are to be three teams of us, taking the three engines . . .''

''Hamian will not have sufficient space suits for the three hundred beasts required to shift all three engines at the same time. You will lead two of the three groups. F'lar will, as planned, head the third. He will be the only one depositing an engine in this time. As you know,'' Aivas went on, overriding Jaxom's protest, ''the locations chosen are not in sight of each other. Since F'lar will think that you are at one end of the Rift, N'ton at the other, he will not know what you are doing.''

''The timing's wrong, Aivas. I cannot be in two places at once. Nor doing that kind of timing without a respite. Ruth doesn't have auxiliary oxygen.''

''You missed the point about insufficient space suits. Your team will have to get out of their suits and turn them over to the members of the second unit. That should allow Ruth sufficient time to regain energy. You will, of course, be certain that he eats well beforehand and can feed immediately afterward to restore himself.''

I could do it the way Aivas suggests, Ruth said amiably.

''I haven't said I'll risk us!'' Jaxom roared, bringing both fists down on the console with such force that he hurt his hands. Rubbing them, he grumbled to himself.

''You already have, or there would not be two craters on the Rift, and there would not have been records of bright flashes.''

''You're inveigling me, Aivas. And I'm not going to let you.''

''You already have, Lord Jaxom. You are the only one who can, could, would, has. Think this proposal over carefully and you will see that the project is not only within the capabilities of yourself and Ruth, but feasible. And essential! Three explosions at *this* point in time will not have the desired effect on the future path of the Red Star."

Jaxom sighed deeply, almost as if he already felt it needful to fill his lungs for a jump timed eighteen hundred Turns away. His mind refused to settle into a logical examination of the affair.

"Since this is a confessional moment, tell me why you are so obsessed with this project you've involved Sharra in? Especially," he added with an ironic laugh, "if you say you know I've already succeeded even before I've begun."

"You do succeed, and there is an easy way to prove it," Aivas said, his tone not quite ingratiating but as close to that as Jaxom had ever heard.

"No, first explain to me about these zebedee things."

"It is extrapolated by the closer examination of the Thread ovoids that there is life, not as you know it, and not even as we see it brought here by the Red Star, but a whole ecology of life-forms throughout the Oort Cloud. Some of them are probably quite intelligent, judging by the complexity of their nervous systems; but when they arrive here, they have lost most of their liquid helium and so can be termed only 'rude mechanicals.' It is these degenerate, warmth-tolerating forms that make it to the surface of Pern; they don't live long enough to replicate themselves there, of course, or on the Red Planet. It is only these 'mechanicals' that can reproduce without helium in Pern's orbit. But if these mechanicals could be contaminated, infected with our disimproved parasite, they would carry it with them to destroy all similar life-forms in the Oort Cloud itself, probably including the more intelligent ones, too. Then, no matter what happens, Pern will forever be freed of this menace. That is why there were Long Intervals: The disimproved zebedees that you will establish—have established long ago—on the surface of the Red Planet, twice in the past and once in the future will infect the Cloud when the Red Star cuts through it twice in every orbit."

"I'm also to be a disease carrier?" Jaxom was not sure which he felt more keenly: indignation, fury, or incredulity at the audacity of Aivas's scheme.

"You will seed the Red Star three times. That is why it is so important to breed up the disimproved zebedees. A triple thrust in two different areas."

"But if I'm to blow the planet out of orbit . . ."

"The perturbation will be slight, and you can seed the zebedees at a sufficient distance from the Rift to insure their safety. There will be plenty of host ovoids on the planet's surface as well as in orbit around it.''

''We saw them on the surface, not in orbit.''

''Were you looking for them?''

''Not in space. Now, tell me how you can prove to me that all these incredible designs of yours will work—have worked!''

''It is very simple. Access the file that gives you a graph of the Red Star's current orbit.''

Jaxom had no trouble doing that. The all-too-familiar diagram filled the screen.

''Hold that on the monitor,'' Aivas instructed.

Jaxom pressed out that command.

''Now, if you will mount Ruth, you can go forward in time fifty years—Turns—using the digital timepiece as your reference.''

''No one goes forward in time, that's the most dangerous . . .''

''Only if alterations will have taken place,'' Aivas replied. ''There will be no changes on the bridge of *Yokohama*. That will be your responsibility. Today you will go forward in time, call up the orbit. Print it out. Then, with that hard copy, return here after a safe interval and compare the two graphs. The doors have been locked. No one is likely to come to this bridge at this moment, or until you have returned.''

Every ounce of common sense Jaxom possessed shouted resistance to a timing forward. And yet . . . to have done so would be a feat no one else could possibly manage successfully. For he had Ruth.

''Did you hear what Aivas said, Ruth?''

I did. Given his assurances, and I know that he would not risk you, Jaxom—

''Or you,'' Jaxom put in.

I would like to see what Pern looks like in the future. I would like to know that the future is going to be a good one.

And so would I, Jaxom thought.

Then, before he could come up with too many arguments against this rash, foolhardy, reckless endeavor, he signaled for Ruth to float over to him.

''You will, of course,'' Aivas said drolly, ''be very sure to keep oxygen tanks full on the bridge for fifty Turns to come.''

Jaxom gave a grim smile. ''I'm not going to take any chances, Aivas. I'll just get into my suit.'' He was becoming quite adept at inserting himself into the space gear. He mounted Ruth and buckled on the riding straps, just to be very sure, in case they emerged in nothingness. He also knew that Ruth would have no trouble any-where—or anywhen—finding his way back to Ruatha Hold.

He read the date exposed on the digital and added fifty to the year displayed: 2577. With that legend firmly in his mind, he told Ruth to transfer to that time.

I know when I'm going, Ruth said cheerfully, and they were abruptly *between.*

Jaxom counted the breaths he was taking and was rather pleased that they were slow and steady. At fifteen, they were back on the bridge—which had not, apparently, altered.

The view hasn't changed, Ruth said disconsolately.

"No, it hasn't," Jaxom said, surprised to see the diagram still up on the screen. The digital clock, however, definitely registered fifty full Turns past his last view of it. He unhooked his straps and floated down from Ruth's back to the screen.

"I suppose I could have put this back up in preparation for my coming," he told himself. "I'll remember. I hope. Is there air up here, Ruth?"

Yes, but it's not very fresh.

Jaxom pulled off his gloves and put them down on the console. He didn't bother to unsuit, since he had no intention of remaining longer than this errand required. He tapped out the appropriate code and saw the cursor outline a second orbit, deviating by several de-grees from the earlier one and with the return path intersecting the orbit of the fifth planet and spiraling in! With trembling fingers, he pressed the print command and a sheet obediently emerged—a sheet that felt subtly different from the paper he had become accustomed to. Much whiter, softer! Bendarek had really improved the quality of paper over the intervening Turns. Then he compared its diagram to the one on the screen.

"Shards! Aivas, the path of the Red Star has shifted. Aivas?" An iciness flowed across Jaxom's midsections. "Aivas?"

How can he hear you fifty Turns into the future, Jaxom? Ruth said in some amusement.

"Oh, right . . . I suppose. Except he'd know when we were go-ing . . ." Jaxom was still uneasy about Aivas's silence. "I guess I *have* got so that I rely on him too much. But he was right. So we're stuck with this new madness of his, aren't we, Ruth?"

I do not think it is madness to be certain we never have Thread again.

"We're not out of this Pass yet, even if it *is* possibly the last one we'll have," Jaxom said, pushing himself off the deck to grab at

Ruth's neck and swing his leg into the saddle. "The old bridge hasn't changed . . . and yet, it feels awful still and unused!"

I thought the view would have changed, Ruth said, clearly disappointed.

Jaxom thought vividly of the digital in his correct present, added thirty seconds to prevent an overlap, and Ruth took them *between*. Exactly fifteen breaths later he was looking straight at the digital advanced the thirty seconds. He did, however, feel very tired, and as he looked at Ruth's neck, he noticed a definite tinge of gray exhaustion in the usually lustrous hide.

"And?" Aivas queried him.

"I must have put the graph up, because it was there when I arrived."

"And?"

Jaxom undid his helmet, determined to spin the scene out for all it was worth. "Well, I must have remembered to keep the oxygen tanks topped up, for there was some, even if Ruth said it wasn't fresh—Shards!" He looked down at his bare hands. "I left my gloves there."

"*Then*. You will have left your gloves *then*." Aivas could play the same game.

Jaxom grinned. "I think I'll just wait and retrieve them . . . later. Here's what came up in the future. Is the variation sufficient for you, lord and master?" He placed the graph from fifty Turns in the future in front of the sensor so that Aivas could see and compare.

"Yes," Aivas said, unperturbed, "that will be sufficient. The explosions have accomplished exactly the desired dislocation. Jaxom, your vital signs show a depletion. You must eat carbohydrates."

"Ruth's a bit gray, too. He needs to eat more than I do."

You should have told me we'd be doing this today, Jaxom. We have flown Fall, and I haven't eaten since those wherries last week.

"As soon as you're feeling able, dear heart, you shall have as many fat bucks and wherries as you can stuff down your maw."

Then let us go now. I really feel very hungry.

"Jaxom?" Aivas said as the white rider started peeling off his space suit.

"Yes?"

"Will you comply?"

"With your mad scheme? It appears I must because I have. Haven't I?"

Ruatha Hold was gay with banners in the bright autumnal air, and folk had been flowing down all the roads to the immense camping grounds near the racing course. One of the first tasks Jaxom had undertaken upon being confirmed as Lord Holder had been to revive Ruatha's breeding of runners. The animals he had produced since had won significant races from time to time at other Gathers, and he hoped that today, racing on home ground, they would perform even better.

He and Ruth had transferred from the *Yokohama* immediately to an upland meadow where the white dragon had replenished his energies on three bucks and two does. He had then glided home, emitting an occasional satisfied burp so that Jaxom could eat a more substantial meal than the handfuls of berries he had found in the bushes surrounding the field. Jaxom had seen his dragon comfortably curled up on the weyr couch, given orders to the first Steward he saw that he was not to be disturbed even if Thread fell out of phase, and grabbed some bread and cheese from the kitchen, which he consumed on his way to his quarters. There, somewhat sated, he removed his boots and riding belt and crawled under the sleeping furs to sleep.

Sometime during that exhausted rest, Sharra must have joined him, for when he awoke just as the sky was lightening, she was there, nestled against him. What had roused him were unmistakable greetings of Gatherers, arriving after an overnight journey. His nose told him that the spits were already turning over open flames in the roasting pits, and his stomach told him that he needed to fill it. He must have slept an entire day.

"Mmmm, Jax?" Sharra murmured, sleepily reaching for him.

"Yes, love, who else were you expecting?" He leaned over and kissed her. "You let me sleep?"

"Hmmm. Ruth said you were very tired. Meer wouldn't let anyone in the room but me."

He angled himself up to a sitting position, scrubbing at his tousled hair, running his tongue around his teeth, and hoping that his breath wasn't too rank. Meer appeared, Talla right behind him, chirping a gentle inquiry.

"We're up, we're up!" Jaxom assured them although Sharra hauled her pillow more firmly under her head, her eyes determinedly shut.

The two fire-lizards disappeared, and very shortly there was a timid scratch at the door of the bedroom.

"Come!" He could smell the aroma of klah as soon as the door opened. A drudge who looked freshly scrubbed and attired entered with a well-stocked tray.

Once he had had some klah and had cajoled Sharra into waking up enough to join him, he revived sufficiently to bathe and dress in new Gather finery.

"Whatever were you doing that exhausted you and Ruth so much?" Sharra asked as she let him fasten her new Gather gown, a splendid affair in the golds and rusts that so suited her.

"Well, there was Fall, and then Ruth and I had to test those new gloves Hamian's produced and—" He waved his hand airily. "I guess things just mounted up. Did you get enough rest?" he asked solicitously, dropping a kiss on her bare neck before he fastened the topaz necklace which had been his nameday present to her.

"Well . . ." she began in the tone he knew was to make him feel guilty, but then she turned in his arms, her face alight with love and mischief. "I did the honors of the Hold for our guests from Cove Hold, and Lord Groghe and those from Fort Hold and"—she grinned up at him—"*they* said I'd better get an early night and they'd make themselves comfortable. Master Robinton was well on the way through the first wineskin, but he was so pleased that you had some of the 'sixteen for him."

A loud halloo from the dawn-lit road brought them to the window, and they saw a huge contingent of riders, bearing Tillek's banners.

"Come, we must greet Ranrel," Sharra said, grabbing him by the hand. "And it's high time the Lord of Ruatha Hold showed himself to his diligent Stewards and staff."

The Gather attracted hordes from every Hold, Hall, and Weyr. This was one of those few days when there was no Fall to be met, and it would be one of the last of the Northern Gathers before winter weather made roads impassable. Jaxom and Sharra, accompanied by Jarrol and Shawan, now a sturdy toddler, walked the long line of booths until Shawan had to be carried and Jarrol revived by one of the first bubbly pies out of the oven. There was an exuberance and buoyancy to the day that affected everyone and was mirrored in the gay new clothing and high spirits. Harpers strolled up and down the Gather line, playing and singing; children congregated in knots to play their favorite games; adults settled in their own groupings or at tables around the huge dancing square where brewers and wine sellers were doing a brisk business.

Jaxom and Sharra hosted a midday meal in the Hold at which those Lord Holders, Weyrleaders, and Craftmasters gracing the day were entertained. Robinton, Menolly, and Sebell gave a special performance of the latest ballads and airs with full orchestral accompaniment, conducted by Master Domick. It was a leisurely meal, and Jaxom enjoyed it, though he noted that Lords Sigomal, Begamon, and Corman were conspicuous by their absence—which caused him to recall the abduction plot.

The racing went very well, with one Ruathan sprinter winning its first race and their other runners taking placings in almost every one of the eight starts. Among the beasts for sale, Jaxom and Sharra found a well-trained little runner to start Jarrol riding, for they had nothing in the beasthold suitable for a beginner. Saddlery then had to be arranged with the Tanner Hall. In between these chores, Jaxom and Sharra circulated among their guests, speaking to all the small holders that looked to Ruatha.

About midafternoon, young Pell brought his intended to meet his lord and lady, and Sharra was warm in her responses to the darkly pretty girl, daughter of a hill holder from Fort. There was nothing in Pell's manner to suggest that he was not totally engrossed in his future as a joiner, especially after his lady showed Jaxom and Sharra the beautiful little coffer Pell had made her.

Ruth, his white hide radiant after a restoring sleep, had emerged sometime in the morning and was on the fireheights, sunning himself with the other dragons. Hundreds of fairs swarmed about the Hold, their cheerful voices a descant to whatever music the harpers were making.

Whether it was the long sleep or the stimulation of the day, or both, Jaxom found himself in fine fettle for the Gather exertions. He and Sharra led several of the energetic dance figures, and then he allowed Sharra to be swirled away by N'ton, then F'lar, while he partnered Lessa. During one of the breaks, he sat at the harpers' table with Robinton, D'ram, and Lytol and made certain that the Masterharper had sufficient wine. A dark-haired young drudge whom Jaxom did not recognize—so many were hired temporarily to assist during a Gather—kept the Harper supplied with food, even bringing some tidbits for Zair.

It was no wonder then that Robinton would need a short nap, and because Jaxom was busy doing his duty dances with Lady Holders, he only noticed as he danced past that Robinton was alone at his table, asleep, Zair curled up beside him.

It was Piemur who discovered that it was not Robinton asleep at the table, but a man dressed in clothing similar to Robinton's Gather suit—a dead man. And it was Piemur who realized that Zair was barely breathing, his color dangerously dull and his weak breath tainted with a sickly odor. Piemur had the good sense not to alarm anyone, sending Farli to summon Jaxom and Sharra, then D'ram, Lytol, and the Benden Weyrleaders.

"This man's been dead a long time," Sharra said, putting her hand on a cold cheek and testing the muscular resistance. She shuddered. "This is too macabre!"

"Robinton's ill?" Lessa asked in a hoarse whisper as she and F'lar arrived. "That isn't Robinton!" First relief and then fury distorted her features. "They *did* abduct him! Right out of a Gather."

She, Jaxom, F'lar, and D'ram alerted their dragons.

"Don't just jump about in panic," Lytol said, even as the big dragons landed quietly in the shadows beyond the dancing square. "Let us decide what to do and who is to search where. There're enough dragons here to cover every possibility. Why did it have to be *here*, where that device of Aivas's won't reach to Landing?"

Sharra was bending over the limp Zair. "He'd find Robinton no matter where he is. C'mon, Zair."

"D'you need your medical kit?" Jaxom asked.

"I've already sent for it." But her face as she turned to Jaxom was anxious. "Lessa, is your healer here? She knows more about dragon and fire-lizard care than I do. Zair's been poisoned, but I don't know what was used."

Jaxom picked up a half-eaten peice of meat from the table, sniffed cautiously at it, and promptly sneezed vociferously. Sharra took it from him and smelled more daintily.

"Fellis, all right," she announced, "but mixed with something else to disguise taste and smell. Poor Zair. He doesn't look good. How wicked!"

F'lar picked up the wine goblet Robinton had been using and carefully sipped. He spat it out immediately. "Fellis in the wine, too. I should have known Robinton wouldn't pass out from mere wine." The Weyrleader was disgusted with himself.

Jaxom groaned. "I saw him sleeping, and I ought to have known he never sleeps at a Gather . . . ."

"Many's the night he's outlasted everyone else at a Gather," Lessa said. "How much of a head start do these miserable fiends have? Which way would they go?"

Jaxom snapped his fingers. "There are marshals on every road. They would have seen who left and in which direction."

"We'll each take a different road," F'lar said, gesturing for all the riders to mount their beasts and check with the marshals. "You stay here as if there was nothing amiss," he told Lytol, Piemur, and Sharra.

But each dragonrider returned shortly. No one, the marshals had assured them, had been seen leaving the Gather, no riders or wagons on any road.

Tell the fire-lizards to search, Ruth said to Jaxom.

"Ruth says to tell all the fire-lizards to hunt for Robinton," Jaxom said aloud.

"That's exactly what Ramoth just said," Lessa said. The noise of sudden winged exodus could be heard above the rollicking dance tune that was encouraging the dancers to outdo themselves.

"If we announce this to the Gather," Lytol suggested, "we'd have sufficient people to search the entire Hold from border to border."

"No," Jaxom said. "There'd be a panic! You know how well loved Robinton is. It can't be more than an hour, at the most. That's not enough time to get to the coast . . ."

"Up into the hills?" Lytol suggested. "There are so many caves up there we'd never be able to search them all."

"The fire-lizards can—and will," Piemur said.

"There are only so many tracks to the hills," Jaxom said. "Ruth and I will start the search. Lytol . . ." And then Jaxom hesitated.

Lytol clutched his arm. "D'ram and Tiroth will take me. I know Ruatha as well as you do, lad."

"So do I," Lessa said roughly.

"I'll go northeast to the Nabol Pass," F'lar said.

"We'll need some Fort Riders," Lessa said.

"And some to follow the river to the sea," Lytol added.

"We'll stay here for the fire-lizards," Piemur said, nodding to Sharra. There were tears running down his cheeks. "Just *find* him!" Then abruptly he sat down, where the shadow of his body fell across the dead man dressed in harper blue.

Dawn was breaking by the time the dragonriders, augmented by Fort Weyr riders, admitted defeat and returned to Ruatha. A few folk were awake, preparing to return home, but most of the Gather area was populated by those sleeping off the night's excesses.

"Not a single wagon is leaving here without being searched," Sharra told Jaxom when he got back. "That was Piemur's notion."

"And a good one," Jaxom said, gratefully taking the cup of klah she handed him. "For there was nothing moving on the tracks, and I went as far as the Ice Lake, and Ruth was particularly vigilant over the wooded areas."

He saw then that someone had thrown a blanket across the dead man's shoulders. Piemur and Jancis sat nearby as if guarding their master's sleep.

"We thought it wiser to pretend it's Master Robinton," Sharra murmured. "Sebell and Menolly know, of course, and her ten fire-lizards have been out searching all night. Sebell's gone back to the Harper Hall to alert everyone. You heard the drums?"

"You can't miss them." She grimaced. "Asgenar and Larad know harper codes, and they were talking of mounting an attack on Bitra."

"They'd never have been fool enough to imprison the Harper there. Sigomal's not stupid. He'd know it would be the first place we'd look."

"That's what Lytol told them, but they feel badly because they heard of the abduction first. Larad says that he ought to have confronted Sigomal immediately and demanded that he forget such a heinous scheme."

"That would have done no good," Jaxom said wearily.

"And it was such a lovely Gather . . ." Sharra said, turning into his shoulder and weeping softly.

Jaxom put his arms about her, smoothing her rumpled hair back from her forehead and wanting very much to give way to the tears that burned his eyes.

"Zair?" he asked, suddenly remembering the little creature.

"Oh! Yes." Sharra pulled herself from his arms, mopping her eyes and sniffing. "He'll recover, Campila says. She purged him and," she added managing a little smile, "he looked so embarrassed. I've never seen that particular shade in fire-lizard eyes before."

"When will he be able to help us find Master Robinton?"

Sharra bit her lower lip. "He's terribly weak and awfully confused. I didn't ask her that, because if they've drugged Master Robinton and he's comatose, not even Zair could find him."

Suddenly the air was full of agitated fire-lizards, shrieking and bugling.

They've found him! Ruth cried. In three mighty hops, he landed at Jaxom's side.

Jaxom was astride the white dragon before he realized his own intention and then Ruth was aloft with such speed that his rider was nearly unseated. Other dragons were airborne as quickly. Like an arrow composed of many bodies—all flying so closely together that many must have been winglocked—the fire-lizards pointed the southeastern direction.

Can you understand who or where from them? Jaxom asked Ruth.

It is not far, and they picture a wagon. You can see the tracks plainly.

And then Jaxom saw the marks, visible over the headlands of fields recently plowed under. The abductors had been clever, taking to the fields instead of the roads, and the cart had to be a small one, or they could not have maneuvered over muddy fields and the rocky terrain beyond the cultivated lands. The dragons had not been airborne long when they saw the first of the foundered runners, splay-legged and gasping, its feet bound in thick rags to muffle its passage. Ten minutes onward, another exhausted beast lay on the ground, breathing its last, its sides covered with bloody welts that indicated how it had been driven.

Tell the others, Ruth, that they must be heading to the sea. Have some riders go on ahead.

They go, Ruth replied, and Jaxom saw spaces opening up all around him as dragons went *between*.

But dragon wings were quicker than the fleetest of runners, even with a head start of some six hours, and at last Jaxom saw the cart bouncing its way down the final slope to the sea and the small ship waiting for this clandestine cargo. Dragons had encircled the ship, and from his vantage point, Jaxom could see men diving from it, vainly attempting to evade capture.

Then Ruth and the Benden contingent swooped down to halt the cart.

There was a brief attempt at innocence by the three men: two on the driving seat, and one inside, lying on a thick mattress and pretending to be ill.

The fire-lizards, however, were far more interested in the unusual dropped load bed, swarming over it, crooning encouragement, bugling triumph. The "sick" man was unceremoniously dumped out of the cart, the mattress rolled out of the way, and the boards of the false bottom pulled free. And there they discovered the Masterharper, looking ashen and almost wizened.

Carefully they lifted him out, rearranging the mattress for his comfort.

"He may just need air," F'lar said, "stuffed in that pit and jostled like a package . . ."

He glared at the three who were struggling in the rough grip of angry riders. Overhead, fire-lizards made as if to bombard them, claws and beaks held in attack readiness.

"We need Sharra," Lessa told Jaxom urgently. "Unless Oldive is still at the Gather . . ."

Jaxom vaulted to Ruth's back.

"Don't meet yourself coming, Jaxom!" Lessa shrieked at him.

Despite his anxiety and fury, Jaxom recognized the sense of that warning; still, he didn't waste any time returning with Sharra and her medical case.

"I think they gave him too much," she said, her face paler than the Harper's. "We must get him back to Ruatha where I can treat him properly."

The limp figure was handed up to Jaxom astride Ruth, with Sharra to help hold the Harper between them. When they arrived back at Ruatha, N'ton was already in the courtyard with Oldive, so Jaxom knew that the Fort Weyrleader had risked timing his errand.

"Hold on, Sharra," Jaxom told her. "Ruth's going to take us straight to our room."

"Will he fit—" Sharra broke off as they reappeared in the large living room; Ruth quickly folded his wings and scrunched down, and managed to knock over only a few pieces of furniture.

By the time N'ton and Oldive arrived, Jaxom and Sharra had the Harper in their bed, his clothing removed. Sharra held the Harper's head, and Master Oldive quickly emptied a vial down his throat. Then he examined Robinton's eyes and listened to his heart.

"We must get him warm," the Masterhealer said, but Sharra was already tucking furs about the lax body. "His body has had a dreadful shock. Who did this?"

"We'll find out who's behind all this. The abductors were nearly to the beach," Jaxom said. "A ship was waiting to take him who knows where."

"We'll have the answer to that, too," N'ton said in a grating tone. "Master Robinton will recover, won't he, Oldive?"

"He must," Sharra said fervently, kneeling beside the bed. "He must!"

18
▾▾▾▾▾▾▾▾

I t was fortunate for the conspirators that Master Robinton recovered from the overdose of fellis and suffered only bruises from
that wild cross-country journey. Until he was certain that Zair, too,
would recover, he was not disposed to charity, but then he started
murmuring about no real harm having been done.

"They have been grossly misguided," he began.

"*Misguided!*" Lytol, D'ram, F'lar, Jaxom, Piemur, Menolly, and Sebell chorused in outrage.

"The very idea that they intended to abduct *you*"—Lessa's expression was so fierce that Robinton regarded her with widened eyes and
open mouth—"to force *us* to destroy Aivas . . . bloody nearly *killing*
you and Zair! And you call them misguided?"

"I've another name for it entirely," Lord Groghe said, his face
flushed with anger. "I'm certain that almost every other Lord Holder
will come to the same conclusion after hearing the confessions we've
heard. Norist has never made any bones about his disagreement, but
for Sigomal to actively assist him! Norist may call Aivas the Abomination, but it is *he* and Sigomal who have acted abominably! Infa-
mously!"

"The masters will deal with Norist now," Sebell said implacably.
Master Oldive was in complete agreement.

A special convocation of both the Lord Holders and the Mastercraftsmen was hastily called for that next evening. Together the two

groups would hear the evidence against the scofflaws, although they would deliberate on their verdict separately, meting out justice as each group saw fit.

"These sessions are rare in Pernese Records," Lytol said, trying to find precedents in now-legible Ruatha Hold records.

"They've rarely been required," Lord Groghe remarked with a snort. "By and large, Hold, Hall, and Weyr have regulated their own members with few grievances spilling over. Everyone knows what is expected of them, what rights, privileges, and responsibilities are due or required."

"It is such a pity," Robinton said, his voice still reflecting his exhaustion, "that they should take such a perverse view."

"Especially when they've had no scruples about using the things which Avias helps us produce," Lytol said in outrage.

"There may be some justification for their attitude," Robinton began again.

"There's no talking to the man," Menolly said, disgusted. "He must still be very tired to come out with twaddle like that!" She gestured for Robinton's visitors to leave.

"It's not twaddle, Menolly," Robinton replied testily, restlessly thrashing about in the bed where Oldive had insisted he remain. Zair, curled up comfortably in the furs by the Harper's feet and looking considerably more bronze than tan, chirped a protest. "We harpers failed somehow . . ."

"Failed nothing!" Menolly said, furious. "Those misbegotten idiots nearly killed you . . . and Zair . . ." She caught Robinton's scowl. "Hah! At least you care about *him*, even if you don't give two hoots and a holler about your own skin. Out, everyone. Robinton must rest if he's to be fit for the Council."

With so much excitement charging the air, few had left Ruatha's Gather site when the dragonriders returned with Robinton and his captors. The riders had then been forced to protect the nine men from being torn to pieces by the incensed crowd. Jaxom had them interned separately in some of the small, dark inner rooms of the Hold, supplying them with only water and dim glowbaskets. The little drudge who had served the Harper the drugged food was found, and although she was plainly of very limited understanding, she was also placed in confinement.

The ship's captain, it turned out, was one of Sigomal's sons, which strongly suggested the Bitran Holder's involvement. It was remarkable, N'ton commented, how willing a man became to talk after he had been dangled awhile in midair from a dragon's forearm.

When a wing of Benden dragonriders had appeared at Bitra Hold, Sigomal loudly and indignantly denied any involvement with such a dreadful, contemptible business; he had bitterly denounced a son who would bring so much dishonor to his sire and his Hold.

F'lar admitted later that he had come very close to smashing Sigomal's lying mouth—only Mnementh had saved the man. The big bronze dragon had been so incensed by his rider's anger that a little curl of flame had escaped his lips, which had had the immediate effect of silencing Sigomal.

G'narish of Igen Weyr and his bronze riders took into custody Master Norist, five of his masters, and nine journeymen, all of whom had been implicated. By then the abduction cart, and the abused runners, had been brought back to Ruatha. Two would have to be put down. To compound the offense, they had been stolen out of a Ruathan paddock. While the Ruathan beastmaster attended to the poor creatures, the woodsmith and Master Fandarel inspected the vehicle that had been used to carry Robinton away. Bendarek found the maker's name on the footrest: Tosikin, a journeyman joiner in Bitra.

"Purpose-made," Fardarel murmured.

"No question of it," Bendarek replied, "with this sunken load bed, padded and long enough to accommodate a tall man like Master Robinton. Look at this lock top, these extra springs, heavy-duty axle, and larger, reinforced wheels. It was made to be used for fast, hard going." Then Bendarek scowled, noticing a poorly mitered edge and nails that had been badly sunk. "And for the one use. Man shouldn't have put his name to such a shoddily made contraption."

"Shall we have him here to speak his piece?" Fandarel asked, his dark eyes sparking as he rubbed his big hands together.

"Might as well. I wouldn't trust Sigomal not to slip out of this if he possibly can."

"I doubt he will this time," Fandarel said somberly.

T he original intention had been to hold the extraordinary convocation in Ruatha's Great Hall. So many people flocked to the Hold, adding to all those Gatherers who had stayed over, that Jaxom, after conferring with Groghe, Lytol, D'ram, and F'lar, transferred the proceedings to the outside court. The weather, while crisp with autumn, remained clear, and by using the dance-square light standards, the court would be brilliantly illuminated if the matter took time. Dragons massed on the fireheights, their eyes glowing with vivid whirling color, added a bizarre display accented by the fairs of fire-lizards whipping restlessly about.

When Lord Begamon sent word that he could not attend, F'lar despatched F'nor and two wings to see that he did, for the Neratian was also implicated. The drudge, however, was excused. Sharra, Lessa, and Menolly had talked with her, kindly enough when they realized how simple she was. She had been told by a man in "beautiful new clothes" to be sure to feed the Master Harper well from special provisions that had been brought a great distance, just for him. She had been shown the wineskins that were reserved only for Master Robinton, and she had also been instructed to feed the fire-lizard only meat from a special bowl.

"Clearly she didn't know she was doing wrong," Lessa said after the interview. Then her expression hardened. "Appalling of them to make use of a simple child like that."

"Clever, too," Menolly said, with a grim twitch of her lips. "Zair would have sensed an open threat to Robinton, so they *had* to use an innocent pawn."

"Clever, but not clever enough, Menolly," Jaxom said. "Where does she come from?"

"A hold near a big mountain," Sharra said, sighing. "And she was so excited to be allowed to come to a Gather and serve someone as pleasant as the man in blue. I'll keep her here. She'll be safe from misuse at Ruatha. The cook says she's very good with the spit animals."

As soon as Lord Corman arrived that evening, he stomped up to Jaxom, who was standing with Groghe, Ranrel, Asgenar, and Larad.

"I don't agree with what you are doing to Pern. I don't like to see so many of our traditional ways and values flouted by what that— that machine is teaching you, but what you others do is your business. What I refuse to do is mine!"

Larad nodded solemnly. "Which is your prerogative."

"Just so that my position is understood," Corman said, his brows running together in a fierce scowl.

"No one doubts your integrity, Lord Corman," Jaxom said.

Corman raised his eyebrows, seemed about to take umbrage at the youngest Holder's comment, then reconsidered and, scowling once more, allowed Brand to lead him to a chair.

A dais had been hastily constructed in the shape of a flat-bottomed V: one side provided for the Lord Holders and the other for the Craftmasters. In the center Jaxom, as resident Lord Holder, would be seated, with Lytol on one side and D'ram on the other. Robinton would sit just below them, facing the accused, who would be accommodated on benches in the space between the wings. Lytol had tried to find an impartial spokesman to represent the accused, following the legal practices about which he had been reading in Aivas's historical files. Harpers generally performed such services but as no harper could be truthfully called "impartial" in this case and no one else could be found to perform that function, it was decided that the accused would have to speak for themselves—if Piemur had remarked, there could be anything that would mitigate their offense since their guilt was already proved.

Promptly at the appointed hour, the accused were brought to the court, where they were jeered at and reviled by the huge throng, comprising representatives from all parts of Pern. It took some time to restore order, but at last all involved were seated and Lord Holders and Master Craftsmen took their places.

Jaxom rose, holding up his arms for silence. Then he spoke.

"Last evening Master Robinton was drugged and taken from the Gather without his consent and knowledge. A dead man who has not been identified was left in his place, wearing similar clothing. So there are two crimes which must be answered tonight: abduction and murder.

"These three men—" Jaxom pointed to each of them, holding his hand up to still the angry murmur from the crowd. "—drove the vehicle which transported Master Robinton without his knowledge or consent. These six men—" Again Jaxom pointed. "—were aboard the ship awaiting them, to take Master Robinton to a place of concealment without his knowledge or consent. I now read their statements, taken in the presence of a Harper, myself as Lord Holder, and Master Fandarel, representing the crafthalls."

Each statement began with the name and origin of the man involved and summarized the job he had been hired to do. Lord Sigomal and Master Norist were named as those who had given the orders and supplied both marks and equipment. The Glassmasters and journeymen also assembled had delivered messages to those involved and passed payments on. Master Idarolan produced a bill of sale for the ship, signed by one Federen, Masterglass-smith, now seated among the accused. It turned out that he had also led the initial attack on the batteries supplying Aivas, and he was the older brother of one of the men involved in the assault that Aivas had foiled. He was very bitter about his brother's punishment and deafness. Lord Begamon, too, was implicated: he was accused of supplying marks, the horses used on the abortive assault on Aivas, and a safe harbor for the ship.

Journeyman Tosikin, a meek and obsequious fellow plainly awed and terrified by the experience, pointed to Gomalsi, Lord Sigomal's son and the captain of the ship, as the man who had commissioned the strange cart. The journeyman had had no idea of its purpose and had tried to argue them into a different sort of vehicle to carry a "delicate cargo." No, he had not known that a man was to be the cargo.

Brestolli had asked to be allowed to speak of what he had overheard. He further provided a positive identification of three of the Bitrans from the ship as those he had overheard in the brewer's. That caused a surge of consternation and recriminations among the accused.

"You will each be allowed to speak in your own defense and inform this panel of any mitigating circumstances," Jaxom said, pointing first to the three men who had absconded with Robinton. But before any of them could speak, Lord Sigomal got to his feet, suddenly rousing from his apathy.

"I am innocent, innocent, I tell you! My son has been misguided, led astray by bad companions whom I pleaded with him to give up, little knowing what they were involved in—"

"I protest!" Gomalsi shouted, jumping to his feet, eyes blazing at his father. "You *told* me to do what I could to discredit that machine. You *told* me to destroy the batteries—and where to look for them. You *gave* me money to hire men—"

"You fool! You imbecile!" Sigomal shrieked back, stepping forward and clouting Gomalsi so hard across the face that the young man fell backward over the bench.

Immediately Jaxom signaled for guards to force Sigomal back to his place and to help Gomalsi.

"Any more outbursts, and Lord Holder or not, you'll be gagged," Jaxom said sternly to Sigomal. He motioned for the guards to remain behind the two Bitrans. Then he pointed at the first of the three actual abductors. "You may speak in your defense. First tell your name and your rank."

There was a soundless conference, and then the oldest of the three stood.

"My name is Halefor. I have no rank, nor hold, nor craft. I hire my services to whoever pays enough. This time it was Lord Sigomal. The three of us struck a price with him and were paid half in advance to take the Harper in the cart to the ship. That was all we was hired to do. Not to kill. That was an accident. Biswy had to drink some of the wine, so the fumes would be on him. But he was not meant to die from it. Nor did we wish any harm to Master Robinton. I didn't much like that part, but Lord Sigomal said it had to be him because he was so well liked. They'd smash the machine to get Master Robinton back." He looked all about, first at the Lord Holders and then at the Mastercraftsmen, gave a sharp nod of his head, and sat down.

From the men who were Gomalsi's crew came much the same story: They had been hired to do a job, to man a ship from Ruatha to an island off the eastern shore of Nerat. Lord Begamon groaned at that and hid his head in his hands. He continued to moan off and on through the rest of the proceedings. When asked harshly by Master Idarolan if any of them were either apprentices or journeymen, two replied that they had sailed a few seasons in fishing fleets but hadn't much cared for the long hours. Master Idarolan looked relieved that no craftsman of his had been involved.

Jaxom could understand Master Idarolan's desire to settle that point in the hearing of his peers and the Lord Holders. In many seacoast holds, boys and girls grew up able to handle a small skiff adequately. Knowing one end of a ship from the other was no crime. What offended Idarolan was the audacity of Gomalsi, who was not trained in seamanship and had thought that he could sail that small craft safely from Ruatha to the eastern coast of Nerat, across the Currents and into some of the trickiest waters of the planet, risking Robinton's safety every wave of the way.

Unlike the others, Master Norist stood proud and defiant.

"I did what my conscience dictated, to rid this world of that Abomination and all its evil works. It encourages sloth and dalliance among our young, distracting them from traditional duties. I see it destroying the very structure of our Halls and our Holds. Contaminating our Pern with vicious complexities that deprive honest men of work and their pride in workmanship, turning whole families away from what has been proved good and wholesome for twenty-five hundred Turns. I would do it again. I will do all in my power to destroy the spell this Abomination has placed on you!" He extended his arm and swept his pointing finger at every one of the Masters who sat in judgment on him. "You have been deluded. You will suffer. And all Pern will suffer because of your blindness, your lapse from the purity of our culture and knowledge."

Two of his Masters and five of his journeymen cheered their master.

Jaxom could see the shocked expression of other Craftmasters. The Lord Holders were solemn to a man. Toric was plainly scornful whenever he looked toward either Sigomal or Begamon. Corman was disgusted and didn't try to hide that any more than he had hidden his own distrust of Aivas.

The Neratian Holder did not choose to say anything in his defense. When Jaxom asked him again, he just kept on shaking his head and moaning and refused to speak.

"Lord Jaxom," Master Oldive said, rising, "my colleagues have just handed me their opinion concerning the cause of the dead man's state."

"And?"

"There is sufficient bodily evidence to suggest that his end was due to a heart attack. There were no visible wounds or damage to his skull. His lips and nails, however, were blue, a common indication of heart failure." Oldive cleared his throat. "His stomach contained a great deal of fellis, which possibly caused his heart to stop."

"Under these circumstances, it would seem that the deceased met his death by misadventure rather than by the design of the defendants, so the charge of murder is no longer applicable." Jaxom noticed the palpable relief of Halefor. "Has the matter of the premeditated abduction of Masterharper Robinton been established?"

He ignored the vehement affirmatives shouted, almost in chorus, from the audience. The Lords Holder duly raised hands, even Corman. Brand wrote down the count. Then Jaxom repeated the question to the Craftmasters. Every hand was raised, Idarolan's as high as he could push his clenched fist in the air. "Then you may retire to the Great Hall to consider your verdicts."

Master Robinton suddenly put his hand up. Surprised, Jaxom allowed him to speak. As the victim, the Harper had the right to be heard, as well as to face his assailants. Jaxom worried that Robinton might plead for leniency, which he thought would only exacerbate the problem—especially with a man as narrow-minded and vindictive as Norist had proved to be.

"For those of you who witness this," Robinton began, speaking not to the Lord Holders or the Craftmasters but to the people outside the court, lining the walls, the ramp, and the roofs of the nearer cots. His voice was weak but true. He cleared his throat and started again. "For those of you here, let me say that Aivas has taught us nothing that our ancestors did not know. He has given us no machines and tools and conveniences that they did not have and use when they first came to Pern. He restored to all crafts only that knowledge which time had blurred or eradicated in Records. So, if that knowledge is evil, then we all are. But I do not think any of us here believes that we are intrinsically evil, or work evil in our crafthalls. For the Holds, he filled in the gaps in their separate histories, so that all know of their past and which of those who traveled to start a new life on Pern started each Hold. And they do not consider themselves evil, or spawned by evil men and women." Master Robinton stared at Norist, who refused to make eye contact.

"For our Weyrs, he gave the promise of deliverance from a long, long struggle, a deliverance made possible by the abilities of our dragons, who were created by our ancestors, and the courage of their riders. They are not evil, or they would have turned the power of the dragons upon us and enslaved us all. But they have not.

"The evil that was done to me by these men was brought on me for the worst of reasons: to force others to destroy our link with our past, our chance of making this world what our ancestors hoped it would become—peaceful, prosperous, pleasant. I have done none of these men harm," Robinton went on, a wave of hand indicating Sigomal, Begamon, and Norist, "nor wished them harm, nor wish them harm now. I pity them for their fear of the unknown, of the unusual, for their violence and unthinking narrowness of vision and spirit."

Master Robinton then looked at the three abductors. "I forgive you for myself; but you took marks to do evil, which is a great wrong. And you were ready to silence a Harper, and that is a greater wrong, for when speech is restricted, all men suffer, not just I."

He sat down, almost as if he could not stand any longer, but when Menolly would have gone to his side, he shook his head.

Groghe bent across Warbret beside him and whispered to him and Bargen; Toric, who couldn't hear, stepped around the table to be where he could. Ranrel, Deckter, and Laudey followed his example. Nessel looked exceedingly uncomfortable with Asgenar on one side and Larad on the other, while Sangel and Toronas disputed a point.

The Craftmasters also huddled close together, Fandarel in the center, his voice lowered to a harsh rumble. Morilton spoke only once and then was silent, though he listened intently to the others. He was representing the Glasscraft on the tribunal, as none of the other Glassmasters had been willing to accept the onus.

"My lords and masters, you may retire if you choose," Jaxom repeated.

"We're well enough here," Groghe said loudly.

Thinking that Robinton might be the better for a glass of wine, Jaxom poured it, then sipped from it himself before passing Robinton the glass, with a reassuring grin. Master Robinton made a little show of distrust but then, after raising the glass to Jaxom, drank eagerly and smiled approval—a little byplay that sent a ripple of applause and laughter through the waiting crowd and succeeded in reducing somewhat the tension that had been building.

"I find that what I resent the most," Robinton said in a guarded aside to Jaxom, "is that people might think I could no longer handle my wine, to see me sprawled asleep like that so early in a Gather."

"We have come to a decision, Lord Jaxom," Groghe announced. The Lord Holders resumed their seats.

"And we," Master Idarolan, said standing up.

"What is your decision, Lord Holder Groghe?" Jaxom asked.

"Sigomal and Begamon have proved themselves totally unacceptable to this Council; they must not govern their Holds. They are dishonored. In the first part, to plot and carry out a punitive action in another Hold or common property, which is the designation of Landing; and in the second part, to abduct a person against his will for purposes of extortion against the best interests of the planet and all of us."

Sigomal took his censure with some dignity, but Begamon began to sob, falling from the bench to his knees.

"Sigomal's third son, Sousmal, is known to most of us, and it is our decision that he should temporarily manage Bitra Hold until further notice by the Council of Lord Holders. As Begamon has no children old enough to Hold in his stead, we appoint his brother, Ciparis, as temporary Lord Holder, also until further notice. Gomalsi is to be exiled with his father for his part in the first attack on the Aivas installation, for his part in the abduction, and because, by setting himself up as a captain of a seagoing ship without qualifications, he has offended all members of the Fishercrafthalls. We suggest that one of the islands in the Eastern Ring be designated the place of exile."

Sigomal groaned, and Gomalsi bit back a cry of protest.

"Master Norist is also stripped of his rank, as are the other Craft members of this conspiracy," Idarolan said. "All are to be exiled. The same place would doubtless give them the company of like minds." He turned to where the other Glasscraftsmen were standing in the crowd. "It is the decision of this body that you must accept Master Morilton as your Craftmaster until such time as we, your peers, decide that you can choose, without prejudice, a man with a more open mind and forward vision than Norist."

Lytol nodded at Jaxom, whose task it was to pass judgment on the other scofflaws. Jaxom had never had to discipline a man for the rest of that man's natural life, but he thought again of the anguish he had felt on that wild ride to rescue Master Robinton.

"Exile!" he announced. Most of the men accepted that, though two of the younger ones looked so desperate that Jaxom added, "Your families may accompany you into exile, if they so choose."

He saw Sharra's slight smile and Lessa's approving nod.

"The convicted will be returned to their quarters and tomorrow will be taken to their place of exile. From this time onward, they are holdless, craftless men and no longer protected by the Weyrs." Jaxom raised his voice over Begamon's frightened babble. "This court is adjourned."

Guards closed in around the condemned, and judges and jury filed into the Hold.

Somehow food had been prepared to serve the unexpected numbers who had come to Ruatha. Sharra told Jaxom in the few moments they had for private conversation that everyone had been exceedingly helpful, Hold, Hall, and Weyr, in accumulating enough provisions to send none away hungry.

"You were, by the way, my love, magnificent," she added. "It was a terrible case to have to judge, but given the evidence and the admissions, no one can fault your decision. The sentence was fairer than they deserved." Her face set in angry lines, and she clenched her fists. "When I saw the bruising Master Robinton sustained . . ."

"He'll be all right?" Jaxom wondered if maybe he had been too forbearing, though he could not have ordered a death sentence. Had Master Robinton died—or had Biswy not died of heart failure—he might have had to decide differently.

Lord Groghe sought him out then, to reassure Jaxom that he himself, had the offenses happened in his Hold, would have done exactly the same. To Jaxom's surprise and a certain sad gratification, Lord Corman also approached him later in the evening.

"Well handled, Jaxom. Only thing you could have done under the circumstances."

The Keroonian Holder did not remain for the evening meal, nor did he ever visit Landing again. But from then on he neither prevented his holders from using the new products nor objected when young folk asked to go South to study. Of Aivas-developed items, Lord Corman purchased only paper, remarking once in his harper's hearing that Bendarek had discovered a form of paper on his own before "the machine" had awakened.

The next morning three Fort Weyr wings arrived at Ruatha to convey the convicted to their place of exile. Delivery of the letters the men had written to their families was promised. Those wishing to join their menfolk would be brought to the island as soon as they were ready.

Master Idarolan had chosen the exile site. "Not too large, not too small, with good fishing and some game, though wherry makes a dull diet. Plenty of fruit and root vegetables. They'll have to work to survive, but that's no more than we must do."

"Threadfall?" Jaxom asked.

Master Idarolan shrugged. "There're a few caves, and you're taking care of the future of that problem. They can endure it or not as they choose. There's also an old volcano and evidence that the island has been inhabited before. It's far more hospitable than Far West Continent, where they'd have only sand and snakes."

When the men were mounted on the dragons, they were handed sacks with basic tools and a few supplies. Then the wings took off *between*.

Jaxom felt enervated as never before, his spirits sunken to a bleak nadir. But as Ruatha's Lord Holder, he had to respond with courtesy and civility to others who were acrimonious in their opinions and harbored considerable rancor for the guilty. Those he admired most among the Lord Holders said little or nothing.

Asgenar and Toronas departed to assist young Sousmal at Bitra. On their way back to Cove Hold, D'ram and Robinton would drop Lytol off at Nerat Hold to apprise Ciparis, who had previously acted as Begamon's Steward, of his new status.

Brand and his understewards were busy arranging for transportation for the many visitors, seeing to travel supplies for those who had exhausted their own and directing the drudges to clear up the debris and repair the damage caused by the large crowd.

Jaxom was perversely grateful when Sharra, looking extremely torn between her responsibilities, asked him if she was needed to help.

"You're wanted back at the laboratory on the *Yokohama*?" he asked.

"Oldive and I both."

He gave her a brief hug and a kiss and nodded. In a way it would be a relief to be able to sort out his thoughts without infecting her with his dejection.

"I'll spend some time with the boys," he said. "I'm not needed right now for anything at the *Yokohama* or Landing."

That was not essentially true, and Sharra knew it. She gave him a quick stare, but then she smiled sadly, kissed his cheek, and left him alone in their quarters.

From his window, he watched her and Oldive mount on the young blue who was now on duty at Ruatha—and that, unfortunately, reminded him of G'lanar.

I am here, Ruth said softly from his weyr in the Hold.

You always are here for me, dear friend, Jaxom said, intolerably weary.

You did as you had to, as you ought to. No blame is yours.

But I am left to deal with its aftermath.

You have acted with honor. Others did not. Can you do more than act with honor?

A good question, Ruth, a very good question. Jaxom stretched out on his bed, hands clasped behind his head. *Could I have avoided this outcome?*

How? By not helping Piemur and Jancis to uncover Aivas that day? The machine would have been found by someone. More good has come of that day's work than any other—except, of course— and Jaxom, hearing the odd satisfied chirp in Ruth's tone, smiled faintly—*the day we brought the queen egg back to Ramoth. And yesterday, when we went forward and assured our success . . .*

Jaxom's smile deepened in spite of his disconsolate mood, as he envisioned Ruth's eyes twirling with blue mischief.

Men think differently than dragons do, Ruth went on thoughtfully. *Most of the time dragons understand their mates. Sometimes, like now, I cannot quite understand why you are troubled. You allow people to think as they wish so long as they do not impose their thoughts on you. You are good about listening to both sides of a problem. I've heard you. You allow people to do as they wish, so long as they do not injure anybody, especially someone you love and admire.*

ALL THE WEYRS OF PERN

Ah, but when we knew that Sigomal was plotting against Robinton, we should have confronted him then, Jaxom said.

Were the plans known?

No, not exactly.

And you took measures to protect the Harper.

Which didn't work, did they?

Not your fault. Who could have thought that they would try something at a Gather, with so many other people about? You must put aside such useless thoughts, Jaxom. You only make yourself miserable. We have much to look forward to . . .

Don't we! Jaxom grimaced as he flopped over onto his stomach, burying his face in the pillow, knowing as he did so that he was merely evading that issue. He made himself think of it: Would he and Ruth tackle the problem Aivas had posed them?

It is not a problem, Jaxom. For it has been solved. Aivas has told you so. He has shown you so.

And you agree with him? You'll risk it?

We went forward to see if it worked. It had. Therefore we will do it because we have done it. It will be quite a feat. Ruth sounded eager and elated. Surprised, Jaxom pushed himself up to his elbows. *It will be even more challenging than saving Ramoth's egg,* Ruth went on. *And even more important for the future of this world. That is what you must think of, not these sad and useless pasts. What has been done, has been done and cannot be undone.*

Did Sharra have a word with you before she left? Jaxom wouldn't have put it past his wife to enlist the aid of his dragon.

She did not need to. Am I not always close to your heart and your mind?

Always, dear heart. Always! And Jaxom swung his legs over the edge of the bed. There was still a lot to be done at Ruatha before he could return with a clear conscience to Aivas and Landing.

19
▼▼▼▼▼▼▼▼▼

A ivas had explained to Fandarel and Bendarek exactly how to alter and reinforce the HNO_3 tanks that were to corrode the metal casing of the antimatter engines. Fandarel followed his instructions, though he thought that the tolerance needed on the alloy of the tanks as well as the padding seemed redundant. He did enjoy constructing the gauges and the nozzles that would let the agenothree drop on the engine casing.

"A slow process, to be sure, but the rate of penetration can be measured and monitored," Aivas told the Smithcraftmaster. "The safety factors built into the great star-crossing engines were immensely sophisticated. The construction data are not available to discover a more efficient way of broaching the antimatter suspension, so this crude method is the only option. Sometimes the simple solutions are best. Therefore, it is prudent to allow a wide window, which has been calculated as two weeks, give or take a few days. By the time the dragonriders transfer the engines to their positions, the corrosion should have penetrated almost to the antimatter capsule."

"Now, look here, Aivas,," Fandarel began. "I know the rate at which agenothree corrodes metal—"

"Not metal such as the builders of this ship used, Master Fandarel."

"That's so." Fandarel scrubbed at his close-cropped scalp. "What puzzles me is the *amount* of agenothree required to reach the antimatter material."

"As has been explained"—a diagram appeared on the monitor in the engineering section: a massive block surrounding a ridiculously small cube in a slightly larger sphere—"the antimatter material is not a large mass, approximately two hundred grams. Even the suspension unit masses only about fifteen hundred kilograms."

"Frankly, Aivas, that's what perplexes me. How could two hundred grams of *anything* power a ship the size of the *Yokohama* through space?"

"Do you not appreciate efficiency, Master Fandarel?" Aivas asked in reply, in a tone that could have been interpreted as amused. Fandarel often had the feeling that the machine *was* amused. "The matter/antimatter engine is the quintessence of efficiency. Only a small amount is ever required."

"With two hundred grams of black powder or even nitro, one cannot explode very much," Fandarel replied.

"Do not equate black powder or nitro, or anything used in mining operations, with antimatter on any count. There is no comparison to the explosive energy released. Despite the distance involved, you will be able to see the flash of the explosion with an ordinary telescope when the antimatter explodes on the Red Star. You would see no trace of an explosion using two hundred grams of black powder, or even nitro. You must be assured that this facility does comprehend the power that is to be discharged."

Fandarel continued to scratch his pate in wonderment, nodding as he tried to accept what Aivas had said.

"You are an excellent craftsman, Master Fandarel, and have advanced at an astonishing pace in the past four years and nine months. Since antimatter, unlike the atom that you have recently been investigating, cannot be studied in laboratory situations, you must rely on explanations. It cannot be exposed to matter as you know it—ore, earth, gases, water. Antimatter can be contained, as it is in the ship's engine, and, with control, become the most efficient source of power Mankind has at its disposal. At this point in your study of physics, you cannot understand these concepts. But you can use them to your advantage—with proper guidance, techniques known to this facility, and the safeguards that have already been explained to you. As you pursue your studies, you will come to understand even the anomalies of antimatter. But not now. Time becomes a critical factor. The Red Planet must be jarred out of its current orbit just where it will later approach the fifth planet of your system.

ANNE MCCAFFREY

"Do you have the couplings to attach the HNO_3 tanks to the engine blocks?"

"Yes," Fandarel said with a sigh, and indicated the metal braces and T-junction that he and his best smiths had built to hold the tanks tightly against the engines in a way that would allow the corrosive material to leak onto the metal in a regulated flow.

"Then you should proceed to install the tanks as indicated." The screen altered to show a new diagram.

"I could do it in my sleep," Bendarek muttered.

"It would be unwise to fall asleep in space, Journeyman Bendarek," Aivas replied immediately.

Bendarek grimaced and shot Fandarel an apologetic glance.

"You will remember to use tether lines while you are EVA," Aivas continued. "F'lessan and his bronze dragon are in the cargo bay in case of an emergency."

Gathering up their bundles, Fandarel and Bendarek made their way to Airlock E-7, nearest the engine shaft. The bulky agenothree tanks, the largest that Fandarel had ever manufactured, ringed the wall of the lock where the rest of the work detail awaited them, all suited up except for helmets. When Fandarel and Bendarek were ready, helmets were donned and secured, each member of the six-man team checking his mate's tank, fastening, and safety lines.

At Fandarel's nod, Bendarek cycled the airlock closed and then opened the outer door. Evan and Belterac took one tank, while Silton and Fosdak took the second. Bendarek handed out the couplers to the other journeyman, checking that each had the tools that would be required. Fandarel swung himself out onto the catwalk that led from the hatch to the great engine shaft.

Big as the Mastersmith was, he was dwarfed to insignificance by the immensity of the metal mass that contained the so-efficient two hundred grams of antimatter. For once in his life, Fandarel felt inadequate as he made his lumbering way: a grain of sand beside a dune. However, there was work to be done, for which he was quite capable, so he suppressed the comparison and, without looking back, gestured for Evan and Belterac to follow him. Pern was spread out below them, and with an accustomed glance, he located the odd pimples that were the Landing volcanoes. It comforted him in the grandeur of space to be able to identify something he knew. He proceeded, feeling the vibration in the walkway as others set foot upon it.

They all had EVA time, were accustomed to moving in free-fall, and were all aware of yet fascinated by the inherent dangers of the new environment. To Fandarel's surprise, Terry, who had been his second hand for so long, could not handle the vastness of space, or even the lack of gravity, though he had never minded going a-dragonback. Still, Master Fandarel thought, space was a different medium altogether than *between* and just as hostile as Aivas told them. There had been those one or two—well, actually five—mishaps, Fandarel had to admit. Fortunately there had been dragons about, and the men who had inadvertently loosened their safety lines, had been hauled back to the *Yokohama*. Belterac was the only one who had overcome fear of a repetition and continued that exercise. But Belterac was phlegmatic by nature.

At last Fandarel's gloved right hand touched the access ladder, which was crafted as a recess into the metal side of the engine shaft, complete with safety-line rail. Beyond his reach, by half a length, were the long, rounded spars to which cargo pods had been attached during the *Yokohama*'s long journey from Earth to Pern. When it came time to move the engines to the Red Star, the dragons, wearing special gloves to protect their flesh from the lacerating cold of the metal, would grip these spars and carry the engine *between*. Aivas, Fandarel knew, still entertained doubts that the dragons, even several hundred of them working together, could move such a mass. He thought that if they must have faith that what Aivas told them was true, Aivas should return the compliment. Fandarel caught a glimpse of Evan and Belterac behind him; then, clipping his line to the safety rail and placing his hands on the rungs, he pulled himself up.

It was a long way up. When he reached the top of the engine block, it was wide enough for five dragons to stand tail to nose. The length of it was four times its width. Fandarel was still not accustomed to thinking in such colossal measurements.

With Aivas's diagram firmly in mind, he stepped carefully to where the tanks were to be positioned, nozzles end to end and joined by the junction that would permit their contents to drip-drip relentlessly into the metal. The waste of all that incredible metal distressed Fandarel, especially after Aivas insisted that they did not have some of the basic raw materials on Pern to reproduce such an alloy. He contented himself with the knowledge that he had seen it, felt it, and yes, even destroyed it. There was nearly as much destruction in smithing as there was creation.

Bendarek and Fosdak had stayed below to attach the hoist cables to the tanks. When those on top had adjusted their lines, they were secure enough to haul the tanks up without drifting off in the effort. The team had been well drilled, and soon the tanks were up, then pressed down so that the ingenious suction cups would keep the tanks firmly in place until the special glue set. The couplings were attached, and the junction installed. Finally the black solar panels were clipped on, so that the agenothree would not freeze, or boil, during the operation. Then Bendarek ceremoniously handed Master Fandarel the spanner to open the plastic nozzles and release the corrosive agenothree.

"One down, two to go," Fosdak said in his usual impudent manner.

"And we will all be careful going down that ladder," Fandarel said, relieved that there had been no mishap. Efficiency was safety, he reminded himself.

He motioned for the others to precede him and checked the gauges that would indicate the amount of agenothree in each tank. There was, of course, no change in the amount yet, but it was second nature for Fandarel to check.

"I know, I know," Hamian said irritably, using both hands to push sweaty hair off his face. He regarded F'lar levelly. Hamian was stripped to work pants in the heat that was part of his discomfort. The major dissatisfaction was the plastic material that he, Zurg, Jancis, and a half hundred other journeymen and Masters of a variety of Crafts were trying to produce in sufficient quantities—and quality—to protect the dragonriders in their epic endeavor.

While the plastic he had produced, using Aivas's formula, was pliable and tough as an outside layer, the filling and cotton lining made assembly difficult. Since the plastic outer skin of the space suits had to be airtight, it could not be sewn. Hamian had been experimenting with glues of every sort, trying to find one that would not become brittle in space and that bonded all three layers. He could not recall now how many suits he had sent up to the *Yokohama* to be tested.

The dragon gloves had been relatively easy in comparison, even if dragon feet differed in length and width as much as human feet did. Still the production of over three hundred pairs had taken some of his work force several months.

"Yes, I know that time is catching up with us, F'lar, but we're working flat out. We've got one hundred and seventy-two finished and tested.'' He held his hands in a gesture of resignation.

"No one can fault you for trying,'' F'lar said.

"Look,'' Jaxom said in a placatory manner, ''if worse comes to worst, we can send the engines in three sections. There should be enough variety of sizes so that the suits can be swapped over.''

F'lar frowned, not liking that alternative.

"Well, it's a suggestion,'' Jaxom said. ''It would take the pressure off Hamian.''

"But this was to be a joint effort . . .''

"You know as well as I do, F'lar, that there's a wide window available,'' Jaxom said, arguing as subtly as he could so that F'lar would not realize that Aivas intended that there be only two hundred suits. Jaxom hated the necessity of manipulating his best friends, but it was essential if he was to bring off Aivas's plan. He didn't like it any better than F'lar did, but he had come to realize that Aivas was not all that confident about the dragons' abilities. The zebedees were a slower way of destroying Thread, but a second option seemed prudent. ''It isn't as if the engines have to be deposited at the same instant.''

"No, that's true,'' F'lar said, absently blotting the sweat off his forehead.

"How long does it take us to shuck space suits now? Half an hour at most, between the two lifts. Hamian needs only to get another twenty—more if at all possible, of course, Hamian, but we've almost enough as it is.''

"And time's running out,'' Hamian said, some of the tension easing from his face and body. He had not liked to fail in this project, but so much time had been spent in little details that no one had considered when they had blithely started. ''Everything takes longer and costs more. Shells! but I hate to fall down on you.''

"Who said you had?'' Jaxom demanded. ''You've got enough kits to do the job right now.''

F'lar regarded Jaxom with faint surprise. Jaxom knew that he had just usurped some of F'lar's prerogative, so he smiled as ingratiatingly as he could, giving a slight shrug.

"Yes, as you say, Jaxom, there are enough suits to do the job right now if riders trade off,'' F'lar agreed.

"Well, then,'' Hamian said, radiating relief, ''I can take time for a bite to eat. Join me?'' He gestured toward the trestle table set under an awning. Some of his large teams were already serving themselves, for meals were taken whenever there was time. "There's always enough in the pot for dragonriders."

Although Jaxom knew that F'lar was scrutinizing him all during the meal he pretended not to notice. He intended to have a few private words with Aivas about easing up on Hamian. The man *was* trying—and could have no idea that Aivas was deliberately rejecting space gear that was probably suitable in all respects. Two hundred finished and acceptable units—and no more—would solve Jaxom's travel problems.

Although Landing bore the brunt of the preparations for the final assault on Thread, there was excitement throughout the planet as the days of the last month were ticked off.

Oldive and Sharra had drafted as many healers as possible and then, at Master Nicat's suggestion, some of the gem cutters who were accustomed to the use of magnifying glasses and small tools. Efforts to find the most effective "disimprover" for the Thread spring were redoubled. Many parasites of the Thread ovoids had been found, and many of those had been infected with a variety of "viruses." While some of the "disimproved" forms had adverse effects on the Thread, none had produced virulent enough reactions, according to Aivas. Massive reproduction had to take place, with the chosen virus— changed to a more parasitic form—able to replicate itself using the material within the ovoid.

Everyone in the laboratory on the *Yokohama*, or in the schoolrooms at Landing, worked long, hard, tedious hours, suffering eyestrain, headache, and back cramps.

Aivas consoled them. "Thread is a very disorganized life-form, not even as organized as the indigenous bacteria you were isolating in biological studies. You cannot be expected to understand reproduction of such a life-form."

"We don't have time!" Mirrim said, speaking through clenched teeth. It was her offering that Aivas had just rejected. Then she brightened. "Of course, we could keep some around to study and learn from, couldn't we?" She saw the horror and disgust of some of her colleagues. "No, I guess we couldn't. Ah, well, back to the microscope. My ninety-eighth batch of trials today. Maybe we luck out at a hundred!"

"Twenty-two more days!" Oldive said with a massive sigh as he, too, turned back to his station.

Afterward, when Lytol wrote up the history of the Aivas years, he would remember the results, not the frenzy that accompanied them, though he gave full credit to everyone involved in the different projects.

At last all the preparations had been completed—two full days *before* the date Aivas had set them.

Two hundred suited riders on two hundred gloved dragons awaited the signal in their Weyrs. Another nine suited riders were ready to do their part in this great enterprise, scattering the "disimproved" ovoids. The three leaders, F'lar, N'ton, and Jaxom, were in the *Yokohama* cargo bay. Lessa was there with Ramoth, who was breeding, and Jaxom did not dare ask how F'lar and Mnementh had timed that so precisely. She had accepted the fact that she would not take part in this venture, but she didn't like her exclusion one bit.

Master Fandarel and Belterac were about to proceed with the separation of the *Yokohama*'s engine shaft from the main sphere. Bendarek was aboard the *Bahrain*, and Evan was on the *Buenos Aires* to perform the same operation. Once that was done, the dragons would be called up to take their places.

Aivas had appointed F'lar to take the *Yokohama*'s unit and deposit it in the approximate center of the great Rift on the Red Planet. Jaxom was to take his group to one end of the Rift, while N'ton was to take his to the other, more or less, close to the immense craters. Only Jaxom knew what had caused those craters—and *when*. The trick would be to keep N'ton from guessing.

Each section would be accompanied by three brown, blue, and green dragons, Mirrim included, who would scatter the sacks of disimproved Thread toroids in a low-altitude flight across the bleak Red Planet's surface and across the flat ring of ovoids orbiting above the planet's equator. Oldive and Sharra had just barely accomplished their part of the undertaking. Mirrim's one hundredth attempt had indeed been the crucial one.

With careful fingers and a frown of concentration, Master Fandarel pressed in the code words that would activate the appropriate sequence to disengage the engines. Aivas had had to delve deeply to find the secret ciphers in the captain's private files.

ANNE MCCAFFREY

"There," the Mastersmith said with an air of triumph.

The monitor displayed lights, and then a message lit up—but not the one that Fandarel expected.

"There is a problem," he said. "The computer refuses to activate."

"The appropriate code word was given, the necessary sequence was provided. Separation should be initiated," Aivas said crisply.

"The screen says 'Unable to activate.' "

"Unable to activate?" There was genuine surprise in Aivas's voice.

"Unable to activate," Fandarel repeated, wondering what the problem could possibly be. The *Yokohama*'s machinery, though it had lain dormant for many centuries, had always complied with the proper action for every operation requested. "I will try again."

"A scan is being run to ascertain if there is any computer malfunction," Aivas replied.

"Master Fandarel?" Bendarek queried from the *Bahrain* on the ship linkup. "Shall I proceed now?"

"We do not have separation here yet," Fandarel said, keenly feeling the failure and hoping it would be momentary.

"Should I not see if the *Bahrain* is more responsive?" Bendarek could not quite suppress his eagerness to begin.

"Aivas?" Fandarel was always a generous man. If Bendarek could proceed, it would be as well.

"No malfunction in the program can be discovered," Aivas said. "It is recommended that the *Bahrain* proceed with separation."

Bendarek had a little more luck than Fandarel. "My screen says 'dysfunction discovered.' Dysfunction of what?"

Evan, on the *Buenos Aires*, initiated the program in his turn and received MECHANICAL MALFUNCTION as his message.

"Which one is correct?" Fandarel asked, feeling somewhat vindicated by the failure of all attempts.

"They may all be correct," Aivas replied. "Reviewing."

Fandarel thought that seemed a good idea for himself as well, and rehearsed, without actually pressing the keys down, the sequence he had inserted.

"It is a mechanical malfunction," Aivas announced.

"Of course!" Fandarel bellowed as he realized what it had to be. "These ships have been in space for over twenty-five hundred years. The mechanical parts have had no maintenance."

"You are correct, Master Fandarel," Aivas replied.

"What's the delay up there?" F'lar asked from the cargo bay.

"A minor one," Fandarel answered. Then paused. "Where?" he asked Aivas.

"The clamps have locked, due to cessation of timely servicing."

"It's not just frozen, is it?" Fandarel asked.

"You have learned much, Master Fandarel. Fortunately the clamps can be lubricated on the inside, through an access, a narrow one." The screen lit up with the schematic of the area between the skins of the *Yokohama*. "It will, however, be necessary to use a special lubricant, for there is little heat in that area, and the oils you ordinarily use will be ineffective. A mixture of liquid neon, liquid hydrogen, and liquid helium must be made with a tiny amount of silicone fluid. That is the equivalent of penetrating oils for use in these very cold conditions. The low molecular weight of gases causes them to evaporate first, but their viscosity is quite low and carries the heavier silicone oil into very thin spaces. That should effect the solution to this minor problem."

"Minor problem?" For once, Fandarel lost his patience. "We do not have those liquids."

"You have the means to produce them, if you remember the liquid-helium experiments."

Fandarel did. "That will take time."

"There is time," Aivas said. "A wide window was allowed for this transfer. There *is* time."

The dragonriders were not pleased with the delay—they had built themselves and their dragons up to this incredible effort and were impatient to go.

"If it isn't one thing, it's another, isn't it?" N'ton said with a wry grin.

"Tomorrow?" Jaxom asked, grinning to allay F'lar's irritated frown. "Same time, same stations?"

F'lar pushed back the lock of hair that never seemed to stay in place and acknowledged the unanticipated delay with a flick of his finger.

"We'll speak to the riders, Aivas."

Despite his lightheartedness, Jaxom had experienced an incredible letdown at having the expedition postponed. More than anyone else, he had had to fortify himself for the tremendous effort required of him and Ruth.

A day makes little difference to me, Jaxom, Ruth said encouragingly. *The meal I had yesterday will last long past tomorrow.*

That's good, Jaxom replied, more grimly than the circumstances warranted—but he had been primed for action today! *Well, let's get back to Eastern and tell my wings to relax.*

It was, in fact, several days before the penetrating oil could be manufactured. Jaxom had Ruth eat at least one small wherry each evening, and Ruth complained that he would be so full he wouldn't be able to complete one jump, let alone two.

"That's preferable to having you fade out on me when we're stuck between times," Jaxom replied.

He waited out the delay at Cove Hold with Sharra, who was recovering from intensive hours in the laboratory. She had lost weight and had deep circles under her eyes. At least he could occupy himself with seeing to her needs. And his. And Robinton's.

Jaxom was distressed to see the change in the Masterharper, a subtle one, but he could tell that Lytol and D'ram were also aware of it. Robinton had recovered from the physical shock but not from the mental one. He seemed himself when in company, but too often Jaxom would catch him deep in thoughts—disturbing and unhappy ones, to judge by the sadness in the Harper's eyes. Also, he seemed to drink less, and with less relish. He was a man going through the motions of living.

Zair is worried, Ruth told Jaxom when he caught his rider worrying about the Harper.

"It may just take a little more time for Master Robinton to recuperate," Jaxom said, trying to reassure himself. "He's not as young as he was, less resilient. And it was a ghastly experience. When this is over, we'll think of something to rouse him from his apathy. Sharra's noticed it, too. She'll talk it over with Oldive. You know how testy he gets when he thinks you're fussing over him. We'll do something. Tell Zair. Now, just once more, let's go through the star pattern for our first timing."

We both know those stars better than the ones above us now, Ruth said, but he dutifully did as Jaxom asked.

The call to assemble came in late afternoon. Fosdak, the slimmest of the smith journeymen, had squeezed his suited self into the interstices and pumped the penetrating liquid and oil into the fine crack of each of the huge clamps that held the engine shaft onto the main ship segment. By the time he had done the *Buenos Aires* and returned to the *Yokohama* to see if the application had dispersed, he was reasonably confident of success.

Once again Fandarel used code-word and key sequence, punched ENTER, and waited. This time the computer acknowledged the commands and responded with READY TO EXECUTE.

"I am ready to execute the order," Fandarel said.

"Go, man, go!" F'lar cried.

Fandarel activated the program. He didn't know if anyone else heard the metallic squealings and clangings, or the final *clunk* as the clamps let go, the noise was loud enough in the engineering section.

"We have separation," he said, and then remembered to activate the exterior optics to view the effect.

"Weyr, alert!" F'lar called, and Fandarel had a fine view of the sudden appearance of the massed dragons, each dropping to prearranged positions along the upper spars. "Magnificent!"

"The *Bahrain* has separation!" Bendarek cried.

Fandarel could not see the *Bahrain*.

Jaxom could, for this was his responsibility. When F'lar had alerted the wings under his command—from Benden, Igen, and Telgar Weyrs—Jaxom had called up his from Eastern, Southern, and Ista. The assembly that answered him was the most impressive he had ever seen in all his Turns. Each arrived in place at the same moment, just as they had drilled. Dragon claws gripped the long spars, and every faceplate was turned toward the spot on the tail section where he and Ruth were perched.

Ruth, give the dragons their direction to the Red Star in star-pattern. Remember, there will be no crater at that end of the Rift.

I do, because we will put it there! Ruth sounded elated.

There would be no confusion over that formality: the dragons expected to receive their destination from Ruth. None of them had been to the Red Star. All the riders had been told that it would appear to be a longer jump than they were accustomed to making, and that they should remember to breathe regularly in the interval.

They understand and are ready, Ruth reported a moment later.

Jaxom took in a deep breath, resting one gloved hand on Ruth's shoulder before he raised it high. *Then we must go*, he said, *before I lose my nerve.* And he dropped his arm.

It was a long jump, even if it was expected. Jaxom counted thirty carefully inhaled and exhaled breaths. Too bad Lessa hadn't remembered how long it had taken her to go back four hundred Turns—that knowledge would have been reassuring. On thirty-two breaths, Jaxom's anxiety began to ooze out of his control.

Here! Ruth announced in a great echoing shout in Jaxom's mind.

And they were hovering inches above one end of the Great Rift. The stars were in the correct pattern in the sky. The desolate landscape at that edge of the Rift was just as bleak at this time of its life as it was in Jaxom's Turn.

Jaxom hauled his mind back to the business at hand. They had ten minutes to let the massive engine down into the Rift.

Those who sow the ovoids are proceeding, Ruth told him.

Jaxom relayed the order for the dragons to lower their burden— and then he grinned broadly. The dragons *had* accomplished this incredible journey! The weight of the engine had been as nothing— because they had not thought of it as anything out of the ordinary. A surge of elation buoyed his spirits immeasurably.

We did it, Ruth! We did it!

Of course we did it. Easy now, keep that thing level, Ruth added, and Jaxom gestured to the rear dragons who were dropping faster than the forward ones. *T'gellan asks how far down are we to go with this?*

Tell him, as far down as we can lower without the dragons scraping their wings. There should be some rocky protrusions that'll hold it in place long enough. Steady now, keep a regular rate of descent.

They were well below the rim of the Rift when Jaxom felt the whole structure jar.

Can we drop down, Ruth, and see if this will do?

Ruth's eyes gleamed off the strata of rock, feldspar, granite, and darker stone mixtures. Then he was below the bulk of the engine.

It will slant a bit if they release it, Ruth said, his sight more acute in the shadows than Jaxom's.

Who's on the bow end? Jaxom asked.

Heth, Clarinath, Silvrath, Jarlath.

Please ask them to lower as far as they can.

They have.

Ask them to release their grip but be ready to grab again. We can't have the thing slipping down into the abyss.

Heth says if the stern will move forward half a length, there is a good shelf of rock for the bow end.

Give Monarth that message.

I have.

Jaxom could see the slight movement as the engine mass settled.

All right. Jaxom gestured to the riders facing him to release their end carefully.

That accomplished, with tension obvious as talons hovered inches above the spars, the massive engine seemed secure. Jaxom glanced at the timepiece strapped to his wrist. Eight minutes had elapsed. They were done.

As he signaled for the wings to rise out of the Rift, he asked Ruth to tell the dragons to land on the rim.

Are the sowers all right, Ruth?

They are, the white dragon said equably. *Mirrim landed Path once to look at the ovoids in the dust. There are many many more than she thought there would be.*

Tell Path that Mirrim is not to bring a sample back. We have enough of them, Jaxom said firmly. The last thing they needed was an artifact from eighteen hundred Turns before.

Path says a lot of them are rotten.

All the more reason to leave them where they are!

Path will not bring one.

Jaxom glanced at his watch. Another minute had ticked by. The dragons and riders were glancing curiously about them.

Monarth says T'gellan says Threads are welcome to this planet, Ruth remarked. *The engine will not explode yet, will it?*

No, not according to the way Bendarek read the gauge when he checked this one over. I wonder how F'lar's doing.

The small hand had circled once again.

Call the others in, Ruth. We'd better get back.

In eight seconds the green, blue, and brown riders rejoined the others.

Now came the dangerous part, the one Jaxom had fretted over since Aivas had informed him of this maneuver: getting all the dragons and riders safely back to their own time.

Impress on every dragon, Ruth, that he is to return to his own weyr. We will have been gone fourteen minutes, so there is really no chance that they will collide with themselves on the way back—is there?

I have told you many times, Jaxom, that I do not think they will become lost. Every dragon knows his way back to his own weyr.

Every dragon is to impress on his rider that there are to be no exceptions to this order, Jaxom insisted.

I will tell them that they are too far away from Pern to disobey. They will not. The dragons certainly will not. Ruth paused briefly. *I have told them. I may not be a queen, but dragons trust me.*

Still apprehensive, Jaxom asked Ruth to rise up over the surface, so that every dragon could see him.

Back at their weyrs, they are to get out of the suits immediately, so they can be collected by browns and brought to Fort Weyr.

For our next trip. Jaxom couldn't believe the smug satisfaction in Ruth's tone. So much for worrying if this double time-jumping was affecting the resilient white dragon. He saw that faceplates were turned in his direction, and he raised his arm, making the hand gesture to go *between.* A second later, he asked Ruth to take him back to *Yokohama.*

Curiously, time seemed to go more slowly on the return. Yet Jaxom reached his thirtieth exhalation just as they emerged in the cargo bay of the *Yokohama.* The first dragon he saw was Ramoth, Lessa beside her, and to one side, F'lar appeared. Jaxom glanced down at his wristwatch: F'lar's trip had lasted the full fifteen minutes that dragons could endure without oxygen. The cargo bay was lit, but not well enough for Jaxom to tell if Mnementh was off color. Looking down at Ruth, he saw no alteration in the lustrous coat.

We've done it, he said. *Everyone safely back below?*

Monarth tells me so. Heth . . . Ruth hesitated, and Jaxom felt part of him shrivel in fear. *Heth says they are all back, but several dragons are in bad color.*

If that's all, it's nothing a good meal won't cure. And you?

I'm fine. We have done very well. So far.

Now if I can only think of some pretext for the Buenos Aires, Jaxom said as he removed his helmet.

You will.

"Yeeeeow!"

Jaxom was so startled by the loud cheer from F'lar that he nearly lifted himself from Ruth's back. The white dragon, eyes whirling in amazement, also turned his head to see F'lar propel himself off Mnementh and go shooting toward the equally surprised Lessa. When he grabbed her, his momentum spun them off in a lazy twirl until they careened into Ramoth. The great gold dragon arched her neck to look down at the extraordinary behavior of the Benden Weyrleaders.

"We did it! The dragons of Pern did it! Aivas'll have to eat sand on this one! He never thought we could do it!" F'lar was yelling at the top of his voice and laughing when echoes bounced back at him.

"Really, F'lar . . ." Lessa struggled to regain her balance, but Jaxom could see that she was smiling. "Yes, it is a splendid moment for the Weyrs! A splendid one! You've kept your promise. Indeed you have. That'll show the Holds and Halls!"

Still grinning fatuously, F'lar leaned back against Ramoth, pushing back his wayward lock.

"In point of fact, Lessa," he said then, his expression turned wry, "we haven't quite done it. There's N'ton's wings to lift the third engine, and then we have to wait. First for the explosion, and then to see if it had the proper effect."

Jaxom rubbed his hand across his lips. Knowledge of the future was a parlous asset. But it was enough that Jaxom *knew* this great enterprise would work.

"All safely down with your wings, Jaxom?" F'lar inquired as Jaxom floated to the deck.

"A few dragons off color . . ."

"Ruth's not," Lessa said, scrutinizing the white dragon and smiling approval at Jaxom.

"He says I've been stuffing him. Which of us gets to tell Aivas?" Jaxom asked, smiling broadly.

"We both do," F'lar said. He clapped an arm across Jaxom's shoulders, and together they bounced across the deck to the cargo-bay console. "You know, I didn't see your wing."

"Nor I yours," Jaxom said, chuckling. "We poor soil-bound Pernese have no appreciation of real size . . ." He spread his arms wide. "That Rift is mammoth. We planted our engine really well down in the Rift on a wide stone ledge."

"Aivas already knows," Lessa said. "I told him you'd all gone and that Ramoth was in touch with Mnementh. Oddly enough," she added, peering at Jaxom, "she couldn't hear Ruth."

"That is odd," Jaxom said, pretending to be puzzled. "Ramoth hears him quite well. But you both forget how far that Rift stretches, and we were at the far northern tip of it."

The reached the console.

"Aivas?" F'lar said.

"You have succeeded. Are all safely returned?"

"Yes. Now do you doubt draconic abilities?" F'lar asked, vindication mixed with the triumph in his laugh. He pulled Jaxom over in a comradely fashion. "You didn't want to believe that dragons could do what we said they could."

"We were right on schedule, too," Jaxom said, allowing himself to chuckle. "My team set that engine down right where you wanted it. No problem!"

"You are both to be complimented on your courage and daring."

"Don't lay it on too thick, Aivas," F'lar said.

"You deserve every credit that will accrue to your valorous deed. You have performed an incredible feat, Weyrleader F'lar. There is no doubt of that. Or that you will have achieved your personal goal—the end of Thread on this planet."

Jaxom grinned at F'lar, pleased at Aivas's unusual rhetoric.

"Your achievement is historically equivalent to that of the first dragonriders to fight Thread. Your name will be remembered with Sean O'Connell's, Sorka Hanrahan's—"

"That *is* laying it on too thick," Jaxom said. "You're the only one who remembered who were first to fight."

"Actually, Jaxom," F'lar said, grinning broadly, "Sebell showed me the corrected Harper Hall Records, and the eighteen riders who participated in that Fall were honored in their Turn. No one ran afoul of any of those dangers you warned us about," F'lar added, savoring this auspicious moment.

"It is wise to prepare for unusual contingencies," Aivas said.

"Well, we've done it."

"And you deserve this," Lessa said, joining them with a wineskin in her hands. "Best Benden."

"The 'sixteen?" Jaxom asked, craning his head for a look at the label.

"What else?" Lessa replied with a coquettish smile before she put the wineskin to her lips.

Jaxom blinked and, recovering, grinned back. It was about time that she treated him as an adult. Then he grew serious as he accepted the wineskin from her and raised it to the Benden Weyrleaders. "To all the Weyrs of Pern!"

"To us for this triumphant day!"

Jaxom took a long swig, then passed the wineskin to F'lar, who drank, then passed it to Lessa. As she sipped, F'lar turned to Jaxom. "You did tell 'em all to shuck those suits for the next round?"

"As planned, brown riders'll bring them to N'ton at Fort Weyr."

"Did your team scatter those treated ovoids as Aivas wanted?"

Jaxom winked at Lessa. "Mirrim wanted to bring back some examples of empty ones she found lying about." Lessa looked outraged, but he waved a reassurance. "I recommended that she didn't."

"How long before the explosion, Aivas?" F'lar asked.

"The HNO₃ gauge readings reassure that there is no stoppage. The corrosion continues."

"That's no answer," F'lar said, frowning.

Jaxom grinned. "That's all you're going to get right now. And we've still the third one to go." Which constituted a major problem for him. He desperately needed a few private words with Aivas, to see if he had come up with any ideas on how Jaxom could insinuate himself into N'ton's flight and get the dragons to take Ruth's coordinates for the second time leap of a mere five hundred Turns. Somehow he *had* accomplished it, for the other crater was there on the southern tip of the Rift. Jaxom had racked his brains and, whenever he was private with Aivas over the past few days, had tried to figure out any way that didn't involve explaining to N'ton. Not that N'ton wouldn't believe Jaxom, or that he wasn't discreet, but the fewer who knew about the time-traveling the better. Lessa would be furious at the risk involved.

So now he looked around him. "Are you the only ones up here, Lessa?"

"Oh, no." She grinned. "Everyone else is on the bridge, peering through the telescope, hoping to see the explosion. Oh, I told them it wouldn't happen soon. They were confident that they'd see the wings." Jaxom's breath caught when she said that. Oblivious, she went on. "Of course, they couldn't. Sometimes, even Fandarel doesn't comprehend vast distances. But today's excitement is being shared."

"How long has it been since we got back?" F'lar asked Jaxom.

"About twenty minutes," Jaxom replied. "N'ton's wings won't be ready yet, F'lar. Does anyone need your suit?"

"I shouldn't think so, but to be on the safe side, I'll shuck out of it. Could you bring it over to the *Buenos Aires* if it is needed?" F'lar handed Jaxom the helmet and, with Lessa's help, started removing the bulky suit. As he laid it over Jaxom's arm, he added, "I think we'll join those on the bridge, and the telescope, and watch N'ton work."

As soon as the lift doors closed on them, Jaxom returned to the console. "All right, Aivas, just how do I get to go with N'ton?"

"That is being arranged," Aivas replied, surprising him.

"*How* is it being arranged?" Jaxom demanded.

"You are quick and clever. You already have a reason to be on the

Buenos Aires. You will know what to do when the time comes. Transfer now to the other ship."

"I'll know when the time comes, will I?" Jaxom muttered to himself as he threw the extra suit over his shoulder. Carrying the suit and two helmets, he made his way over to Ruth. "Hand this one up to me, will you?" he asked, giving the white dragon one of the two helmets so he would have a free hand to mount. "How's N'ton doing? Has he got all the suits yet?"

As he arranged F'lar's suit in front of him he caught a whiff of sweat. Well, he didn't smell that sweet himself after his exertions.

N'ton says that some suits have to be sponged, and helmets have to match the suit.

Washed? Dragonriders tended to be fastidious in their personal habits, and dressing in a sweaty suit might be distasteful to many. *Oh, yes, perhaps they might at that. I don't understand about the helmets.*

There was a pause while Ruth inquired of Monarth, N'ton's bronze.

They forgot to put the suits back together—Ruth was obviously repeating something he did not quite understand—*and the helmets got mixed up.*

How long is sorting going to take? And suddenly Jaxom had a glimmer of an idea. With nearly a hundred suits to match to helmets, it could take several hours. He hoped it would take a long time.

Monarth didn't know. N'ton is not happy.

Reassure Monarth and N'ton, would you please, Ruth? Because this is going to work for our benefit. I think we can now put in an appearance on the Buenos Aires.

There were three blues and two greens waiting there, all from Eastern Weyr, and Ruth was greeted with considerable awe by the young dragons. Knowing that the white dragon would enjoy their deferential attention, Jaxom left him there and took the lift up to the smaller bridge of the *Buenos Aires.*

"What's holding up N'ton's wings?" Fandarel asked, relieved to see Jaxom. "That was a splendid sight, Jaxom, watching all those dragons lifting the engines like they were so many firestone sacks. Aivas has informed us that all went well." Fandarel looked concerned. "Why isn't N'ton here?"

"Because no one thought to keep helmet and body suit together," Jaxom said. Then he realized that he should also appear concerned and managed a frown. "I don't think it's going to matter in the long run," he added thoughtfully as he made his way to the nearest console. "Aivas, there is going to be a delay. Helmets weren't kept with suits, and they've got to match."

"That could be inconvenient if the delay is prolonged," Aivas said.

"It's three-quarters of an hour since we went off. How long before N'ton has to have different star-pattern references? It would be disastrous if he arrived at the wrong time and his engine went off either prematurely or too late." If Aivas expected Jaxom to use his wits, he hoped he would see what he was aiming at.

"A consideration to be sure. Reprogramming contingency." The screen altered from the current view of the *Buenos Aires* engine to rapid shifts of star configurations. "With any lengthy delay, the star picture will be slightly different."

"Is there going to be a problem?" Fandarel asked.

Jaxom smiled reassuringly at the Mastersmith and the others on the bridge, Masterminer Nicat, Master Idarolan, Jancis, and Piemur. Jaxom wished Piemur were not there: they knew each other far too well. "I don't think it's insurmountable. As you heard, Aivas is already programming contingency plans. I'd better inform Lessa and F'lar of the delay."

When he had done that, a call came through from Evan in engineering, patiently waiting to complete the separation. Jaxom was glad it was he, rather than Fosdak, in charge of that task. Fosdak had no patience.

Of all on the three bridges, Jaxom was the only one delighted that it took N'ton and his wings nearly four hours to get suited up. N'ton was usually a calm, easygoing, and relaxed Weyrleader; his patience had been sorely tried by the delays.

Monarth says they're ready. Ramoth says they must get the new configurations from you. Aivas is giving you the new star patterns to memorize and give Monarth. Ruth delivered the various messages just as the new configurations came up on the monitor. They were, as Jaxom knew, those for the five-hundred-Turn jump with the Red Star in the same relation to Rukbat at the Eighth Pass. Aivas had made a slight time alteration on those original coordinates, judging by the position of the Wheel and the Plow constellations on the horizon.

"Lessa," Jaxom said, toggling the ship-to-ship link, "I've got the visuals here. I'll give them to N'ton. Can Ramoth tell them to transfer in five more minutes? I have to get Ruth from the cargo bay."

"Just give N'ton the coordinates, Jaxom," Lessa said.

"That's what I intend doing," Jaxom replied mendaciously. "Fandarel, five-minute warning for Evan?"

The smith nodded enthusiastically, for the waiting had made everyone edgy. Waiting, in the smith's lexicon, was inefficient. As Jaxom took the lift to the cargo bay, he wondered if Fandarel ever rested. Here he had completed the most complex and exhausting work of a lifetime and he still fretted over inactivity.

We go? Ruth asked Jaxom, his eyes whirling with excitement.

We don't really have to go, you know, Ruth, Jaxom said. *Lessa said we only have to give N'ton the new coordinates . . .* Jaxom chuckled as he saw the disappointment in Ruth's eyes. He mounted and, crowning his head with the helmet, twisted it shut. *That will get them there safely enough but . . . I think you'll make an error and go, too. You feel all right about that?*

I have rested, and this is the shorter trip, isn't it?

I hope so. Between the first jump, fretting over how to join N'ton's wings, and the long wait, Jaxom was feeling slightly frayed. He took care not to let Ruth sense that.

Monarth comes! Excitement colored Ruth's tone.

"Fandarel, do you see them?" Jaxom asked through his helmet link.

"Yes, magnificent. I have given Evan the order to separate."

Let's get to the stern, Ruth.

Jaxom took a deep breath, but they flashed *between* so fast that he had not quite completed the inhalation when Ruth reappeared gripping the stern. Monarth and N'ton were beside them, and below, the bronze dragons of Fort, High Reaches, Telgar, and Ista ranged along the top spars.

Jaxom held the image of where they were going vivid in his mind. *Give Monarth and N'ton my compliments and ask Monarth to take our destination from you.*

N'ton threw Jaxom a salute, but Jaxom couldn't see the Fort Weyrleader's expression, obscured as it was by his faceplate. He gave N'ton a deferential salute.

Monarth says we go!

They went. The cold of *between* seemed to penetrate Jaxom's space suit, and he could hear his breath coming raggedly. He forced himself to slow down.

I'm here, Ruth said in encouragement.

As always, Jaxom replied, and continued to count his inhalations. Eighteen, nineteen, twenty, twenty-one, twenty-two.

And then they were hovering inches above the southern tip of the Rift.

Monarth says where's the crater?

Tell him that Aivas picked this spot, so here's where we'd better deposit the engine. We don't have time to find that bloody crater!

Jaxom turned toward N'ton, who was looking at him, arms raised in query. Jaxom gave him an exasperated shrug in reply.

Monarth says N'ton understands. They proceed.

N'ton was signaling to the auxiliary dragons to begin their task of sowing the zebedees. Then he turned all his attention to the lowering of the massive engine into the Rift. The maneuver went well, even better than Jaxom's, taking just ten minutes.

N'ton waited another few moments, allowing the dragons a chance to rest. Then he called in the auxiliaries.

I have told Monarth that everyone must return to their own Weyrs. But to keep the right helmets with the right suits this time, Ruth told Jaxom.

We're not likely to need two hundred slightly used space suits again, Jaxom said, trying to contain his elation until they were safely back. *We must go back to the* Yokohama.

I have told Monarth. N'ton says he is grateful and apologizes for the delay.

Tell him that it all worked out well in the end.

It did, didn't it? Ruth added. *Shall we return now?*

Please yes!

Once again, the return seemed longer than the outgoing journey, but it wasn't. Finally the comforting dimness of the big cargo bay of the *Yokohama* surrounded them. And they were immediately attacked by Ramoth and Mnementh.

Where have I been? Ruth exclaimed, rearing back away from Ramoth's savage expression and dodging Mnementh's massive wings. *I'm fine. I'm fine. So is Jaxom. He didn't tell me not to go!*

"Jaxom!" F'lar was bellowing the moment he stepped out of the lift, with Lessa on his heels.

Jaxom loosened his helmet. "So we went, too," he said, raising his voice to top the angry ones of the Benden Weyrleaders. "Ruth's not even a trifle off color. Not his fault. I forgot to tell him not to follow Monarth. But the job is now completely done!" He glared back at F'lar and Lessa and slid down Ruth's side, patting his foreleg. "I could certainly use another pull at that wineskin, Lessa, if you wouldn't mind . . .'"

He spoke with no trace of regret or apology, and he felt rather too battered to bother with the deference the Weyrleaders deserved from him. He undid the first of the suit's fastenings, knowing that they were still angry with him and hoping they would give it up.

"Here, I'll help," F'lar said unexpectedly. "Lessa, this Lord Holder deserves another swallow of that 'sixteen!"

Jaxom gave F'lar a sharp look and then grinned back. By the first Egg, so he had finally come into his own in the cargo bay of the *Yokohama*.

20

A few riders in the third group suffered some physical attrition. M'rand, one of the older bronze riders of High Reaches, returned long after the rest of the Weyr and in terrible condition. He was tormented by bad dreams, insisting that he had returned to his Weyr but it had not been *his* Weyr. Tileth had been frantic, recognizing none of the other dragons there and finding a strange bronze asleep on the ledge of his Weyr. M'rand couldn't understand at first, but he had heard that bronzes could slip through time. He kept his wits and had tried to get home again, giving Tileth the most vivid images of their favorite view of High Reaches, with the blue M'rand knew was that day's watchdragon. That time they had emerged in the right place and the right time.

"Sloppy visualization," Lessa said when she and F'lar had also spoken with M'rand and the others: two in Fort Weyr and another in Igen. "And they're all older riders, leaving more up to their dragons than they ought."

Jaxom noticed that N'ton was regarding him with a quizzical expression, and he responded with a perplexed grin. He himself had felt woefully tired after the exertions of that momentous day, pausing only long enough to let Ruth feed on a juicy buck before returning home, and no one thought it odd that he slept nearly a day. Sharra was equally exhausted by her last few days in the laboratory, churning out zebedees.

Despite the fact that Aivas had repeatedly told everyone that the explosion would not take place for several more days and then would not be immediately visible due to light speed—which he had to explain again to some—a twenty-four-hour vigil was kept on the *Yokohama*. Every screen in the various areas on the ships where air was available was adjusted to the ships' main screens and the big telescope, aimed at the Red Star.

"Jaxom, aren't you going to watch?" Sharra asked. "You of all people ought to have the right!" She was baffled by his apparent indifference to the event.

"Frankly," he said, "I have a lot of more important things to do here in Ruatha than floating about on the bridge, waiting for the thing to blow. Unless, of course," he added considerately, "you really want to see it."

"Well . . ." Sharra paused, then smiled at him. "I've got those cultures going right now and . . ."

Jaxom grinned at her. "If there's enough warning, Ruth'll get us there in time."

Sharra gave him a startled sideways glance.

"All in a good cause," he said, trying for nonchalance, "and a minute or two isn't going to disrupt the universe. I'll ask Ruth to keep an ear open, if you like. There's always some fire-lizards or a dragon or two up at the *Yokohama* these days. Easy enough."

"If he can stay awake long enough to listen," Sharra replied, having noticed that Ruth seemed to be taking an unusual amount of sleep.

"He can sleep with one ear open," Jaxom said, and then they each went about the concerns of the day.

Brand had also observed Ruth's somnolence, and while he and Jaxom were checking the brood mares, he mentioned it.

"I don't think it's so very unusual, Brand," Jaxom said easily. "N'ton said that all the bronzes who went with us are also sleeping a good deal. I suspect none of the dragons care to admit that they had to work pretty hard to transfer those engines." Then Jaxom noticed his Steward's hesitation. "Why? What's wrong?"

"It's just that there have been some complaints about Fort Weyr."

"What do you mean, Brand?" Jaxom and Ruth had not flown the most recent Fall with the Fort wings. "Have I missed something?"

Brand had shrugged expressively. "Well, because the bronzes are a big logy, they haven't been as, well, diligent in chasing airborne

Thread. There have been a lot of unhappy groundcrews. And that's the other problem."

"Tell me."

"Somehow—" Brand paused to frame his explanation. "A lot of people thought that there'd be no more Thread *now*. That once the dragonriders had done this explosion thing, Thread wouldn't fall again."

"Oh!" Jaxom made a face. "Bloody shards, Brand. Don't they ever listen? Harpers have been explaining for the last four Turns that we can't stem *this* Fall, but there won't be any more!"

"They don't see it that way, I'm afraid, from the accounts I've heard. And Holder Grevil isn't a stupid man, as you know, but *he* hadn't understood and feels aggrieved, especially when a clump of Thread came down on his best field."

"I can appreciate his annoyance. Did you manage to soothe him?"

"I did, but he's sure to approach you on the matter the next time he can. I thought I'd warn you. And you should know that he blames the Aivas."

Jaxom compressed his lips against rash words, momentarily defeated by this news: especially coming from Grevil, who was usually a moderate man. "I thought we'd straightened all that out at the trial."

Brand shrugged, holding his hands up in an impotent gesture. "People will hear what they wish to hear, and believe what they want to. If they put the blame on Aivas, however, that absolves you, Jaxom, and even the Weyrs to a certain extent."

"I can't really count that as an advantage," Jaxom replied. "Why should Aivas bear any blame after all he's done to help Pern?"

"Ah, but the help is not so visible to some," Brand said. "It'll all sort itself out, Jaxom. But I did feel you should know current opinion."

"Hmmmm, yes, I should. How many has that new stallion covered of this lot?" he asked, welcoming the chance to change to matters less complicated.

The more he thought about it, the more he felt obliged to let the Harper Hall know, and those at Cove Hold. He hated to disrupt the mood of euphoria and triumph they would be feeling. He sent Meer, who had been shadowing him constantly while Ruth slept, with a message to Lytol, who could mention the report at an appropriate moment.

"What I don't understand," Sharra said when he mentioned the matter to her over their midday meal, "is that with all that has been explained so carefully to everyone who would listen, how they can possibly misconstrue what you and the Weyrs were doing, and its immediate consequences."

Jaxom grinned. "They probably stopped listening after the words 'Thread will be forever destroyed.' " He sipped his klah pensively.

F'lar and Lessa are up on the Yokohama, Ruth said in a sleepy voice. *Ramoth says Aivas thinks the explosion will be any time now.*

Sharra politely cocked her head at Jaxom, knowing that Ruth had spoken to him. "What woke him up?"

"It should be any moment now. The explosion. Want to go?"

"Do *you* want to?"

"Let's not play the you-first, no-you-first game. Do you want to go?"

She blinked rapidly, considering, and looking so like Jarrol that he grinned. "No," she said with a sigh. "I think I've seen quite enough of the insides of the Yokohama to last me the rest of my life. And everyone will be crowding about up there. But you want to go . . ."

He laughed, reaching for her hand and bringing it to his lips. "I think I won't. This moment should be F'lar's."

Sharra eyed him long and thoughtfully, her eyes beginning to sparkle. "You're a good man, but I do not concede that it is *all* F'lar's triumph."

"Don't be silly," he replied. "It took all the Weyrs of Pern to do it."

"And a white dragon!"

As she turned back to her soup, Jaxom wondered exactly what she meant by that. Could Sharra have guessed Ruth's unusual role?

After so many long days of watching the round ball that was the Red Star, the explosion, when it became visible, was an anticlimax. An orange-red fireball blossomed on the side of the wanderer planet.

"Only one?" F'lar exclaimed, feeling a certain chagrin that half the planet had not exploded, too, after all Aivas had told them about the awesome power of the antimatter.

"That is how it would appear at this distance," Aivas replied.

"It *is* rather spectacular," Robinton murmured.

"Then all three engines went off at the same time?" Fandarel asked.

"It would seem so," Aivas said.

"Well done, Aivas, well done." Fandarel beamed, evidently not bothered by a tinge of disappointment. "That junction was successful."

"And efficient," D'ram said, unable to resist the opportunity to tease Fandarel.

"It's odd, you know," Piemur began, more to Jancis than the others. "You work your butt off to achieve an end, and suddenly you've done it! And all the excitement, frustration, sleepless nights, and involvement are over! Gone!" He snapped his fingers. "In one large and impressive fireball! So what do we do with all that extra time we have on our hands now?"

"You," Robinton said, pointing a stern finger at the journeyman, "will now have the unenviable task as a harper of explaining the true facts of the achievement to those who didn't understand that this effort would not alter the path of Thread during the remainder of this Pass."

To Lytol's surprise, Robinton had not been at all dismayed by Jaxom's report. In fact, the Harper had seemed to expect such disgruntlements.

"Menolly's already composed one ballad," Robinton went on, "with a chorus to hammer home the point that this is the Last Pass for Thread, that Pern will be forever free from the end of this Pass."

"A point!" Piemur said. "Is that certain, Aivas?"

"That is now guaranteed, Piemur. You must realize, of course, that an immediate alteration of the Red Star's orbit will not be perceived," Aivas said, "for some decades."

"Decades?" F'lar exclaimed, surprised.

"Naturally. If you consider the size of the object you were trying to move," Fandarel said, "and the scale of this solar system, there is no such thing as sudden change. Even chaos takes time to develop. But in several decades, that alteration will be measurable."

"Rest assured of that, Weyrleader," Aivas added in a tone so laden with certainty that F'lar's consternation eased.

"It's too bad Jaxom and Sharra didn't come," Lessa said, slightly irritated by their absence. "I knew that Ruth would strain himself, taking part in the second lift."

"Jaxom is quite capable of making his own decisions now, my dear," F'lar said, amused at her proprietary concern for the Ruathan Holder.

"There is one more minor adjustment to make, however," Aivas said, "which it is recommended to be undertaken by the lesser colors."

"Oh? What?" Lessa and F'lar were very much aware that the brown, blue, and green riders were somewhat aggrieved by their exclusion from the project. "All the Weyrs of Pern" had been limited to most of the bronze dragons and only a few of the other colors, even if it had been obvious that there wasn't space enough on the spars to accommodate every dragon who wished to take part, much less space suits to protect their riders in space.

"The matter of the *Buenos Aires* and the *Bahrain*."

"What about them?" F'lar asked just as Fandarel emitted an "ah" of comprehension.

"Readings on the orbits of the two smaller ships have shown a marked increase of frequency of adjustments. The adjustments take more and more power, and the prognosis is that their orbits are likely to decay over the next decades to the critical point. The *Yokohama*, of course, has the fuel to remain in a stable orbit and must be maintained as long as possible, since its telescope will be used to track the Red Star. But the other ships ought to be moved."

"Moved?" F'lar asked. "Where?"

"A slight alteration in their speed and altitude will break them out of orbit and send them coasting harmlessly off into space."

"Eventually to be captured by the sun's gravity and pulled into it," Fandarel added.

"Burned up?" Lytol asked.

"A heroic end for such valiant ships," Robinton murmured.

"You mentioned nothing of this before," F'lar said.

"There were more urgent priorities," Aivas replied. "It is certainly a task that must be accomplished sooner rather than later when the orbits have decayed, and while the skills your riders have learned for the more essential task are still fresh in their minds."

"It would certainly ease the tension in the Weyr," Lessa said. "We hadn't anticipated that."

"What exactly does this entail, Aivas?" F'lar asked.

"As stated, the dragons are to alter the direction of the two ships and give a 'push'; that is, transport the ship *between*, all moving at the same cue. There are many handholds on the exterior of the ships to give dragons a grip. Judging by what you were able to accomplish in transferring the engines, such a maneuver is well within the scope of your smaller creatures."

F'lar grinned. "You're no longer skeptical about them?"

"In no way, Weyrleader."

"What is the time frame on this?" Fandarel asked.

"Preferably within the next few weeks. There is no immediate danger, but do not let the dragons and riders lose the edge."

"I think that will be good news," F'lar said, nodding acceptance.

"Then you will set a time for this maneuver?"

"As soon as I can discuss it with the other Weyrleaders." Oddly enough, F'lar's spirits rose with the thought of another project. Flying Threadfall had become less exciting since the removal of the engines to the Red Star.

"It seems ungrateful to condemn those ships to death," Lessa murmured.

"It's a crime to waste all the material," Fandarel added.

"These ships were never designed for planetary landings, Master Fandarel," Aivas said.

"In one piece, that is," Piemur added.

"Yes, Piemur, the pieces could have lethal consequences if they were to enter the atmosphere without disintegrating entirely."

"I'll let you know," F'lar said. "Shall we go, Lessa?"

Watching the fireball soon lost its appeal for many on the *Yokohama* bridge that day. Shortly thereafter, when D'ram and the Eastern Weyr rider were ready to take the last watchers back to the Landing, Fandarel and Piemur cycled the life-support systems down to the holding mode.

"I'm glad we're able to keep the *Yokohama*," Piemur said. "I've gotten rather fond of this old girl." He let his fingers trail along the console.

"She has served long and well," Robinton said, sighing deeply.

"Why don't you write a ballad about her, Piemur?" Jancis suggested.

"You know, I think I will!"

As the last one entering the lift, Piemur palmed off the bridge lights.

J axom heard about the second expedition from N'ton, who dropped in to Ruatha Hall two days after the Red Star explosion. N'ton had been on the *Buenos Aires* with half a dozen of his wingleaders.

"I feel an affinity to that little ship," N'ton said, with a wry smile. "I'll be sorry to see her go."

"I wonder why she needs to," Jaxom said. "Surely the solar panels . . ."

"Aivas said that there have been too many corrections and the panels can't handle them."

"Hmm, that's quite possible."

"He also recommended doing it while we're still accustomed to working in weightlessness. There is, I might add," N'ton said with a broad grin, "great rejoicing among the riders of browns, blues, and greens. At that, they know that there are only two hundred and some suits available, so they'll have to draw lots. But that's fair enough."

"Let's hope the helmets are with the right suits this time."

"Oh, we made sure of that." N'ton rolled his eyes. "What a mess that was! I tried on twenty helmets before I found one that would attach snugly to the collar. Then I had to get the wingleaders to check every rider to be sure all the bloody things fitted properly. Some riders were just cramming helmets on any old way."

"The important thing is that everyone did get rigged out and we got where we were supposed to go."

N'ton regarded him for such a long moment that Jaxom wondered if the Fort Weyrleader had somehow guessed what had happened. Considering his disoriented bronze riders, a man as intelligent as N'ton might extrapolate the truth. As long as Jaxom didn't admit it, N'ton would be kept guessing.

"Maybe that's what happened to those disoriented riders," Jaxom went on as if the thought had just occurred to him. "Maybe they had badly fitting helmets and lost air."

"I hadn't thought of that," N'ton replied. "You know, that would certainly explain a lot."

Jaxom nodded in agreement, saying nothing more.

"F'lar's not best pleased to have to wait, yet again, to be sure the blastings did the trick," N'ton went on.

"Aivas was evidently satisfied."

"Yes, but he always sounds certain."

"Everything he's sounded certain about has worked just as he said. He's never prevaricated. I don't think an AI facility can."

"You'd know better than I." N'ton grinned at Jaxom over his wineglass. "We certainly can't fault Hold and Hall, then, for disbelief if the Benden Weyrleader is still skeptical."

"Again, Aivas has been right so often we have to trust him this time." Jaxom had a whimsical desire to confide in N'ton that he knew, incontrovertibly, that Aivas's great Plan had worked, at least as far as the orbit of the Red Star was concerned. That he had seen it with his own eyes—fifty Turns in the future.

"As he trusted our dragons?"

"Well, he did, in the end, didn't he?" Jaxom replied. "No, N'ton, don't fret. It'll be as Aivas has predicted. You wait, you'll see."

"Ah, but F'lar might not. And he's the one who wants to know for certain, or he will not have kept that promise!"

Maybe, Jaxom thought, he could just reassure F'lar.

I wouldn't, Ruth said. *You'd have to explain everything to him then.*

Not necessarily, Jaxom replied.

Ruth's silence indicated complete disagreement.

"So," N'ton went on, "now that we've solved the world's problems, what do you intend doing with all that spare time you've got?"

"What spare time, N'ton? I've only just scraped the surface of the information in Aivas's files. I was in the process of organizing Hold affairs before I resume my studies—at an easier pace, now that the urgency is over."

"We've Threadfall in two days. Are you and Ruth rested enough to join us?"

"I'd better, what with all these misconceptions about the end of Thread."

"Indeed!" From that succinct but heartfelt comment, Jaxom knew that N'ton had been heavily criticized for letting Thread get through the Fort Weyr wings.

"I'll be there!" Jaxom promised.

"Master Robinton, it is good to see you," Aivas said as the Harper entered.

"I've been meaning to come for the last week," Robinton remarked with a droll smile. Even that short walk down the corridor had taken more breath than he had in his body.

"You are well?"

Robinton laughed softly and eased himself into the chair he had occupied for so many hours in the recent past. "Can't fool you, can I?"

"No."

Robinton sighed and stroked Zair, curled asleep on his shoulder. "I did forgive them, then, you know," he began slowly, so his words would not come out at the end of a gasp, "at the trial. I'm not so sure now that I would."

"The effects of inappropriate fellis administration?"

"Yes, I must assume so."

"You have not consulted Master Oldive?" Aivas's tone was sharp.

Robinton waved one hand, dismissing the advice. "He has enough to do, teaching his healers all the new techniques he learned while doing your work. That will take him the rest of his life."

"You must consult—"

"Why? You can produce no cures for worn-out human parts, can you, Aivas?" When there was silence, Robinton went on, still stroking Zair's soft body. "Neither Zair nor I will recover from that abduction. Sometimes, I think he stays out of spite."

"Or love of you, Master Robinton?"

The Harper had never heard that particular tone from Aivas.

"Quite likely, for they can be exceedingly loyal, these fire-lizards."

Robinton had his breath back now, and being in this room brought back some of the excitement of the early days of discovery. He felt at ease here in the Aivas room as he did not at Cove Hold, especially when Lytol and D'ram kept treating him like an invalid. Which, he had to admit, he was. He heard the chatter of students changing classes in the hall.

"The classes continue?" he asked, well pleased that they did.

"The classes continue," Aivas said, using that soft, almost rueful tone that had surprised the Harper before. "The machines now harbor all the information this world will need to build a better future."

"The future which you have given them."

"The priorities for this facility have now been met."

"That's true enough," Robinton said, smiling.

"This facility now has no further function."

"Don't be ridiculous, Aivas," Robinton said somewhat sharply. "You've just gotten your students to the point where they know enough to argue with you!"

"And to resent the superiority of this facility. No, Master Robinton, the task is done. Now it is wise to let them seek their own way forward. They have the intelligence and a great spirit. Their ancestors can rightfully be proud of them."

"Are you?"

"They have worked hard and well. That is in itself a reward and an end."

"You know, I believe you're right."

" 'To everything there is a season, and a time to every purpose under heaven,' Master Robinton."

"That is poetic, Aivas."

There was one of those pauses that Robinton always thought was the Aivas equivalent of a smile.

"From the greatest book ever written by Mankind, Master Robinton. You may find the entire quotation in the files. The time has been accomplished. This system is going down. Farewell, Masterharper of Pern. Amen."

Robinton sat straight up in his chair, fingers on the pressure plates, though he hadn't a single positive idea of how he could avert what Aivas was about to do. He half turned to the Hall, to call for help, but no one who had the knowledge—Jaxom, Piemur, Jancis, Fandarel, D'ram, or Lytol—was near enough at hand.

The screen that had paraded so much knowledge and issued so many commands and diagrams and plans was suddenly blank, lifeless. In the right-hand corner, a single line blinked.

" 'And a time to every purpose under heaven,' " Robinton murmured, his throat almost too tight for him to speak. He felt incredibly tired, overwhelmingly sleepy. "Yes, how very true. How splendidly true. And what a wonderful time it has been!"

Unable to resist the lethargy that spread from his extremities, he laid his head down on the inactive pressure plate, one hand holding Zair in the curve of his neck, and closed his eyes, his long season over, his purpose, too, accomplished.

D'ram found them there, for Zair had breathed his last as well following the Harper as selflessly as any dragon followed his rider into death.

Tiroth lifted his head, his keening alerting all those at Landing and, indeed, broadcasting to every Weyr, every dragon, and every rider on Pern, and throughout the Halls and Holds, from mountain to plain, from sea to sea on both continents.

D'ram was so tear-blinded that he did not notice the opacity of the screen, or read the blinking message.

In Ruatha Hold, Ruth gave out a bellow of anguish that had everyone in the Great Hall rushing to the door.

The Harper! The Harper!

Jaxom didn't think. He grabbed Sharra by the hand and propelled her down the steps to where Ruth had reared, head back, wings extended.

"Jaxom!" she exclaimed.

"The Harper! Something's happened to the Harper!"

She needed no more urging. They scrambled astride the white dragon.

"We need Oldive for this, Ruth," Jaxom said. "Take us first to the Healer Hall."

They emerged almost immediately in the central court of the Hall, Ruth just barely managing to avoid setting down on anyone. Oldive, jacket flapping from one hand, his medical case in the other, was limping down the stairs.

I told him! Ruth said.

Just then the Fort Hold dragon began to keen, and swirling storms of fire-lizards, ululating in weird descant, flashed in and out of the court.

"What has happened to the Harper?" Oldive demanded, handing his case up to Sharra and struggling into his jacket. "Neither of you has a jacket!"

"Don't worry about us." Jaxom sat, leaning down to grab Oldive's arm and haul him up. *Is it Landing? Or Cove Hold?* he asked Ruth.

Landing!

"Take us there! We must be in time!"

Neither Jaxom nor Sharra even noticed the dread chill of *between* in that anxious trip. Dragons were arriving from all directions, so Ruth, ducking low, skimmed the tops of the houses and landed in front of the Aivas building, once again missing collisions with those on the ground rushing in response to the emergency.

It is too late! Ruth said, and folded his wings over his head.

"It can't be too late! Move aside, let us through. Let Oldive through!" Jaxom pushed their way through, one hand hauling the Masterhealer along beside him, the limping Oldive somehow keeping up with him. "Make way here. Make way!"

At the doorway, he came to an abrupt stop. Piemur, Jancis, D'ram, and Lytol stood around the chair, the Harper's silver-haired pate visible where it rested against the back. Choking back the sobs that threatened to overwhelm him, Jaxom slowly approached, moving to one side so that he could see. The Harper looked as if he were merely sleeping. Zair, gray with death, curled against his neck.

"He just—went—to—sleep," Piemur said brokenly. "He's not even warm anymore."

"I thought he was just asleep," D'ram said, "the last time I looked in. I never thought . . ." Hand to his face, he turned away.

"*Aivas!*" Jaxom roared. "Aivas, why didn't you call someone? You must have been aware—"

"Look," Sharra said, touching his arm and then pointing to the screen and the blinking message there.

" 'And a time for every purpose under heaven'? What is that supposed to mean, Aivas? Aivas!"

Only then did Jaxom realize the difference in the screen, as lifeless as it had been the very first time he had entered the room. "Aivas?"

He pressed a "restore" sequence. Then, cursing at fingers that fumbled, he tried other codes, but got no response.

"Piemur? Jancis? What do we do?"

Sharra grabbed his trembling hands and held them, her tearing eyes bright with the knowledge that he could not accept.

"Aivas has gone, too," she said, her voice rough. "See the smile on Master Robinton's face? Just as you and I have seen him smile so many times. The message was for him as it is there for us."

"We'll go back, we'll go back to when he was still alive—" Jaxom began, reaching for Master Oldive and heading toward the door. If he and Ruth could time it . . . F'lar and Lessa stood in the doorway. He didn't care if they knew he meant to time it.

Oldive grabbed his arm, shaking his head, his eyes blurred with tears. "We could do nothing for him, Jaxom. 'A time for every purpose under heaven, Jaxom.' And it was time for the Harper."

"He wouldn't let us tell anyone," Sharra said to Jaxom, "how serious his condition was."

"It was only a matter of time," Oldive murmured, peering up at him, his long face grooved with sorrow. "His heart was badly strained by the abduction. This was a kind ending, Jaxom, no matter how abrupt and unexpected."

"I know Robinton wasn't well," Jaxom went on, shaking his head, tears coursing down his cheeks. "But I don't understand about Aivas, too."

"He tells us plainly enough," D'ram said, having recovered his composure. He pointed to the message. "He has served his purpose in helping us destroy Thread. You will come to realize just how wise Aivas was in this. We were beginning to count on him too heavily."

"Machines can't die!" Jaxom chewed the words out resentfully.

"The knowledge he gave us will not," F'lar said, and stood aside to let Menolly and Sebell enter the room. "Now let us all honor Masterharper Robinton."

The day was inappropriately beautiful when the Masterharper, wrapped in a harper-blue shroud, was laid to rest in the beautiful blue-green waters of his beloved Cove Hold. Master Idarolan had dispatched his fastest ship and came a-dragonback to captain it himself. Master Alemi, with his sloop from Paradise River, and the small ketches that fished in Monaco Bay, assembled to accommodate the many people who would escort Master Robinton to his resting place.

All the Weyrs of Pern hovered in the sky, and while fire-lizards made sad swirls around them the ship sailed out of Cove Hold. Lord Holders and Craftmasters lined the decks amid harpers of every degree.

Sebell and Menolly sang all the songs that had made the Masterharper so beloved by everyone, Menolly remembering the day that she had sung farewell to his father, Petiron, the day that had begun the major change in her own life.

And as the ship moved into the Current, scores of shipfish led the way, slipping, diving, gliding, and weaving among the ships' bow waves.

When his body was consigned to the sea, the dragons bugled one last note for Masterharper Robinton.

Jaxom, aloft on Ruth, watched the ripples spread and then meld into the waves. After a bitter night, he had come to terms with his grief for Master Robinton and his wild notion that he and Ruth could or should have forestalled that peaceful death.

But he could find no surcease yet for the bitter blow of losing Aivas. He felt that he had been abandoned just when he had the most grievous need of Aivas's wisdom and support. Had he not done everything Aivas wished? Put himself and Ruth in danger to fulfill those bleeding priorities of the ungrateful machine?

I understand your grief, Jaxom, Ruth said quietly, his head, like that of every other dragon, watching the scene below as the ships tacked about for their return to Cove Hold. *Why do you harbor such anger and resentment?*

"He left us, and with Master Robinton gone, we need him now more than ever."

Not we—you. But that is the wrong way to think about this. Aivas left behind all the information you need—and you have only to access it to solve problems now.

For the first time in their long association, Jaxom resented Ruth's words.

Probably, Ruth said at his drollest, *you know I'm right. I think that Aivas was as tired as the Harper, having waited all those long Turns to complete his tasks and keep faith with his makers.*

Though Jaxom resisted the thought, the words of Aivas's last message reverberated in his head. How much Robinton had enjoyed Aivas! Had Aivas ended his existence before, or after, Master Robinton had fallen into his last sleep? Surely if Aivas had been aware of Robinton's condition, he would have summoned help. Those options had exercised everyone yesterday. But everyone had agreed with D'ram that Aivas had achieved those ancient priorities—with great honor.

Then give Aivas the honor that is due him, Jaxom. Anger and resentment cloud your mind and heart.

Jaxom sighed, accepting the gentle reproach of his white dragon. "I haven't been thinking straight, have I?"

Think of what we have done together, you and I, to show Aivas that we could. We did the impossible because I knew where and when to do it. It's as well you cracked my shell that Hatching Day, Jaxom, or where would Pern be now?

Laughter burst from Jaxom, provoked by the dragon's sly cajolery. But draconic logic had lifted him out of his depression.

" 'And a time for every purpose under heaven'!" he cried into the air about them. What Ruth said was true: Only he, Jaxom, Lord of Ruatha Hold, and Ruth, the white dragon, could have done what had to be done to free Pern forever from Thread, serving their world as only dragon and rider could, united in mind and heart to their purpose.

And so Jaxom and Ruth turned back to Cove Hold, ready to delve into the legacy of knowledge that Aivas had left for them.

ABOUT THE AUTHOR

ANNE MCCAFFREY shuttles between her home in Ireland and the United States, where she picks up awards and honors and greets her myriad fans. She is one of the field's most popular authors. Her Dragonriders of Pern® novels constitute a *New York Times* bestselling series.